Defiant Unto Death

Master of War
Defiant Unto Death

David Gilman

W F HOWES LTD

This large print edition published in 2015 by
W F Howes Ltd
Unit 4, Rearsby Business Park, Gaddesby Lane,
Rearsby, Leicester LE7 4YH

1 3 5 7 9 10 8 6 4 2

First published in the United Kingdom in 2015
by Head of Zeus Ltd

A CIP catalogue record for this book is available
from the British Library

ISBN 978 1 47129 600 0

Typeset by Palimpsest Book Production Limited,
Falkirk, Stirlingshire

www.printondemand-worldwide.com of Peterborough, England

For Suzy,
as always

CONTENTS

*T*he wounds of war still bled.

The greatest army in Christendom had been slaughtered ten years earlier at Crécy, when Thomas Blackstone and his fellow archers stood their ground and rained death on knight and horse, prince and commoner. It was from that squalid field of death that Blackstone had risen, fought hand to hand and saved the English King's son. Dragged from the blood-soaked mud, the badly wounded Blackstone had been given the last sacrament and honoured by his King. There was no greater accolade than to be knighted in battle and Sir Thomas Blackstone's broken body withstood its agony and eluded the dark mantle of death. Over the years since that day King Edward had continued to press his claim to the French throne. He still held Calais, the gateway to France, but that mighty nation was not yet on its knees.

Pestilence had ripped through the two kingdoms, stripping away lives and revenues, leaving both monarchs unable to finance war, or to bring about a decisive battle. Not yet. That would come when Norman lords,

1

tricky and aggressive men who craved more power within France and who harboured resentment against their King, finally became strong enough to challenge him.

PART I

THE SAVAGE PRIEST

CHAPTER 1

It was said Thomas Blackstone was like a ghost in a graveyard. A man could sense his presence but by the time he turned to face the spectre the chill wind of death struck him down. No one knew where this scarred-faced Englishman might strike next. That he was protected by Norman lords deep in their territory was known, but when mercenary assassins, disavowed by the French King, rode into the forests of the Norman stronghold to seek him out, their bodies were found hanging by the roadside.

His fierce reputation might have suffered had his enemies seen him on this windswept day. Spume ripped from the wave tops as the tide raced against a swirling offshore wind that flailed the sea into a saw-toothed, gut-wrenching swell. The thirty-ton cog, its rudder being wrenched by the turbulence, needed two of the fifteen mariners aboard to hold its tiller. The tide was rising and they hoped that the sandbar ahead of the ship was covered by sufficient water to save the protesting timbers from running aground and casting those on board into the mercy of the waves and the sucking mud that lay beyond. Blackstone's mentor from days gone by shouted a simple command into his mind. *Choose your ground to fight!* Sir Gilbert Killbere's voice insisted. Sweet merciful God, this was not *ground*! This was the heaving hulk of a ship, one of the hundreds that had taken Edward's army to France ten years ago. And ten years was too short a respite before being put back aboard a cork-bobbing hulk, no matter how seaworthy her master insisted she might be.

Blackstone welcomed the stinging salt on his face and sucked the cold air deep into his lungs as he gripped the gunwale of the lurching ship. Vomit rose and he retched across the bow, knowing there were men behind him clinging as he was and now, no doubt, sprayed with his previous night's dinner.

'How much longer?' he yelled at the master who, unlike Black stone and his men, stood braced, legs apart, on the raised quarterdeck, and cupped a hand to his ear to catch the knight's words.

'I'll tell you when I know, Sir Thomas! When I know! Not a damned moment before!'

Blackstone balanced himself, twisting a ship's rope about his arm. He brought the silver figure of Arianrhod from around his neck, and kissed it with spittle-flecked lips. The pagan goddess had been given to him years before by a dying Welsh archer in the ferocious battle for Caen and her protective mantle had served him well, but misery made him reach further in his quest for relief.

Sweet Jesus, I have turned my back on you many a time. I place my faith in pagan superstition, but I swear to you, by all that is holy in heaven, that if you bring me through this torture I will give my share of spoils from this battle to the nearest, poorest church I find.

A figure staggered up next to him, but the man who held the ship's side for support showed no sign of illness. He pulled his hair back from his face with the help of the biting wind. 'Promises to God are seldom kept, my lord. Better to pray to your stomach for comfort,' said Guillaume Bourdin, Blackstone's squire, as if he had read his lord's mind. The young fighter was unaffected by the raging waves. Blackstone could barely raise his eyes without his gorge rising. He squared his shoulders, shamed by his squire's lack of discomfort. Blackstone had not been on a ship since that crossing to invade France ten years ago, when his brother Richard had been the only man unaffected, yet here he was breaking the vow he had made never to repeat the experience. Every second of the heaving horizon twisted his stomach. Nothing had changed.

'The men?' Blackstone demanded, half turning just in time to see the stern rise on a mighty wave, making the small ship dip her nose into a trough that threatened to pitchpole her end over end. Blackstone and Guillaume clung to their handholds. The master shouted an unheard command and the ship slid across the face of the wave, shuddered and then steadied back on course. The single sail fluttered, its iron-hard wet canvas cracking like the snap of a mighty oak being felled. Blackstone could see the packed deck, men huddling behind their shields, shoulders jammed into their neighbour's, steadying themselves. 'Can they fight?' Blackstone demanded.

'A third are too weak; half have a chance to reach the castle walls; the rest might have the strength to scale them and fight.' Guillaume squinted through the spray. The shoreline and its feared sandbar were getting closer. The *Saint Margaret Boat* was twice as long as she was wide, overladen with men and rundlets of tar and oil. She wallowed like a drunken pig.

'You're smiling like a monk with a candle up his arse! Don't mock your sworn lord, Guillaume – he can make your life more hellish than this!'

'Forgive me, lord, but from what the sailors say there's no need to worry about assaulting the castle. There's a wicked cross-current at the mouth of the estuary and beyond that bogland that will suck down man and horse. Taking the stronghold is the least of our worries.'

Another bone-jarring crash and Guillaume bent his body to accommodate the turbulence. He was lithe and strong, taught to move rapidly with sword, axe and mace. A fighting man, nineteen years old, with the immortality of youth, who had fought at Blackstone's side through desperate hours of battle since the squire had forged his pact of loyalty.

A warning cry carried on the wind. The master had urged his sailors to put their weight on the slab of sail. 'You'd best ready yourself, Sir Thomas!' he yelled. 'Lose a man here and he's gone to the devil!'

Blackstone took another turn on the rope and felt the ship surge, lift and crash in a bone-jarring jolt. In the sudden, unexpected contortion, Guillaume's fingers tore loose from their purchase and his body slammed into the ship's side. The blow took his legs from him and he grabbed wildly to find a handhold. Blackstone loosened his grip on the rope, its coarse fibre stinging his palm as it slid through his hand. He snatched Guillaume's tunic and took his weight, but knew, despite his strength, that the heaving, sluicing deck would soon wrench the squire free and he would be lost. The young man's set face showed the determination Blackstone had first recognized when his squire was a boy, and had held a trembling dagger close to Blackstone's face to protect his dying master. But now there was sudden panic in Guillaume's eyes. Neither spoke, but with a final, desperate glance at his sworn lord, Guillaume was snatched from him by a churning, malevolent green wave, shrouded in white spray, that tore across the ship's bows.

Helplessness and regret engulfed Blackstone. He should have left the ship's master, Jennah of Hythe, on the alehouse floor in Bordeaux with a knife at his throat and let the drunken German mercenaries, who had started the fight, finish it. But Blackstone had kicked the heavy-set murderer aside when the men pinned Jennah's arms. Knife fights in harbour taverns often ended with someone dead or maimed, but holding a defenceless man down was worse than pig slaughter and so Blackstone stopped it. Men in alehouses should know better than to challenge strangers, he had said to the German who threatened him. Foolishly, the drunken knifeman lunged – a futile attempt, as Blackstone and Guillaume quickly disarmed their attackers. Then Blackstone's captain, Meulon, the throat-cutter, did the rest, quietly and with a cut so deep the men had no breath left to cry out. The old whore who ran the alehouse screamed abuse, but Meulon showed her the blade and raised his shaggy eyebrows. No words were needed. The woman kicked the child servant and the floor was sluiced; then sawdust was thrown across the spilled blood as the men's bodies were dragged through the back alley that led to the wharf. The splash as they hit the water twenty feet below was barely heard. The Prince's invading army would not miss three of their men.

And Master Jennah was grateful. After a dozen shared bottles of rough red wine and a plate of mutton, his rambling stories of sailing the grave-yard coast of France's western shores mentioned a castle garrisoned in the French King's name that held a key bridge across a river fifty miles to the north as the crow flies. Rumour had it that it held weapons that supplied the French king's supporters. It was too far north for the Prince of Wales to attack and the castle's key location kept his loyal Gascon commander, the Captal de Buch, from warring beyond Bordeaux. The English Prince wanted booty and victory, not a prolonged, bone-aching siege in the marshlands, which is why he took his army south: the Prince had landed in Bordeaux late the previous year and was raiding south and east from Bordeaux. Like a cork in a bottle the castle sat at the head of an estuary, a foul, mist-laden place of stinking marsh gas like a whore's fart and a powerful, surging tide. And when that tide turned it left a devil's maw of a quagmire.

Blackstone gazed through the haze-laden room. The logs in the grate crackled and spat and men's eyes watered from its smoke. Figures swayed and moved to and fro; a gust of cold air swept through the room when the door opened and closed, but the stench of stale sweat lingered as men slept where they fell. The alehouse woman kicked them and swore, but, like tufted stumps of marsh grass at low tide, they remained unmoving. Marshland. Could a boat get upriver? Had he asked the question or had it formed only in his thoughts? Someone said that only a madman would attempt an attack upriver even if a ship could ever get that far along the storm-ravaged coast and, in case the Englishman didn't know, a cog, with its flat bottom, couldn't sail in a headwind.

11

Did Jennah of Hythe know those waters? Blackstone was nearly as drunk as the wine-sodden ship's master, a vainglorious plan forming in his mind, a plan that would put coin in his purse and inflict a defeat on the French: his King's enemy. He was sworn by honour to Edward and his son.

The sailor's face was the colour of tanned leather. Broken veins from drink or weather reddened his cheeks and nose. He wiped an arm across his lips that dribbled wine through blackened teeth. 'Know it? These past twenty years' worth of knowing. I've run m'ship from Bordeaux to Southampton and back carrying my King's wine from Gascony. I've had twenty-odd men lashed together like barrels when we invaded France back in '46. Twenty! No other carried more than a dozen. Less! I took them lads across and they had dry feet when they landed. You were there, were you, Master Blackstone?'

Blackstone nodded. He could never forget that hellish crossing even when drunk, though it had been nothing compared to what awaited him on the battlefields.

Master Jennah grasped Blackstone's shoulder, his eyes nearly closed with impending drunken slumber, and slurred a stumbling declaration. 'I have never slaked my thirst with a knight before, Sir Thomas. The honour is mine, and had my ship not been arrested by the serjeant-at-arms, and pressed into service, and my cargo taken – my cargo! Aye! I've lost my contract, right enough. I'm out of pocket serving my King – but . . . that said . . . if she were mine to offer . . . she would be yours if she could ever be of service.' Jennah's head slumped onto the table, the wine spilled. Blackstone stumbled across the floor, shouldered the door into the night and took his ambitious idea to the Gascon commander.

Jean de Grailly, whose sworn troops fought for the Crown, belonged to one of the noblest families in the Bordelais. It was the English King's good fortune to have him on his side. He was one of the youngest and ablest commanders, from an august family, who had secured some of King Edward's greatest victories and who still carried the feudal title, Captal de Buch. He was known across France for his audacious attacks that bolstered the English King's territorial claims. He was, Blackstone decided as he stood before this great seigneur, perhaps two or three years younger than his own twenty-six. It was unusual for such a high-ranking lord to grant an audience to anyone he regarded as of lesser rank, but Blackstone's reputation and acceptance by Edward and, if rumour did not lie, the Norman lords, was not to be denied. De Grailly studied the dishevelled man before him. Blackstone was at least a two-week ride from home. Over the years the scarred knight had enjoyed sanctuary with and protection from local English seneschals and Gascon nobles when he raided cattle and food in the warmer climes beyond Normandy. Blackstone was not involved in the fighting and the Prince had made no demands on the Englishman. Here in the south-west, noblemen carried on ancient feuds between themselves. Some could be bought, others defeated to secure territory in war, so why had Thomas Blackstone come to his headquarters? de Grailly wondered. The Englishman had already turned for home with the fifty men who rode with him, herding livestock and carting victuals to replenish his winter supplies. Had the Englishman made a new alliance with a feudal lord so far south from his own domain?

Blackstone was sober, but when he explained his daring plan it felt as cold and hard in his heart as the morning frost underfoot. What had fired his ambition the drunken night before now seemed a damned foolish idea and he had no need to suggest it, but it had been a long, hard winter that was not yet over, and Blackstone was always in need of money and weapons for his men. He accepted the cup of spiced wine he was offered and, keeping his uncertainty at bay, he outlined his plan.

De Grailly listened attentively; he was one of the few who could put aside the arrogance of rank when a seasoned fighter offered a plan that could bring victory, and personal glory.

'You want me to release his ship?' said de Grailly, surprised not so much by the request itself as by the objective that Blackstone had outlined.

'I do. And if he gets us through, return his cargo and let the man make a profit if he gets back to England.'

'Thomas,' de Grailly said, uncertain whether the boldness of the plan was that of a man possessed or a feat of daring that would allow him to strike farther north into French territory than he could ever have hoped, 'you know how many men that small cog can take? A dozen – perhaps a handful more. It can't be done.'

Perhaps de Grailly was right, Blackstone thought. To throw himself on the mercy of the sea and then sail upriver with a fast-turning tide behind an enemy stronghold, with little knowledge of its fortifications, could be a quick way to die. The ship's master had told him that a spit of land, like a small island, lay to the seaward side of the stronghold and provided the tides had not risen too high and made the ground impassable, then men could get across it and scale the walls. Beyond that, little was known. Blackstone hoped to burn down the main gate and force the garrison of – how many? Sixty or more? – to defend themselves within the courtyard. De Grailly's weight of numbers had to arrive in support and on time.

De Grailly said: 'The French control the river and the road. They will have barges patrolling downriver. A barge can turn and outrun a ship. They will be waiting for you.'

'Master Jennah tells me the tide will be in our

favour, running from the sea. We run with it. Barges from upriver won't go against the tide.'

Silence settled between de Grailly and Blackstone as both men considered the idea. De Grailly realized that if he could swoop north and deliver a deep wound into the French underbelly, he could then turn his troops inland and drive south in a pincer movement that would throw his enemy off guard and allow him to seize Périgueux, a major French-held city. He tapped his finger nervously on the table. Too far too fast? Too exposed on his flank? How much longer could this English knight lead a charmed life?

Blackstone broke their silence. 'Take the garrison, seize their armoury and you inflict a wound that'll bleed them dry. You'll control the river, your men will command the road north, your back will be protected and the Prince will kiss you on both cheeks and shower you with glory.'

'And for you, Thomas? What is in it for you?'

'I take whatever weapons I can carry. I take their plate and silver, relieve them of the coin they'll have for paying the garrison and those local nobles who support King John. You take the victory; I take the rewards. I can't pay my men with glory alone.'

De Grailly was nodding. The Englishman was taking the greater risk.

'You would have to be on that road to secure it,' Blackstone said, knowing the route to the castle was the key. Reinforcements could pour down it and overwhelm Blackstone's small force. 'Be there when I burn down those gates and get inside the walls. If you don't I'm trapped.'

'And if you don't get inside? Then I'm exposed. I can't turn back six hundred men. The French see my approach and they have me. My head would be delivered to the French King and the Prince becomes vulnerable.'

'And a horse could stumble walking across a stable yard, throw you and break your neck, or a thief could slip a knife between your ribs. Death is waiting for us all. The trick is to cheat it long enough,' Blackstone answered.

The wave that took Guillaume tumbled him away along the deck. A pitch and a roll and he would be lost. Blackstone could do nothing; his hand already bled from the coarse rope, and as he swung like a flailing pulley-block in a tempest, making a final, desperate effort to grab him, he saw a dark shape separate itself from the huddled mass. The burly figure, his eyes barely visible, his black beard matted with salt, threw the weight of his body onto the helpless man, wresting Guillaume from the roiling water. It was Meulon who pulled the smaller man to him like a shield, and he in turn was grabbed and held by Gaillard. They had enough muscle between them to force half a dozen men to the ground with ferocious ease. The sea god's anger was denied its sacrifice – and, like a burrowing animal, Guillaume disappeared beneath the shield wall.

17

Blackstone took a tighter grip on the rope, lost his footing, and was slammed into the ship's side. Pain burst through him, but gave him a surge of anger that doubled his strength. And then the boat shuddered, the ominous sound of wood scraping across the sand bar. The clinker-built cog was like a fat-bellied sow; its bowed ribs made it wallow, but its flat-bottomed hull allowed it to enter shallow waters, and with a following tide the ship lurched across the gravelled mouth of the estuary. There was an immediate halt to the violence as the ship found calmer water in the broad reach of the river. For two hundred paces each side of the ship, the mudflats rose into a stubbled landscape of rotted tree-stumps that caught the wind and howled dismally.

Blackstone swung himself around to face the huddled men. 'On your feet! Up! Now!'

The men staggered uncertainly, found what balance they could, locking arms, bracing legs, weapons in one hand, comrades held fast in the other. There had been enough vomit spewed that day to empty men's stomachs and Blackstone saw the gaunt look of illness on every man's face. As the ship steadied, Master Jennah ordered the sail lowered and secured.

'Wind's against us good and proper now, but this tide will carry us upstream,' he shouted to Blackstone. 'Get the water out!'

The ship was heavy with seawater trapped knee-deep with nowhere to go. Blackstone grabbed a bucket and followed the mariners' example, scooping water and passing it to the next man. Without needing to be told his men slung their shields and, ignoring the cramped deckspace, bent to the task. The boat would settle if they did not empty it of the shipped water. Jennah watched the veering wind scatter spray and foam and shouted his helmsmen to keep their course. The command was merely a ritual in these shallow rivers, but the men who steered the ship had been pressed into service most of their lives and had taken trading vessels like the *Saint Margaret Boat* up many inlets.

Master Jennah had told Blackstone of the river's long, twisting curves, of the mudbanks that broke the shallow surface and the wasteland that stretched into the distant forests. If they reached the river mouth by the time the sun was above their heads, he had told Blackstone with a look of misgiving, then when they heard a distant church bell ring for prayers they had less than half the daylight remaining. That was when they would turn the final bend in the river. Blackstone looked at the riverbank and guessed they were moving as quickly as a horse trotted. If Master Jennah was correct, then by the time they reached the garrison there would be only a short time before darkness fell. That was the better choice. It was what he had hoped for: a few short hours to get close to the walls, then fight and secure. They would attack and hold until the next morning. De Grailly would not bring his troops up in darkness. With luck the

19

Gascon commander would be waiting a few miles away, hidden in the forest so that at first light he could secure the road. A soldier needed good fortune on his side, a calming hand from the angels that allowed him to survive; looking at the state of his men, shivering and hunched, limbs aching and bellies empty, he reckoned he needed the earth spirits' blessing as well.

It was not given.

Blackstone threw the bucketful of water over the side. It was whipped away by the wind, half of it stinging his face. The wind had turned.

He looked to where Jennah stood with his helmsmen and the ship's master nodded in silent acknowledgement. The wind was now behind them and, with the flowing tide pushed them ever faster towards the enemy, they would reach the castle with more daylight than he had wished.

There had been no appetite for the ship's rations of salted fish, so once the water had been cleared he gave each man a generous ration of brandywine. It would settle the effects of the voyage and put strength back into their limbs, and Blackstone knew its effect would calm the uncertainty that sat in every man's mind. There were only twenty of them – two more counting Blackstone and Guillaume – and there could be no expectation that the mariners would join in the assault. There was likely to be at least twice the number behind the castle walls to hold a stronghold such as this, but Blackstone prayed that their meandering approach through the mudflats would go unnoticed. The French nobleman who commanded the garrison would expect any challenge to be made from beneath the castle walls. Men of honour did not slip quietly behind the enemy like assassins in the night.

Honour, Blackstone told himself, meant different things to different men.

There was no church bell ringing as the *Saint Margaret Boat* eased around the headland of the river's final bend. His men crouched below the ship's sides as Blackstone stood with Jennah and watched the stronghold ease into view. What he saw was a poor defensive structure that depended on the natural lie of the land. A timbered wall faced the river and Blackstone guessed that the wet ground had been too yielding to secure a stone fortification, which he could see extended beyond the rear wall of the castle where the ground must have been firmer. Drainage ditches had been dug and abandoned over time. There had been little need to expend further effort on a defensive wall where the quagmire and tide formed seemingly impregnable defences. The timber would be chestnut or oak, strong as iron, but with its feet in the soft ground. The castle rose fifteen feet above the river and he could see that what was once a broad reach of water narrowed into smaller channels, finally disappearing into little more than fingers of water that seeped into a distant water meadow. No wonder the castle held the road; there was little chance of an assault by land.

'Not too close, Master Jennah,' Blackstone told him. Wild grassland and reeds smothered what remained of stunted trees, sodden with brackish water, which obscured the small ship. Bulrushes bent in the wind, scattering their fine down.

'I can run aground on that mudbank there, Sir Thomas,' he said, holding the boat pressed against the riverbank, 'and I'll float free when the tide turns. You and your men will have to go through the reeds, and it'll be hard going, particularly if you have to carry them rundlets.' He nodded towards the lashed casks, half the size of a wine barrel, but which would still weigh a hundred pounds or more. Master Jennah grimaced – more, was his guess. Blackstone had loaded a dozen of the tar-filled half-barrels with the intention of burning down the main gate, but he now saw that was impossible, since the river did not allow access to the front of the stronghold. It swirled away beneath the road bridge, its strength diminished as it spread out into the shallow tributaries of the water meadows beyond. It was obvious that the only place Blackstone could place them was beneath the timber wall. Wading through marshland carrying the barrels under cover of bulrushes was a task he did not envy his poor seasick men. The reeds might obscure their approach but only so far. A narrow tributary flowed beneath the walls, thick with the stinking black slime of rotted vegetation, and then rejoined the river. It was better than a defensive ditch. If that approach was Blackstone's only means of attack, Jennah realized, it meant those walls would take a long time to burn, which would give sufficient warning for the garrison to summon reinforcements. Ten years before, he had anchored his boat beyond the great city of Caen and watched its destruction from upriver. In those days the King's army had brought up barges loaded with archers and their firepower had bought time for the soldiers. This place was no Caen, but with only twenty men, no archers or floating platforms, it might as well have been.

'Can you get your ship down that ditch?' Blackstone asked, pointing to the water that ran below the walls.

'I'd get her down but I won't be able to get her back. She'll be held fast.'

Blackstone kept his steady gaze on Jennah's face. It took only a moment for the ship's master to grasp what Blackstone meant.

'No! I'll not make this a fire ship!'

Blackstone's legs were still unsteady from the tormented voyage, so the stocky man had strength enough to push him aside. Jennah snarled at the helmsman: 'Hold her fast! Keep her bow there!' he said, cutting the air with the flat of his hand in the direction of the riverbank. The following tide still kept his ship pressed snugly out of sight from the French. He glowered at Blackstone. 'A master of his ship swears an oath to save his cargo and the lives of his men. And a ship is never lost unless master and crew are dead, that's the law! The law, Sir Thomas! And I'll not sacrifice my ship or my men for you. I owe you my life, but nothing more.'

'You'll earn the Prince's blessing,' Blackstone told him, in the hope of stinging the man's loyalty.

'Ay! The Prince! God bless him! He'd take the shirt off a man's back if it meant he could freeze the poor bastard to death. The Prince has no need of my ship to go up in flames though!'

The scarred knight had him outnumbered. Jennah spat and rubbed his cropped head, scattering flakes of scurf into the wind. His salt- and wind-cracked hands had healed too many times to remember, but they had strength enough to grasp a knife and a knotted rope to fight the man who wanted to burn his ship.

Blackstone knew the threat was a brave man's stand. Jennah was three strides away but Meulon and the men drew their swords. Blackstone raised an arm and halted any violence against the sailors, whose death would have been slaughter, for they could have made only token resistance.

'You'll not have my boat, by Christ's tears you will not, Sir Thomas,' said Jennah, readying himself. 'A knight would fight for his pennon or banner; he'd have to be dead before he let his sword fall from his fist. It's no different for a mariner. We swore an oath. The *Saint Margaret Boat* is my vessel. Heart and soul.'

It would have been an easy task to disarm the angry man but killing him would serve no purpose. Blackstone did not have the skill to use the tide and nudge the ship beneath the walls, and to blackmail the old man with the killing of one of his innocent crew was not an option that Blackstone would consider – it could only ever be a bluff. Besides, Master Jennah had kept his part of the bargain and brought the fighting men to the shore.

Blackstone said: 'How long before the tide turns?'

'Three hours at most,' answered Jennah, still holding the knife warily.

Blackstone nodded and turned to the waiting men. 'Meulon. Send Gaillard ashore with a cask.' Blackstone turned back to Jennah. 'Lower your blade, Master Jennah. You'll take no harm from me. Your ship is yours. Men need no better reason to defend that which they love.'

Jennah hesitated, but when Blackstone went down onto the deck he slid the blade back into its sheath. He watched as one of Blackstone's soldiers, as big a man as Blackstone himself, but with a heavier build to his shoulders, clambered over the side of the ship carrying a tar barrel. There was no doubting the man's strength or determination as he attempted to make headway through the soggy ground that sucked his legs down to the knee. With the rundlet on his shoulder he tried to keep his balance, but within ten paces he fell. He staggered to his feet, hefted his burden back onto his shoulder again but made no more than three or four paces before he squelched down again.

Meulon took the signal from Blackstone and gently whistled a single note, then beckoned Gaillard back to the ship. Every fighting man knew that if Gaillard's strength could not even reach twenty paces, then none would ever reach the base of the wall, more than three hundred cloth yards away, and then negotiate the quagmire and stream.

Blackstone weighed their chances. Attack too soon and the garrison would send a messenger for reinforcements. Then, no matter how strong de Grailly's force might appear, they could be ambushed on the narrow road and the English would suffer a defeat that could have a devastating effect on the Prince of Wales's war of attrition. Attack too late and Blackstone and his men could be cornered like rats behind the walls. His successful raid, which had occupied the past several weeks, meant that his men were ready for the comfort of their women and a good fire in a grate rather than wet ground and bitter fighting. Now they could end with their heads on poles. He cursed himself for being too ambitious.

He should have been halfway home by now. He had promised Christiana that, once he had re-supplied the towns he held and paid the men who followed him, there would be time for them both before his son's birthday. There were few raids undertaken over the winter months so he had scraped out the foundations of a new wall, embedding stone so that the winter rains would sluice through them and not damage his planned construction. They had carted rock from the fields and quarry and he had spent two cold months in his barn cutting and shaping the stone to his liking. When they had first taken over the old Norman manor house after they were married, he'd discovered signs of an ancient settlement. In their time the Romans had laid cut-stone pathways and built shelters for the animals with defensive walls, but like many old French towns they had tumbled and lain shrouded by undergrowth. Ancient warriors had encamped in these parts until wars of conquest had dragged them away. The place gave Blackstone a sense of belonging, somewhere he would live in relative peace with Christiana and the children. And they had desperately wanted another child. That was all part of his promise to her. Six months before this raid for food and supplies she had lost the child from her womb. The women who attended her had wrapped the infant and hid it from him, but Blackstone had unfolded the bloodied linen and gazed at the small creature that lay curled in sleep-like death and who would have been his second son.

A friend, Joanne de Ruymont, who had never shared her husband's friendship with the Englishman, had comforted her. She was a woman constrained by the manners dictated by her high-born family, a woman who held a deep-rooted resentment against Thomas Blackstone, an archer who had slain members of her family at Crécy. It was her husband, Guy, who served as peacemaker between the two families, given his close friendship with Blackstone's mentor, the Norman lord Jean de Harcourt, but it had been Christiana that Joanna visited when the men were away fighting. It had been she who had held Christiana through the torturous time of her miscarriage.

And now all Blackstone wanted was to go home, comfort his wife, and build his wall.

'Sir Thomas?'

Meulon's voice broke into Blackstone's thoughts. 'What are your orders?'

Blackstone looked at the men who awaited his command.

'Can any of your men swim, Master Jennah?'

'Swim? Other than me – no. I'm the only man aboard with a chance to reach the shore if we were ever wrecked. There's no swimming to be had here, Sir Thomas. Not with this current.' It made no sense to the sailor. 'Swim where?'

'Rope each barrel of oil with another of tar. Someone has to take them beneath the bridges and into the water meadows. And then light them. Send flames across the sky and draw out those inside. But it will take at least two men.'

'Well, I'm too old to be doing that. The water is cold and a man can be snared by what lies beneath. And to keep tinder dry to fire the barrels will be the devil's job.'

28

Blackstone looked to his men. Guillaume stepped forward. 'I'll go, lord. But I'll need time to float them into position.'

He had no wish to see his squire go into the water. Whoever lit the barrels might easily be seen by crossbowmen on the walls. Enough quarrels could be loosed to cut through reed beds without even aiming.

'Meulon, you lead the assault. I'll go into the water with Master Guillaume.' There was no choice. Blackstone had swum in the river that flowed by his village since he could walk.

'My lord,' Meulon said quickly. 'Taking the walls can be done, but it needs you to lead us. We could flounder inside the stronghold as badly as a drowning man in the water.' There was a murmur of agreement from the men. A wiry man, muscular despite his slight build, stepped forward. It was Perinne, one of the men who had fought with Blackstone these past ten years. A wall-builder like the man who led him.

'I thrashed across a pond once, Sir Thomas. Give me a shaft of wood to cling to and I'll get myself out there with a bit of help from the current. We can't have Meulon here taking all the glory for seizing the place. Besides, it's safer in the water than having Gaillard sticking his spear up my arse every time a shadow moves.'

The men laughed and muttered their agreement; the tension of uncertainty was broken.

'Right enough,' Guillaume said, 'but when you

fire the tar barrels make sure you're upwind or you'll have less hair than you have now.'

Perinne's thinning, close-cropped hair showed bird's-feet scars across his scalp. 'I might not have the locks of a girl, Master Guillaume, but I'll wager my old head has snuggled between more tits than your own.'

Guillaume Bourdin wore his hair to his shoulders and, with his fine features, could easily be mistaken for a young woman – a mistake soon corrected when the fighting started – but it was seldom they had seen the young squire take a whore. The young man's pride was easily hurt when it came to such matters, but to fight with men like these meant pride had best learn to suffer its own wounds; by now Guillaume's carried as many nicks and cuts as Perinne's scalp.

Master Jennah said: 'Merciful Christ, Sir Thomas. A lad and a man who can barely float on the tide like a turd? Is that your plan?'

'If victory were governed by how we look and whether shit floats we would all be Kings of France. I'll swim with them until the barrels are in place and then return. Now, Master Jennah, you'll keep your boat safe and tucked up here, because when the tide turns we must pray they don't send river patrols out from that garrison. If they do, your ship is gone and your crew dead – and you with it. I'll not be able to help you, because we will have put ourselves below that wall, waiting for the fire to take their attention.'

Jennah wiped a hand across his face. The risk of being discovered and attacked was more of a reality now than it had ever been.

'Sir Thomas, I can't anchor here for long. They'll see my mast sooner or later. You need the tide to float the tar barrels; you don't need my ship. Give me leave to sail when the wind turns.'

It was Meulon's voice that carried: 'You abandon us?' The tightly packed men jostled forward, their mood quickly changing.

The ship's master took a step back. These violent men were as great a danger as the enemy. He crossed himself, uttering an invocation to Jesu, Son of God. Blackstone stepped between him and the men.

'Master Jennah has done what I asked. He's right: we have no further need of his ship. We either take this stronghold and are relieved by the Captal de Buch and his forces, or we die. And I for one would not go another hour on this bucket and leave my innards for the fish. I'll fight, but I'll not die on my knees, retching my arse through my throat!'

His deliberately crude comment had the desired effect. 'Amen, my lord,' said Perinne.

Others agreed. Meulon took his lead from Blackstone. 'Then we'd best get ourselves beneath that wall while there's daylight and try to stomach some of Master Jennah's salted fish, because it will be a long night.'

CHAPTER 2

The eddies settled as the tide turned. Within hours twenty feet of the riverbanks would be exposed as the water raced for the sea. Blackstone stripped off and slipped naked into the chilled water. He gasped with the cold, feeling his muscles tighten. Guillaume and Perinne followed him, but they would be in the marshes all night so stayed clothed, their weapons wrapped securely in oiled cloth. Using the calmer water to drift beneath the road bridge, each man pushed two of the half-barrels roped together, their staves already cracked by axe and covered in sackcloth to hold back their seepage. At times the men's feet touched the bottom, giving them purchase as they pushed through into the water meadow, easing aside lush grass and reeds, praying that the breeze would cover the reeds' movement. Once they were beyond the stronghold's walls they dared to look back and saw the iron-studded doors and gate-house, where the gloom of the closing day revealed the figures of two sentries guarding their posts. There was no sign of any others. The French commander had grown complacent. So well placed was the garrison it seemed obvious that the only way an enemy could approach would be along the road.

Blackstone took one of the channels into the marshland; Guillaume and Perinne, who had tied a piece of wood beneath his chest, pushed their way into others. In the distance a church bell rang. A hundred yards further and they wedged the casks into the knotted clumps of vegetation and prised the cracked staves further open. Their flint and steel, and the tinder they carried beneath their leather caps to ignite the oil, would be kept safe and dry until the signal was given. Somewhere across the wasteland that same church bell would ring out in darkness, its lonely chime signalling the time to attack.

Blackstone paddled back to the two men. The wind had dropped and the stench of marsh gas that bubbled from beneath the surface soured the back of their throats. Smoke drifted lazily from the garrison, the cold, heavy air pushing it down towards the river's surface. They shivered not only from the wet and cold, but from the belief that lost spirits of the dead, trapped between heaven and earth, could rise from the bubbling, stinking underworld. Blackstone grabbed Perinne's shoulder, forcing aside his own fear of the place.

'They won't rise at night, Perinne. If they manifest it will be now in the half-light. Don't confuse that curling smoke with anything else. Get yourself onto this clump of reed and stay out of the water. You know what to do.'

'Aye, Sir Thomas. I know.'

'My life depends on you, as it has in the past. I need your courage tonight more than ever. And if there are spirits about they'll be of our dead friends sent to protect us.'

Perinne grinned. His teeth had almost stopped chattering. 'Next you'll be telling me my mother wasn't a whore,' he said.

Blackstone pulled himself away through the tangled undergrowth. Arianrhod sat in the hollow of his throat, listening to his whispered prayer for protection as his naked body was caressed by submerged weeds and rotting fingers of roots. But his mind pictured the floating dead reaching up for him; it was all he could do to keep from crying out. The place was rank with evil. Yet he swam back twice again with the uncomplaining Guillaume, pushing his own fear aside and the remaining barrels into place. Guillaume would keep Perinne close to him. Two men's courage was better than one man alone in the cloying mist. It was almost dark when Jennah's men hauled the shivering Blackstone aboard and, as Meulon reported that he had sent Gaillard and two others forward with coils of light rope to mark the way, he rubbed himself dry with sackcloth, scouring his skin back to warmth. He could feel the boat moving in a gentle rise and fall as it scraped against the mud bank, straining for its release in its desire to join the ebb tide. A sullen bell marking vespers – the end of the day – sent its haunting sound across the marshland.

Meulon took the men over the side and onto the riverbank, waiting for Blackstone.

'Your two men in the water, their shields are still aboard,' Jennah told him.

'We can't take extra weight with us. Do as you wish with them,' said Blackstone, slinging his own shield across his back. 'They'll be given others to replace them.'

'Then we'll keep them with some pride, Sir Thomas. Mist is settling,' Jennah said, thankful that it would help cover his departure. 'It'll sit around those gullies and cover you and your men till you climb over that wall. I wish you well and that God blesses your endeavours, but I have to let loose my boat and be gone from here.'

Blackstone finished dressing. 'Your cargo's waiting for you, Master Jennah. The *Saint Margaret Boat* is yours again.'

Jennah bowed his head while Blackstone secured his shield as the men ashore had done. 'I'm a sailor, Sir Thomas. Your world frightens me. But I would have fought you for my ship, even though you would have killed me.'

'Go and secure your profit and your freedom, Master Jennah of Hythe. I would rather die here than face that sea again. We each fight in our own way.'

No mention was made of Jennah's debt of life, or that his ship had also been spared. He watched Blackstone lead his men away into the darkness. No words passed between them; each fell into place, with every man knowing what was expected of him. The only sound Jennah heard was the soft squelch of their feet moving through the soggy ground.

The boat turned into the tide. Master Jennah raised his arm in farewell.

But Blackstone never looked back.

They stood knee-deep in black, stinking quagmire, their backs pressed against the wooden wall. It had taken slow, painful hours to cross the spit of land, wary of their movement being seen by any sentry patrolling the rear ramparts. They had forded the tributary as the tide turned, each man helping the other as at times they waded deep into the foulness. Exhaustion was claiming them as a swell of water rippled like a great dark snake. The church bell had rung once more, telling peasant and lord, wherever they might be, to retire for the night. The next bell would be rung later in the night, calling the monks to prayer – and that would be the signal for Guillaume to set alight the tar barrels.

And Blackstone now realized that it would be too late.

Twenty men shivered and prayed as the water rose higher. Blackstone knew that Guillaume and Perinne would be clinging to the roots of the bulrushes. And that oil would have seeped through the tangled mass, but the tide was coming in faster than Blackstone had thought possible. If Guillaume had fallen asleep or did not realize the quickness of the tide, the men against the wall would soon have a simple choice: drown or scale the walls and fall into the enemy's arms.

They heard the rushing tide before they saw the darkness move towards them. The river had spilled into the tributary of the spit of land and as it curled around the narrow headland the force of the water swept into the riverbank. The mud they had been standing in was now water tugging at their thighs. If they waited any longer the men would have no purchase beneath their feet to balance the throwing of the grappling irons twenty feet above their head.

'Throw!' Blackstone hissed.

Ropes snaked up into the darkness, their iron claws biting into the top of the wooden wall. Twenty men, six ropes. Blackstone put his weight against one of them and tested its strength and then without another word began to climb hand over hand as his feet tried to find some grip on the slimy wood. Others were scrambling on either side of him, grunting with effort, overcoming the protests of stiff muscles and chilled bodies. Blackstone was first over the wall, crouching, lowering the outline of his body against the dark sky. The dull glow of flickering torches came from the four corners of the courtyard. The stronghold was little more than a glorified earthwork that had been fortified over the years, a piecemeal strengthening as demands dictated. Across the open expanse on the far side from where Blackstone and his men now stood the gatehouse silhouette reared up. A horse whinnied from a stable block. The men froze. Had the breeze carried their scent? A few muted voices came from one of the buildings below the wall. A dormitory door opened; torchlight flickered as a soldier stepped out and walked a few yards to another building – the latrines.

Light up the night, boy! Now!

When the soldier returned he would be facing directly where Blackstone and his men now crouched. No matter how low they tried to keep below the rampart, the shape of the wall would change and living in a garrison gave a man an animal sense of something altered.

The door opened. They could see the man's face plainly now.

Burn it, Guillaume! Don't wait for the damned bell! Light the oil!

Coiled in tension the men dared not move. Blackstone sensed Meulon turn to face him, waiting for his lord's command. Better to get down into the courtyard than be caught on the wall. Was there a chance they could run for the gatehouse and seize it? Blackstone wondered, his mind weighing the odds of survival rather than the chance of success.

Better to fight and find out.

And then the night sky flared into a curtain of fire.

Sentries screamed their alarm and within moments the garrison was alive with shouting men as they gathered their weapons and ran for the front parapet. Blackstone signalled. Meulon took half the men to the right; he with the others skirmished left, each group running for the steps that would take them into the mêlée below. Beyond the walls reed beds caught in the flames flickered like burning stars that rose and died. Men shouted, a door slammed open and a bareheaded knight with a squire at his side ran out, buckling belt and sword, and joined the men sprinting for the gatehouse and the walls.

Thirty, forty, men – at least. Kill them – how?

The sky blazed and Blackstone spared a moment's thought for his squire and Perinne. If they were badly placed there would be no escape from the inferno that would catch every dry reed. A memory flared: a windmill engulfed in flames when he was an archer lying close to death on the field of Crécy, his bloodied fist gripping the Bohemian knight's sword that had slain his young brother. The blade that bore the mark of the running wolf. He had wrenched it from the knight's hand and in a final brutal contest had killed him with it.

Blackstone gestured with Wolf Sword to Gaillard, who took his six men and ran into the shadows of a building to protect Blackstone's flank. Meulon had already positioned his men. Blackstone would take the centre ground and start the killing. When the time was right Meulon's crossbowmen would loose their missiles into the unsuspecting soldiers. None of the garrison had yet looked behind them, unaware that the darkness held such deadly threat. They clambered up ladders and jostled onto the parapet as the soldiers already on the wall called to each other, trying to find where the threat might be coming from, pointing at shadows that swayed and deceived.

Blackstone made his run across the open ground towards the ladder to kill the men who flocked together at that end of the wall.

Horses whinnied when they heard the cries of panic and scented fire in the air. Some kicked at their stalls. A small group of four or five Frenchmen turned and ran back to the stables, their thoughts concentrated on calming the horses. It was they who saw Blackstone and his half-dozen shield-bearers run diagonally across the courtyard. These wild-eyed intruders looked briefly their way but, incredibly, chose to ignore them. In that moment, even though they were common soldiers, the Frenchmen recognized the shields' design of a gauntleted fist clasping a cruciform sword and knew who was within their walls. That moment of fear held them fast as they turned to yell a warning. They died where they stood, disbelief and agony etched on their faces as Gaillard's spearmen struck from their blind side, thrusting their long blades into their backs and then melting back into the shadows, by which time Blackstone was already at the steps, looking up at the crimson light that flooded the sky. If the garrison commander had allied noblemen within twenty miles then they too would know violence had befallen the garrison. Blackstone ran past the first dozen men, his shoulder banging and shoving them as he made his way along the parapet. None turned. In their efforts to reach the wall the soldiers had jostled and barged one another, so in their minds whoever it was who ran behind them now were others doing the same. Mesmerized by the racing fire that seemed to have set the vast water meadow alight, they watched as streams of burning oil and floating tar cut through the chan-nels, blood-red claws raking the land.

Blackstone was halfway down the line of men. His luck would not hold much longer. He rammed Wolf Sword into the back of a man whose sudden contortion turned the man next to him. Terror-stricken, the man's face twisted into a macabre mask as he tried to bring up his blade. Wolf Sword severed his arm and Blackstone shouldered the screaming man aside with his shield. The alerted soldiers turned and attacked. Blackstone heard the clash of arms behind him: his men already savaging the startled defenders. There was little room to manoeuvre on the narrow rampart and, as he sidestepped the first attacker, someone behind him thrust a sword into the man's chest. Blackstone's men fought at his shoulder, lending their weight as the next Frenchman met his shield and strength as he braced against the surge of soldiers now bearing down on him. The sudden whisper of crossbow quarrels became muscle-tearing thuds as they struck home. Meulon had gauged the threat and his men loosed their bolts as their sworn lord was under attack, slamming into the dying and wounded men who fell on top of each other, some tumbling into the courtyard. Blackstone turned back. At least twenty enemies lay dead, for the cost of two of his own. That section of the wall was now secure. Meulon had not wasted time reloading the crossbows but led the men towards the gatehouse. Ragged knots of French defenders ran out of the half-light from across the courtyard towards the fighting. Confusion splintered them further as sudden attacks from Blackstone's men from the shadows, led by a heavy-set bearded man, cut and thrust at them, killing and maiming, and then retreated quickly. Another group of armed men attacked near the gatehouse. Screams and incoherent commands among the besieged French caused chaos. There was no place to make a stand. The attackers seemed to be everywhere.

Two square-built towers rose thirty feet on either side of the gate, joined above the entrance passageway. The two rooms above the vaulted doorway formed the gatehouse that held the port-cullis's winding mechanism and the guard commander's quarters. Meulon ran to the east tower as Blackstone's men hacked at the bolted door with axes. Resistance was sporadic now as

Gaillard's group still engaged in random violence against the disorganized defenders and Meulon's men held the other side of the gatehouse. Blackstone knew there were at least twenty or thirty Frenchmen left alive and sooner or later someone would realize how few the attackers were and organize themselves into a fighting unit. Then Blackstone's isolated raiders would be cornered and picked off. As the wooden doors splintered amid the shouts of alarm from those inside the tower, Blackstone looked beyond the crenellated walls and saw two bedraggled figures drag themselves onto the narrow road out of the smouldering clumps of reed beds.

Agonizing screams soon faltered into whimpering pain and then fell silent as the wounded were put to death. Blackstone stepped into the tower and saw Meulon cutting a wounded man's throat. His men stood gasping for air, their lungs heaving, this final assault sapping the last of their strength. Blackstone knew they all needed sleep, food and a safe haven, but there were still men in the stronghold who could gather their wits and their weapons and hunt them down.

'Bring it up,' he commanded. Meulon and two others took to the windlass as Blackstone stepped back out into the night and called for the others. 'Gaillard. The bridge! Lower it! And open the gates!'

Gaillard's unmistakable lumbering figure led others from the cover of one of the low stone buildings towards the two counterweights below. Once they were released the ten-foot drawbridge would drop into place across the defensive ditch and join road and castle.

Inside the tower his exhausted men secured the windlass and slumped against the wall. Only Meulon remained standing, but Blackstone could see that even he had little left in him to carry on the fight.

Blackstone said: 'The garrison's not yet surrendered. Meulon! Two men who bear wounds remain here for the portcullis. They see French reinforcements – drop it. Everyone else outside.'

They had neither slept nor eaten a decent meal in three days, had vomited their way across a violent sea and fought quagmire and enemy. For a moment it seemed the gaunt-eyed men might refuse as he turned back through the door, not wanting to risk his order being questioned, not knowing what he would do if it were. As he reached the courtyard he heard the men chase down the steps after him. The gaping space in the vaulted archway was without portcullis and gate. The way of escape was now open.

'Gaillard, Meulon. Form up the men, shield high. We'll chase the wolf from its lair.'

Of the twenty men who had followed him over the wall, three were now dead, two bore wounds that would need a barber-surgeon and everyone else, including himself, carried lesser hurts. He stepped forward, followed by fourteen men who brought their shields up and advanced across the open courtyard. The scattered remnants of the garrison's force saw their discipline and their swords held ready to strike and, as Blackstone wheeled the men like beaters driving game, they ran for the open gate and safety beyond the garrison's walls.

One group did not.

A strengthening wind whipped torchlight flames, distorting the shadows, making the small knot of men indistinguishable from the building they defended. Were there more than the handful of men that Blackstone could see, who stood in front of a lone bareheaded figure? They made no advance to attack, waiting instead for Blackstone to turn on them. He halted his men; the stronghold was theirs except for these soldiers. The bareheaded man was the knight he had seen running across the courtyard. His shield was distinguished by a boar's head, and the men's jupons bore the same emblem. Blackstone realized it was the garrison commander and led his men forward slowly; the outnumbered Frenchmen had to be fearful, as every man is when death approaches, but Blackstone could see their resolute stance in defence of their lord.

'Hold the men,' Blackstone told Meulon, and stepped closer to the group. The torchlight around them showed them to be older men, most, Blackstone guessed, having known battle for twenty-odd years; taken into their lord's service when they were little more than boys. Probably about the same age as Blackstone's fourteen-year-old brother when he had gone to war with him ten years before. And if these men had survived this long it meant their fighting skills were honed. The knight reminded him of Sir Reginald Cobham, the unyielding warrior who had commanded at Crécy. Older. Aggressively proud. Fearless.

Blackstone stopped ten paces from them.

'I am Thomas—' he began, but was quickly interrupted by the knight.

'I know who you are, Thomas Blackstone. A routier and a murderer. A man without honour. I am Henri de la Beaumont, Count of Saint-Clair-de-la-Beaumont and guardian of this, my lord King's castle.'

Blackstone knew in that moment that the old man would never surrender and that more of Blackstone's men would die in this fight.

'This place is lost, my lord. I claim it in the name of Edward, King of England, and his son the Prince of Wales. Lay down your weapons.'

The old man sneered and spat into the dirt. 'To a handful of cut-throats? Your bodies will float back on the tide like turds from our latrines.'

Blackstone heard his men shuffle into a half-moon formation behind him. They would envelop these few men and the long night of bloodshed would finally end.

'I desire no more slaughter, my lord. Take your men and leave this place,' said Blackstone. 'I will not even ask for your surrender because you think me a lesser knight than yourself. If you stand fast and wait until morning then Lord de Grailly will take your surrender and ransom you to your King.'

Blackstone saw the look of defeat move across the old man's face. If the Captal de Buch was so close then he had struck further north than had been thought possible. This was no mere opportunistic raid by a daring independent captain; it was an attack designed to give King John's enemies a strategic advantage. For a moment Blackstone thought the old fighter would see the helplessness of the situation. There was no shame in surrendering to someone of such rank as de Grailly. But de la Beaumont's eyes narrowed with contempt.

'Jean de Grailly is a Gascon arse-wipe for your English King.'

Blackstone could refuse to engage the old man and wait until de Grailly arrived and took command, but the shuffling feet and gathering of shields meant the men were ready to fight and die. It took only an instant for it to happen; a brief warning as men's eyes steeled themselves. Then, like men in a dream wading helplessly through mud, the French came forward. Shields clashed and the illusion ended. Blackstone barged and hacked, feinted and killed. Wolf Sword's blood knot bit into his wrist and kept its slippery grip firmly in his hand. Spears lunged past him as Meulon beat down with a mace, hammering a man's helmet and skull into pulp. The old knight waited behind his men, determined not to yield whatever lay in the building behind him. It would be Blackstone who would kill him – a swift, vicious fight that would end in the knight's death. Blackstone beat his way forward, men at his shoulder. A sudden blow caught him as a wounded Frenchman went down wildly swinging his sword; the flat of it slammed across the back of Blackstone's head. He fell hard, rolled quickly, covering himself with his shield. Contorted faces of his dead men glared at him. Images of them when alive flashed through the pain in his head. He scrambled to his feet, but his men had pushed past him and he saw Meulon parry the knight's blows, allowing men behind him to ram their spears into the old man, pinning him to the door. He squirmed, coughed blood, looked wildly at Blackstone – a man of rank and honour being slaughtered by lesser men – seconds before others mobbed him and hacked him down. The old boar was dead. The fight was finally over.

Blackstone ripped the silver belt from the knight's body and passed it to Meulon. It was his reward.

'Search the garrison. There'll be plate and Sir Henri will have clasps and silk. Gather whatever you find before Lord de Grailly's men arrive – they'll strip the place.' All except Meulon and Gaillard grabbed torches and ran. 'Go out and find Guillaume and Perinne, then close the gates,' he told them.

The two men defied their exhaustion and lumbered into the night as Blackstone dragged Sir Henri's body aside and pushed open the door that he had guarded. The spluttering torch lasted long enough for Blackstone to see barrels packed with crossbow bolts and swords. Spears were stacked against the wall. The French had used the garrison for supplying local lords to support the southern borders against Gascony. There was no sign of coin until Blackstone shifted some of the weapons and then pulled aside planks shrouded in old sackcloth covered with a few shovelfuls of earth. The space dug below the floor was big enough for several barrels, but he found only two remaining – enough, Blackstone realized, to keep the men who served him until they raided again next year, and enough to deny the French King the means to pay his vassals in the area. It would be a good, long year when Blackstone's men could rest and he would lie with Christiana beneath the shade of the great willow down at the riverside. They would make another baby and the year would end with its birth. This fight had been worth every damned minute of its misery.

Within the hour Guillaume and Perinne, barely conscious from their hours spent lying in the cold water, were wrapped into blankets and kept close to a blazing fire the men built in the centre of the courtyard. They lay with their backs to the warmth, with their booty gathered near them, and let the fatigue of battle finally claim them.

When the distant church bell rang for matins, Jean de Grailly's troops moved down the narrow road between smouldering reed beds. He had kept his word and secured the route from the south. A sentry, barely awake, called out the challenge and then allowed de Grailly to ride forward with a handful of his men, taking in the sight of the battleground within the walls. It was too soon after the fighting to see anything other than Blackstone's filthy and exhausted men. Their bodies, caked in dried mud and blood, gave them the appearance of a wild, ancient tribe. He had a fleeting thought that he would rather have this scarred fighter on his side than not. French defenders' bodies lay scattered where they had fallen across battlements and court-yard, as smoke still drifted over the wasteland. A handful of dead men lay butchered in front of a building, their stench already rising like the morning tide. De Grailly had half expected to ride down the road and find the French garrison intact. He had planned for skirmishers to ride out and lay ambush should the French come at him in force. There would have been no shame in turning back and admitting he had gone too far north.

But Thomas Blackstone and his savage-looking men had offered him glory.

'You will have made a grave enemy of the King of France for this success, Thomas,' said de Grailly as he dismounted.

'I took it in the name of Edward. You'll hold it for him, my lord?' said Blackstone, aware that de Grailly had not extended the hand of friendship, nor made any gesture to embrace a fellow knight.

'I'll garrison it with a hundred men and send a messenger to the Prince. Is there food here?'

'I dare say, but we've slept this past couple of hours. We needed that more than food.'

De Grailly nodded, looking about the scene. And saw the boar-head shield lying near one of the dead. 'You slaughtered Sir Henri. A ransom could have been earned.'

'He placed too high a price on himself.'

De Grailly studied the Englishman. 'As have you after this attack. They'll want your head on a pole for the King to see. The hornet's nest has been badly beaten with a big stick. You will soon be even more famous than I am. In truth, you are already. Very well, Thomas. I'll have the rest of your men brought from the rear of the column.'

'Thank you, my lord. I need your barber-surgeon for my wounded.'

'Then you will have him. And my cooks will feed you. I'll have Sir Henri's body sent home for a Christian burial; the others we'll let the tide take out to sea.'

Blackstone looked at those who had survived the fight. 'There's a church somewhere near; we've heard its bell. I'll take my dead and bury them there and have prayers said for them.' He looked at the unstained surcoat of the knight. If there had been fighting it had not been done by de Grailly, although Blackstone knew that if there was killing needed doing de Grailly would be happiest in the turmoil, using his sword. Whatever

51

conflict they had faced coming up from the south must have offered little contest for the Gascon war leader. His fighting was still to come.

'See to it. Your plunder is safe here. None of mine will touch it. Honour your dead.'

Finding the church was easy enough; they simply waited until the next call to prayer was chimed and followed the dull, mournful sound. The poorly cast bell from an inefficient foundry offered no hope or joy in its sullen clanging. The marshland gave way to forest and then a clearing, with tree stumps still unearthed, that supported a timbered enclosure with a wooden belfry. It was a modest foothold for a humble monastic cell that supported only half a dozen monks, who lived in hovels and spent their time scratching a living from the soil and keeping a few goats for their milk. The undernourished monks and their mud-caked habits told their own story of toil. As Blackstone led his hard-bitten soldiers into the clearing the monks gathered in a fearful knot. One of them stepped forward. He was younger than some of the others; his dirt-ingrained hands gripped the axe he had been using to chop wood, but it was held close to his body, suggesting it was more for comfort and assurance than any intended act of violence.

'We have nothing here of value, but we have broth we can share. Your soldiers look hungry,' the monk said with some trepidation in his voice.

These dangerous-looking men had obviously been involved in the fighting the night before that had set the night sky alight. Appeasement seemed the only option. There was so little to plunder but that did not mean that killing for its own sake was not their intention.

Blackstone looked at the man's veins, which pulsed from the pressure of his grip. The monk's face was etched with weariness, making him look older than his years, but his eyes glared with a determination that meant he would die defending the holy cross that no doubt had pride of place in the wattle and mud chapel.

'Is there a prior here?' Blackstone asked.

'No, we are little more than a cell for our order. The priory itself is a week's walk to the east. We have not yet cast a vote to see who among us should lead us. We make our choices by common consensus. I am Brother Clement.'

'We don't want your food, Brother. I came to bury my dead and have prayers offered for them.'

The monk glanced to where the small cart had been brought to a halt behind the horsemen. 'We have two of our own buried in sacred ground.'

'My soldiers won't care whose company they keep. Their souls need forgiveness and their bodies a Christian burial,' said Blackstone wearily. He wanted to rid himself of this damp place and get home. His towns would be resupplied with the weapons and money they had gained and his men needed women and ale. Blackstone looked at the bedraggled monks; they seemed in greater need of care than his own men. 'Is there game here?'

'There is plenty in the forest, but we have no weapons and Sir Henri forbade anyone but himself and his men to hunt.'

'Sir Henri's arrogant soul has not yet been laid to rest, but his ghost can't prevent you taking game. Have your monks dig the grave, one will do, long and deep enough for my men.'

He spurred his horse forward. Fresh venison or boar would fill his men's bellies and reunite body and soul.

By the time he returned the watery sun was halfway into the afternoon. And where his men's corpses had lain in the back of the cart there was now a roe deer that would feed them for the next few days, a supplement to de Grailly's cooks' pottage, and another for the grateful monks.

A wooden cross was hammered into the dirt; Blackstone's men knelt in the mud and prayed while he stood behind them and fingered the silver goddess. Brother Clement spoke a Latin liturgy, but cast a disapproving look in Blackstone's direction.

'Humility before God costs a man nothing but his pride,' he said, taking the risk of chiding Blackstone as the men gathered their horses.

'I'm not proud, Brother.'

'Then what?'

'Angry.'

'With God?' the monk quavered, alarmed that the man who stood before him, wounds bandaged and features disfigured by war, might be an agent of Satan.

'It's none of your business,' Blackstone said, adjusting the belly strap on his saddle.

'There are abandoned souls who haunt these desolate marshlands at night. We hear them cry out in the forests. Make your peace, lord knight, and He will save you. Cast aside that pagan goddess you wear and let your men see a holy warrior lead them.'

'What you hear are wolves calling their brothers to the kill. My goddess is of the marshlands and the trees, she's in mountain and stream. She's everywhere I need her.' He pulled himself up into the saddle and tossed a sack full of silver plate and a bag of coin at the monk's feet. 'And she does not kill a deaf-mute boy. My brother was slaughtered like a beast ten years back, too soon for my anger to cool. But on my journey here I promised God that I'd give my share of the spoils to the first poor church I found. I keep my promises. Just in case He's watching. Spend it wisely or I'll hear of it.'

Blackstone turned the horse away as Brother Clement's disbelief gave way to joy when he tipped open the sack. He called after Blackstone: 'My lord! We shall! An infirmary and more! Sir Thomas, you will always find a welcome here!'

'You hear that,' Meulon said. 'You'll be an honoured guest in this slime pit.'

'Then let's hope we never ride this way again,' said Blackstone.

Meulon turned in the saddle and looked back at the gathered monks, embracing in their joy and clasping hands in grateful prayer, eyes raised to heaven, for the bounty delivered by the scarred Englishman.

'Your share might have been better served by bribing a town's burghers to open their gates to us. It would save another fight.'

Blackstone dug his heels into the horse's flanks. 'We have all we need. No more towns, Meulon. We're going home. We've missed Christmas and my son's birthday. There'll be no more fighting this year.'

CHAPTER 3

The street urchin scurried through the muddy backstreets of Paris that he had known all of his eight years, avoiding the jostling crowds on the main cobbled thoroughfares that carried carts and carriages. He sidestepped the piles of human faeces that congealed and stank in his path and in doorways. Although the city's ordinance stipulated that each resident was to carry these deposits to disposal tips, the boy, whose only given name was Raoul, knew of no one who obeyed the Provost. Instead, Raoul, and others like him, shovelled it away for them. A crust of stale bread or a near-worthless coin was payment enough to ensure he pleased those who squatted and relieved themselves while he hovered, like one of the flies above the steaming pile, ready to scoop it up. When the stench-ridden alleyways became too fetid he carried buckets of water from the city fountains to sluice the doorways and the gutters that ran down the middle of the narrow streets. From dawn until the Angelus rang at eight at night he would move from one workplace to the next; it was a routine that would not pay a man enough to feed himself or his family, but enabled the feral child to survive another day. No task was too menial.

He had once taken a young whore to the man who ran one of the public baths. She was no more than thirteen but she could pleasure the fat old bastard as had the daughter who had run from his incest and was found drowned in the Seine. Some said he had killed her himself to avoid eternal damnation by the local priest to whom she had confessed. Suicide condemned her anyway. It was of no matter to Raoul; his service was rewarded when the old man allowed him to carry the buckets of hot water into the communal tubs. The steam soaked away the grime from his skin and loosened his matted hair, and gave him warmth in the winter months when the King commanded that the baths be kept open despite the cost of fuel. No wonder they called him 'le Bon'. The 'good' King gave alms to the poor and was pious before the face of God. The great lords and other men of influence and power were in the city to swear allegiance to their King. They would pledge loyalty and money to support his plans to raise a great army of thirty thousand to stop the Prince of Wales in his scourging of the south – and where crowds gathered there would be purses to cut, because once these nobles emerged from their ceremony with the King they would join the merchants, artisans and commoners in the Place de Grève where the unemployed gathered to be hired for whatever work could be found. But there would be no work today. In its stead there was to be a spectacle.

It would be a cut-purse's gift from God when the divine King had one of his Norman lords beheaded in the square.

And that was why Raoul avoided the crowded main streets.

'Raoul!' a man cried as the urchin's bare feet ran lightly across the soiled streets. 'Clear this shit!'

Not today.

King John II of France, resplendent in his royal robes, waited in the ante-rooms of the Great Chamber of the Parlement. His irritations chafed like an ill-fitting piece of armour. Being king meant having too many decisions to make. He was here to face those who wished to control the royal purse. That, and consider for the last time whether to grant clemency to Count Bernard d'Aubriet, a Norman lord who had surrendered his land to the English. The uncertainty was like a knife in his gut. Beyond the walls, across court-yards and roofs, he sensed the unseen population going about their daily business, isolated as he was in the Royal Palace on the Île de la Cité, the island in the middle of the River Seine. The Grand Pont was the way he crossed the river but it was an excursion infrequently undertaken unless the French Parlement convened or he rode to war. He seldom laid eyes on his subjects; it was their repre-sentatives, the Estates General, who spoke on their

59

behalf; it was they who made their demands, fawned and bowed while scheming how best to protect their local wealth, how not to gather the taxes he needed. Well, he needed their money now. A demand had been sent from the Estates in the south, demanding – that word was more insulting and humiliating than being spat upon in public – that he send troops to defend them against the marauding Prince of Wales, whose army, albeit small, wreaked havoc, scorching the land, plundering city, town and village. They *demanded* he do his royal duty and protect them. And now news had reached him of trusted noblemen in the south who had betrayed him to the English Prince.

The King suddenly rose from his chair, his thoughts propelling him to his feet. His Lord Chamberlain and close advisers were startled and shuffled back from him, but the King barely saw them; instead he saw disaster looming and the crushing defeat of his reign if he did not force the English to cease their depredations. He needed more money. And once he had shown his command of the situation he would bring the troublesome Norman lords under control, and once he had them brought to heel he would, at last, confiscate his son-in-law's lands and lock the scheming, murdering bastard Charles of Navarre away in the Châtelet.

John needed the Estates General of the Languedoïl, who represented the people of northern France. And he needed the people of Paris. He needed their support, their belief in him and their taxes. He needed a subsidy to pay his army. It was of no concern to him if his subjects did not love him as their King, be they peasants or merchants. And following the great pestilence, half the damned so-called nobles had bought their rank and status. His father had made them pay for it though. He had prised the last coin from their grasping hands. Which was about the only good thing he did before he died. The rest? Bankruptcy, dissent and the damned English.

Seeing the King's torment of uncertainty one of the other men stepped closer. Simon Bucy was unafraid of the King's outbursts; he and others like him were the strength behind an uncertain monarch. All were considered friends, and each of them had benefited from John's largesse. They were capable men who worked diligently for the Crown but, more than high office, wealth was their rank.

'My lord?'

'Simon, what are we to do?' the King asked in barely a whisper. 'Do we execute d'Aubriet or reprieve him? Will his death spark a Norman rebellion? We needed more time. We should have given him a trial – a public trial. Now the Normans will see that we alone have condemned him.'

'Perhaps, my lord, a generous gesture would placate the Norman lords.'

The King's temper flared. 'Our generosity is our failing! We manoeuvre ourselves between a son-in-law who plots intrigue, who nurtures the weakness of our son the Dauphin against us, who gathers the barons ready to strike when Edward invades to support the Prince of Wales – and invade he will!'

He hurled his goblet of wine across the room. Courtiers and advisers ducked and swayed but those nearest their monarch could not avoid being spattered. King John leaned across the embossed, intricately carved table, his fingers curled like talons. The table, like the kingdom, had been inherited from his father who had squandered the glory of France at Crécy ten years earlier and died months after his noblemen failed to take back Calais. John also inherited empty coffers, drained by years of war. In those years since his father's death and that final humiliation at Calais, he had raised taxes, secured loyalties, brought errant knights and dissident noblemen back into the royal fold. But it was still not enough to rid himself of certain Norman lords and the English captain, Thomas Blackstone, who tore at his flesh. It was as if France were a boar on a spit, turning slowly over the coals, fat dripping into the spluttering flames and flaring up as had the southern provinces, burned and looted by the English and Gascons, who seized towns and trade routes. And Norman lords still defied him; still made demands; continued to deny they protected the English adventurer Thomas Blackstone, who stole his towns like a thief in the night.

'Are we a flagellant? Are we to be whipped

publicly into further humiliation? Do we not bleed enough for France?' he bellowed, spittle spraying those who had avoided the thrown wine-cup, but who now dared not flinch from the royal phlegm. The royal house of Valois fought burning fires of discontent on a wide front, which at times encircled the King like hounds around a cornered beast.

'Very well. It is done. We will show them! The people of Paris need to see that their King does not grant mercy to those who place France in jeopardy.'

He turned on his heel and strode towards the door. Simon Bucy glanced at the others in the room. None could quite conceal their despair at their impetuous King, but when their advice was cut at its root, there was no stopping him. He did not learn from past mistakes, and now he was about to make another.

King John 'the Good' sat on a divan raised on a platform beneath a broad canopy at the far corner of the Great Chamber of Parlement. The principals of the realm sat along the wall at the King's left; to his right were the peers and barons. At a lower level were the representatives of the towns with five hundred inhabitants or more. The impressive barrel-roofed hall was dominated by a wall painting of the crucifixion. The image of divine suffering seemed to be so often reflected in the King's pained expression.

Power and majesty were two sides of the same

coin. The Normans were resplendent in their tabards – larger than surcoats, they were made of silk embroidered in sumptuous style, emblazoned with the nobleman's coat of arms. Sir Godfrey and Jean de Harcourt sat with Guy de Ruymont and other Norman lords, among them the older statesmen de Mainemares and Jean Malet, the Lord de Graville – men who would rather see a more capable monarch settle his backside onto the silk cushions embroidered with the fleur-de-lys. They bore their impatience with grim determination as the Chancellor, Pierre de la Forêt, droned on like a glorified moneylender of the difficulties of waging a defensive war from the coffers of the royal treasury alone. More money was required, taxes would be raised and the loyal support of the Estates General was needed in this time of national crisis. The murmur of uncertainty echoed around the vaulted hall. The Chancellor waited a moment, then turned to the King, who nodded; such meetings were always stage-managed. The Estates would want something in return for giving the Crown the money it needed.

Like a common street entertainer the Chancellor captured his audience's uncertain expectation. A salt tax would be raised, he told them. That had a calming effect, because salt was an expensive commodity, enjoyed only by those who could afford it. And the rich would be taxed 4 per cent on their wealth. Now it was the bourgeois's and nobles' turn to feel the Crown's lash. Their loyalty would be proven by agreeing to these terms. Refusal was the first step towards treason.

Godfrey de Harcourt turned to those close to him. 'He's using the taxes to bind us to him. Can we bargain for d'Aubriet's life by agreeing?'

Guy de Ruymont, who was one of the younger nobles and had a less forcible approach than most, was at de Harcourt's shoulder. He had befriended Blackstone when the young archer was still recovering from his wounds at Jean de Harcourt's castle all those years ago. He had helped close the gulf between common fighting man and nobles. It had been a slow journey of friendship, because his wife Joanne had lost family beneath the archers' arrows at Crécy and her hatred for the English intensified when she learnt Blackstone had been one of the men who had slaughtered French nobility. The glue that now bound the two families was her friendship with Blackstone's wife, Christiana, and their children. Joanne de Ruymont had been kind to Christiana over the years and at times seemed to have softened her animosity towards Blackstone. When there were feasts and celebrations de Ruymont and his family would share it with the Blackstones and their children often played together. They were less than half a day's ride from the Englishman's manor, which made them and the de Harcourts the closest neighbours.

He bent low, his voice barely audible above the rumble of disconcerted voices in the great hall.

'He will want taxes, our loyalty and Bernard's life. We should swear it and plead for mercy.'

The barons considered what he said, and quickly nodded their agreement.

The older Baron de Mainemares said, 'Swear it and test his intentions. If he then executes Bernard, we know he'll bear down on us all sooner or later. Swear it and we will deal with the consequences in our own time. Edward will invade from the north sooner or later. We buy such time as we need until he does.'

The King waited impassively, observing the hubbub as it went back and forth among the delegates, but the Norman lords said nothing. He knew he had cornered them and that they would be forced to swear their allegiance, at least for the time being, and that was all he needed, because events could alter men's decisions and loyalty. The more time he had to root out those who plotted against him, the better. He had already found one of the Norman lords was prepared to betray the others. A promise of greater wealth and additional domains that bequeathed his family and their successors riches for generations. Give a traitor such wealth that he would fear losing it and he was enslaved to the Crown.

He gazed at them, relishing the thought that they did not know there was a Judas among them.

John turned to face the Provost of Merchants, chosen by the leading citizens, who bowed his head and addressed the King directly.

'Our loyalty is undiminished, despite the losses our beloved France has endured, but we see no point in protecting the realm by defence alone. Our great King should gather the army and call for the *arrière-ban*, to bring together every lord, knight and soldier and then to attack!'

There were cheers from the crowded hall. The Provost raised an arm, as if sweeping the wave of enthusiasm across the audience towards the King. 'If France is to survive, the English must be defeated, not contained. Defeated and made to suffer such grievous losses that they dare not set foot again in France,' he said with a flourish.

'Ignorant bastard knows nothing of war and killing,' said de Graville and spat casually down at those below him.

The hall settled into a murmur. The Estates had gained the great concession of having their own officers in charge of collecting the taxes. The business of the day was almost done. The King was about to rise, but as Godfrey de Harcourt moved to stand, Jean de Harcourt grabbed his arm. 'No, Uncle. I'm head of the family. I'll do it.'

And before the seasoned campaigner could get to his feet Jean de Harcourt was standing, calling across the hall, his voice clear and challenging. 'Sire!'

King John and those next to him looked at the man who now stood as if ready to throw down a gauntlet. The King raised a hand, indicating that

67

de Harcourt should speak, and as the gesture ended he picked a piece of imaginary lint from his garment in a gesture of disregard that was not lost on the gathered Norman lords.

Jean de Harcourt ignored the slight. 'Sire, we too seek a benevolent concession from your highness.'

'We know, Count de Harcourt, but we are a prisoner of circumstance. Our hands are tied,' the King said, knowing full well what question would be put to him.

De Harcourt took a step forward, a pace away from the others, so that he might be seen even more clearly by the hundreds of delegates and advisers. Best to make his Norman sentiments known, in public, so that the King could be seen for the unjust monarch he was. 'Sire, my father and I fought alongside your father at Crécy. We suffered and bled for France, as did Bernard d'Aubriet. He has caused you no harm. Release him, sire, is what we ask.'

'The Lords of Normandy ask this of us?' the King answered.

'We do, my lord,' said de Harcourt.

'Then you side with a traitor of France,' said the King with the flicker of a smile.

'Bernard d'Aubriet is no traitor. He has given more than most here for his country.'

The King gestured towards the gathered delegates. 'These men represent France on our behalf, Count de Harcourt. Your friend surrendered vital land to our enemy. To France's enemy. What choice do we have but to punish him for placing Frenchmen in jeopardy?'

The King's gentle taunting was too much for Godfrey de Harcourt who stood and pointed at the gathered men. 'You do France an injustice! These men in this hall are merchants and artisans who will go to the people and ask for money to pay for the army. It is not these *tax collectors*,' he said with as much derision as he could muster, 'who will take up the sword, but men like Count d'Aubriet, who bind themselves to their honour!'

This time Simon Bucy could not prevent King John from giving rein to his temper.

'Honour, Sir Godfrey! You speak of honour? You who sided against our father! Who fought for the English!'

A decade before Godfrey de Harcourt had risked execution by begging forgiveness from the old King. The defeated French monarch pardoned the lame knight's treason and settled for Godfrey's oath of allegiance and public humiliation. Wearing nothing but a shirt, and with a hangman's noose around his neck, Godfrey had been paraded before the court. King Philip was aware that the Norman barons would sip long from the cup of resentment if he put Godfrey to death. But Philip, like John who followed him, was a poor decision-maker, whose failings had been shown up starkly during the English invasion – and sparing the duplicitous Godfrey de Harcourt was certainly a mistake. Ten years after the battle of Crécy, the traitor's heart was about to turn again.

Godfrey de Harcourt was not to be cowed by an intemperate King cocooned by such self-serving men as Bucy. 'Honour is every man's creed as he understands it. I fought your father because of a wrong done against me. One of his favourites was given my lands. My honour demanded I sided with he who would help me recover them. If honour is our shield then pride is our downfall. I begged forgiveness. I was humiliated. I bore myself through these streets of Paris in nothing more than an undershirt with a halter around my neck. I prostrated myself before your father!'

'And he forgave you!' said King John.

'He forgave me because he knew that if justice was to be served then he would need me to fight for the Crown again. You make the same mistake, my Prince: you kill a man who could be put to better use.'

'His death is the better use!'

'No!' Jean de Harcourt pushed his uncle aside, because he could see the King's mood was becoming dangerous. Simon Bucy was at the King's shoulder, his hand hovering close to his sovereign's arm in case the King went forward to face the Norman lords. The armed guards had shifted position, readying themselves. 'Sire,' he said in a more measured tone. 'When Bernard d'Aubriet was captured by the English last year his ransom was more than he could secure in a lifetime.'

Bucy's closeness and de Harcourt's even-handed manner mollified the King momentarily. 'He gave his castle to the English in payment and now they occupy it. Our border is compromised,' said the King.

'Every border has its weakness, sire,' de Harcourt answered.

'Aye, as Normandy is to France!'

The direct insult to the Norman lords went unchallenged as Jean de Harcourt held up a restraining hand, warning the others to remain silent, but the challenge caused a rippling murmur among the delegates.

'You gave Count d'Aubriet little choice,' de Harcourt said, raising his voice, wanting even those who stood at the back of the hall to hear his accusation. 'You had confiscated his lands to recoup taxes, land that could have been redeemed to pay his ransom. He had no choice but to surrender what he had left. Give him his life, sire. An act of justice, an act that would show your gracious mercy.'

The King turned to face the packed audience, averting his gaze from de Harcourt and the others. 'The punishment is just,' he declared. And then he faced the Normans. 'All those who weaken France by betrayal and false fealty shall meet their reckoning.'

He strode from the hall. Bucy spared a non-committal glance towards de Harcourt.

'By the blood of Christ, this King is a worthless

man and a bad ruler,' said Jean de Harcourt, pushing his way through the crowd.

The men fell silent and gathered their cloaks. It would be hard to see d'Aubriet die. He was one of their own.

The crowd gathered, jostling and pushing forward to get closer to where the King's soldiers formed a barricade twenty feet in front of the scaffold. Godfrey de Harcourt limped to take his place with the other Norman lords and to give their friend sight of them. Even if he could not draw courage from their presence, his pride would be strengthened enough for him to die well in front of his friends.

The Place de Grève was almost full; the jugglers and street entertainers had taken what few coins they could, but the crowd was eager for more brutal entertainment. Men and women peered over the heads of others; children were lifted onto shoulders.

Jean de Harcourt could barely contain his seething anger. 'These bastard peasants should be chased into the Seine. Let them drown like the rats they are.' He beckoned de Ruymont. 'Send some of our retainers into the crowd, let them mingle. Have them keep their ears open for any words of dissent against the King. It will help us to know just how much unrest there is among the people of Paris.'

Guy de Ruymont nodded and pushed his way through the merchants and city officials who crowded behind them. Beyond the enclosure

72

where the privileged lords and merchants stood to witness the execution, Raoul twisted his way through the crowd. He kept his short-bladed knife beneath his sleeve, and as soon as the drum beats started to announce the arrival of the condemned man, necks would crane and eyes would peer towards the place of execution, and then he would slip quickly through the crowd. By the time the nobleman's head was severed, so too would a handful of purses be separated from their victims' belts. An execution was a profitable time for those even less fortunate than an arrogant lord fallen foul of the King.

Bernard d'Aubriet was held in the Châtelet's ancient building, a small fortress that once guarded the entrance to the city. The passing years had seen the city walls extend and the Châtelet's role become redundant so it was turned into the state prison that also housed the Provost's offices. As its gates opened the crowds were already gathered to accompany d'Aubriet on his final journey to the scaffold. Stripped to his undershirt, wrists bound by coarse rope that chafed his skin, he gripped the side of the tumbril, not wishing to endure further humiliation by losing his balance and falling before the jeering crowds. The cart's iron-shod wheels rattled onto the streets within sight of the Seine and, as it passed the Grand Pont that led to the Royal Palace on the Île de la Cité, the King's banner and pennons fluttered mockingly, as if celebrating his victory over a Norman lord. D'Aubriet shivered from the chill breeze coming off the great river, but his trembling was also from fear of his fast-approaching death. They had at least granted him a priest, who assured him that the kingdom of heaven awaited his immortal soul, but it was his mortal body that would suffer beheading. A death in battle was forged in the fire of desperation and urgency, but the thought of this cold-blooded demise put ice water in his bowels.

Had he been a common criminal the tumbril would have continued along the Grand'Rue, north towards the plain beyond the city where such men were executed, but instead it turned east, away from the sprawling suburbs where merchants' bourgeois mansions flaunted their wealth beyond the butchers' stalls of Paris's market quarter and the stench it held. The narrow irregular streets gave the crowds an opportunity to spit and shout abuse at the condemned man, who kept his eyes resolutely on the streets ahead and the light that shone into the open space of the Place de Grève. At least his title meant that no torture had been inflicted upon him in the King's name; no part of his body had been torn with red-hot pincers and burning oil poured into the wounds. The privilege of his rank would give him a clean death. Not for him the crude hacking of the executioner's axe on a block, but a swift blow of the sword. The last thing he would hear, other than the crowd's gasp, would be the long blade whispering through the air.

The Norman lords watched as the cart drew level with the scaffold's steps. Soldiers stood aside as d'Aubriet found his footing on them – steadying himself; willing his legs not to tremble and expose his fear. The crowd roared when he appeared on top of the platform. The hooded executioner stood to one side as the captain of the guard released d'Aubriet's bonds. He rubbed his wrists, eyes scanning the crowd, seeking out the brightly coloured tabards of his fellow barons. Sir Godfrey raised an arm.

'Bernard! Your friends are here!'

The condemned man gave a rueful smile and nodded; then, as if eager for it to be over, he took the gold coin kept for him by the captain and handed it to the executioner, who cupped his hands like a begging bowl and dipped his head in acknowledgement. The executioner's assistant stepped forward, but d'Aubriet made a small gesture declining his help and tucked the hair from the nape of his neck under the plain white linen cap. He turned once again to face his friends, ignoring the baying of the crowd, and held up his palms to them – man leaves this world empty-handed.

A muffled drum roll began to silence the crowd.

The cut-purse Raoul felt the wave of silence engulf the onlookers, their attention locked onto the scaffold and the kneeling man. The masked executioner quickly bent, took the sword from beneath its cloth covering and with practised concentration swung the blade.

The sound of its edge biting bone was plain to hear. The crowd gasped. The dull thud of a head falling held their attention a moment longer.

Raoul parted a purse from its owner's belt as voices roared approval. The corpse jerked, spraying blood. No sooner had the boy cut the purse than he felt a man's grip on his neck and looked up into the scowling face of one of the Norman lord's men.

Jean de Harcourt and the others had already turned their backs on the bloodied platform and saw nothing of a street urchin being apprehended.

'We must ready ourselves,' Guy de Ruymont said.

'And Blackstone could be useful to us in these coming months,' added the Lord de Graville. 'Where is he?'

They shouldered their way out of the throng, feeling the chill winter air even more. 'I don't know,' Jean de Harcourt answered. 'Raiding somewhere.'

'You don't know? We might need him,' said the older Norman. 'He's your man!'

Sir Godfrey de Harcourt answered before his nephew. 'He's no one's man; you should know that by now. Wherever he is, he'll come home, and then we'll approach him.'

CHAPTER 4

When Blackstone had recovered from his wounds, sustained those years ago at Crécy, and shown his skill with Wolf Sword, Jean de Harcourt had taken him to the arsenal at Clos des Galées, near Rouen, and paid for a suit of armour, its steel made from the best iron ore in the region, mined at Pont-Audemer. Impoverished knight that he was, the armour not only protected Blackstone but also proclaimed his status as a man with powerful friends. It was while journeying back to Castle de Harcourt on this occasion that he and Christiana discovered the place that would become their new home. The Risle valley, north-west of Harcourt, had known mixed fortunes. The English had pillaged it; the plague had caused the deaths of many more; but Thomas and Christiana had found an old fortified manor, abandoned and partly ruined, in a hamlet within sight of the river, protected from the north-east wind by a forest of ancient chestnut trees.

Several families farmed the surrounding land and, when the young, battle-hardened knight claimed the manor and its domain as his own, they submitted to his vow of protection. Now the fifty or so peasants were well fed and prospered through their own efforts and the generosity of their warlord, who had declared them free men. Lord de Graville had bequeathed Blackstone a retainer, Hugh, to act as his steward. The old man could read and write and was accepted as Blackstone's authority on the land when he was absent. Christiana, though, was a strong voice when it came to organization and she often clashed with the old steward. It was a contest she seldom won because the hunchback knew the land and could gauge a shift in the weather better even than Blackstone himself. The Englishman whose bent arm would never pull a war bow again and the crooked-backed Norman understood each other perfectly – and both knew that Lady Christiana would inspect the ledgers and spot any errors. To that end she was mistress of her husband's lands. Mutual respect was established.

As Blackstone led his weary troops along the forest track, the scent of woodsmoke pulling him home like an invisible thread, he turned to smile at those who followed. Guinot, the Anglo-Gascon, raised his bent and aching back from the saddle and caught the smell from the fires and the mouth-watering aroma of freshly baked bread. The half-dozen soldiers urged their horses forward, their long ride almost behind them. Food, rest and safety were within sight.

There were horses tethered in Blackstone's yard

and he saw that they and the squire and page who attended them belonged to Jean de Harcourt. And there were other horses at hitching rings. The sudden anticipation of returning home turned quickly into uncertainty as the sight of a dozen soldiers loitering by the stables with the horses told him it could not simply be a social call from his old friend.

'Should we hold back, my lord?' asked Guinot.

'No, they're friends. Take the men and the supplies to the stable yard.' Blackstone spurred the horse forward as his own men-at-arms appeared, hands on sword hilts in case the approaching horsemen were enemies. They quickly recognized Blackstone.

'Sir Thomas! My Lords de Harcourt and de Ruymont are here,' one of them told him, standing aside as Blackstone's horse clattered through the archway into the courtyard. Guillaume dismounted and held Blackstone's reins.

'Christiana!' he called. Servants were scurrying back and forth, bobbing in curtsy or bowing their heads as they saw him.

There was a sudden flurry of people from the entrance hall. Christiana lifted her skirts and almost ran towards him; Jean de Harcourt and Blanche were only a few steps behind, as was Guy de Ruymont and his wife, Joanne.

'Thomas!' Christiana cried, and embraced him.

Blackstone's uncertainty was soon explained when Jean de Harcourt gripped his arm. 'We had news that you were dead. God has answered our prayers.'

Christiana wiped tears away, bravely bringing her emotions back under control, as befitted a knight's wife. Blanche had moved to her side. 'Thomas, you caused your family and friends great distress. The moment we heard we all came here to be with Christiana and the children.'

'Don't look so mystified, Thomas,' said Guy de Ruymont, 'we never know where your raids take you. News of your death should come as no surprise to any of us.'

'As you can see,' Blackstone said, 'I may stink, but I'm alive.'

'We had news from Brittany that a ship sank in foul weather and that your shields were washed ashore in the wreckage. There were no survivors, and only three bodies were found.'

Blackstone felt a pang of regret at hearing the news. So, Master Jennah of Hythe had drowned.

'We used the boat to attack a stronghold to the south. The ship's master was a good man. His skill gave us success.'

'Then we'll offer up prayers for him,' Blanche de Harcourt said.

'You've been away from us too long. There's a lot to tell you,' de Harcourt said quietly. He was more subdued than usual, thought Blackstone. His friend looked drawn and pale; his features were gaunt, like those of a man recovering from a wound.

'Bernard has been executed in Paris and the King does not realize the mistake he's made,' added de Ruymont quickly.

'D'Aubriet? For surrendering land? Are the King's men riding into Normandy?' Blackstone asked. If this was a determined strike against the Norman lords, then they needed to prepare their defences.

'No, it was a gesture to show us his authority. He is in no position to come here,' said de Harcourt. Blackstone could see the concern and anger on the men's faces.

De Ruymont's wife intervened. 'Guy, this is not the time or the place to berate the King or—'

The amiable Norman turned suddenly on his wife. 'Do you presume to know when I should speak on matters of importance?'

Joanne de Ruymont blushed and lowered her head.

The embarrassed silence was quickly broken when de Ruymont smiled at Blackstone. 'Now, we must leave you to celebrate your safe return.'

'No, we'll stay!' said de Harcourt. 'This calls for a party, surely. Something at last to cheer us!'

There was still an awkwardness between Guy and his wife. Blanche de Harcourt, being from the senior family present, exercised her right of decision. 'Another time, Jean,' she said gently. She knew the passion she had for her husband whenever he had returned from battle and Christiana and Blackstone would need their privacy.

'You are all welcome to stay,' said Christiana

hospitably, hoping the invitation would be seen for the social politeness it was.

It was Guy de Ruymont who stepped down to his friend de Harcourt and murmured something into his ear. De Harcourt's sudden look of understanding could not be disguised. He laughed. 'It's been too long since I fought, Thomas; I'm getting old and fat and dull-witted. When your wounds have healed and you have rested,' he said, 'then ride over and spend a day with us so we can tell you what has been happening in your absence and hear of your success.'

'And we will discuss the arrangements for Henry's party. It won't be all politics,' said Blanche de Harcourt.

The women kissed each other's cheeks and Guy de Ruymont pressed Blackstone's shoulder. 'Is it true Saint-Clair has fallen? We heard rumours.'

Blackstone nodded. 'We took it.'

'You are a madman, Thomas, I've always known it,' said de Ruymont, then lowered his voice so that his wife would hear no blasphemy: 'Sweet Jesus, you have either an angel or a demon at your shoulder.'

Despite de Ruymont's caution his wife heard what he said and, risking her husband's admonition, could not resist a barbed comment. 'Your wife is your angel, Thomas; it is you who gives sanctuary to the demon. More time on your knees in a chapel would not serve you ill. You seek treasure and fortune elsewhere, but they are here under your own roof. You should stay at home more often.'

Before Guy de Ruymont could say anything, Christiana stepped between them. 'Joanne, Thomas knows what he has, and what will always be here when he returns,' she said, slipping her arm through his.

Attendants brought the horses forward; the escort of soldiers was already formed up. Jean de Harcourt gathered his reins. 'You forget, Joanne, Thomas did not inherit his wealth, he fought for it. Christiana, I'm counting on you to make him come and see us.'

She nodded, grateful for her friends' companionship and care. Blanche de Harcourt had turned out to be more than the guardian she once was. 'I thank you all, for being here and comforting me.'

'We're the closest thing you have to family beyond these walls, and Normans look after their own,' said de Harcourt. 'Thomas! We'll want to hear everything! A week! No longer! There's only so much sleep and – *rest* – a man needs,' he added gruffly, and then turned his horse and led the others from the manor's courtyard.

There were times, Blackstone thought, that it might seem to others as if Christiana cared more for his squire than she did for him. Whenever they rode home from their time away it was always the same, her greeting to him was always controlled and then she would turn her attention to Guillaume. Blackstone's youngest child, Agnes, would throw herself into his arms, her chestnut hair flicking like a pony's tail from beneath her embroidered linen cap. This time was no different. No sooner had the horses left the yard than the children ran from the house. Blackstone felt a surge of affection for the freckle-faced child whose eyes were as green as her mother's; Blackstone cherished her joyful innocence. Village children worked; noblemen's were cosseted; but this child knew happiness. Her giggling and shrieks of laughter as Blackstone nuzzled her with his close-trimmed whiskers made her hide her face behind her hands. His son Henry stood, as always, at a respectful distance and waited to be called, unlike the dogs that snuffled and whined at their master's feet. The handful of servants scurried from room to room of the small manor house, making a last-minute attempt to replace any soiled reed flooring with freshly cut stalks and to sprinkle fragrant herbs into the fires.

'There was no word of you coming home other than the news of the shipwreck. Would it have been so difficult to send a messenger?' Christiana asked as she touched his face tenderly and kissed his lips.

'A messenger can be waylaid, and then the next thing it would be routiers or the King's men trying to ambush me. Best I just arrive. Besides, I thought you liked surprises?'

'Of your well-being – not that you lie in the depths of a savage sea.'

His daughter wriggled and demanded to be hoisted on his shoulders as Christiana murmured a non-committal sigh. 'I age a year with every day you are away,' she said, regret tingeing her voice.

'No you don't,' he said and kissed her lightly, but the child was turning his head, running her finger down his scarred face.

'Agnes may have you for now, but I will need you soon,' she said, letting Blackstone see the lust for him in her eyes. She turned her back and eased Guillaume away to flatter him, telling him how much the children missed the games he played with them. She would patiently tease from the young squire where her husband and his men had been and what they had done, because she knew that Blackstone would give her few details of the danger they had faced. Christiana's comfort of knowing that the young squire had become such a fine soldier meant that there was yet another determined fighter at her husband's side. Such family reunions after a raid were a ritual, not unlike the courtly dance that Blackstone had never mastered. Christiana gave little away in public in front of her husband, a few words here and there, almost with a sense of indifference, but it was all to do with her being mistress of the house. Her emotions seethed, but she maintained a cool composure. On the one hand, Blackstone liked the way the other ladies, Blanche de Harcourt and

Joanne de Ruymont, had versed her in the duties expected of a knight's wife in command of her own household; on the other, he wished the wild, temperamental, auburn-haired girl, with the fire of passion in her eyes, who had once held her favours from him for so long and then had given herself with abandon was still that spontaneous. As Blackstone had learnt during his recovery, the woman who had bathed his broken and bleeding body and who slept by his side breathed the same rebellious air as her mistress, the Countess Blanche de Harcourt et Ponthieu. If a woman was to be accorded respect beyond the role of bearing children, a steely determination and a willingness to suffer hardship for the honour of their men and their family name must overshadow their lives. It had taken all of Blackstone's patience to wait until the true expression of her love and passion could be experienced in the privacy of their own bedchamber.

As usual, Blackstone had warned his squire not to relate too much information to his wife, but there was little cause for concern; the squire was as dextrous with his words as with his sword. Blackstone lacked the boy's easy charm, a result of Guillaume's early education at the hands of a kindly master, one who had died in the great pestilence, and who had given his young charge the tools to conduct his life with confidence. There was no doubt in Blackstone's mind that his own son, Henry, who was soon to have his belated birthday celebration, received similar schooling in reading and writing, nurtured in the appreciation of fine manners and poetic endeavours required of a nobleman's son. But Blackstone was no member of the nobility and his son should have been trained for the past two years in the use of weapons and an understanding of combat. It was this undercurrent of disagreement that could suddenly erupt between him and Christiana. In Blackstone's mind the boy had had sufficient education and needed to be toughened up so that he could be sent to a nobleman's household and brought up as a page in preparation for being a squire.

The formality of Blackstone's arrival home had been played out. As he walked into the great room where a fire blazed and the dogs followed, Christiana grabbed his arm and went on tiptoe to kiss him in a stolen moment before the servants intruded.

'I want you,' she whispered. 'I lust after you every night you are away from my bed. I am short-tempered with the servants and I lie in fear of you never returning to me.'

Those few whispered words aroused him, but no sooner had his hand touched her breast than she turned away quickly with a mischievous smile, saying she must oversee the food for the men who still accompanied him. He cursed his vulnerability to her teasing and would have kicked the dogs away and taken her there and then on the woven woollen rug in front of the fire. His unwashed and stinking body would have smothered her sweet-scented smoothness. But those carefree days of spontaneous carnal pleasure were in the past. The house, the servants and the men who loitered, guarding the palisades, saw to that. Success as a knight had brought restrictions to their lives. He followed her out into the courtyard, watching her body sway, allowing his imagination free rein. As she turned towards the kitchen he saw Old Hugh waiting in the yard, head bowed as Blackstone's eyes fell on him. His jerkin was pulled tight by a broad leather belt over a belly that had known famine and feast. That pot belly was from the lack of food when the crops failed – and how many times had that happened during the old man's lifetime? Blackstone wondered. His steward had not moved, his ankles deep in mud; the cold must be clawing up those spindly legs like grappling irons. He had obviously waited in the yard since Blackstone had first arrived home, rooted like the old hawthorn stave he gripped to help keep his balance. He had attended his duties, and now waited to greet his master.

The men's horses were already stabled, rubbed down and fed oats and chestnuts to rebuild their strength before the soldiers left for Chaulion, the nearest of the towns Blackstone held. Blackstone had barely been out of the saddle, but acknowledged the man's stoic determination to show him that all had gone without mishap during his absence. As they walked across the yard towards the arched gateway, Guinot appeared from the latrines, pulling his hose tighter beneath his jerkin. Blackstone gestured for him to join them, so the Gascon, after clearing his throat and spitting out the stench of the shit pit, tucked his calloused hands into his belt and fell in alongside Blackstone and Old Hugh. Why his sworn lord allowed the old hunchback cripple to haul him around his own domain like a stable lad he never understood but, like anyone else who served Thomas Blackstone, he knew the Englishman had his own reasons and there was never a good time to question what they were. Guinot, like the others, was glad that they were the last to return to their duties and would be fed before they continued their journey. During Blackstone's ride home men who were stationed in his towns had been dropped off at their garrisons and at every stop food, money and weapons distributed so that by the time he reached his own manor only a handful of men remained with him. Meulon and Gaillard had returned to their post and the responsibility that Blackstone had given them of holding one of the towns in the chain of six that formed his defensive line down through Normandy. These towns, along with other Norman lords and Charles of Navarre, who held swathes of lower Normandy, meant the King of France had barely a foothold in the duchy. Chaulion was the first town Blackstone had captured years ago and, being a few days' ride, was closest to his home. Guinot, his tough, no-nonsense commander, would leave Blackstone's home the next morning with his half-dozen men and return to garrison duty.

Blackstone allowed Old Hugh to set the pace as the three men moved into the clearing beyond the manor where fields stretched into hedgerows and orchards. There was little chance, if anyone came by night, that they could flank the manor.

'Guinot? Do you think we've moved everything near enough?' Blackstone asked his commander of Chaulion.

The Gascon saw that since their last bout of raiding some of the villagers had been moved closer to the low walls.

'Better than it was, Sir Thomas. It's unlikely anyone could get through them without the alarm being raised by the mange-ridden dogs you've got around here.'

'I keep them for a good reason. They bark at the scent of a fox or even if they hear the distant snuffle of deer in those trees,' Blackstone said, pointing to the nearest copse of birch.

Guinot was a solid man with a keen eye for defence and that was why Blackstone had kept him on behind the walls at Chaulion. He was strong enough to exert discipline, although he was getting too old to fight with any pace. His belligerence could entrench him like a boar in a thicket and keep an enemy at bay, but the way Blackstone fought, a man needed enduring strength and will-power. When Blackstone had sailed for Saint-Clair the balding man complained at being kept back from the fight and left in charge of the baggage train, but he probably knew in his heart by now that Blackstone had been right. Not that it lessened his desire to fight.

'You can't do much else, Sir Thomas. It's as good as it can be without bringing a hundred men to build a damned castle, and, let's face it, these Normans whose lands surround yours are as good as walls,' he said, letting his eyes wander across the meadows and the obstacles and precautions Blackstone had created. Over the years Blackstone had built new houses closer to the manor's palisades to act as a buffer and a warning by bringing some of the fenced animals closer. Penned geese and those mangy dogs Guinot had referred to made fine sentries.

Old Hugh walked like a crab, using the gnarled hawthorn staff to steady his gait, but he was quick enough for Blackstone's long stride. As usual the old man complained.

'You're not taking enough, Sir Thomas. Lord de Graville knew how to make the land work for him,' said Hugh. 'Take more from these damned peasants and you'd spend less time away from home resupplying us.'

'I raid for all the towns I hold, you know that,' Blackstone answered, knowing the lecture would not be halted, and saw Guinot suppress a smile.

'Aye, I do.' Hugh was determined to gently chastise his master. 'And I know you'd be better off,

91

with respect, my lord, if you let me loose on those towns of yours' – he directed a glaring look towards Guinot, which in turn allowed Blackstone to smile and raise his eyebrows – 'and the *patis* you take from the villeins,' the old man continued gruffly. They crossed the footbridge over the stream, upsetting geese that panicked like haughty noblewomen, long necks pushing their nostrils into the air as they flapped to a safer distance, honking with annoyance. Separate wicker pens now held chickens, pigs and domestic geese nearer to the rear of the stables, whose back walls had always been the most vulnerable to escalade. The poultry yards for the manor and the orchards were kept separate from the villagers' own vegetable gardens – not that there was anything in the frost-hard ground now. Turnips and cabbages had all been taken and used for winter cooking.

The steward pointed across the fields with the stick. 'We'll be laying the manure in the next ten days. God willing, we'll have a good spring for sowing. Aye, Lord de Graville knew all right,' he went on, as always peppering his report to his master with repetitive memories from his days as steward with Jean Malet, Lord de Graville. 'He had these lice-ridden serfs sorted good and proper, he did. Ten casks of honey, three hundred loaves, a dozen casks of strong ale and cider and he never took less than a couple of oxen and a dozen of geese – fat ones mind you – cheese, butter – a whole cask of butter he'd take from them—'

'And salmon. Don't forget those, Hugh,' Blackstone interrupted. He knew de Graville's rent from his vassals almost off by heart. Old Hugh never failed to deprecate his own largesse to the villagers.

'I had not forgotten, my lord, I had not yet reached that part in the telling.'

Smoke from the village fires settled like a newborn's caul. 'I can see you've been busy,' Blackstone told him, his eyes scanning the open land. The hedges had been laid, adding yet another line of defence between the forest and the track to the manor's gate. Also, the land to the west was rough and would not be cultivated this year, so Blackstone had instructed that all branches and cuttings from the tree-felling be laid on it, making yet another obstacle for any intruders to navigate.

The cold air took his breath and he saw that the old man was wheezing. 'I'll go around the village tomorrow then we'll ride out and see the rest,' he said, excusing them from the inspection.

'Lord,' said Old Hugh and bowed his head. 'You are too generous with us all. I fear for your profit.'

'For once I agree with him, Sir Thomas,' said Guinot.

Blackstone shook his head. A peasant's life was hard enough, eking out a bare subsistence. He had endured it as a boy and saw enough drought and flood ruin crops and put families in their graves. The shire where he was born and grew had a strict master – Lord Marldon; he was not afraid to inflict punishment, but was not heavy-handed towards his villeins. Blackstone remembered those early lessons as an example. 'There's enough,' said Blackstone. 'I've no desire to break a peasant's back so I can eat another mouthful.'

The old man shrugged. What could he do with the young English knight? He had no cause for complaint. Blackstone and Lady Christiana had taken him in, an old hunchback whose brain was of more use than his body. Lord de Graville had ordered him to serve and serve he would. He was grateful he had not been abandoned because of his age.

Blackstone poured water from a pitcher into a bowl nestling on a stand in his chamber. His son waited.

'Henry,' Blackstone said, 'did you accompany Steward Hugh when he inspected the fields and checked the oxen?'

'I did, Father,' the boy answered.

'And who gave out the gifts to the village families at Christmas?'

'I did, as you told me to before you left home.'

Blackstone peeled away the sweat-sodden clothes and threw them into the corner of the room. He would bathe later with Christiana, but for now he sluiced down his torso from the bowl, its cold water raising goose pimples on his skin.

'Were there enough bundles of wood for them all?'

'Hugh had the men cut and bind them and kept them in the barn. Every family had their share. And we had enough fodder in storage for the cows so there was extra milk.'

'Good. You stand in my place when I'm not here. Old Hugh will see to the running of the land and the villagers and your mother will stand over Hugh as she must, but you are lord of this domain in my absence. It will always be that way.'

'I do my best to honour you, Father.'

Blackstone placed a hand on his son's shoulder and gave an affectionate squeeze. Did the boy flinch? 'Son, I'm sorry I missed your birthday, but I told you before I left that we'll celebrate before the spring sowing. We'll ride down to your god-father and spend some time at Harcourt. Everyone's going to be there. You'll have some fun with all the other children.'

'I'm not a child, Father.'

Blackstone regretted the words as soon as he had spoken. But the truth was that Henry had not yet grasped the seriousness of his age or what was expected of him. There was a gentleness to the boy's character that he acknowledged; something of himself that he recognized. His own sworn lord, Sir Gilbert Killbere, had confessed to him that it had been thought Blackstone would not be suitable for war, that his own heart was too gentle.

'Of course you're not,' said Blackstone unconvincingly.

An uneasy silence settled between them.

'Besides, you're getting a bit old for things like birthdays,' he said, trying to make good any damage to the boy's feelings, but by the brief look of despair on Henry's face, it only made matters worse.

'Yes, Father. You're right,' his son answered dutifully.

Blackstone grunted and towelled himself dry. He promised himself he would spend the summer with the boy and bring them closer together.

'Reach into my saddlebags,' he said.

Henry did as ordered and pulled out an ivory-handled dagger. He gazed at it for a few seconds and then carefully withdrew it from the silver-etched sheath.

'I took that off one of the King's lords.'

'Did you kill him, Father?'

'Meulon slew him with a spear thrust, up through the belly and into his chest. He squirmed like a worm on a hook. You remember Meulon?'

Henry nodded but his eyes stayed on the blade as he slowly slid it in and out of its scabbard.

Blackstone pulled on a shirt and fresh jerkin. The wind had picked up and he needed to check the men and see that the barn had fresh straw laid for them. He knew it would have been attended to by the old steward, but he wanted to see for himself before fatigue and hunger claimed him.

'I think that must have come from his family.

That grip is ivory, the crossguard looks to be a fine steel like the blade, so perhaps his ancestors brought it back from the crusades. You know the dagger Guillaume carries?'

'The one on his belt? He always has it.'

'Yes. It's special to him. Had it since he was younger than you,' said Blackstone, remembering when that dagger had quivered inches from his face, held by the then nine-year-old Guillaume, a terrified page who wanted only to protect his Burgundian master after the river crossing at Blanchetaque. 'We all have a weapon that's special to us. We cherish them and keep them close. Give it to me.'

His son could barely hide the disappointment at relinquishing the knife. Blackstone held it and felt its weight.

'This is a nobleman's knife, Henry. It's one of the best I've seen. That's why I took it from him.' He paused and then extended the knife. 'For you. For your birthday.'

That night, when the men in the barn slept and Blackstone had checked the sentries, he and Christiana bathed and afterwards she rubbed oils into his bruised muscles, tending the cuts that had festered from lack of care. They languished in their great bed, bolstered with cushions and woven blankets, a smouldering fire in the grate, his dogs whimpering at the door until his voice commanded their silence. The children slept in another room, but were close, so Christiana's cries of passion were muted and buried in the pillows. Before he had left on his latest raid she had finally overcome the loss of her unborn child. Nights of prayer had kept her from Blackstone's bed, testing his patience until their arguments increased. The loss, she said, was a divine punishment, though Blackstone had failed to discover what crime had been committed to make God pull the child from her womb, but she could not be consoled. The months had passed and as the winter bit hard Blackstone had taken himself into the barn to cut stone for his wall. That slow, determined stonemason's skill had never deserted him and it mollified his anger to see something built rather than destroyed. And then one storm-driven day she came to him and they lay in the warm straw and banished the barren months with a desperation to their lovemaking. Theirs was a strange fate: bound together out of the conflict of war, but it was a bond that strengthened them, each having fought and cared for the other.

Somewhere a loose door banged in the wind, and a muted sentry's voice shouted for it to be closed. Blackstone stroked the fullness of her breasts and whispered a breath across her nipples. They rose to his lips and he teased them with his tongue. They had already sated their lust and now was the time for the quiet, slow enjoyment of lingering sex. She eased her arms around his back, her fingers stroking his old scars, and as she felt the raised welts across his muscles from his latest battle, a shudder went through her. Fear and passion fought each other until his deliberately slow movement within her suppressed her anxiety and bathed her in warmth and love, drifting into the dim candlelight.

Christiana settled into the crook of his arm. 'I have prayed to our blessed Virgin Mary for a baby, Thomas. I want another child,' were her final whispered words as she fell asleep.

CHAPTER 5

Guillaume Bourdin had never yet managed to rise from his sleep before his sworn lord. Blackstone had the ability to wake at least an hour before the first glimmer of dawn crept into the sky, no matter the season. Before first light he would be found in the solitude of the exercise yard, practising with Wolf Sword. There were times when the young squire thought his master fought demons. Several years ago, when he was still a boy, Guillaume had survived the plague and ridden thirteen days in search of Blackstone, who had once spared his life. His own lord, Henri Livay, lay dead from the hideous black swellings inflicted by the Great Pestilence. The boy's will to survive brought him to the man who granted him the honour of being his squire and taught him to fight. He inherited Livay's fine sword, and learnt how to use it well, but as young as he was and as skilled as he had become, he had never witnessed such relentless fury in a fighter as that in his sworn lord, Sir Thomas Blackstone, a knight whom the Norman lords declared to be the most ferocious they had ever seen. And yet that fury, which men revered in a war leader, was never witnessed by family or friend.

The story of how Blackstone came by the sword, with its maker's mark of the running wolf, had been known for years and Guillaume never tired of the telling. The great swordsmiths of Passau in Germany had learnt their skills from the Saracens following the crusades. And Wolf Sword had been a gift from a German count to his son, who campaigned with the King of Bohemia, an ally of the French. It had been the German's misfortune to have slain Thomas Blackstone's brother on the field at Crécy. It was there, Guillaume thought, that his master's demons had been unleashed. For, as the German knight came within striking distance of the young Prince of Wales, the English archer took the fight to him and killed him despite being badly wounded himself. No devil or god could have expected muscle and sinew to do what Blackstone did. And every time Guillaume burnished his lord's armour, he would recite the legend to Blackstone's son, Henry, who had yet to learn the ways of fighting men. He was still like a child who played with younger children, a source of contention that Guillaume was aware of, but it was not his place to pass comment or to encourage the boy beyond telling him stories and pleasing Lady Christiana by playing with the children when time from his duties permitted.

He suspected that Blackstone shared her gratitude, but it was a matter that was never discussed between them when they campaigned together. And now that there would be no fighting for the rest of this year, Guillaume would spend more time with the boy and help him with his Latin studies. He knew, though, that Sir Thomas would never cease their training schedule and that when the weight of his domestic life bore down they would ride out to the other walled towns so that Blackstone could be with his men and ensure their readiness to fight. And to absent himself from the women who would visit Lady Christiana and share his hearth. And gossip.

Blackstone's manor was not large: a cluster of buildings in the yard housed stables and a few servants; its kitchen stood close to the great hall. Although each room had a fireplace all the socializing was done where the fire burned the brightest, in the great hall, its chestnut bressummer mantel spanning four cloth yards. Blackstone was gracious enough to spend time with these infrequent visitors, grateful that they showed sufficient concern to be with Christiana while he was away campaigning, but he did not have the luxury of those Norman barons who had sufficient income from their lands. The tithe that Blackstone took from his villagers was sufficient to keep the house warm and food on the table for the handful of hobelars who lived with their women and guarded the manor's boundary. Each town under Blackstone's control took a similar *patis*, offering protection for the peasants in return for the feeding of his soldiers and a percentage of any goods sold in local markets. But payment for these men had to be in plunder and that was why he undertook the campaigns that he did, reaching ever further from the safety of his home to take on those loyal to King John and stripping them of coin, plate and livestock. In attacking other men-at-arms or noblemen he deprived them of their own supplies, which meant that those peasants who farmed their lord's land would suffer. Some might even starve. But they were of no consequence to him. His own people looked to him for protection and to ensure they got through the winter with enough food on their tables. That was his duty to them as much as they had theirs to him.

Blackstone was held in esteem by those who knew his worth and feared by those who thought him a common butcher, elevated by the English royal house from the lowest ranks, renowned for their slaughter of the greatest knights in Christendom: the archers.

In the chill barn where Guillaume cleaned his lord's armour he glanced at Blackstone, who seemed to be concentrating too hard on sharpening his archer's knife.

'Is Henry going to be so useless that he'll be packed off to a monastery?' Blackstone asked. The dumping ground for weaklings, half-witted children of the nobility or the inbred peasant.

Guillaume knew Blackstone's son was a worry

to him. 'My lord,' he said, 'he's intelligent in his studies and well versed in other matters as befits an educated boy.'

Blackstone had taught Henry to ride and swim, taking him out into the river's deep pools so he could feel the cold, teaching him how to cease the shivering by concentrating his mind and ignoring his body's suffering.

'He's not that strong,' Blackstone argued, wanting to hear that he was wrong and that his son had shown the squire a side to his nature that he himself had not seen.

'No,' Guillaume answered, 'he's not, Sir Thomas. But he tries hard.'

That was the truth, and he could always rely on his squire to be truthful. It was a virtue that sometimes bordered on the painful. Blackstone loved his son; cherished him as much as he adored the boy's sister, Agnes. It was a joy kept hidden from most lest anyone think the poorer of him, though who that might have been was a question he could never answer. Still, showing too much affection to a son could be detrimental to the boy himself. He would be thought weaker than he was, derided by other children as being shielded and protected by an overprotective father. Eyebrows had been raised when he forbade the priest from whipping Henry because of his lack of progress in his Latin studies. What damned difference did it make if he could not learn the language of lawyers and monks? Unless he became one.

'I should spend more time with him. He'll be nine this year.'

'Yes, lord. Let him feel the weight of your sword in his hand and experience what it is you feel when you grasp it.'

Blackstone knew that the surge of power and violence that coursed through him when Wolf Sword lay in his grip and the blood knot was fastened around his wrist would never be experienced by his son. Those feelings had nothing to do with the balance or the finely honed steel of its blade.

'Aye, let him feel its weight, but find more time to spend with the training sword. He needs to feel what its edge can do to a careless boy who does not shield himself properly.'

Guillaume began burnishing the armour again. He had no desire to contradict his sworn lord, nor did he wish him to see the doubt in his eyes. Henry lacked the grim determination that every boy needed to go through the punishment of training. 'My Lady Christiana will notice any bruising, lord.'

'Then strike him where it will not show. He has to learn, Guillaume.'

The squire faced his master. 'I will lose his trust if I hurt him, Sir Thomas. He's not—'

'Strong?' Blackstone interrupted. 'You think I don't know that? I don't care if he hates us both. If we do not teach him, then the day will soon arrive when he must go to a nobleman's house and learn the harsh reality of being alone and punished for every wrong step.'

Blackstone left his squire to continue his duties and took away his own doubts about his son and his inability to be a good father.

Simon Bucy, the man who wanted to deprive Henry Blackstone of his father, pondered the fate of France and the vital role he could play in saving her. From his magnificent urban estate close to the Abbey of Saint-Germain-des-Prés he gazed from the window of his mansion across the gardens towards the Royal Palace. So much turmoil had been endured by the people of this great city. It was only a few years ago that half its population, some fifty thousand, lay in wretched death on its streets. The great paved streets that led through the city suburbs to the countryside had seen no royal procession but bore witness to the crippled rhythm of cartwheels as they lumbered, stacked with the dead, towards the communal graves. But now Paris was alive with street traders and commerce, and must never fall into the hands of the barbaric English soldiers. Let Edward increase his foothold in Gascony for now if he must, but those who secretly supported him, and who could hand the keys of this great city to his King's enemies, must be stopped. He had to find a way to cut the root of the Norman lords' power, to disinherit them of the strength they possessed. There could be no sudden violence inflicted upon them; instead they must be drawn in, snared and dispatched. But how to destroy the man who could rise up in their support, bringing hundreds of the men who garrisoned his towns? What was his weakness that could be exploited? If Thomas Blackstone stayed entrenched at his home in Normandy, as the King's spies informed Bucy, then little could be done to draw him out.

A servant's footsteps scuffed the floor. Bucy gestured the man forward and took the folded note from the silver tray that was offered. The ink-smudged paper showed a decent hand from a poorly sharpened quill, but it had been written in haste. Bucy had sent word to the one Norman lord who might answer the question that preyed on his mind. The traitor could not be seen visiting Bucy's residence; instead a messenger would rendezvous with him and unsigned notes would pass between them. No seal or mark to reveal the writer.

Honour and fealty, or a quest for wealth, could take a man across the world to fight an enemy he never knew. But what kept such a man at home? He needed to find the means to geld the scarred Englishman. He tore open the note.

Bucy swept down the cloisters of the abbey church of Saint-Magloire that stood north of the city. Messengers had gone before him to keep the monks out of sight. This secret meeting needed no witnesses and the church had been endowed with enough money for the prior to know when absence was required. Two of Bucy's guards stood at the great doors that led to the vaulted darkness of the church. As he stepped across their threshold they closed behind him, their sullen echo reverberating across the flagstones. A cloaked figure stepped out from the shadows, his tabard hidden; the hood of his ermine-lined cloak covering his face. Bucy glanced left and right, a matter of habit to ensure there were no other witnesses to the meeting, that no monk lay prostrate in the near darkness, humbling himself before God. He knew it was unnecessary, because his guards had already swept through the side altars and pressed beyond the massive pillars to explore the shadows by torchlight. Only the traitor stood waiting.

Bucy strode towards the altar and the candlelit figure of the suffering Christ. There was little humility within Simon Bucy – he was a political survivor – but he bent his knee. The Norman lord who was to betray his friends settled onto a bench. Bucy rose and approached him. He pulled his own cloak tighter around himself, the chill damp of the chapel penetrating his old bones, although he felt a gratifying sense of warmth at being another step closer to finding the means of destroying Thomas Blackstone. Neither man spoke for a few moments and Bucy sensed that this Norman was teetering in his betrayal.

'Are we to sit in silent prayer?' he prompted, his breath pluming in the chilled atmosphere.

'The garrison at Saint-Clair-de-la-Beaumont has fallen. Blackstone seized it,' said the traitor. A brutal hammer blow that had the desired effect.

Bucy's eyes widened; then his shoulders slumped. A vital stronghold had fallen and Bucy was the one who would have to break the news to the King.

'I have the name of a man you can use to entrap and kill Blackstone,' the traitor said. 'But I want the King's assurance that I and my family will be granted protection.'

Bucy recovered quickly. 'It is I who will ensure your protection. That you and I meet is a gesture of the King's gratitude. Tell me what you have so we may rid ourselves of your Norman trouble-makers and the damned Englishman.'

The Norman wiped a dribble of snot away. The cold air was as punishing as Lent. 'I have two sources that I can use against Blackstone. One is someone close to him.'

'Who?' Bucy asked.

'That is for me alone to know. But it is someone that the Englishman or his family would never suspect.'

'Very well. Who is the other?'

'Years ago I was at Castle de Harcourt where Thomas Blackstone was being sheltered after suffering injuries at Crécy. The old King heard that an Englishman was there and sent men to seize him but de Harcourt tricked them and handed over a wounded messenger that Blackstone had rescued from a mob in one of the villages. The King's men took him but he died less than a day later. It was a good trick and Blackstone was saved.'

The Norman was taking his damned time. Leaking the story like a barber surgeon bleeding the sick. Bucy kept a rein on his impatience, but there was no soft cushion to sit on, and the cold stone floor made his legs ache. That the traitorous Norman could not have chosen a ride in the countryside beyond the city walls was annoying, but his actions reflected the fear and uncertainty that he felt. Perhaps, Bucy thought, being in sight of the tortured son of God, who died for mankind's sins, offered some solace – and if that was the case then perhaps this Norman hoped his own sins, now witnessed, would be forgiven. Bucy almost shrugged as he thought of it: forgiveness was not his to give, so let it be in the hands of the Almighty.

'Yes, we know Thomas Blackstone leads a charmed life, but how does that event so many years ago help us now?'

'It is a case of understanding where the seeds of fear are planted,' said the Norman. 'And then you harvest the crop.'

'Quite so,' Bucy answered, 'but my fear is that I'll be catching my death if I sit in this dank place much longer.'

'Too much soft living, my lord.'

'A state of comfort I intend to continue, *my lord*.'

The traitor held back any further retort. 'There was a man who rode with the King's mercenaries that day. He was an underling then, a scab on the arse of the routiers; but he has power now; he has built a raiding band of routiers. And he can be bought.' He paused, letting Bucy's thoughts churn a moment longer. 'This man is the weapon you use to kill Blackstone.'

Bucy tasted the pleasure of imminent success. Could he use this man to destroy the King's enemy without the King being involved? The King might still have a chance to negotiate with the barons once the threat of Blackstone had been removed. Events might then unfold that could force the Norman lords to yield their ambitions with the English crown and Charles of Navarre and swear fealty to John.

The traitor leaned forward. 'I know where he is. Send for him – and he will come to you.' His voice fell to a whisper. 'But be careful. Be guided by fear. He is the great destroyer.'

CHAPTER 6

Blackstone seldom ventured beyond the walls of the manor without taking a diversion through the kitchen. Scent-laden steam filtered through the open window and the sound of ladles scratching iron pots as the pottage was stirred always brought back childhood memories. If ever there could be contentment in his life it was here, at home.

He stepped inside to find four boys from the village preparing trenchers of coarse-grain bread ready to receive the topping for Blackstone's men. As he entered, the boys stopped what they were doing and bowed their heads and when Beatrix caught sight of him she dipped her knee. The kitchen was a domain of its own; Christiana seldom went into it, but Blackstone did not care for servants to rule without an occasional challenge.

The heat from the fire and the steaming pots made Beatrix's face seem more flushed than usual. She seldom saw Blackstone even when he was not on campaign and had to gather herself for a moment, not wishing to be seen flustered in front of the kitchen boys.

'Beatrix, the men are hungry, so I pray you won't be offering salted fish; we've had a belly full of that,' he said, smiling at her. But she was a peasant Frenchwoman who had no understanding that her English lord's ways meant his words were often spoken in gentle jest. It was better not to try and interpret them in any other way than what she heard.

'You will have pottage and mutton, my lord.'

'No white sauce or beef?' he said, once again gently mocking her.

Beatrix scowled. 'There's never been delicate food from this kitchen except when my Ladies de Harcourt and de Ruymont have visited and then my mistress commands me to serve fine cuts with a sauce. You've no need to worry about your men, Sir Thomas. They'll bed down in the straw with full bellies and sleep like farting pigs.'

She fussed the boys and gave a gentle slap to the back of the head of one of them, urging them to carry on with their duties and to lower their eyes when their lord and master came into the kitchen.

Blackstone looked around the shelves laden with pottery storage jars. There was honey and butter and he could smell mint and sage, and one of the boys was grinding fresh garlic with the pestle and mortar. In a cool corner of the kitchen there was wine and olive oil that had been traded with merchants or taken on one of his raids. He dipped a finger in a jar of congealed honey and sucked

113

the cloying sweetness to the roof of his mouth. There was an astringent tang of herbs that tasted like rosemary and lavender. He grimaced. There were delights to be had from having a home surrounded by the richness of its countryside, but this was not the best honey he had tasted. Beatrix could blend seasoning to suit most palates when guests visited, but Blackstone's requirements for food remained simplicity and quantity. He swallowed and scraped a finger across the roof of his mouth, then reached for a morsel of meat.

'Put venison on the table as well. They deserve it,' he said. 'I have Gascons with me, so make sure there's extra garlic and they'll have ale instead of cider, but keep the cider ready because they'll have a thirst on them. You've been told how many men?'

'Aye, Sir Thomas. And we've made up a balm for those with any wounds,' she said, taking from him the jar whose contents he had just tasted.

Blackstone hid his foolishness as Beatrix reclaimed her authority in the kitchen. A fighter knew when to retreat and Blackstone left the heat of the kitchen for the cool air of the open fields. There was a wall to be built, and his skill in choosing and laying the stones was a welcome distraction. He remembered that there had been some unhappiness from the men who served in the kitchen when Beatrix came to the house, shuffling down the road with her bundle on her shoulder, bent as double as Old Hugh, whom she followed. Where one was sent the other trailed behind, and so Christiana inherited not only a steward to look after Blackstone's affairs while he was away fighting, but a cook from Lord de Graville's castle, a woman, ruddy-faced from years standing over flames and steaming pots, with broken veins in her face that crawled like rivers on a map. Thirty years in the kitchens was experience that would benefit the Englishman and his wife, de Graville had decided. It was a known fact among the French noblemen that the English scorched their food and ate coarse bread, and if Christiana insisted on breaking tradition by breast-feeding her children, then it would do no harm to have a woman cooking in the kitchen rather than a male servant. And Lord de Graville had not gifted the servants simply out of the goodness of his heart or a wish to help Blackstone and his wife in their new home. The servants were old and their strength would soon fail, and then they would be mouths to feed without any return of work.

But Beatrix and Old Hugh had shown a willingness to serve their new master with what seemed to be grim determination. Perhaps it was the generosity with which Blackstone and Christiana governed their house. There was firm rule, but both Christiana, the daughter of a penurious knight, and Blackstone, a village stonemason whose strength and courage had brought him honour, understood how peasants could be treated. Beatrix had proved more competent than expected. Her previously undernourished body gained weight and, despite her slender frame, she had no difficulty hauling the chains above the great fireplace in the kitchens when meat had to be smoked and roasted, or when lifting the cauldrons of boiled ham or pottage when Blackstone fed his men.

Christiana saw to it that older children from the village were employed to fetch and carry and scrub floors in the kitchens, and the discontent among the men who would have served as cooks was soon quelled when Blackstone suggested they might prefer to return to being bondsmen rather than have the freedom he had given them. Over time the Blackstone domain became productive and well organized, its master liking nothing better than taking his son into the forests with Guillaume, showing Henry the tracks of fox and wolf while they hunted venison and boar whose meat was smoked or salted for the winter months. The manor's grain stores had been repaired and were dry and airy, keeping the bushels free of mould. Old Hugh supervised the crop rotation, instructed the blacksmith and beat the stable-hands if they were not diligent in their duties. He was as tireless as his master. There was little time for rest except on holy days and special occasions when the peasants did not work. But on any of those days Blackstone was seldom behind the stone walls that surrounded the courtyard. The outlying domains of the Norman lords offered him protection, but he created his own defences, cutting back the treeline, using the timber as a palisade that created an additional barrier to anyone wishing to strike suddenly. A stream had been dammed to form a small lake with sluice gates, where fish bred and were caught when the winter frosts were not too heavy. It had all taken great effort because he was so often absent, but the rewards were there for all to see.

Blackstone remembered the ruined manor when they first rode into the weed-grown courtyard. They had both worked like peasants to clear it, and the villagers gradually submitted to his promise of protection. Over the months that followed Christiana decorated their chambers with tapestry and silk, covered floors with carpets that Blackstone brought home from his raids on French lords. Her own resourcefulness was often tested, not least when Blackstone was away fighting. Once, a thief had slipped through Blackstone's patrolling soldiers; she had remained calm despite the desperate man menacing her with a knife. She talked to him until he eventually agreed that she would have him fed and given food for the road. She gave him her word to cement the promise. When the man had gorged and had a sack of supplies given to him, Blackstone's men held him, ready for their lord's return and the hanging that was sure to follow. Christiana demanded they release him. Her word was Blackstone's bond as well as her own. Reluctantly they did as she ordered but, like all vagabonds, he left a mark on a stone near the manor, a sign to tell others like him that there were easy pickings to be had with the lady of the house. The next thief who slipped through the kitchen window held Beatrix at knife point, but this time Christiana summoned the sentry. The promise she made the intruder was also straightforward. Harm the cook and he would be hanged, drawn and quartered by Count Jean de Harcourt, on whose land the thief had trespassed in order to reach Blackstone's domain, or surrender and be hanged on a full stomach without mutilation. The thief surrendered, she fed him, and had him strung up at the crossroads. No thief ever again entered the manor's land.

The handful of soldiers who served in the village were never idle, often working alongside their sworn lord as he reinforced broken walls, or carted fresh stone for another. They were low-caste men; some had committed murder; all had served in one army or another. Some were deserters, others men displaced by fractured treaties, but as Blackstone seized towns and garrisoned them with soldiers drawn by his reputation, he handpicked some of the basest characters to settle in his village with their women. Such men, he knew, would fight with great viciousness in defence of the privilege bestowed on them. Their worth had been proven on the occasions when the King sent marauders into the duchy. The Norman lords would send word to Blackstone and it was men from his village who would ride out and do the killing. It was a strange relationship between the English knight and these men, but he had shown a firm hand and paid them well and they served as his first line of defence should intruders ever slip through the forests and assault the village. The domain served them all and its master was unrelenting in his determination to see it prosper further still. He wondered if the time might come when the violence between France and England would cease and that King Edward would relinquish his desire for the French crown. Even if such a thing came to pass, the killing would not stop in such places as Brittany and Gascony, because local lords would feud and the last thing men trained for war wanted was peace.

But here in Normandy, which was like his home country, the lush fields and rich orchards were a haven that could feed his family and allow him to watch his children grow.

'You're daydreaming,' said Christiana, carrying a basket over her arm as she walked to where he had been cutting and laying the stone wall.

Blackstone looked quickly at her. 'Was I?'

'Yes.' She threw down a blanket next to a large piece of stone that had yet to be cut and shaped. 'Your mouth was open, your eyes were glazed and flies were starting to gather,' she said as she sat, settling herself.

He threw down the mallet and chisel, and bent to kiss her. 'I was thinking,' he told her.

'It looked painful.'

'Yet I felt no discomfort.'

'You were grimacing,' she said and pulled back the linen cloth that covered his food.

'Thinking can be hard work,' he said, and nuzzled her neck, breathing deeply of her scent.

Christiana shrugged him off. 'I'm not here for sex, Thomas. It's too cold and this stubborn frost would seize my bones.'

'I'd warm you. You would be aflame with desire and be grateful for the cold earth to cool your passion. Isn't that what a courtly-love nobleman would say?'

'Do you want cheese or meat?' she asked.

'Either,' he said and smiled. It made no difference what food he ate, but he could not ignore the stirring of passion for her.

She cut a chunk of rough bread and handed it to him with a wedge of cheese and an apple whose skin was beginning to wrinkle.

He rolled the apple between his fingers. 'Have we been married too long?'

'Are you saying I'm as wrinkled as that?'

'I'm saying we used to rut like deer,' he told her and took a big bite of cheese, pushing a torn piece of bread into his mouth at the same time.

'You're a peasant, Thomas,' she said, not unkindly, to which he grinned and nodded. She held the wrinkled apple. 'It's one of the last on the rack in the barn,' she said. 'Maybe it *is* like me. Left abandoned over winter to age alone. Letting my juices dry.'

'You could take a lover,' he said, pulling the cork on the stone flask from the basket and taking a mouthful of cider. 'God's blood, this could turn a man blind.' He grimaced.

'Well, it certainly can't make you any more stupid,' she teased as she slipped a slender slice of apple between her lips.

'Why, because I suggested you take another man to your bed? You never would. I know that.'

'No, because the sun is burning off the mist and we are here far away from the house and children, where there are no servants or sentries, it's as secluded as I could hope for. You obviously don't need the cider to turn you blind.'

He swallowed and looked at her propped on her elbow, watching him, saying nothing, the swell of her breasts pushing against the dress. Like a child trespassing on his lord's domain, Blackstone popped his head above the wall and peered across the fields and orchards. They were alone. Blackstone pushed aside the food basket and lay next to her.

'Why don't you just say you want to lie with your lord and husband?' he said, teasing her nipple beneath her dress with a fingertip.

'Thomas, that's not how the game is played,' she replied, and pulled his scarred face towards her lips.

CHAPTER 7

Paris and the Île de la Cité shone in the spring sunshine, a welcome change from the river fog. Notre-Dame's towers finally broke through the shroud that had covered them these past several days. The city's stench had shifted as the breeze turned and King John felt that the future would reward his determination to protect this jewel of a city, with its renowned university and Notre-Dame's magnificent homage to God. The court astrologer had predicted that momentous events would occur, that a great battle would be fought, and that could mean only one thing to the impetuous King – that Edward of England would be vanquished and hurled back across La Manche, the sea across which the bastard Duke of Normandy had once invaded and claimed the land beyond as his own. Like a blade being twisted in a wound, history since that day had inflicted its agony on the French and caused an abiding mistrust and bitterness between them and the Normans.

The King, despite the apparent physical strength of his body, was prone to chills and ill health. His chair was drawn up close to the fire when Simon Bucy entered the royal apartment. John looked at him and for a moment Bucy thought that he looked like a sick old man despite his thirty-seven years. The King pulled his ermine robe closer to his neck. He was not in the mood for the leader of the Parlement to bring him affairs of state.

'We have a new falcon and thought to release some cages of doves. A distraction from the tedium of this gilded cage where I am kept duty-bound,' said John.

'Sire, we have news,' Bucy said. 'From the south.'

Bucy quickly gestured the attendants away and they pressed back against the walls, well out of earshot. He took a slow, deep breath. He needed it to calm his own trepidation before delivering what would be another mighty blow to the King's already shaky confidence. 'Jean de Grailly led a mixed force of Gascons and English and struck north from Bordeaux away from the main force and then turned east. He has taken the city of Périgueux.'

King John's breath expelled like a deflated bladder. 'What?' he whispered. 'Impossible. The garrison at Saint-Clair-de-la-Beaumont holds the road and the river. De Grailly would need to take it. He could not. No one could lay siege at Saint-Clair. Sir Henri would have sent word. We would have heard.'

'I'm afraid it's true, highness. Thomas Blackstone

123

sailed upriver and attacked through the marshes from the rear. Sir Henri is dead and his men with him. De Grailly has garrisoned it with a hundred troops or more and Blackstone seized the weapons and the coin Sir Henri held to pay the local lords. We cannot raise further taxes and must find other means to pay those who are still loyal to us there.'

'Blackstone,' said John, as if the very name was poison on his tongue.

Bucy stepped quickly forward, eager to alleviate the bad news. 'Sire, I have found the man who would dare to draw out Thomas Blackstone, and by so doing enable us to diminish the Norman lords.'

The light of sudden interest sparkled in King John's eyes. He nodded for Bucy to sit.

Bucy began to relate all he had learnt from the Norman traitor. 'He is the son of a minor family. He is educated, literate and has intelligence, even if more feral than most.'

'We do not want these lesser nobles thinking we will grant them land and favour because they believe themselves to be capable of going against the Englishman. How many fools have dreamt of that and now look down on their folly from heaven?'

Bucy shook his head and spoke quietly. 'It has nothing to do with his family. They abandoned him, glad to rid themselves of him. He stole from a family while he was a guest in their home—'

The King interrupted: 'All nobles are thieves,

my friend, like gutter rats snatching at scraps. They preen themselves with spittle for their enemies. A man who covets a silver goblet and is prepared to kill for it is a shallow character. To be a master thief with ambition is to steal a nation,' he added dismissively. 'Look to Edward for a lesson in thievery.'

'This man is more than a thief, sire. He began killing when he was young. He befriended a widow's son so he could attempt her seduction. But she rebuffed his advances.'

The King's attention was held. 'And he killed her for it?'

'No, her chastisement made him flee, but he helped himself to whatever jewellery he could find. When the woman's young son accused him of the theft he murdered the boy.'

'A matter of honour because he was falsely accused or was there proof?' asked the King.

Bucy licked his lips nervously. What frightened him was not the machinations of politics but of having any close contact with the violent men who scoured the country, be they of the nobility or base-born, like the routier horsemen. Rape and slaughter were an everyday occurrence. The King granted licence for torture and the Church never questioned a confession of heresy obtained by breaking and burning a victim. And yet Bucy hesitated. He was about to deliver to his King a man so vile in nature that the devout John might refuse to have him do the Crown's bidding.

'It was a matter of revenge against the woman. He took her son in the night and tied him to a tree within sight of his mother's bedchamber. When she awoke the first thing she saw were his slashed and bloodied remains. It was a vicious evisceration that curdled even the hearts of men who had fought in war.'

'He would have been condemned,' said the King. 'And hanged.'

'He very nearly was. The scandal could hardly be contained. His family was on the point of ruin. Reparation to the injured widow would have meant the loss of their estate and financial compensation that would force them into penury.'

The King raised a glass of wine to his lips. He could see his adviser was frightened by the very thought of this man. If fear could be spread like contagion then perhaps he had found his plague carrier.

'How was he not punished?'

'The solution was suggested by the killer himself. Were his family to buy a benefice from the Archbishop, their land would be retained, he would be saved from the hangman's noose and the widow could not contest the forgiveness that would be granted.'

'And the killer was made the archpriest of the diocese?'

Bucy nodded. 'And in so doing the Church gave him the opportunity to secure his own authority and wealth.'

Both men fell silent. The solution of the benefice offered a blessedly simple way for the killer to gain influence, and his family were well rid of a brutal and troublesome son who guaranteed their ruin. Bucy recounted what he knew.

'This man sold sinners to the Bishop; those accused of blasphemy he whipped and tortured; he exchanged holy oils for gifts, rosaries for carnality and, when visiting the dying, would strip them of their jewellery. The abomination ended only when the Bishop realized that his priest was taking more from his victims within the dioceses than the Bishop himself. The killer lost his benefice, but by then he was well used to the pleasures that money could buy.'

Bishops were powerful, archbishops more so, and the Pope may as well have been the voice of God incarnate. The Church's power and authority could often be a direct challenge to the authority of the Crown despite a king being thought divine, but that they should have taken into their fold such an evil creature and stripped him of office only when they discovered he was more successful at extortion than themselves gave the King dispensation to use him. Doubts crossed the King's mind. A brutal murderer might not be the answer to weakening the Norman lords' power by killing Thomas Blackstone.

'Simon, it is not enough to let a rabid dog loose across the countryside. A man like this will never be assuaged by blood; he will kill simply for the

127

enjoyment of killing. He is not the man we seek. His desires make him too unreliable.'

'Sire, there is more.'

The King's eyebrows lifted. A slaughterman who tortured his victims could have no further qualities that could be put to good use.

Bucy said, 'Ten or eleven years ago he became obsessed with the daughter of an ageing knight, Guyon de Sainteny.'

King John remembered loyalty as much as he did treachery.

'De Sainteny? He was a Norman. Yes, he served our father against Godfrey de Harcourt and the English. What happened to de Sainteny?'

Bucy barely withheld the sigh that threatened to escape from his chest. The King was easily distracted.

'I don't know, sire. Killed in the fighting before Crécy, no doubt. He was of little importance. What we know is that he was poor and a widower who could not keep his child in safety. Even a convent was no sanctury.'

'Then this creature violated his daughter? Is that it?'

'No. He attempted to entice her into marriage. He threatened Sir Guyon but the old knight was made of sterner stuff and knew he would never be able to offer the protection his daughter needed because he was often away from home serving his sworn lord, so he sent her to a household that he would never dare challenge.' Bucy paused for effect. 'Countess Blanche de Harcourt.'

The glass of wine was held suspended without reaching the King's lips. Bucy knew in that moment that John's interest was finally caught.

'Harcourt?' the King murmured. He sipped the wine, his mind whirring with anticipation of taking the first steps towards wounding the Norman lords, enticing him to consider engaging this beast of a man.

'If he kills Blackstone let him have all that Blackstone possesses. His territory. His towns. It is what he desires. Or part of it, anyway. Pardon him and use him,' Bucy urged him.

The King faltered. His agreement would give the killer official status and a lawful source of income. John thought about it. The fear this man created from the violence he inflicted was worth more than could be bought.

'Is he Satan's spawn?'

'He professes to be the instrument of God's anger, sire.' Bucy hesitated, considering whether he should mention the killer's sobriquet to the devout monarch. 'He is known as "le Prêtre sanguinaire".'

King John swallowed hard, the flutter in his chest a quiver that rippled through him. 'His name?'

'Gilles de Marcy.'

It meant nothing to John. A fear of God was most men's inheritance. But clearly not this man. Great lords stripped their wealth and prostrated themselves before the Church as they neared death in an attempt to renounce worldly desires and success. Such desperation for absolution and to expunge pride from their souls was a final plea for mercy before being swept into the heavens with Satan's imps biting and clawing at the ankles. But a man who claimed to embrace such heavenly vengeance was possessed . . . of what?

'This Savage Priest. A fanatic, then. Dangerous,' said King John.

Bucy did not try to hide his own sense of disgust about de Marcy's macabre past, his savage acts that had become a scourge, despised by any God-fearing man, be they peasant or aristocrat. 'More than dangerous, my lord. He is a twisted creature. He takes pleasure from torture, salivates at the thought of pain and inflicts it with relish. As for being an instrument of God's anger – if that's what he believes – then he is unstoppable,' said Bucy.

King John understood the game. He knew Bucy was holding back, waiting for the moment when he would reveal some vital scrap of information. 'Very well. What else does he want?'

'We give him the woman he has always desired. De Sainteny's daughter.'

'She could be anywhere.'

Bucy hesitated again, wanting to draw out the final moments of suspense as the traitor baron had done to him.

'She is Blackstone's wife, and may God help her if we let loose this man.'

The King gasped quietly as a sense of victory eased his disquiet.

The winter sun had burned the river mist into vapour. He would ride out with his favourite falcons and watch them tear the flock of helpless doves into bloodied terror.

CHAPTER 8

Blackstone had waited almost three weeks before visiting his friend, needing time to reflect on his decision not to campaign for the remainder of that year and to keep his towns intact, well fed and disciplined during the coming months. Meulon and Gaillard could be relied upon to keep their garrisons in order, and Guinot would never allow anyone to challenge his authority. But Blackstone would still have to travel throughout the summer to ensure that his own leadership remained unquestioned among those smaller garrisons and manors that had sworn fealty to him. Fighting men needed to fight and if there was no common enemy they could turn upon their own. Count Jean de Harcourt was due the respect and friendship of a visit and Blackstone was happy to accord it to him – on his own terms. He was an independent captain of men who sought favour from no one.

Blackstone nudged his horse onto the path around Castle de Harcourt's outer moat; its breadth and depth still as formidable as when he first paddled across it as a young archer on the orders of Sir Godfrey de Harcourt. Richard, his brother, had stood in the skiff and his great strength had supported Blackstone as he clambered through the lower window that he could now see as they turned their horses towards the outer walls. Hidden within the confines of the castle had been brigands who had slaughtered the servants, but thankfully not the de Harcourt family who were elsewhere. But the treasure that Blackstone found hidden in a narrow passageway was the young girl he took to safety: Christiana.

'My Lord de Harcourt holds you in great esteem, Sir Thomas,' Guillaume said as they rode within sight of the castle. 'I see they've cut the treeline back further beyond the north gate as you suggested.' He raised himself in the saddle. 'And there are more men on the walls.'

'Each of us must prepare for the worst, Guillaume,' said Blackstone as the gate sentries called out their challenge, which Guillaume answered.

'Then do you think we should bring Gaillard and Meulon with some extra men to the manor?' asked the squire as their horses passed under the arch, and de Harcourt's sentries called for servants to run forward and take their horses.

'By the time anyone came through the valley we would know about it in good enough time, and no one can lay siege to us with Norman lords at their back. And remember, Guillaume, no one in Paris knows which of my towns I'm in at any given

133

time, so the King would not risking alerting us by a random strike.'

Blackstone saw Blanche de Harcourt appear from under the raised portcullis and cross the wooden bridge over the inner moat. Ahead of her, Marcel, her personal servant, ran towards them and bowed his head respectfully.

'My lord, Sir Thomas, welcome as always to my master's home. We rejoiced in your victory. My Lady Blanche bids me to take you to her.'

Blackstone looked at Blanche's faithful servant. He had been there when Christiana had nursed his wounds and it had taken some time for him to realize that the old man was Blanche's confidant rather than her husband's. Marcel nodded in acknowledgement to the squire.

'Master Guillaume, it is good to see you again.'

The horses were led away by stable-hands and Blanche de Harcourt was almost within earshot.

'Are you well, Marcel?' asked Blackstone as he looked at the bruising on the servant's neck and face.

'I am, Sir Thomas,' he answered without a moment's hesitation, making light of the injury. 'I took a fall down the cellar steps. I fear that age has made me more clumsy than I would wish.'

Blackstone saw the momentary look of distress in the man's eyes. He was lying.

'Aches and pains are the curse of us all who live in this clinging damp place, Marcel.' Blackstone extended his crooked arm as far as he could. 'I too feel its pinch in my bones, and I have some years yet to go before I reach your age. And by the way you ran across the outer ward there is little sign of it getting the better of you.'

Blanche de Harcourt joined them and kissed Blackstone on each cheek.

'At last, Thomas, you come to us. Now, let me take you to Jean, who is in the library. He will be even more pleased to see you.' She turned to Marcel. 'Take Master Guillaume to the kitchens and make sure he has whatever he needs.'

Guillaume bowed in thanks. 'My lady.'

Blanche put her arm through Blackstone's and led him towards the château's entrance. He let his eyes follow the line of curtain walls, interrupted by half-towers. They had been reinforced in several places since he had last visited the castle.

Blanche de Harcourt seemed nervous, though she controlled her voice carefully. 'Jean is fervent in his prayers. He's still bitter about Bernard d'Aubriet's execution, and I can't blame him, Thomas. The King made a cruel and unjust decision. Since my husband returned from Paris he spends his time between the chapel and the library. He locks himself in there and plans what should be done.' Blackstone felt the squeeze of her hand on his arm. 'He needs you, Thomas. At times the tension is unbearable because he feels that this is the breaking point for Normandy and his chance to influence what happens with the King.'

'And he fears an attack,' Blackstone said, glancing at the walls.

She knew Blackstone was observant enough to notice the changes in the place where he had spent those years recovering from his wounds and being drawn into the Harcourt family, where he and Christiana still visited every few months. She nodded and he sensed more sadness than fear.

He looked at her. 'Marcel has never tripped over his own feet in all the years I've known him. He could walk around this castle at night in pitch darkness and not stumble. He's loyal to you, Blanche. What's going on?'

For a moment she did not answer. Blackstone felt her body sag, as if grief claimed her – it was barely noticeable but he felt it; then she stiffened in resolve, iron in her bones, and relented. 'Guy de Ruymont was here last week. Jean saw him talking to Marcel in the stables. He gave Marcel a silver penny. Jean thought Guy was questioning him about what went on here – that Guy did not trust him to take this burden on his shoulders.'

'Jean beat Marcel.'

She nodded. 'It was stupid. Guy was rewarding him for attending to Joanne and the children when they were here. You know Marcel is good with children; they ride him like a donkey. Jean's fears grow out of all proportion. He thought he was being betrayed and he hit Marcel. I had to stop it. Trying to keep the lords who support Charles of Navarre in line is proving difficult. Jean takes the strain badly. And if he goes on like this he'll make an even bigger mistake. We all know Navarre is not to be trusted. What would it take for him to turn his back on Jean and the others? Nothing more than another arrangement with the King.'

They reached the inner hall, where burning torches in iron sconces threw uneven light down the corridors. Blackstone thought it made the stone corridors feel like a crypt as its chill settled in the gloom. A sudden crash of something thrown echoed from the great hall followed by the yelp of a dog. She suddenly held his arm, unmistakable concern etched on her face. 'Thomas, be careful. He's been drinking.'

Jean, the fifth Count of Harcourt, one of Normandy's most prominent families, was drunk. He raged against the shadows that tormented him in the great hall as firelight cast its demons across the walls. His bellowing anger and cries of self-pity kept servants and family alike away from his violent outbursts. Stools and benches were thrown and usually favoured dogs cowered in the far reaches of the room, whimpering with fear and bewilderment.

De Harcourt stumbled, drew his sword and slashed at the tapestry that mocked him: a great hunting scene of a nobleman with a falcon striking a dove, a deer pierced through the heart by a spear and an adoring woman by his side. Golden threads were woven through the figures' finery. A noble lord and his lady. A time of great joy. And what else? Wealth. Confidence. Authority.

Wine spilled down his gown as he slurped from the glass. Honour had deserted him. What greater shame could befall a man?

Blackstone waited a moment longer before putting his weight against the heavy door. Blanche de Harcourt's face was gaunt with strain.

'How long has he been in there?' Blackstone asked.

She hesitated, not wishing to condemn her husband's actions. 'He arrived home just after dawn. He's been in there all day. I have never seen him like this, Thomas.' She turned away from him. 'He met William de Fossat and Rabigot Dury. There were others. I don't know how many.' She turned her face towards him, as if accepting the inevitable. 'And Charles of Navarre.'

William de Fossat was once Blackstone's adversary, but they had since fought side by side. However, now de Harcourt's association with Charles of Navarre and other disaffected nobles raised the spectre of violent men intent on inflicting their will against the French King.

'I don't know where he's been these past three days but when he came back this morning his clothes were bloodstained.'

Blackstone pushed open the door into the great hall and then closed it carefully behind him. Firelight was the only illumination in the room and he had to look into the shadows to find the half-slumped form of Jean de Harcourt. Blackstone moved forward warily. A drunken knight with a dagger at his belt and a sword in hand could draw an army of demons from within himself.

'Jean,' Blackstone called gently. 'Jean, it's Thomas. Do you hear me?'

De Harcourt raised himself, staring uncertainly towards his friend. Blackstone stood head and shoulders above many men and the firelight cast an eerie, looming shadow behind him. The Norman lord recoiled as if one of Satan's imps had come for his soul. And as the scar-faced Blackstone stepped closer de Harcourt pushed his back against the wall, ready to fight.

'Keep back! No closer!' de Harcourt snarled.

Blackstone saw the drunken fear and knew his friend had not recognized him. Trapped within his own torment de Harcourt would see nothing but what his distorted mind projected.

As Blackstone stepped closer, he raised a calming hand to try and soothe the wine-fuelled madness. 'Jean, put down your sword. It's me, Thomas Blackstone. You're scaring the shit out of Blanche and the children.'

Like a cornered beast, de Harcourt readied himself to strike out.

'Lower your sword!' Blackstone shouted, hoping the command would penetrate the man's consciousness.

It had the opposite effect. With a defiant yell de

Harcourt lunged, a high guard sweeping the blade down and across, enough to sever an arm, or cleave a man from neck to chest. Blackstone turned on the balls of his feet, allowing the attack to throw de Harcourt off balance. He clubbed his fist into his friend's skull and his friend fell as if pole-axed. As Blackstone bent forward and grabbed his friend's clothing to haul him onto a chair one of the faithful dogs ran snarling to his master's defence. Blackstone half turned, offered his tunic-clad arm and felt the crushing jaws close on him as the other dogs began their attack. Blackstone drew his knife, severed the dog's throat and kicked its quivering carcass at them. For a moment their companion's blood unsettled and confused them, leaving precious moments before they resumed their attack. Blackstone dragged his friend to the door and unceremoniously threw him into the passageway, slamming closed the doors as the barking dogs reached him, their snuffling and scratching persisting as he faced the shocked servants and Blanche de Harcourt.

'Take my lord to his rooms and care for him!' Blackstone commanded, breaking the spell of uncertainty.

Willing hands gathered the crumpled body of their master.

'Sweet Jesus, Blanche, what has he done?'

She shook her head, a fist unconsciously clenched and pressed to her mouth. Blackstone saw tears well in her eyes, and then she quickly brought herself under control. 'Whatever he's done, it's torn into him and blackened his heart.' She reached up and kissed the Englishman's scarred face in gratitude. 'Stay with him through the night, Thomas. He won't want to see me until his head is clear and his turmoil subdued.' She turned on her heel.

Blackstone muttered curses. Wet-nursing de Harcourt might test the ties of friendship. He'd slain a favoured dog and pummelled the Lord of Harcourt to the ground. There was nothing to be done other than to follow the sounds of the straining servants as they carried their master. It would be a long night.

Daylight brought its bone-aching chill. De Harcourt retched, his hands clasped in supplication across the privy's seat. He vomited again, spitting the residue clear from his lips. He groaned like a man suffering a battlefield wound, and then rolled clear of the stench. Blackstone offered him a pitcher of water; he took it with shaking hands and tipped it over his head, heedless of the water that soaked his clothes and puddled on the floor.

'It's done, Thomas. You can't stop murder when people are set on it.'

Blackstone remained silent and threw a cloth for de Harcourt to wipe his face. His friend and mentor staggered to his feet and began to pull off his clothes until he stood in only his shirt. He slumped into a chair and poured wine, his eyes watching Blackstone over the rim of the goblet as he drank thirstily as if waiting for Blackstone's anger and disapproval.

Instead, he was tossed a bed covering for warmth. 'You're no murderer, Jean. I know that.'

De Harcourt dragged the blanket over himself and turned his gaze away. The Norman countryside stretched to the horizon as far back as his inheritance reached – to the days of the Vikings. His noble family had served French Kings since the first holy scribe could be found to set down their history. That history had already been fractured by divisions, but despite the intrigue and conspiracy, all de Harcourt had ever wanted was for the Normans to remain autonomous and decide to which lord their fealty should be pledged. If only King Edward had seized the crown when he had the chance after the great battle at Crécy all those years before. If only.

Blackstone sat on a stool, watching his mentor and friend, whose involvement in his life was like a tapestry of his past. Each woven knot bound them together ever more tightly. After Blackstone's first great battle it had taken a year for his wounds to heal, and another before his strength returned, by which time the Great Pestilence had swept across Europe from the plague-ridden ports of Genoa and Marseilles. Back then the harsh winter had isolated the villages and towns around Castle de Harcourt, checking the plague's onslaught and extending life until the following spring. Fifty thousand died in the papal city of Avignon alone; even more in Paris. Throughout France black flags were raised above each village blighted by the plague. Bodies were tipped into mass graves; some stricken families were walled into their houses and burned.

But no plague threatened when the young Blackstone had been kept secure in the castle's safety on the orders of the English King. The threat at that time was from other Norman noblemen who loathed the archers who had slain so many of their countrymen. Blackstone had spent hours each day building strength back into his body. His broken arm meant he would never draw a war bow again, but would instead carry a shield that absorbed the heaviest of blows delivered by sword, axe and mace. It was these months of harsh training in sword skills under the tutelage of Jean de Harcourt that turned the archer into a fighting man-at-arms and neither de Harcourt nor any of the battle-experienced knights he counted as friends could best Blackstone in combat. Rather than risk injury they yielded when he beat them into submission. The relentless savagery of his attack reminded the French of other Englishmen they had witnessed in the van of battle: Cobham, Killbere and de Bohun, but they could not know that what seeped into Blackstone's muscle and sinew was caged anger and remorse. Each blow delivered with the sword seized from the German knight who had slaughtered his brother at Crécy was a desperate attempt to hack away his guilt for failing to protect him. It was a violence harnessed over the following years as he took town and village and left his mark on the French. And now he had been called to save his friend – from what?

'I didn't raise my hand in time to stop it,' de Harcourt answered, and related the foul act. 'We killed a man we thought was leading us into a trap. A clandestine meeting with the King's son was arranged. One of the others became suspicious. And we were mistaken in our suspicions.' De Harcourt shook his head. 'We discovered the poor bastard was innocent of any deception. And worse still . . . a distant cousin . . . to Blanche. Sweet Jesus, she has no idea the lad was involved. If she ever finds out . . .' He swilled out his mouth again and spat. 'We buried him and slunk home like feral dogs.'

Blackstone knew that his friend would never forgive himself for not stopping the killing. He was branded with the invisible mark of a thief: a thief who had stolen his own honour. There was no point in dragging out the man's misery. This was no time for sympathy.

'Stay silent and she'll never know. Trust me, I know about keeping secrets that blacken the soul. For Christ's sake, he was a victim. You play this game of kings, Jean, and people will die. See it for what it is,' Blackstone said, deliberately provoking his friend to stir him from self-pity.

'Don't you understand? It's not just the lad's

death. The risks increase the more we gather other barons to our cause. We cannot find our way clear to remove this King. We are too few. We're helpless!'

'You're weak!' Blackstone retorted. 'You whimper. You stumble around like blind men in a dark room. Keep those you trust close to you. Be your own master. Sooner or later the King will discover just how much his son is prepared to listen to you, that you plot with Navarre to put him or the Dauphin on the throne. And then he will strike against you. He will wait for the moment. He wants you to put your own head in the noose. He's a hot-tempered fool but he will not strike against you until he is ready. Whatever path you take, keep your nerve. Choose your ground and fight.'

De Harcourt stood dazed, as if slapped by Blackstone's response. After a moment he nodded. He was a Norman lord and this common man he had entrusted with his friendship had brought him to his senses.

'Get dressed,' said Blackstone, 'I'll have food sent to the library.'

De Harcourt grimaced.

'Not for you, dammit. I'm starving.'

CHAPTER 9

The library was as it always had been. Crammed with scrolls and manuscripts, maps spread out across the slab of chestnut that served as a table, the room warmed by the arc of heat radiating from the stone fireplace as Blackstone finished the plate of food ordered for him. No mention had been made of what had happened in the bedchamber. Sober, de Harcourt seemed more like his old self, but there was still an unmistakable tension to him.

'You were to be here in a week, Thomas, that's what you promised.'

'I made no promise, Jean. It's what you asked for. I could not leave home before now,' said Blackstone, pushing the plate away.

'A man's wife should not hold his shirt tail,' de Harcourt answered, pouring them both wine.

'I have villagers to attend to and accounts to be tallied. And I wanted to spend some time with Christiana and the children.'

Blackstone watched his friend shrug and turn his attention to the flames.

'There are bigger issues pressing upon you. I'll listen, but don't ask me to be involved.'

It was obvious that the Norman barons had not yet agreed on a course of action to support Charles of Navarre in his quest to usurp the French crown. Messengers rode daily between each of their domains, safe in the knowledge that French troops would not infiltrate their lands, but cautious enough to ensure that the messages were brief so that should one of the messengers fall by chance into the French King's hands, his knowledge of the information that he carried was limited. But no matter what course of action was eventually taken, de Harcourt would prefer to have Blackstone and his men, from those scattered towns across Normandy, to be ready to fight on their side should the need arise.

'The Prince of Wales slashes his way across the south, Thomas,' said de Harcourt as he pushed another log into the fire. Blackstone was scratching one of the dog's ears as it rested across his knee, its wet snout comforted by the smell of his cloak. 'And we, as docile as that hound, await King Edward's word of support,' he added, unable to keep the edge of irritation from his voice.

'What of the others? Are they in agreement? You're in contact with them?' Blackstone asked.

'Daily. All except de Graville . . .' He hesitated, uncertainty in his voice.

'What about him?'

'He spends time in Paris,' de Harcourt admitted.

'Is he talking to the King?' Blackstone asked. Traitors could be found anywhere.

De Harcourt shook his head. 'He courts the Dauphin and stays quietly in the background, whispering words of encouragement when he must. The Dauphin is our key to the door.'

'But the Dauphin is mostly in Rouen. Not Paris.'

De Harcourt knew what Blackstone was asking. 'De Graville is loyal, Thomas. He sent you his old servants as a goodwill gesture, didn't he?'

'Then why Paris? Is there a favoured whore there?' Blackstone insisted.

'De Graville!' De Harcourt laughed derisively. 'He's not like our friend de Fossat, who rides away from that sour-faced wife of his each week to bed a merchant's daughter.'

'William has a lover?' Blackstone said.

'Aye. Milk-white tits and as shy as a rosebud in spring. I hear she blossoms at his touch. He's promised her father to help buy an ennoblement. No, de Graville goes to Paris to see a priest. You know how damned religious he is. Hard with it.' He raised a finger quickly. 'And before you ask, it's the priest who confessed him at Rouen for twenty years and is now in Paris. A man and his confessor can be closer than a man and a favoured whore.' De Harcourt refilled their glasses.

Blackstone wondered how far de Harcourt and the other Norman lords would go to take the crown from John. Would they try to kill him, as rumour had it? He had heard that a plot by the King's cousin and son-in-law, Charles of Navarre, and other unnamed barons had been foiled months ago, but the fact that the King's son, the Dauphin, was allegedly involved had brought no recrimination. Hearsay was that he had bought off his son's debts in an effort to keep the boy close. Who knew? Rumours were as common as fleas on the dog that was snuffling his hand for attention.

'Jean, you know as well as I do that Edward doesn't trust Navarre. You told me so yourself. How many times has the man made deals with Edward and then used those promises to negotiate a better contract with King John? Navarre plays both sides and you and the others can't see it.'

De Harcourt worried the burning logs with an iron bar. 'We use him to influence the Dauphin. If the boy can be influenced by anyone it will be by Navarre. Charles is of royal blood – let's not forget that – and has charmed half the French court, so little by little we will get closer to securing what we want. I'm leaving tomorrow for a meeting at Guy de Ruymont's. Some of the others will join me.'

He stopped stabbing at the fire and threw down the bar in a small gesture of frustration. 'Edward will see that Navarre's charm and silver-tongued persuasion will yield us the crown. We will use Navarre to help us convince the Dauphin that he should rule in his father's place or we will let Charles settle the crown on his own head. Either way we will triumph – and we Normans will at last have control of our own destiny. What Edward must do is invade and come at King John hard and fast through Normandy – the Prince of Wales in the south and Edward in the north. We'll deliver Normandy to him and I swear even more French lords will come onto our side,' he said, flopping into the fireside chair. He savoured the comfort that there had been no incursion into any Norman territories after the news of Blackstone's success, which had deprived King John of a strategic garrison, and which had allowed the Gascons to go on and secure an even greater victory.

'It's a sign, Thomas.' De Harcourt pushed his boots onto the hearth. 'John's weak, he has no money; the best he can do is to fortify Paris. Why do you think he had Bernard executed? He needs the people and the merchant's guilds ready to fight. But you hurt him. You took his money and stung his pride and weakened him. And he can do nothing about it. Nothing!' he said with barely contained triumph. 'We will finish this King if we can convince Edward to come sooner rather than later. We are starving John of taxes. None of us here will pay.'

Blackstone eased the dog away and leaned forward. The Normans were blinding themselves to reality. 'That's the wrong decision. That will give him further excuses to find a way to strike at you, and withholding your taxes is treasonable. You escalate the stakes unnecessarily. Pay what you owe. That buys you more time and gives him no cause.'

Jean de Harcourt looked at the man ten years his junior; long gone was the boy he had trained to become a man-at-arms. This weather-beaten knight before him had survived and succeeded where many thought he would die in failure. He had a good head on his shoulders that worked as deftly as his sword. 'We should have made you our ambassador to Edward. You see the issue clearly and quickly. You're right; I'll ensure some of them pay, as a showpiece. That's all. Not support. We will suffocate his treasury, but would he dare risk sweeping us aside without an army?'

He needed Blackstone to join them, but Blackstone was right, they were too fractured in their conspiracy. All the greater reason to persuade him. De Harcourt weighed his words carefully. 'Thomas, the King can raise an army of thirty thousand if he calls for the *arrière-ban*. Our barons have only a few hundred, mostly peasants, a handful of fighting men. You can see our problem.'

What Blackstone could see was that the Norman lords were playing with fire and that he was in de Harcourt's debt for his friendship and protection all these years. 'Then pay what he asks and keep him at bay as long as you can,' he answered. Blackstone had no desire to be drawn into his friend's conflict. 'Do as you think best, Jean. Navarre has troops. He can bring them on ships from the south to Normandy ports; he has garrisons here, he has the support of the other lords. You don't need me.'

He could see that de Harcourt would not hold onto his patience for long and he did not wish to strain their enduring friendship – a spirited friendship that had often seen disagreement, but the two men's mutual respect formed as close a bond as a sword to its scabbard.

'You hold your towns in the name of Edward—'

'I know this argument, Jean,' Blackstone interrupted. 'I have five hundred pounds a year stipend from the English treasury. It's not enough. It's a reward for my loyalty and what I did at Calais, that's all. I still have to raid and fight to keep those towns in his name. If Edward calls for my help, he shall have it.'

'And us?' de Harcourt said angrily.

Blackstone turned his face away and stared into the crackling fire. A spark in the wrong place could set Normandy ablaze. King John would go to war with the Normans if he was forced to – they were playing a fool's game. They were not ready to strike, not yet. They needed the Dauphin to side with them, to be guided under the tutelage of Charles of Navarre. Here was a man whose charm could sway the nobility to secure the crown for the teenage Dauphin. And then what game would follow? Would Edward see the boy as a weaker opponent? Would Navarre use his own royal blood to claim the crown? Blackstone silently cursed the power-hungry ambitions of them all.

He was a fighting man who held his domains, fed his family and men. But he was an Englishman sworn to his King. He barely disguised a sigh as the truth stared him in the face. Was he any better? He had fought for and seized land to extend his own territory. There was no doubt there were men who desired what he had and would take it if they could. It was a game that would never play itself out.

'Edward waits too long, Thomas,' said de Harcourt. 'We must do what we must to rid ourselves of this King. And the sooner the better.'

'Tread carefully,' said Blackstone. 'Navarre is not to be trusted. I can't know Edward's mind, but he plans carefully. As should you. He'll strike when he's ready. Slow down, for God's sake; history will wait for you.'

De Harcourt was suddenly on his feet, a fist clenched in rage. 'We *are* fucking history! Damn you, Thomas! Look to your own forefathers. It wasn't the French who invaded your barbaric island, it was us! Normans! We changed history and we will change it again. Your Kings come from here!'

A vein pulsed in his temple. Blackstone could not remember seeing him this way before. What could be done to calm him?

'Jean, is my presence here in Normandy a hindrance?'

The question flustered de Harcourt's thoughts for a moment. 'What!'

153

'My being here. After what happened down at Saint-Clair. Does King John want my head so badly that he would cut through Normandy to take it? Am I his excuse for coming after you now rather than waiting for you to make your next move?'

'He cannot strike us and he knows it,' de Harcourt answered, his mind distracted by Blackstone's questioning.

'Because if that was the case I would take my family south to Bordeaux. Edward's seneschals will give us refuge among the Gascons until your business is settled.'

'Sweet Jesus, Thomas! One minute you're as wise as Solomon and the next playing the village idiot! I want you *here*! I want you ready to raise your men and support us.'

'Then, when that time comes, and Edward needs you, I will be ready. I serve my King, Jean, no matter where his ancestors came from.' He smiled and let his assurance mollify his friend. De Harcourt gritted his teeth. It was a good enough answer. He nodded in acceptance, but said nothing. Blackstone wondered how long it would take for these Normans to make their move. He looked out of the château's window; he was in the heartland that had nurtured him and given him life. That he was in Jean's debt was undeniable, as was his love for the man and his family that was almost as deep as that for his own. He knew his friend yearned for peace, but not at any price. His was a great family burdened with honour, and lesser nobles looked to de Harcourt for leadership. Fighting men needed to find strength – seldom spoken of but shown by gesture and courage – that often came from those who fought alongside them.

'Jean, I serve my sovereign lord, but I would lay down my life for you,' Blackstone said quietly.

De Harcourt's grim demeanour became a sullen scowl as his eyes welled with tears.

Blanche de Harcourt was a noblewoman in her own right. When her father, the Count of Aumale, died sixteen years ago, the inheritance and title passed to her. She had independent wealth and authority within her home region but that had been put to one side when she took on the role of mistress of Castle de Harcourt and wife to a warrior lord. Years before, when the English had invaded and her husband had gone to war against them, she had armed herself and defended her mother's castle at Noyelles. It was there – when the Englishmen had forged across Blanchetaque and slain so many knights of Burgundy – that she had offered sanctuary to a wounded pageboy and his dying lord. How close that memory was: her ward Christiana had been saved by one of King Edward's archers. Blanche had been assured that the castle would not come under assault; had she not she would have struck down the man who accompanied the girl: the archer she came to know as Thomas Blackstone. Nothing would have made her countenance the company of such a loathed enemy had she not learnt later that this enemy had offered succour to the wounded knight to whom she had given sanctuary and hidden in a side chamber. Even then there had been little forgiveness in her heart . . . but God's mystery unfolded further after Crécy when Thomas Blackstone was brought to them near death. As Christiana nursed him Blanche had slowly learnt to tolerate his presence and then . . .

She lowered the embroidery in her hands and let the images unfold from across the years. And then . . . they had come to embrace and love the man-at-arms he had become.

Now she was content to safeguard her husband's well-being. Behind the scenes she ensured that her husband's steward attended to his estate duties and that the household servants went about their business in an efficient manner. The celebration of Henry Blackstone's birthday was only weeks away and that would bring all the families together. She was glad. At least there would be some entertainment and the women could catch up on news, gossip and rumour. And it was a distraction, thank the Lord: a time when she could shrug off all the fatigue of her daily life that had become so fragile in its uncertainty. She quickly pushed the needle through the stretched material, the image slowly but surely taking shape. Anything that would alleviate this mounting tension was welcome. No matter what happened she was determined the party would go ahead, and admitted to herself that it benefited her and their friends more than the children.

Blanche's chamber was a place of comfort where the large window gave her good light to sit and concentrate on her needlework. But her concentration wavered and the stitches were often pulled out when, at times like this, her hands trembled. She was frightened of the dangerous game that her husband was playing. She had been almost relieved that Blackstone had been absent on campaign these previous months, because it gave her a reason to share Christmas with Christiana and then to stay with her, giving Jean the excuse that a woman needed comfort when her husband was away fighting. Christiana might well be married, but in Blanche's heart she was still her ward. Except now it was the guardian who needed the comfort of the younger woman's company. As a countess she would never confess her fears to the younger woman, but simply being in the company of youth, with its resilience to misfortune and blessed ignorance of what might lie beyond the horizon, was soothing.

Her eyes settled on the rich velvet cloth beneath her fingers, through which she stitched green and gold threads. She heard voices from the inner ward and peered down as Jean and Blackstone walked across to the southern bridge between the half-towers. She noticed that there was no animosity between them and for that she was grateful. After the execution in Paris her husband and the other Norman lords seemed determined to avenge d'Aubriet's death. She had never before seen her husband so coiled with tension. Something had gone wrong two nights ago and despite her gentle influence with him she knew there were some matters that would never be shared. Perhaps, she reasoned, her husband sought to keep her ignorant as a means to protect her. Blackstone must have calmed him – how a man so steeped in war could do that she did not know, but was thankful for it nonetheless.

She would let them talk longer: seeing them together steadied her hand as she stitched silver thread onto the gold strand. The figures were taking shape and their richness would soon display her widely envied skill. The English had developed a much-admired style of stitching with gold and silk – *opus anglicanum* – but she had brought a special finesse to the technique and had spent weeks carefully sewing the figure of a dark-haired boy enticing a dove from a small tree. The *aumônière* was a gift for Henry Blackstone, so that the boy could have something of quality and beauty tied on his belt for his coins. She hesitated as the needle was about to pull through the silk. Was she being naive? Seeing the hardened knight now raised doubt in her mind. Would the gift be a problem? she wondered. Christiana's son was attracted to these fine purses – his mother had a dozen of them – but Blackstone himself preferred a plain and simple leather drawstring pouch. Blanche mentally chastised herself for being foolish. Blackstone was an Englishman. His French mother had died when he was two years old; he would never appreciate the delicate intricacy of such things, no matter how much they had taught him. Perhaps that was why Fate had smiled on Henry, who would have as a legacy the formidable legend of his father and the appreciation of beauty from his mother. A fine purse was a sign of a gentleman.

Blanche smiled at the thought. The barbaric archer had been made civilized under this very roof and now the next generation had been nurtured to appreciate beauty and courtly ways. Christiana had always insisted that Blackstone had a tender heart, but Blanche was convinced the de Harcourts' influence and duty had smoothed the Englishman's inherent roughness. She knew that, God willing, they would all come through this turbulent time. She prayed every day that Blackstone would stand ready to help them, kneeling on the cold uneven floor of her chapel until she was certain of it. She and Jean had been instrumental in forging the individual strengths of Thomas and Christiana into one. Not unlike what Blackstone called his Wolf Sword. A blade tempered by ancient skills at the hands of a master. She liked that comparison. It gave her fortitude.

'All is well, my lord?' Guillaume asked guardedly as they rode away from Castle de Harcourt, twisting in the saddle to look back at the white towers and speckled flint walls.

'Never look back, Guillaume,' said Blackstone, spurring his horse gently forward as it mounted the rising earthworks that were part of the château's defence.

'You always say that, Sir Thomas.'

Blackstone shrugged. 'There's no point looking to where you've been or to those you leave behind. The road ahead is what must always concern you.'

Guillaume said nothing for a moment. 'Your friends stand and wave farewell, though.'

'That's good manners. They're nobles. It's a sentiment. You know what I mean by that?'

His squire hesitated. 'I'm not sure,' he said.

'It's a yearning within them to feel they're a part of you.'

Guillaume thought about that for a minute. 'Friendship and loyalty mean the same thing, don't they?'

Blackstone smiled. As a boy he had once asked his sworn lord, Sir Gilbert Killbere, a similar question when they first embarked for France – ten lifetimes ago. 'It might well be so, but behind you is the past, it's already gone. And there may be no remnant of it when you return. Sentiment, Guillaume – that's the rope's knot that sits beneath your ear before Fate kicks the stool away. Don't die with regret in your heart.'

Guillaume Bourdin was not certain he understood exactly what his lord meant: it was something his master felt deeply, that was certain. Perhaps looking back was the first step towards regret. At leaving.

Sir Thomas was not a man to talk unnecessarily. They could ride for days and barely speak, except perhaps a few words to explain the flight of a goshawk or falcon, the settling of grass that showed where a fawn had lain and the way the clouds changed shape to tell him what would happen to the weather. He would point out hunting tracks through the forest and grassland, scars across the earth where animals travelled, guided by their instincts. Smell the wind, and you know where men are, Blackstone would tell him. Look to the land and sky to tell you where you are and what might befall you. And so it had always been for Guillaume under the training and protection of his lord, Sir Thomas Blackstone.

'Now, Guillaume, you tell me. Is all well at my friend's domain? I know you've spoken to the servants. How many horses a day come and go?'

'Their feed stores are full, but my Lord de Harcourt brings more in each day to replenish what is used.'

'From his villages?'

'Aye, Sir Thomas. He takes what they have. At least two riders a day are sent out and return with messages. There's a lot of activity between all the Norman lords. Servants work late into the night. Men ride by torchlight with escorts.'

'And my Lord de Harcourt? What scandal and lies do the servants tell about him?'

Blackstone always expected his squire to move among the servants, to listen at the kitchen table and to take note while their horses were tended.

'He uses harsh words at times, worse than he has ever done before. He whips a man for not performing his duty, but then relents and gives him extra food or pay. No one knows what to do. The soldiers stand long night watches. I doubt they are lies and no one would dare spread scandal. Marcel would not speak of his injuries, but I could tell he is distressed. He's served them the longest and whatever's going on causes him worry. Perhaps Lord de Harcourt is too heavy-handed with everyone,' he said finally, clearly implying that Marcel's master had been the one responsible for his injuries.

Blackstone glanced at his squire. There was as much trust and loyalty between them as there was between him and Jean de Harcourt. Guillaume always gave a straight answer and his eyes and ears were for Blackstone alone.

'Was I too harsh in what I said or how I said it?' Guillaume asked, concerned at his master's silence.

Blackstone shook his head. 'I already knew it. The Count admitted as much to me himself. The Norman barons are a gathering storm. They rumble with dissatisfaction and uncertainty as to how the King will deal with them or they with him. Count de Harcourt carries too much responsibility and wishes none of the Norman families to suffer needlessly. His temper is short. I grieve for him.'

'If you grieve for him, then . . . is that not sentiment, Sir Thomas?'

'Most likely,' he answered.

The young squire thought for a few moments. 'Then you do not look back because you carry them with you,' he said, finally understanding. 'In your heart.'

Blackstone glanced at him; then he turned his eyes back to the road. And without the young squire seeing, allowed a smile. A smile tinged with regret. He was grateful he had no part in the Norman conspiracy. His was a straightforward life of soldiering, with men who fought their enemies face to face. Being a common man had its advantages. Still, it was with a sense of unease that he rode home to his own wife and family.

CHAPTER 10

Far beyond Blackstone's horizon to the east, a fire burned in the smothered light of a forest. Gaunt-faced men, teeth bared, ran gasping for breath from the terror that pursued them. Thick smoke curled beyond the treetops as their village burned. The survivors grunted with exertion, pushing aside children who slowed their escape into the clearing. Women sobbed, their stricken faces showing clearly the bitter choice they must make; cast aside the infants they carried or cleave them to their bodies and falter. Most dropped them or threw the frightened infants into the spring-flooded streams. More children could be born, but a mother needed to be alive.

Those villagers who had escaped the brutal attack tore their flesh against bramble and thorn as they squirmed desperately through the undergrowth. Bewildered children stumbled, arms raised, their filthy bodies soiled further in their distress, their cries and screams soon silenced by sword and spear. The killers laughed and shouted, alerting each other to where survivors had broken free, giving pursuit as if on a boar hunt.

The terror revealed itself to the two riders who had tried to settle their horses as they witnessed the assault but the bloodletting and screams came upon them too quickly. The killers were behind them, sweeping onto the clearing's flank, so those being pursued were caught in the grassland arena.

Had it not been for their livery and the quality of their horses the bloodied mercenaries who hacked down the escaping villagers would have slain them. The horses spooked, the men fell and quickly went on to their knees, hands clasped in prayer, calling out their master's name, yelling at the top of their lungs that they were messengers. One of the men's bowels gave way in fear, its stench adding to that of the dead and dying. A bearded blood-cloaked ruffian noticed their livery and heard their pleas.

'Not these!' he ordered, and ran towards the villagers who were being quickly surrounded.

Two of the routiers put their boots' heels into the messengers' backs, slamming them down into the wet grass, where they were held, unmoving, stricken by fear. The encircled men, women and children retreated back to back into a circle, crossing themselves in supplication, yielding to the inevitable. The routiers barely paused for breath as they hacked into them.

The messengers were bound and dragged towards the burning village. Little more than a handful had escaped the settlement to be slain in the clearing; here in the ruins at least seventy or more villagers lay, slaughtered. The pathways between what remained of the hovels were churned to mud glistening with silken ribbons of blood. The stench of charred flesh caught the back of the men's throats as it mingled with the smell of smouldering thatch.

Wide-eyed with fear they squelched in the footsteps of their captors as they were dragged towards the small stone church that indicated the centre of the village. A fire burned, flames spurting as the deep-seated embers were fed with more dry wood, fuel that would have seen the villagers through to summer.

There was no sign of monk or priest and the church seemed not to have been violated, unlike the screaming women being assaulted and raped by routiers. A man stood by the flames tormenting the embers with a stick as he watched their approach. His dark cloak concealed his mail and his bare head was free from the aventail. A broad silver-studded belt held a silver-pommelled sword, which indicated he was a rich man or a killer who had taken it. A heavy wet patch of blood darkened the black cloth further beneath an ebony crucifix. Both men averted their eyes. They were kicked to their knees, hands clasped, despite their bound wrists, utterances of prayer and pleas for mercy. Neither man dared raise his eyes to face what they thought to be the devil's disciple.

The man who had soiled himself shuddered,

unable to control his fear; he rambled incoherently, spilling his words as he told the mercenary leader whom he served and why they were sent and how his own master was a voice for the King. The second man finally gathered courage, raised his head and delivered the message that his lord had told must be given clearly to this murdering brigand.

'We are to tell you, my lord de Marcy, that Thomas Blackstone has killed Henri, Count of Saint Clair-de-la-Beaumont, and seized the fortress, handing it over to King Edward's allies. He is rich in coin and weapons.'

De Marcy's brow furrowed. Blackstone. The Englishman went from strength to strength. Blackstone raided with impunity and then returned to the sanctuary of the Norman lords. And now the French King was suddenly willing to use Bucy as a go-between. Gilles de Marcy knew he was a pariah. The nobility abhorred his actions; some of them had tried at times to entrap him and put a rope around his neck. But it was they who suffered the terror from his retribution. They and their families. He fingered the ebony crucifix at his neck. Divine violence was his to dispense. It served his purpose to employ God's anger for his own benefit. It was a blessing that protected him. The closest he had come to being apprehended was buried in the past, a few weeks after the English had invaded and fought their way across Normandy into the streets of Caen where a quick-witted archer had slashed the finger from his hand. A chance encounter. A brief moment of pain. But he had escaped from a despised enemy. The memory slipped away from his thoughts.

De Marcy stabbed at the messenger's livery with the charred stick.

'Bucy sent you?' he said, dark eyes settling on the messenger's terrified face, who quickly averted his gaze.

The men nodded vigorously.

'To tell me of the Englishman's success? News I would hear soon enough from travellers I rob and kill?'

'My lord,' said the stronger of the two men, 'our master wishes you to enter Paris and meet with him.'

'With my men at my back? He wants us inside the walls?' he said disbelievingly.

'Alone, lord, with a small escort. To meet with him in secret.'

'And what is his offer?'

'For you to be the instrument of the Englishman's death. To succeed where others have failed. To be offered a pardon, wealth and acceptance as the King's man.'

The Savage Priest's attention hovered on a ring on his finger. Ten years ago the great killing field at Crécy had given him enough wealth from the slaughtered French nobility's jewellery and weapons to hire men of his own. And now the King summoned him – welcoming his thirst for killing. De Marcy grunted and worried the stick's smouldering tip into the man's chest. These messengers would have no more information other than what they had given. Was it a trap? Mercenaries were bleeding the countryside dry. King John did not have the resources to fight them, but drawing in those who commanded the routiers, one by one, that could diminish their strength.

'Who else has been summoned?'

'Lord?' the messenger asked uncertainly.

'Who else has been sent for, to rid the King of the Englishman?'

The man shook his head. He looked bewildered. 'None. We are our master's messengers, we have served him all our lives, we are trusted. No others from our master's house have been sent. But I cannot answer for what my King might have done.'

That was the truth, de Marcy decided. Bucy was the King's confidant, he was a power behind the throne, and the King would not send his own messengers and risk being seen to align himself openly with such a ruthless mercenary. The politicians were fools; they saw armed men as blunt instruments. A commander needed his wits about him to draw out his enemy, to outflank him, to have the animal instinct to savage a foe after he had out-thought him. These men carried no sealed document, there was nothing to link the King to their mission, but Bucy would not dare sanction a pardon without the King's permission.

'And nothing else was said?'

The man hesitated. 'A benefit that would please you.'

'He offers me a place at high table?' the mercenary sneered.

The messenger faltered. Bucy had spoken the woman's name almost as an afterthought when he had given them their orders. 'Sainteny. Christiana de Sainteny. I do not understand everything that I am commanded to say, but that name was given to me.'

The Savage Priest's reaction to the name that was a long-abandoned desire was barely visible, but his breath faltered. His pulse quickened. How easily the years had erased the youth who had first laid eyes on the auburn-haired girl. That once shining instant had never left him. A boy, already a killer, had seen a woman whose beauty had cleaved a path through his darkness. A rare moment of light in a life of lust and violence. It lasted less than the blink of an eye. Whatever it was that had seized his heart had also squeezed it dry when she had rejected him.

It was a decade or more past. A scurrying de Marcy was shouldering his way through the crowded market place, eager to leave the stench of the alleyway behind him. The girl was carrying a basket over her arm, her back to him; he was no more than a half-dozen strides away when he saw the stooped figure of the old beggar neatly slice the purse from the cord around her waist.

Why de Marcy faltered in his escape across the square he never knew. A petty thief was none of his concern, but he altered his stride, gripped the old man's arm, his strength forcing the beggar to open the palm of his hand. In the instant when the old man yelped with pain the girl he came to know as Christiana de Sainteny turned.

Nothing had ever explained that moment. Her green eyes flashed in alarm and then quickly understood when she saw the purse. She had said something about not causing the beggar harm and while de Marcy held him she took back her purse and pressed a coin into the old man's still-open palm. Under the girl's beseeching gaze de Marcy released the beggar. She smiled and thanked him and then turned to go about her business, her fingers tucking a strand of auburn hair beneath her cap. Like a prisoner held in a dark pit who sees a shard of light, a glimpse of sky, and then has it taken away, he reached out and caught her arm. She turned again and before he could utter the words that fought his tongue those same eyes blazed with anger. She saw the bloodied hand that gripped her and he realized he had not cleaned the gore that clung to it after the murder he had committed in the alleyway only minutes before. She pulled free, her shout of alarm alerting others. Reality brought de Marcy to his senses; a hue and cry would have him cornered and at the end of a rope before the day was over. He pulled his hood over his face and escaped into the crowd.

171

The months passed and de Marcy tracked her down. His persistence in his pursuit of her was met with increasing hostility from her father and those who served him. The threats held no fear for de Marcy. He offered what inducements he could – even marriage – but then one day she was gone, spirited away to a place of safety. And now she was being used to draw him in. How he did not yet know, but here was an opportunity to be welcomed back into the nobility and an offer of wealth with the bonus of a woman he had once coveted. He grimaced at the soiled messenger.

'Your stench offends me.'

He barely raised his eyes to the man behind the kneeling victim. The mercenary rammed his spear into the man's back and forced his body into the fire. Flames leapt as the squirming man was pinned like a writhing insect, his screams smothered by the searing embers.

'Tell your master what you have seen today,' he said to the second messenger who was staring in horror at his companion's fate. 'And tell him that I am coming.'

CHAPTER 11

Simon Bucy, the King's adviser and friend, observed, when he arrived at the church, that a dozen men loitered in various parts of the cloisters. They were not grouped together, but stood separate, and he could see that they acted as guards for the man who was waiting inside. Bucy had agreed to meet the Savage Priest and it was obvious that the mercenary did not trust those he was dealing with. Had it been a trap set by King John, using Bucy and his offer as bait, then it was clear that the mercenary had planned his escape.

As Bucy strode along the uneven flagstones towards the iron-studded doors, the men's casual demeanour changed and the brigands became more alert. Bucy's escort of a half-dozen soldiers moved closer to his shoulder, but Bucy raised a hand.

'Captain, you will wait here.'

The captain of the guard hesitated; it was easy to kill someone of importance in the gloom of a church and, from what he had heard of the man that Bucy was about to meet, his fears might well be justified.

'I am charged with your safety,' the captain insisted.

'And you will stay here until I call you. I am on the King's business, and no ill fortune will befall me today. Do not approach any of those men; I want to create no opportunity for anyone to cause trouble. So keep your men here and keep them silent.'

The captain was unhappy about the order, but the powerful Simon Bucy was not to be contradicted. He nodded his understanding of his orders and watched as Bucy went on ahead without him.

Bucy had so far managed to keep his fear under control but as the arched doors swung open it felt as though he was stepping into a beast's lair rather than a place of worship. One of the brigands nodded him through the archway and then pulled the door closed behind him. Bucy moved no further into the near darkness. It was a windy day; heavy clouds darkened the sky, and the church's windows were dull with grime. He shivered beneath his woven cloak and pulled the fur collar around his neck, clutching it tightly for a moment, forcing his hand to stop trembling. He moved further into the gloom and tried to make out if there were figures in the side chapels, but he could see no one. As he turned to face the transept a hooded monk appeared at the far end carrying a candle as thick as a man's arm and placed it on a spiked stand. In the yellow light that it cast was the cloaked figure of a man hunched in prayer. Bucy squinted, trying to focus on the man's back, unable to see whether it was his traitor or the man he had come to meet. He glanced nervously left and right, his mind playing tricks. These Normans were all treacherous bastards. A sudden panic gripped him. What if he had been played like a fish on a line and they had planned his capture or murder all along? That would give them one of the King's advisers, a man who knew what the King thought and planned to do. Simon Bucy was a source of information that could be of great value to Charles of Navarre and the Norman lords. My God, he thought, I've been a fool. It was all he could do not to call out for the soldiers to rush into the darkness and get him back to his accustomed warmth and luxury.

The hunched figure stood and turned, the cowled face still in darkness. Whoever it was raised a hand and gestured him forward. Bucy caught his breath as if Death's emissary beckoned him. He faltered, unable to make one foot move in front of the other. It was not the traitor – it was the killer who was here to do the King's bidding. Bucy's eyes had become accustomed to the shadows and saw that this man was of a bigger and heavier build than the Norman lord.

'Come closer into the light,' the man said, his voice echoing as he stood waiting.

Without realizing it Bucy had started to walk towards him. He felt drawn to do the man's bidding without question and his actions caught him by surprise. He stopped halfway. It was time to compose himself and exert his own authority – only that could dampen the fear.

'Declare yourself,' he said, pulling himself up, trying to feel as tall as possible, knowing the figure who waited in front of the altar stood head and shoulders above him.

The man tugged back the hood of his cloak and stepped closer to the candlelight.

'I am the man sent to do your bidding, my lord. I am Gilles de Marcy.'

Bucy could not help himself from moving closer to see the man's features. 'Are you alone?' he asked nervously, his eyes drawn to the gaunt, sallow features of the man who had not yet made any other move towards him. Bucy was transfixed by the man's eyes, which seemed not to reflect any of the light, but appeared as black obsidian stones pushed into their sockets. He shuddered, imagining that face close to a victim's, the last vision of hell on earth.

He felt foolish the moment the question passed his lips: 'You are le Prêtre sanguinaire?'

'Is that what I am called?' de Marcy answered.

Bucy felt the irritation rise at his own pathetic demeanour. 'You know damned well what you are.' That was better. He was getting back some control now. Being sent to a freezing cold church to meet a creature discarded by all that was holy was a duty he had begged the King not to send him on. But King John refused to have the man brought to the palace. And he would have no personal contact with the mercenary leader. There were conditions that John would insist upon even if the man succeeded in the task of killing Thomas Blackstone.

Bucy felt some comfort returning to him as he thought of his role as the King's envoy. He took a few more purposeful strides, trying to show that he was not afraid of the black-cloaked figure and that he was the one controlling the meeting.

De Marcy took a step back allowing Bucy to settle himself on one of the benches on the other side of the aisle. Bucy flicked his hand in a frustrated gesture of having a lesser being in his presence. 'Sit. The sooner this is done with the better.'

De Marcy did as he was instructed, but showed little concern for the older man's status. They were both there to serve a purpose. A contract would be agreed upon and both parties sought the same conclusion.

'We have failed to kill Thomas Blackstone. He nestles in the heart of Normandy. We have sent routiers, men who cannot be linked to the King, but they fail. Every time,' Bucy said, exasperation tinging his words.

Bucy waited for a response from the dark creature, for that was how he seemed, half-shadowed, wearing the darkness like a sorcerer's cloak, but he remained silent, letting the King's trusted ally squirm a little longer. Like a man beneath his boot and a sword through his throat.

'You do not kill a man like that with brute force, unless God favours you in battle,' he said.

'Can you kill Thomas Blackstone?' Bucy asked.

'I can.'

'Then you will tell me how before I go any further.'

'I will not risk my plan by telling you or anyone else. Secrets seep away in the King's court like a leaking privy. Enough for you to know that I will draw Blackstone away, without his men, isolate him and then he's mine.' He smiled. 'You will let me have him so that I can determine how long it takes for him to die.'

Bucy turned his face away. 'I have the authority to offer you payment and recognition for the services that you will provide the King. Kill Blackstone and all the towns he holds are yours. You take the *patis* from those who pay it to him. You will control his land, take his home – everything.'

De Marcy said nothing for a moment. His silence was broken by the sound of the older man's breathing. It was almost laboured. Like a man afraid.

'Christiana de Sainteny. Where is she?' the Savage Priest asked quietly, knowing he was handing back the advantage to the King's adviser.

Bucy grinned. 'You want her?' he taunted.

'Tell me,' de Marcy whispered. The softly spoken demand carried an unspoken threat.

De Bucy held his nerve. He looked again at the killer, wanting his authority to be acknowledged.

'Not yet. Our King makes another demand upon you.'

Bucy already felt the taste of bile at the back of his throat. Over the years of serving the King's father, and now the King himself, he had played every political game in order to advance the King's best interests as well as his own rewards. He knew brutality was common on a battlefield soaked in blood in order to secure a nation, but sitting here smelling the damp walls and the scent of sweat and woodsmoke from this man's clothing brought him too close to the reality of it all. Bucy had never wielded a sword in anger. He realized that his gaze had drifted towards the spluttering candle. Like a moth, his mind had sought the flame and its comfort and, like the moth, he was perhaps also being drawn to destruction. He had advised the King to take this irreconcilable path of murder. It did not matter. The dice were thrown. Victory was the prize. So, better to stare at the mesmerizing flame than at the face of the Savage Priest.

'What is it?' de Marcy asked without concern or irritation, catching Bucy by surprise, making him avert his eyes from the flame and back to his face.

Bucy stood up; he wanted this day over. 'Hundreds follow you. When the time comes you and your horsemen must serve the King in battle against the English. There will be a great need for fighting men. But you will receive no payment for this duty,' he answered brusquely.

'And if these terms are not suitable to me?'

'Then you will never have the domains that Thomas Blackstone commands or the glory of having slain the Englishman. The woman you once desired will be warned that you seek her and she will disappear from your life forever.'

De Marcy shrugged as if he didn't care. 'It's Blackstone I want. I keep the taxes; I keep the land and towns. And I am given the King's pardon and brought into court.'

'You wanted the woman once, and you are the kind of man who would not let a desire escape him.'

Bucy knew he was right and so did de Marcy. The old bastard held the line tight and the hook was deep. How long would he allow himself to wriggle on it?

'As remote as the possibility is, what if Blackstone escapes me and I fail to kill him?'

'You are still obliged,' Bucy said.

'And if I agree and then change my mind?'

'There will be no hiding place for you in this country, or any other. And if you doubt that, understand that my sovereign lord can call upon others wherever you sell your sword, be it to the Holy Roman Empire, the Italians, the Germans – anyone. You will be seized and you will suffer a fate that will inflict the greatest pain.'

Bucy waited a moment longer. It was time to throw the vile creature his bone.

'Christiana de Sainteny is Blackstone's wife.'

Gilles de Marcy's lips drew back, smiling like a

rat baring stained fangs. 'I accept,' he said and extended his hand to seal the bargain.

Bucy glared down at the bony hand that extended from the cloak's folds and saw that half of the little finger was missing. He had seen worse disfigurements before but for some reason the thought of taking that hand into his own made him recoil.

Without another word he turned on his heel and walked away as quickly as his dignity would permit, forcing himself not to break into a run, but unable to disguise the desperation in his voice.

'Open the doors!' he shouted. 'Open the doors!'

CHAPTER 12

Wourilliam de Fossat had once been Thomas
Blackstone's enemy, and one of the
group of Norman barons who had
fought the English King a decade ago, but their
simmering disappointment at the French
monarch's poor leadership had led him to side
with Blackstone and fight the French at Calais.
He was a man who seized opportunities, and
admitted as much. For him there was no shame
in waking from a stupor to realize that the honour
of France no longer lay in the hands of a pathetic,
indecisive King. That was why he joined other
Norman lords who sided with Navarre.

De Fossat cared not. He had married a widow
with land, and his honour and wealth was once
again intact. There were nights, though, when he
knew the price had been high as he lay in his
bedchamber listening to his wife's snoring, when
her heaving carcass threatened to tear her night-
dress like a snorting boar ploughing the forest
floor. If his prayers were answered she would one
day choke on a fish bone and he would be free to
do as he pleased. He had sold his body to the

widow, which gave him wealth, and the estates were secured under his protection, but there was hope yet to salvage his soul. The widow's lands were now his and they nestled in the safety of the Breton marches, a place where the French King might still dare to venture should he dislodge the English from the south. De Fossat remembered with a mixture of regret and fondness his siding with Blackstone. War forged strange alliances, even friendships, and if it came to more fighting he would ride with the Englishman again.

As his horse meandered along the forest trail his thoughts flitted between past memories of those times and the Norman lords' simmering conspiracy against the King. It was a good alliance between him and the Englishman even though Blackstone had once nearly killed him in a challenge. Despite being an opportunistic nobleman, de Fossat was bound by honour, driven by ambition and sworn to stand with the other nobles who secretly planned a conspiracy to remove the French King and replace him with his son, the Dauphin, Duke of Normandy – whose bequeathed title meant little to the Normans. As if clearing an unpleasant thought from his head, de Fossat leaned from the saddle and blew snot from his nostrils. It was not these thoughts of conspiracy and treason that now held his attention and which made him careless. In his mind's eye he was already easing the undershift of Aloise, the eighteen-year-old girl he had been lying with this past year. Her freshness invigorated him and when he woke with arousal each morning it was because of the thought of her and not the demands of his wife insisting they attend church and kneel in humility on a cold stone floor for an hour so that some half-witted inbred, fit only to become a parasitic monk, could chant a pious litany. It was the thought of Aloise's pink nipples and her unblemished skin, not the pock-marked battle-field of his wife's arse, that seeped warmth into him and which lowered his guard.

He did not notice the well-travelled path through the forest, a route that was seldom used except by himself and those of his household, or the tram-pled ferns beneath the bare branches – such obvious signs of horsemen making their way into the forest's shadows.

The French King's assassin waited patiently in the forest's gloom as his victim rode towards the trap he had laid. The mercenary scum he led were anxious to spring the ambush, but fear of their leader stayed their hands. The sallow-faced horseman with the pinched features had the ear of a fearful King who trusted few of those around him. Even the King's own son, the Dauphin, was suspect – more for the weakness the seventeen-year-old boy exhibited, naively believing the false promises of the Normans, than any blatant act of treachery. The son was the easy route to the King's heart and throne. Like a diseased wound the Normans' poison crept ever closer to the heart of

France. De Marcy knew it was better to allow a routier like him to go where the King's men could not and to do the killing for which the King could deny responsibility. Like a poacher in his own royal forests, he would bait the trap. Sooner or later Thomas Blackstone and those who secretly supported him would step, one by one, into the snare.

The undergrowth exploded as men leapt from their hiding places, launching themselves at de Fossat. The greed-driven fools underestimated the knight's fighting skills and he reacted so quickly that his spurred horse trampled three of them underfoot. Bones crunched from the force of iron-shod hooves, and where moments before his hands held only the reins, he now wielded his sword. De Fossat had only ever been bested by Blackstone, and these carrion fighters would pay dearly in trying to take him alive. Heeling the horse he wheeled it around in a fast tight turn, caught another two, swung the sword and felt its edge bite into skull and shoulder. Men cursed; others screamed in pain. But as a pack of wolves pull down a stag their numbers soon overwhelmed him. Grasping hands held the horse's bridle; knives plunged into the beast's neck. It whinnied and fell as others beat down on him.

'Don't kill him!' de Marcy called.

One of the mercenaries snarled, spitting blood from his mouth from where de Fossat had smashed his sword's pommel. The command halted his knife's lunge into de Fossat's throat, but was not enough to stop his retribution of plunging it into his thigh. The Norman cried out but twisted free, swinging his fist into the routier's neck and having the satisfaction of hearing bones crack from the force of the blow. Grasping one of the men by his belt he yanked the man off balance and pulled the dagger from his belt. He left the blade embedded in his leg to slow the blood flow and ducked beneath a flange-tipped mace that skimmed close to his head. The attacker was off balance and de Fossat rammed his own knife beneath the man's armpit, then feinted, using his weight to shoulder away another. What was supposed to be a simple ambush had now turned into a deadly battle of life and death as de Fossat picked up the fallen mace and his sword. The knife still protruded from his leg, hampering his agility, but the force and speed of his sword strokes maimed and killed. Within minutes four more men lay dead and another two fatally wounded. Blood was splattered across the crushed ferns as he edged back on the track. There was little doubt in his mind he was going to die. He was too far from home for anyone to hear the men's screams and not close enough to any village for a runner to bring help, but if he could kill these remaining two then there was only the man on the horse to kill. His life was not yet forfeit. Not yet. There was always hope. But a glimpse of the man astride the horse brought a brief, almost unconscious realization that he had seen the man before. Years ago. But where? There was no time to remember. These brigands had been paid good money and the surviving pair put their shoulders together and threw themselves at the embattled knight. Better to fail against de Fossat than endure the slow death that le Prêtre sanguinaire would inflict.

One of the men struck at the knife blade in de Fossat's leg and the fierce pain caused him to drop his shoulder, allowing the second mercenary to slash down with his blade which de Fossat parried, but he was unable to keep the other man from seizing the advantage and ramming him, punching his sword's pommel into his head. The renowned Norman fighter went down and would have been killed had the men's orders not forbidden it. The soldiers kicked and pummelled him until, breathless, heaving from the exertion, they staggered back from his unconscious, battered body.

The Savage Priest spurred his horse forward and looked down at the fallen man. He had no recollection of this knight ever being at Castle de Harcourt all those years before when he rode with the King's routiers, but the Norman traitor had told Simon Bucy that de Fossat was there. It made no difference. He was not here for the whoring knight; he was here to find his bait. A wounded lamb staked out for the wolf.

CHAPTER 13

Blackstone waited patiently as Christiana sat in front of the fire in their great hall, twisting the piece of linen in her hands. She laid it on her lap and spread it lovingly, resting her palms on the image of the small blue bird in flight. It was a similar emblem of love that she had once given to the young Thomas Blackstone as he went into battle. A token of her affection for him and her desire for him to return to her safely that had always nestled beneath Blackstone's tunic. But now the distress that Christiana felt made Blackstone's mind seethe with uncertainty.

'And who told you about this?' Blackstone asked, keeping his own anxiety hidden. He had returned that morning from de Harcourt's, and in his two-day absence unsettling news had arrived at his doorstep, bringing with it fear that could tear his family apart.

'Joanne de Ruymont sent it by messenger.'

'From Paris?'

'Yes.'

'And you questioned the rider who brought it?'

'No, I was with Henry and his lessons. He is

learning a poem for his birthday recital. Old Hugh brought it to me. It was wrapped and enclosed with a note from her. She came across this in Paris,' she said, lifting the embroidered cloth as if it were rare silk. 'She bought it from a street seller.' Her voice hovered between joy and distress. 'And when she questioned further she learnt that an old man, living in poverty, had sold it.'

'And the note is in Joanne's hand?'

'Yes . . . of course.'

'But you can't be certain?'

'But who else?'

Blackstone could see that she was barely able to suppress her excitement.

'This means my father could be alive after all these years,' she said. 'No one could know I embroidered such things.'

Blackstone's stomach fluttered. He knew that his own token of her affection, given to him years before, which he had carried through battle, still bore the bloodstains ingrained in its weave. It was the exact same coat of arms that had been embroidered on the tunic of the first man he had killed during the great invasion ten years before. The old man was a poorly armed knight with a group of crossbowmen who had lain in ambush, but Blackstone, raw and frightened, had outflanked him. It had been the young archer's arrow that had killed the French knight and allowed the English to move safely through the crossroads. It was only weeks later, as the battles progressed and

Blackstone's heart had been captured, that he realized the old man must have been Christiana's father.

And that secret could never be revealed.

'You lived at Harcourt for years. What about the servants? They knew. Other wives knew. Women talk about embroidery, don't they? It was hardly a secret.'

'Quite so,' she said patiently, 'it is not a secret, but no one could copy my needlework. This is by my hand.'

'Surely there's doubt?' he asked carefully. 'That embroidery could have been taken by one of the servants when you were living at Harcourt. Some of them go to Paris with Jean and Blanche. Who's to say that when you lived with them it wasn't stolen and sold in the city?'

'Perhaps,' she conceded. She examined it again, as if the simple pattern on the old and worn material might expose more of its journey. 'A simple piece of linen, Thomas. Worth barely anything, but still precious, and to be kept close to one's heart.'

Blackstone tugged his own piece of linen free from the folds of his shirt and laid it open in the hope that there would be a difference between the two squares of cloth. Christiana took it from his fingers and laid it on her lap next to the other.

'Look, Thomas,' she said in hushed tones, 'what little difference there is shows only in the threads I used. He must be alive and living somewhere in Paris.'

Blackstone had no idea how he could convince her otherwise without confessing his part in the old knight's death. Life's mystery had brought Christiana to him and the misfortune and co-incidence of her father's death burdened him whenever she told stories of how they once lived. Time had passed and their lives had moved on, but this news felt like a jagged piece of broken mirror reflecting a ghost.

'Christiana, remember all those years ago when Godfrey de Harcourt came to warn Jean about King Edward being unable to pursue the French crown, he told you then – I was there; we were all there – that your father was dead. I can understand how you would wish it otherwise, but this piece of cloth proves nothing.'

She folded Blackstone's piece of linen carefully and brought it to her lips and then passed it back to him. 'Thomas, you have never relinquished this token from me. No matter what happened to you, you held it tightly, as a symbol of our love for each other. And so it was between my father and me. If he is alive, he's desperate enough to sell it to stave off hunger, and if it was stolen from him then the thief must know where he is.'

'Christiana! How many pieces of this embroidery have you ever done? How many times have you left a piece of cloth such as this lying around over the years? See it for what it is! Taken by a servant and sold in the city. It's nonsense to think otherwise,' he said, unable to keep the agitation from his voice. Or, as he admitted to himself, the sense of panic that refused to settle. His words were badly chosen and he regretted uttering them as soon as he saw the pain on her face.

'Why would I not hold onto the dream of him being alive?' she said, looking at him in disbelief.

Blackstone quickly softened his voice. 'I would do anything to have him live, Christiana, because that would soothe every blemish in your heart caused by his loss. But it's been ten years and if he were alive surely we would know of it by now?'

She wiped a tear from her cheek, but showed him a brave face. 'Well,' she tried to reason, 'an old man caught up in battle, most probably wounded, and taken to a monastery, and then, when his wounds were healed, and perhaps with his memory as injured as his body, he would wander penniless and without knowledge of who he was from village to village, like a beggar. How many beggars have we seen who fought?'

Blackstone's hands smothered her own that held the cloth. 'It cannot be, Christiana, it cannot.'

'I believe it can,' she said quietly.

He knew there could be no argument. Once she had decided on a course of action there would be no deterring her. He had proven that to himself over the years, and it had started with her determination, in defiance of her guardians, to love a wounded Englishman.

'All right,' he said. 'I'll speak to Guy and Joanne and ask them to send people into the city to find out what they can. You know I cannot go; King John's soldiers would like nothing better. Will you be patient and let me deal with this? I'll pay for any information that we can get. It will take some time. Can you be patient?'

She nodded and smiled through her tears. 'Thank you, Thomas.'

He eased her face to him and kissed her gently, as he would an injured child. And as he left her at the fireside he cursed himself for the lies he had told her, but thanked God that he had bought time and the means to convince her that her father was long dead.

'Hugh!'

The old man turned from directing men stacking sacks of grain in one of the barns as Blackstone strode towards him.

'My lord?'

'Did you recognize the man who brought the message for Lady Christiana?'

'No, Sir Thomas. He was not known to me. The sentries did not recognize him either and refused him entry through the gates.'

'Was he from these parts? Could you tell by his accent?'

'He was a common man, my lord, and he barely spoke. He said he had come from my Lord de Ruymont's domain and that being a day's ride away I offered him food and shelter for the night and to stable his horse, but he refused.'

'Then he would be travelling back in darkness?'

'Aye, my lord, but he seemed intent in doing so.'

'You think that strange?'

'I thought it commendable that he would serve his master so well,' Hugh answered.

Blackstone thought on it for a moment. A servant with the opportunity to spend a night under a roof lying on dry straw with a belly full of hot food was more likely to seize the chance of such comfort.

'And he did not ask for me?'

'No. Only that I deliver what he offered to Lady Christiana.'

Blackstone nodded and turned away. What to do? How long could he ignore Christiana's request? For as long as possible was the only answer he could find, but sooner or later Guy or Joanne de Ruymont would visit, or send a message to enquire as to the outcome. Damn. He would have to speak to them. But not this week, or the next. He would wait until Henry's birthday party and hope that before then something would occur to him on how to handle the matter. It was foolish to think that – and he knew it. This was a threat that had to be dealt with sooner.

Haunted, he walked to the stables with the dogs at his heels, glad of their company. The freshening breeze raised their nostrils; one of them barked. They had freedom to go wherever they chose, but they would not leave the immediate confines of the house and grounds where invisible chains of familiar scents held them. But if their master chose to go further afield then they skipped and jostled each other as they did now, knowing Blackstone's mind before he had made the decision. Guilt and uncertainty gave out its own stench. Dogs knew it, horses too, as did soldiers who crowded at your shoulder waiting to strike. If such feelings lingered like stale sweat then it was best that they be flushed away.

'Hugh!' he called back to the old man. 'Have them saddle my horse!'

It was a bastard of a horse – an ugly beast. The fine French heritage of his dam had been spoiled by a rogue stallion and what came from their breeding was a creature unyielding in its belligerence. A neck as thick as a man's waist supported a head like a ship's prow, oversized and misshapen, that was lowered in battle like a battering ram. His yellow teeth, as firm and strong as grindstones, bit at Blackstone whenever opportunity offered. Its ears would swivel in opposing directions in a constant state of alertness as they sought whispers of movement from here and there. Its hooves, the breadth of a man's hand and powered by bulging shoulder muscles that encased a tireless heart, bore iron shoes that tore the ground. Battle-scarred, it was cast – so it was said – into this world by the devil forging a pact with the animal kingdom. There had been few men who could abide its awkward gait when it ambled, but when the reins were eased and a strong rider gave it his trust, the horse would run without faltering day and night.

Stable-hands knew better than to enter its winter stall alone. It took two determined men to put a halter on it and coax the beast out. Blackstone's other horses, especially his big courser that he rode when hunting, was kept apart from this wild-eyed animal, which would tolerate no competition from stallion, gelding or mare. It had smashed stalls and bitten and kicked lesser horses that raised their heads and stiffened their ears, muzzles snorting in naive expectation of exerting their superiority over it. When mounting Blackstone always held taut the opposite rein, tugging the horse's head away from where the snap of teeth would nip him if he were so careless as to forget past experience, but Blackstone had never laid a whip on the beast. Each measured the other – and each gave way when necessary. Every week Blackstone rode the horse hard, ridding it of its aggression, pounding across meadow and hills, plunging him into swollen rivers to clamber up mud-slicked embankments, placing his life into the horse's care as they challenged the demands of twisting currents and uneven ground, neither rider nor horse prepared to shy away. And Blackstone swore that he loved this horse more than any other because it bore as fiery a soul as any fighting warrior he had witnessed.

His dogs had faltered miles back, lolling tongues slavering as they lay with heaving ribs. Despite their loyalty to their master they could not keep pace when he rode out with the dappled black horse whose coat looked as though it had been singed by hell's embers. The dogs would soon recover, then lope home where they would wait until the wind brought them knowledge of man and horse returning.

Guillaume followed a good half-mile behind Blackstone, his horse unable to catch up, but that suited the squire; it allowed him to keep an alert eye open for any sign of danger. His sworn lord was a wanted man and, despite the Normans' protection, it was not impossible for a lone assassin to penetrate their domains and lie in wait. Movement was easily observed in a landscape that never changed except by the seasons or where it was grazed or cultivated, so its landmarks were familiar to those who knew it. Blackstone had taken a hard route but it was a shorter distance than the usual road. There was no doubt that he was heading for Guy de Ruymont's castle where the Count de Harcourt and others were meeting. It was the fluttering of birds rising from the depth of the forest that alerted Guillaume. Blackstone would have been close enough to the treeline to think he had disturbed them. The squire spurred his horse, cutting diagonally across the uneven ground, risking his horse stumbling. The birds had been disturbed by horsemen who emerged from the forest.

Guillaume's anxiety should have been tempered with more confidence in his master and the horse he rode, but fealty to a knight like Sir Thomas was a privilege that could be bestowed only once in a lifetime and the young fighter would die before an enemy struck down the Englishman owing to any failure of duty on his part. He needn't have worried. Blackstone's horse had already alerted him. Its ears had picked up movement even before the birds rose from the branches; and Blackstone too had heard the snap of dry twigs from the weight of horsemen approaching. By the time the men appeared Wolf Sword was in his hand and the devil's horse was turned to face them: rock steady, ears forward, muscles quivering momentarily as it smelled the other beasts. His master's shift in weight told him a contest was approaching.

Jean de Harcourt rode through the edge of the forest, twenty men or more at his back, pennons flying. He raised a hand when he saw the lone knight waiting, and in the distance Guillaume Bourdin at full gallop towards them.

'Thomas! God's blood, man! You ride alone?' de Harcourt said, easing his horse forward.

Blackstone sheathed Wolf Sword and tugged a rein. 'Just as on any other day, Jean. I was going to Guy's. I thought you'd be there with the others.'

'Aye, well, after what's happened we're biding our time and staying behind our own walls until we see what lies ahead.'

'Has trouble befallen them? I need to speak to Guy and Joanne.'

Guillaume slowed his horse, cantering the last hundred yards, then stopped and bowed his head towards de Harcourt, who nodded acknowledgement and then answered Blackstone.

'No. They're safe. But we are uncertain whether the King is planning a strike against us. We think not, but we'll keep ourselves to ourselves for a few days and watch out for each other. When I saw you ready to fight I thought you might have heard, but of course you could not. A messenger came from Paris. One of Guy's informers at court. They've taken William.'

For King John to strike at a Norman lord, especially one whose domain straddled the Breton marches, was a daring move. 'They attacked his castle?' Blackstone asked, knowing that if that were the case then men might now be attacking his own manor.

De Harcourt eased his helm and mail away from his sweat-matted hair and rubbed his scalp. 'No. Men took him on his way to visit the girl I told you about. It was an ambush, pure and simple. The fool rode right into it. There's been no threat made to others. No sign of troops, no indication that King John is planning to ride against us. From what we have gathered, they were mercenaries. We had hoped for a ransom demand, but none has been asked for.'

'When was he taken?'

'Three, perhaps four days ago. He's being held by one of the King's seneschals, Sir Rolf de Sagard, but whether John has sanctioned this we don't know. He's either picking us off one by one or this is a rogue attack by bastard routiers who have taken refuge behind his walls.'

'A planned attack, then?'

'God knows. You remember I told you that William had promised to help the girl's father buy an ennoblement? Well, our friend had not yet fulfilled his promise. Too interested in cunny. So, I wouldn't be surprised if her father isn't behind his capture.'

'Are you riding to meet the other barons to release him?' Blackstone asked, looking at the well-armed soldiers.

'Save William? And show our hand? If it is the King's work then we'll need to be ready, if it's not then our plans are still in place and we'll go ahead with our meeting with the Dauphin and Navarre.'

'De Fossat's one of you!' Blackstone said sharply.

'And his own man!' de Harcourt retorted.

'He's been your ally throughout. He deserves your help.'

'No, Thomas. If William's cock has brought about his downfall then he'll have to sweat it out in the man's dungeon until demands are made.'

Their tempers eased. A friend and ally, no matter how self-serving a character, was in danger, but Blackstone knew that de Harcourt was right.

'I'd get home if I were you. Stay watchful for a few days,' the Count said.

Blackstone felt a nagging conflict rise within him. William de Fossat's ambush and capture could not have happened at a worse time. De Harcourt saw the concern crease Blackstone's face and knew his friend only too well. 'Sweet merciful Christ, Thomas, you can't be thinking of an oath made years ago.'

'I'm in his debt. He saved my life. He's my friend.'

'A fair-weather one!'

'A friend! It's who you pledge your word to that counts!'

De Harcourt snatched at Blackstone's bridle, but the horse's strength was too great and it snorted, yanking itself clear of the grasping fist. 'I'm your friend too. And I beg you not to be foolish. Who would care if a pledge was not kept because a man couldn't keep his cock under control?'

Blackstone brought the horse back under control. 'I gave my word, Jean,' he said quietly.

Their rush of blood had settled. De Harcourt sighed, and nodded in defeat. 'I know.'

'Listen, Jean. It's better I ride south with my men. That keeps you and the Norman lords out of it. If I can free William then we'll get him home and lock the horny bastard in his own dungeon until this blows over. You must see I'm right.'

De Harcourt grunted, refusing to answer immediately, but he already knew that Blackstone had made up his mind. 'Sir Rolf de Sagard has about sixty or seventy men behind those walls. Does that make you think twice?'

Blackstone's men were weary from their winter raiding and the battle at Saint-Clair, but now he would demand even more from them.

'Ride straight to Christiana and take her and the children to Harcourt. Keep her there until I return. Two weeks. No more.'

'Merciful God, Thomas. Her spleen will burst. You promised her no more campaigns or fighting this year. You gave *her* your word as well.'

'And you think I could sit by the hearth and do nothing for William?'

De Harcourt settled his helm. 'We'll ride there now. And tell William when you see him that he should be more diligent in his prayers and thank God he has you as a friend.'

He nodded in farewell and yanked his horse away, cantering for the road that led to Blackstone's manor – and Christiana's displeasure.

CHAPTER 14

The retreating soldiers squelched through blood-soaked mud, their labouring breath desperate from exertion as they ran for their lives, pursued by men as breathless as themselves but who sensed victory was in their grasp. Swords' tips cut through the air, their sting nicking hamstrings and leg muscles. Those who fell tried to turn and raise a sword arm in defence but their attackers snarled their venom and plunged sword, knife or axe into the screaming men. Bodies split open, entrails spilled across their legs as feeble hands tried to gather their guts moments before blades severed heads and limbs. Fighting men stood in their enemies' innards and then clawed their way up the hillside. A butcher's yard slick with gore.

Those in retreat saw the man leading the killers in pursuit was always a half-dozen strides ahead of those who followed – all seasoned fighters anxious for victory and the spoils of war. As the fight crested the hill ten horsemen from the castle spurred their horses forward to trample the attackers beneath their hooves. Those on the run, those men who had survived the baying horde behind them, somehow managed to run between their own cavalry's mounts, buffeted by the riders' careless disregard for their safety. Relief surged through the survivors. Safety! The savage bastards who sought to take the stronghold had failed because now the castle's horsemen would set about their killing. They were wrong. The moment of exhilaration faded as quickly as it had occurred. When the riders crested the hill they were at their most vulnerable. The snarling horde levelled pike and spear and lunged at the horses' bellies. The beasts' agonizing screams echoed across the hills to the castle walls.

Disembowelled and mortally wounded horses reared up, throwing riders into the attackers' midst who swarmed across them in an unforgiving and relentless tide. Sweat stung knights' eyes, their vision a narrow slit through a helm's visor, unable to see the mayhem being wrought. It was a half-blindness that became a terrifying claustrophobia when the horse beneath them fell, throwing them and the eighty pounds of armour that encased them like a worm in an iron coffin to the ground. One of the first to fall felt a final, helpless terror, piss spilling down his leg as the final sight of life was of a wild-eyed attacker snarling a curse as a knife came through the narrow slit and pierced eye and brain. Heels drummed the ground in death throes – flailing into the darkness, realizing that the howling scream was his. And that God did not exist.

Before the man's bowels let go his killer was already stepping on his lifeless body and attacking another.

Almost there! Suck the air and spit the fear. Wild-eyed and unstoppable, the attacking men surged over the brow of the hill and saw the enemy run for the safety of the castle walls. The portcullis was up; men on the battlements screamed for survivors to hurry. A siren wail of pain and terror told the defenders that unless the portcullis was dropped death would be among them. Those being pursued were overtaken by the lone surviving man-at-arms who mercilessly spurred his horse to escape the savagery that pursued him. The retreating men heard the bastard screaming to lower the portcullis as soon as he reached the castle's gate. Their hatred for the privileged horseman lent power to their legs. They heard his horse's hooves clatter across the bridge. Fifty yards. Forty. Only thirty now. Thirty rapid strides to safety. A groan came from the chain tower as the mighty winch holding the portcullis released the tension of its burden. The portcullis slammed into the ground. The survivors were only ten yards from safety and their screams of anguish echoed up the walls. They were dead men.

The dozen or so soldiers, bloodied and exhausted, turned to face the men who would kill them. Their backs against the barred gate they threw down their weapons and knelt in supplication. Mercy was their only hope.

None was given.

The butchery lasted only minutes despite spears and rocks being hurled down onto those doing the killing. There would be no burning pitch or oil, no siege was in place, there had been no warning to defend the castle. The assault had caught the garrison by surprise when the supply wagons were attacked on the approach road. There had been so few men surging from the forest that the garrison commander thought they could only be a roving band of disorganized routiers – mercenaries who raided for supplies. And that was why Sir Rolf de Sagard had sent out troops and horsemen to inflict punishment and rescue his supplies – but the ragged band soon formed into a cohesive knot of disciplined fighters led by one man at the point of the phalanx. Now the attackers were closer, the Frenchman saw the man's armorial blazon: a mailed fist clenching the cruciform of a sword. His heart sank – Sir Thomas Blackstone. There was only one reason for him to venture this far south into such hostile territory; Blackstone was after the prisoner held in the castle's dungeon. But how could the Englishman hope to secure the castle with so few men? Was this the best he could muster – fewer than fifty fighting men? Perhaps Blackstone's legend had been embellished? He seemed to be little more than a common brigand with ambition beyond his capability. Sir Rolf de Sagard's hopes soared. Below his gate the scar-faced Englishman and his men huddled beneath their shields, sheltering from his men's barrage. He bellowed his orders to his men on the wall. 'Kill them! We have them! More rocks!'

Glory would be his and the King of France would reward him for delivering the head of the man who had plagued him for so long.

Blackstone and his fighters knelt, shield straps tightened and locked above their heads as the thud of rubble and spears pounded down upon them. Their boiled leather knee guards protected them from the stony ground but it would not be long before the shields would crack like eggs and then Blackstone and his men's mangled bodies would join those of the slaughtered men.

'Holy Mother! He'd best hurry!' Meulon shouted above the noise of the assault hammering down.

Blackstone twisted his head and looked at the black-bearded man whose eyes glared from behind his helmet's nose guard. Meulon and the others – Gaillard, Perinne: sworn men at his side for these past years – crouched like beasts in the field fearful of being struck by lightning.

'He'll be here!' Blackstone yelled, and prayed that his squire had done exactly as ordered because his own attack was a feint to draw the men in the castle to the front wall.

Guillaume Bourdin clambered across the rear parapet from the scaling ladder that had wobbled precariously when four of the rungs gave way beneath his weight. He led the assault but almost lost his grip when he crashed the length of his body down the ladder. His feet slammed into the man below, a muffled grunt and a curse was all the nineteen-year-old squire heard as he hauled his weight up hand over hand. Shield and sword were strapped across his back, which meant that he would be vulnerable as he breached the wall. But no soldiers lay in wait; the cries of battle were beyond him from where Blackstone led the frontal assault. Despite the broken ladder men poured across the wall after him, running along the battlements, peeling left and right to secure the walls and watch towers. They ran silently, bringing their shields across their bodies, readying axe and spear. None wore armour, their swiftness of foot and agility in battle demanding that they wore only mail shirts beneath a gambeson that bore Blackstone's coat of arms. There was no distinction between knight and common soldier. The castle's inner ward was protected by a curtain wall and as Guillaume ran towards the front battlements he saw others clamber like rats across a sinking ship's bows to the keep, where soldiers would be guarding the garrison knight's family. The young squire gave them little thought. If the men followed Blackstone's orders the women and children would not be harmed, but if any showed resistance they would be slaughtered.

Guillaume and his men had got further than they thought possible before being detected as the defenders concentrated their efforts on destroying those below the shield wall. Ten men ran behind him in support, another dozen or more raced along the other parapet and they would soon meet resistance from the watchtower, but the men on the ground who had run down the steps to the courtyard would have to secure the gate as rapidly as they could, while those above took control of the tower and raised the portcullis. Guillaume saw the rolling gait of Guinot the stocky Gascon, his short hair bristling grey in the dull light, his leather jerkin stretching tight across a broad back as he wielded an axe in one hand and a mace in the other. He and the men with him carried no shields for protection; they were going to carve a path into the soldiers behind the gates. Fifty men were now inside the castle walls. Guillaume knew that despite every one of his men being worth two of Sir Rolf de Sagard's, Blackstone had, for once, attacked with a superior force.

The garrison commander half turned as men behind him screamed a warning. Sir Rolf's worst fears were realized as he saw the enemy swarming within the castle walls. He yelled a command and ran at Guillaume along the parapet, which was only wide enough to allow two men shoulder to shoulder. Blackstone had spent the past five years training each day with his young squire, and the remorseless demands Blackstone made on his men were what secured the towns he held and the fear he created. Ferocity in attack, he always told them, drives the heart and strengthens the sword arm, but also puts the fear of Christ into others. Now, however, the greatest challenge Guillaume faced was to carry out his lord's command not to slay Sir Rolf. He wanted him alive. How, the young squire asked himself, was he supposed to do that and survive? The garrison commander held back, ordering his men-at-arms to halt the attacking men. Guillaume bent his shoulder behind his shield and scraped its edge along the parapet wall, allowing another of his men to squeeze in next to his shoulder. As the man cut viciously low into the legs of the soldiers defending Sir Rolf, Guillaume skewered and jabbed his sword beneath raised arms and exposed throats. They fell gasping and squirming and were kicked to the yard below.

Sir Rolf turned to retreat to the safety of the keep but Guillaume screamed to Guinot below: 'Guinot! Stop him!' and jabbed with his sword in the direction of the knight.

The sweat-slicked Gascon ran forward, cutting off the man's escape, and, as Sir Rolf killed two of his attackers, Guinot hurled his mace straight at the man's head. The strike whipped the knight's head back, rocking him onto his heels, and then one of his knees gave way as he staggered. Stunned, he half turned, desperately sweeping the sword in a wide arc, catching another of Guillaume's men across the throat. By then Guinot was on him, throwing his weight over him, ripping free the helm and punching him in the temple. Sir Rolf de Sagard lay unconscious in the mud, his beard clogged, his ears and nose leaking blood. As the cry went up that their commander was down his soldiers grouped together and formed a defensive knot, crowding themselves into a corner. They had already witnessed the lack of mercy given to those who had tried to surrender on the other side of the portcullis. There was no choice other than to fight. Guillaume shouted for others to assault the gatehouse and as the men he led plunged spear and sword into the fifteen or so men who stood their ground he joined those who were using a granite horse trough as a battering ram against the keep's stubborn oak door.

He heard the portcullis clank upwards and men heaving aside the gates. Blackstone strode into the outer ward flanked by the bear-like figures of Meulon and Gaillard. Within half a dozen strides Blackstone had barked out an order to spare the few remaining survivors who now crowded behind their fallen comrades. The moment the order was given the French threw down their weapons and knelt in surrender. Blackstone's men reached into the group and hauled them into the open yard.

'Where's de Sagard?' Blackstone called as he and the others walked between the fallen men.

'My lord!' Perinne shouted from where he had propped the hapless commander against the wall, wrists bound and shackled to an eyelet in the wall. Sir Rolf was still groggy from the blows and blinked uncertainly as Blackstone reached him and lifted his chin with his gauntleted fist.

'Where is William de Fossat?'

The battered man shook his head, mumbled and dropped his head down onto his chest.

Blackstone pinched the knight's nose. 'Don't feign unconsciousness with me, you turd!'

Sir Rolf gasped for air.

'You know who I am,' Blackstone said threateningly through gritted teeth.

Sir Rolf nodded.

'Good,' said Blackstone, as he heard the keep door shatter and saw Guillaume lead the men inside. He twisted the man's head so he could see what was happening. There was a clash of steel and shouts of alarm from within. Men cried out; a woman screamed. 'But you don't know my men. And what they'll do to your wife and children. Where is de Fossat?'

'He's not here.'

Blackstone pushed his head back against the wall, making him grimace as the rough stone rubbed his scalp.

'You'll spare them? I beg you, Sir Thomas, don't let your men dishonour my wife and daughter.'

Blackstone glared at the beaten man, saying nothing – and then relented. 'I'll spare them,' knowing full well his orders already stood for them to remain unharmed.

'The truth, Sir Thomas. William de Fossat is not here. He is no longer my prisoner.'

This time Blackstone slammed Rolf's head back hard, stunning him. 'Stay with him, Guinot.

Keep the bastard alive. Give him water when he comes to. Meulon, with me. Gaillard, you and Perinne take the men. Search everywhere.' He strode quickly to the keep and pushed his way through the crowded stairwell as his men came down with bolts of fine cloth, silver plate and jewellery.

'Stand aside!' Meulon cried up the stairwell. 'My lord is here!' And forged through the throng of men as Blackstone followed on his heels. Blackstone's men pulled the bodies of dead defenders out of his path. Men pressed themselves back against the wall of the twisting stairs. Blackstone spoke a word here and there, mentioning men by name, congratulating his fighters.

'Next landing, my lord. Master Guillaume has them,' one of the soldiers said as Blackstone pushed past him.

Blackstone stepped into the broad room where long-plank floors creaked under his weight. Murder holes sent slits of light into the chamber where the last of his men pillaged tapestries from the wall and grabbed pewter cups from cupboards. Candlesticks and table coverings were already stripped and one of the men had a woman's fur-collared cloak over his shoulder. Blackstone pulled it from him and muted any protest of stealing the man's booty. 'I'll pay you for this, Betyn. More than it's worth.'

'Aye, my lord,' the soldier answered. Silver from Sir Thomas was better, easier than trading the cloak for a whore's pleasures for a month or more.

Meulon ushered the last few men out of the room as Blackstone looked towards the huddled family. A woman, beyond her thirtieth year, he guessed, held a protective arm around a girl of about eight years. She would have been raped by now had it been anyone other than Blackstone leading the assault. A boy of similar age stood to the front of his mother holding a broken-shafted spear. As Blackstone stepped forward towards the shivering woman the boy made a stabbing motion. Guillaume half sat on the edge of an oak table, his sword point resting on the floor, waiting to see if the boy was going to lunge. He was unconcerned at the feeble threat. 'A memory, my lord, of another boy in another castle in another time.'

'Aye, but not as determined as you were,' Blackstone said, and nodded for the boy to be taken care of.

His squire moved so quickly that the child had no chance to bring the spear point to bear. Guillaume snatched it, pulled the boy off balance and cuffed him behind the ear. The woman gasped; the girl cried out. Blackstone held the cloak for her.

'Madam, the castle is taken. No one here will harm you. It's cold and you will need this.'

She snatched the proffered cloak and wrapped it about her, pulling the trembling girl in beneath it. Guillaume hauled the boy to his feet and smiled at Blackstone. He picked up a fallen bench and sat the boy on it and then gestured for the woman and her daughter to sit with him. They did as they were told, but kept darting nervous looks at the black-bearded man who hovered behind them.

'Meulon, you're making the lady nervous. Step this side of her,' said Blackstone.

'It is said his mother died of fright when she gave birth,' Guillaume said to the wide-eyed boy. 'He was born with that beard.'

Meulon grinned and did as ordered.

'That's enough,' Blackstone told Guillaume. 'We've no time for humour here.' He looked unsmiling at the woman. 'Your husband was not prepared to save you, my lady,' he said. 'He lied to me. I know William de Fossat is here.'

She shook her head.

Blackstone pushed Wolf Sword, still wet from blood, through its holding ring on his belt. 'I will give you safe passage to the nearest lord who supports King John, but I need to know where my friend is being held. I see no place for a dungeon.'

'I don't know anything of William de Fossat. I know he was brought here and I believe he was taken away after spending only one night chained in the outer ward.'

'Who brought him?'

'I do not know the man.'

He could see her confidence was returning. She was the Lady de Sagard again, disdainful of the barbarian soldiers in her home. Blackstone had given his word that she would not be harmed and that gave her security. He put his face closer to hers, watching as her eyes widened fearfully again. Blackstone lowered his voice and spoke to her in measured terms so that she would gather in his words. 'You and your children are safe but your husband will die today unless you tell me what has happened in this place. You will be a widow without protection. Your children orphaned. I will burn this place to the ground. The King will take your lands. Save yourself and your lord.'

She faltered, but the thought of being widowed like so many others she knew, and the hardship that it could bring, broke her resolve.

'There is a dungeon, beneath the north wall. A trapdoor . . . in the armoury.'

Gaillard dragged his boot across the straw-laden floor as Blackstone and Guillaume stood by with Meulon and half a dozen others who held burning torches.

'It's here,' said Gaillard, grunting as he bent down and grasped the iron ring of the trapdoor and heaved the heavy wooden slats up, then let the weight of it crash down. 'There are steps, my lord.' But as he spoke he recoiled from the stench that wafted up from the darkened cellar. The smell reached the others and they pulled an arm across their nose and mouth. Blackstone took one of the torches and eased himself down the steep stairway.

'Stay here,' he ordered.

As he descended the smell became worse and he

could hear the muted buzz of flies. He realized he must be at least fifteen feet below the floor, and could see the rough-hewn stone foundations. As his hand reached out to steady his step on the narrow staircase he felt water running down the wall. The place seeped with moisture from the ground above and the sticky smell of putrefaction mingled with the damp air. When the steps ended he was in a vast space where the flames from his torch did not reach. As he made his way forward he saw manacled chains hanging from wall rings and a brazier, cold, its grey ash half burying the irons used for torture that pierced its dead embers. He listened but there was no sound except that of the spluttering torch that he held away from him, sweeping through the darkness.

'Guillaume! Meulon! Bring more light!' he called. 'William? Are you down here? William! It's Thomas! Can you hear me?' There was no echo to his call, the heavy walls deadening all sound. There was no response; perhaps the woman had told the truth that William de Fossat had been taken elsewhere. He heard Guillaume and Meulon clamber down the wooden steps, heard them gasp, and then spit the foul taste from their mouths. The light from the torches broadened across the dungeon, but still there was no sign of de Fossat. Blackstone turned his head and listened. The dull buzzing sound was somewhere over to the right. He stepped carefully forwards, the others with him, and then they saw the figure against the far wall.

Blackstone went quickly towards the man who hung from the ceiling chains, manacled at the wrists; his head was slumped on his chest, the long mane of black hair covering his features.

'Merciful Jesus,' Meulon whispered, and crossed himself.

Blackstone could not comprehend what they had done to his friend and it took a few moments for his eyes to search out the answer and then for his mind to understand. William de Fossat was naked, his arms fully extended bearing the weight of his body, or what was left of it. The broad slab of muscle across his back and chest was not covered in black hair as Blackstone remembered, but rather in a trembling mass of flies. He heard Guillaume choke and then retch as Blackstone's torchlight exposed the lower half of the man's body. What had taken Blackstone so long to comprehend was that the shredded clothing that hung from below de Fossat's chest was not cloth from any shirt but rather what remained of the skin that had been flayed from his body.

Blackstone's throat tightened and he was barely able to speak. 'Guillaume, fetch a bucket of water and a cloth, and take that woman's cloak from her and bring it here.'

Blackstone heard his squire scurry back and then seconds later the scuff of his footfall on the steps. Blackstone kept his eyes on his Norman friend, praying that there was no life left in that tortured body. He extended his arm to one side. 'Meulon, take this and bring both the torches closer.'

218

Meulon did as Blackstone asked and stretched out his arms wide, giving his sworn lord as much light across the injured man as he could. Blackstone waved the flies away; they swarmed momentarily but he kept his arm moving until they scattered. He gently eased the wounded man's hair from his face. One of his eyes had been gouged and the inflamed flesh was as swollen as the bloodied mass of his cheekbone. Blackstone's hands hovered, uncertain what to do next. He let his fingers gently ease across de Fossat's arms and he could feel through the bulk of muscle that the bones were broken.

'William, who in God's name did this to you?' he whispered to himself.

He laid his bare hand carefully on de Fossat's neck but could feel no pulse of life. Guillaume returned with a bucket of water and rags and put it down a few steps away from the man's ripped torso. Blackstone did not need to turn to see the horror on his squire's face.

'Bring it closer, Guillaume. I need it here,' he said quietly.

The young squire took the bucket to his master's side, but kept his face averted from the shredded skin and the heaving mass that returned to feed on the torn flesh. Blackstone held one side of de Fossat's face, supporting his head. 'Soak the rag and give it to me,' he said, keeping his eyes on the tortured man's face. Then he took the dripping cloth and soothed the battered skin, dabbing the broken and cracked lips. He felt a slight tremor and knew the Norman was still alive. He squeezed more water to his lips.

'William, it's Thomas Blackstone. Can you hear me?'

He listened and was sure he heard the rasp of breath at the back of the man's throat.

'Guillaume, find a manacle key. We must get him down.' Blackstone placed his mouth close to de Fossat's ear and repeated his name. This time there was a definite sound within the big man's chest that found its way to his lips.

'Thoma—' he sighed.

'Yes, yes, I've come for you,' he said quickly.

De Fossat said something else, but Blackstone could not hear, and moved his ear closer to the man's lips.

'As you prom—'

'Yes. As I promised,' he said. 'We're going to get you down.' Blackstone half turned his head to where Guillaume frantically searched for a key among the other chains and manacles. 'Hurry,' he urged.

De Fossat's head was moving against Blackstone's hand and he heard him whisper. 'No . . . Thomas . . . no.'

Blackstone's helplessness embraced him. 'William, I'll take you home. I swear it.'

Again the man's head moved slightly, his un-injured eye opened, blinking in the torchlight.

'Lower it,' Blackstone quickly told Meulon, who

brought his arms down, letting the shadow soften on de Fossat's face.

Blackstone felt tears sting his eyes. 'William,' he whispered. 'You're broken. Everything has been broken.'

A breath escaped the tortured man. He tried to speak, but the words did not form. Blackstone turned in anguish to Meulon and saw that through gritted teeth the bear of a man wept.

Blackstone choked back his own tears, wiping those that cut across the grime on his face. He sniffed back the phlegm and steadied himself. De Fossat was trying to say something. Blackstone held his breath, heart pounding, wishing it would quieten.

'Pain . . .' de Fossat murmured. Then bravely forced more words from his lips. 'Too . . . much pain . . .'

Blackstone's voice fell to a whisper. 'Who did this, William? Tell me. Was it de Sagard?'

For a moment it seemed de Fossat's life had deserted him, but then his lips moved again. 'Priest . . . Thomas . . . priest . . .'

It was a hopeless moment. 'There is no priest to comfort you or absolve you, William,' said Blackstone, unable to help his friend further.

His gaze locked on Blackstone, who looked uncertainly at him. Then de Fossat nodded, and his lips moved.

Blackstone heard the words clearly, and stood blankly for a moment. Then he shook his head.

'I cannot. I will take you home. I swear.' But as he uttered the promise he knew it was false. There could be no means of taking the man down without the suffering squeezing the last drop of courage and breath from him.

Guillaume stood at his shoulder. 'I have a key, Sir Thomas.'

Blackstone turned to the two men, his look of anguish plain to see. Meulon nodded. He knew.

'Wait,' he told Guillaume, his voice barely audible. He placed his face next to de Fossat and then kissed him on each cheek. De Fossat nodded again.

'Better . . . my friend . . . than this hell,' he murmured. 'Even . . . though you're an Englishman.' The corner of his mouth rose attempting a smile.

Blackstone embraced the bloodied body that had been both enemy and friend and pressed his knife upwards into his heart.

The rain fell steadily. Not hard like arrow shafts driven by an angry wind, but an even, soaking veil that drenched and stung the eyes. A fine rain that disguised a man's tears.

Meulon and Gaillard brought de Fossat's body from the dungeon wrapped in the woman's cloak. It took six strong men to carry him to the yard where the others gathered, silent and uneasy. Blackstone had tied off the loose folds with cord; the man was too tall and broad for the cloth to afford him any dignity, but it made no difference, torment such as that which had been inflicted on him had stripped dignity away when the first knife cut had encircled his body and the skin peeled off. Rain splattered his grey, lifeless face, absorbed by his thick hair and beard as the fur collar wilted. Sir Rolf and his family were made to stand in the mud, soaking and shivering, to watch as Blackstone had de Fossat laid out in front of them all. He cut the tie cords and threw back the cloak, exposing de Fossat's naked torso and what had been inflicted upon it.

A murmur went among the men as the woman gasped and drew her children to her. Sir Rolf looked at the body and then turned his face away, tilting his chin as if disclaiming any interest or knowledge of the dead man.

'Broken and then flayed,' Blackstone told the onlooking men.

'Peel the bastard, my lord. Let him feel the misery,' one of them called.

'Make them dig his grave!' Perinne shouted. 'And then skin him!'

A ripple of agreement went through them. Sir Rolf's fate was in the balance.

'Tell me if this was done by your hand,' Blackstone said evenly. The chill of his voice was not lost on Sir Rolf.

'You promised us safe passage,' the knight answered. 'For us to be taken to a French ally. Your word, Sir Thomas. As a knight!'

Blackstone nodded. 'It was given and it remains so.'

De Sagard nodded, finally succumbing to Blackstone's pledge, his voice tinged with relief. 'Your friend was brought here under custody of a man I did not know. He bore the King's warrant. I was told William de Fossat was to be kept here. That no one would know where he was held. I acted without malice. I was fearful for our own lives, Sir Thomas. All I did was allow him entry. I knew nothing of what he did to Sir William. Nothing. I swear it on my oath. We are vassals of the King and we obeyed his orders. On pain of death we obeyed.'

'And the name of this man?'

'Gilles de Marcy. I heard the routiers call him the Savage Priest.'

Blackstone realized that de Fossat had not whispered his need for a priest but was telling him the name of who had tortured him.

'You heard no screams?' Blackstone asked, looking at the knight and his wife. Both shook their heads vehemently. They were lying. William de Fossat was a great fighter and a man who could endure more pain than most, but Blackstone knew that had he been manacled in that dungeon and endured the same fate his own screams would still be echoing around the castle walls.

'No sound came from below?' he asked again. 'No howl from a man being broken and flayed? Even through these walls?'

Again the man and wife shook their heads.

Blackstone looked down to the trembling child,

held close to her mother's skirts. She was probably close in years to his own daughter. Taking Guillaume aside he spoke to him quietly. 'My face will scare the child; yours shows tenderness. Question her,' he said, and told his squire what information he needed.

Guillaume turned to the child, bending so he could look into her face. He lowered his voice. 'Did you sleep these past nights, little one?' he gently asked. He saw the mother's arm flinch, pulling the girl another inch closer. Guillaume waited. After a moment when the child understood that the fair-haired young man with the soft eyes was making no obvious threat to her, she shook her head.

'Was it something you heard in the darkness?' Guillaume asked, his smile softening the question.

The child nodded.

'What was it you heard?' he asked, going down on one knee, but not moving closer to her.

'The night demons,' she said. 'They were screaming.'

Sir Rolf was about to chastise his daughter but Gaillard stepped quickly between him and the girl, preventing her from seeing the look on her father's face. His knife pricked the knight's throat into silence.

'Is that what your mother told you?' Guillaume asked, teasing the truth from her.

The girl shook her head. 'Father said they were demons sent by the devil to frighten naughty children.'

Guillaume smiled reassuringly at her and then stood. The mother's face was drawn, gaunt from the child's exposure. Blackstone turned to Sir Rolf.

The Frenchman's fate was sealed and he knew it.

His wife suddenly ran to him, pushing aside her child, and clung to him as he embraced her. She wept into his shoulder and then faced Blackstone. 'An honourable death, Sir Thomas. Grant him that. Do not butcher him—'

'As he allowed my friend to be!' Blackstone shouted. The woman flinched. Gaillard dragged the hapless knight away as Meulon grabbed and held her. The girl wailed for her mother and ran to her skirts, but Rolf's son stood stoically watching the unfolding events.

Blackstone stepped to the middle of the yard where Gaillard kicked away the man's legs, forcing him to kneel, ready for execution.

'Let him up,' Blackstone ordered.

For a moment doubt made Gaillard hesitate, but then he obeyed.

Sir Rolf stood like a cornered animal, trembling before the pack of men who surrounded him. Gone was any arrogance of rank and privilege.

'You said that no one was to know that William de Fossat was being held here,' he asked.

Sir Rolf nodded.

'But a Norman lord received word that my friend had been captured and brought here. And that information was passed to me. It was expected

226

that I would try to rescue him. How many men did this Savage Priest ride with?'

'Only two of his men survived. De Fossat killed the others.'

Blackstone realized that this was no strike against Norman lords. No great band of routiers or the King's men had ridden through Normandy. If such an incursion had taken place their presence would have been noted. This had been little more than an ambush party. Whoever had planned it had drawn Blackstone away from the safety of his own domain and the Normans who surrounded him. They knew he would attack here in force and that he could not be taken.

'So I am not their prey,' Blackstone muttered to himself, the hollow pit of his stomach chilled with fear. 'Meulon! Give him your sword!'

Meulon gave it quickly and stepped back into the press of men.

'You deserve no mercy but you can die with dignity,' Blackstone told him, drawing Wolf Sword.

Sir Rolf looked once more towards his wife and children, raised the sword in a high guard and took three determined strides towards Blackstone.

His attack was well paced, his balance firm, and his strike could have proved deadly had Blackstone not quickly moved outside the sweeping cut. By the time Sir Rolf's momentum took him a stride beyond the Englishman, his severed head pitched forward into the mud as his flailing body staggered on a few more paces and then crumpled in a final spasm.

Fire consumed the castle, sweeping Blackstone's anger through every cranny. The billowing smoke would be seen for miles but it was doubtful any Frenchmen would venture beyond the safety of their own walls until the sky cleared. Blackstone had Lady de Sagard and her children escorted to a local lord by her husband's surviving soldiers. Sooner or later scouts would venture out and they would confirm the destruction of Sir Rolf's stronghold and that his severed head adorned a pole in front of the main gate. And they would know who had made a rapid and successful raid on the castle and slain one of King John's trusted knights.

William de Fossat's body was packed in salt, swaddled in linen and stitched into canvas to be accompanied home by a dozen of Blackstone's men. His friend's burial was his widow's affair. The man's soul had passed through Blackstone's embrace and a prayer would be said and an invocation made to the goddess whose image hung at his neck. Angels or pagan spirits could do the rest. There was little doubt that de Fossat being tortured in such a manner was a declaration of an enemy who cared little for the blessings of angels. So what strike would come next? If de Fossat had been used as bait to draw out Blackstone and his men then for all he knew an attack to retake his towns might have already started. He had raked his spurs into King John's flanks when he had seized Saint-Clair-de-la-Beaumont and yet the more he thought it through the more he realized that it made no sense. King John would not, could not, risk such an enterprise. Even with routiers in his pay there were not enough men to lay siege to several towns at once and risk turning the Norman barons against him. Despite his doubts he sent Meulon, Gaillard and Guinot and the men hastily back to their duties. Patrols would be doubled and the towns made ready to bring the villagers inside the walls. Blackstone gave his willing horse full rein with Guillaume at his side. They would sleep in the saddle and stop only when the horses needed rest.

Talons clawed his heart.

The Savage Priest's threat was aimed closer to home.

CHAPTER 15

Blackstone's children were safe. He arrived at Castle de Harcourt to be greeted by Blanche and Jean with their usual warmth and affection, but with the worrying news that Christiana had grown impatient and, despite their objections, had travelled to Paris in search of her father.

Both men and their horses were exhausted, but Blackstone gathered the children to him, pushing his anger with Christiana away from the tenderness he allowed for Agnes, and a more reserved yet no less affectionate embrace for his son, Henry.

'Father, I told Mother that she shouldn't leave without you, but she wouldn't listen to me,' Henry said, standing respectfully in front of his father.

Blackstone held Agnes on his knee, brushing strands of the child's hair behind her ear. As he kissed her forehead she wrinkled her nose. 'You smell like a horse,' she said.

'Shall I go away until I've bathed or will you put up with the smell?' he asked.

'You can stay,' she told him and settled into her

privileged position, scraping a nail on the dirt and blood-encrusted jupon.

'Was she angry?' Blackstone finally said to his son.

'No, Father, but she was unhappy that you weren't here.'

There could be no denying that he expected anything less. 'I had work to do,' he answered.

'Did you save Lord de Fossat?' Henry asked, his palm resting on the silver scabbard of the knife in his belt.

'No, but I held him as he died.'

'Did you kill the man who captured him?'

'One of them,' Blackstone said, and eased his daughter to the floor. 'I have to go now, Agnes.'

'To bathe?' she asked, brushing a hand down her skirts, smoothing the material as he had seen Christiana do a thousand times.

'I'll bathe when I come back,' he reassured her.

'Are you going away again?' she asked, reaching for his filthy hands and slipping her small fingers into his palm.

'Yes, I'm going to find your mother.'

Blackstone rejoined Jean and Blanche de Harcourt in the great hall and told them what had happened: that he thought the ambush had been staged to draw him away from his home. He spared no detail of the torture inflicted or the revenge he exacted. The wine they drank did little to ease the sour taste of how de Fossat had died. Blanche crossed herself. There would be prayers said in their chapel for him.

'There's been no incursion anywhere near your domain, Thomas,' Jean told him. 'No troops, no routiers. Nothing. None of us believe that the ambush was anything other than a personal matter. There is no sign of any build-up of troops.'

'Is it coincidence that de Fossat is taken when Christiana finds a token she believes is her father's?' Blackstone asked.

'What else? Joanne told me herself that she had sent it to her,' said Blanche.

'Who told you about the ambush?' Blackstone said, studying Jean de Harcourt's face, looking for any tell-tale signs of dishonesty, while cursing himself for having such thoughts.

'De Graville. One of his informers in Paris sent word when we were at Guy's castle.'

'His confessor?' Blackstone said and swallowed the last of his wine, but keeping his eyes on his friend's face.

De Harcourt shrugged. 'Thomas, I've no idea. De Graville wouldn't tell us even if we asked; it would be too dangerous for whoever gave him the information.'

Blackstone knew de Harcourt was not lying. But the fact that de Graville spent a lot of time in Paris, praying with and confessing to a priest he'd known for years, was both a risk and an ideal subterfuge – if one was needed. Doubt festered. Was the pious de Graville a traitor? He had not only sent word of de Fossat's capture but had placed Old Hugh and Beatrix in Blackstone's household. Such a betrayal would only show itself when the Norman lords made their move against the King. And the Normans' strength could be blunted by killing Blackstone.

'And nothing else unusual? No further agreements with Navarre or the King's son?' said Blackstone, seeking out anything that might give him a clue as to the cause of recent events.

'None. Other than extra guards at the city gates,' de Harcourt said without suspicion.

'For what reason?'

'The King gets nervous. It happens now and then.'

Blackstone helped himself to more wine. 'Christiana should never have left the children. She promised me she would wait for me to sort this out.'

Blanche touched his arm and tried to reassure him. 'The children are safe and have been well cared for, Thomas. Marcel keeps Agnes amused and Jean instructs Henry every day,' she said as Blackstone let the flames from the grate warm him.

'Thomas,' Jean urged. 'Christiana is self-willed. Were she not she wouldn't have ignored our advice and married you!' He smiled in a vain attempt to relieve Blackstone's anxiety. 'And Henry is coming along. He strikes well and he's becoming more aggressive with a training sword every day.'

Blackstone's mood could not be soothed. 'She's abandoned her children for an impatient quest that might place us all in danger.' He looked at them both, wishing he could explain why he knew with certainty that what he said was the truth. 'Her father is dead,' he said coldly.

The two men stared at each other. Read my eyes, Blackstone willed him. See what I saw that day when my arrow gutted the old man.

De Harcourt felt Blackstone's intensity, and realized that whatever secret his friend held it was obviously something that could never be spoken aloud. By whatever means Blackstone had come across the knowledge, it was obvious Christiana's father was dead.

Blanche de Harcourt mistook Blackstone's unspoken agony as worry for Christiana. She touched his arm and smiled. 'I've arranged hot water and food for you and Guillaume.'

Blackstone's hair was matted; the grime in his hands and face witness to the days of travel and conflict. Whatever weariness nagged his muscles he ignored. 'I'm not staying, Blanche, I have to go and find her.'

'Did we think you would not?' said Jean, handing him another glass of red wine. 'Eat and bathe at least.'

Blackstone shook his head. 'If I go into Paris I have to be seen as a peasant.'

'Even those of low birth in Paris bathe, Thomas. Don't worry, you'll stink enough by the time you get there.'

He could not deny that a hot bath would ease the discomfort in his mind as well as sluice the foulness from his skin. He dipped his head in acknowledgement to Blanche. She smiled and turned away to instruct her servants.

Blackstone waited until she had left the great hall. 'Jean, listen to me. If I am hunted by the King's killer how best would I be taken? In my domain? Here, in the heart of Normandy?' he asked quietly.

'No. They could never take you here. So, they draw you away by capturing William. Then why not kill you when you went to try and rescue him?'

'Because I had my men with me. Sir Rolf's castle was not that well defended. I rose to their bait, Jean. I went to honour a debt to a friend and my wife was deceived into going to Paris. Can I take my men into Paris?'

It was a question that needed no answer.

De Harcourt wrung his hands. 'Sweet Jesus, Thomas, you go alone into a trap.'

'What else can I do? Christiana is in danger. They know I'll go.'

De Harcourt shook his head. 'Joanne de Ruymont would not be a part of this. She cares as much for Christiana as Blanche does. These women are bound with care for each other.'

'Jean, a simple piece of embroidery by Christiana's hand has been used to entice her away. What better way to draw her in than by using a friend? With every good intention Joanne de Ruymont has unwittingly played into the King's hands. She and Guy might also be in danger.'

'A Norman lord would never be harmed in Paris, Thomas. Even the King is not that stupid. Dear Christ, have I brought this upon you with our plotting?'

Blackstone leaned forward and gripped his friend's arm. 'No, Jean. They must want me because I hurt the King by taking Saint-Clair.' Blackstone drank the last of his wine. 'You say they've doubled the guards, then how do I get past them? And how do I find Christiana?'

One of de Harcourt's allies had a contract with the city to supply grain and food and his barges travelled down the Seine into the city. A peasant with a strong back was always welcome, especially when no coin changed hand and it was done as a favour that would one day be repaid.

The barge carrying Blackstone eased its way along the twisting current. Stripped of his mail and jupon, he looked no different from any other peasant working on the transport barges. The boatman steered with a confidence learnt since boyhood, but he eyed his broad-shouldered passenger with curiosity. He was no aristocrat, that was certain. His grime and muscles denoted a working man but his manner was too sophisticated to be that. He had spoken quietly when he came aboard, offering his thanks and asking what he should do. Whoever thanked a bargeman? Sit down and keep quiet and he'd be told when the time was right, is what he was ordered to do, and like a damned sheep he had done exactly that.

It would be unwise to question the stranger, but a safe passage without mishap would do the boatman no harm in his employer's eyes. A man's business was his own, but he would wager his payment from these sacks of grain that the man ushered aboard twenty miles upstream was up to no good. A killer, perhaps. A score to settle. River trade seethed with men with knives, but that was for tavern brawls, nothing more. No, this man was put aboard in secrecy for a reason that he had no wish to learn. Christ's tears, he thought, it wasn't only the Seine that ran deep with treacherous currents a man couldn't see. He was grateful he had only the wharfside authorities to deal with, and hoped scar-face did nothing stupid if challenged because then they could all be for the lash.

Blackstone watched the tableau of village and countryside drift by, but as the boat eased around a bend he saw the distant pillars of smoke rising from house chimneys that seemed to fill the horizon. As far as he could see the city walls embraced Paris. If Edward's great war ever reached here he would need to lay siege to it for a man's lifetime. The river could be blockaded, but Blackstone knew that if Edward wanted this crown then the French King would have to be drawn from this stronghold and defeated outside its walls.

As they passed the outskirts of the city birds

swirled over gibbets, the victims' bodies hanging for raven and crow that feasted on their rotting flesh. One great structure was built to hang ten or twenty at a time, standing like a monument to death in the wasteland beyond the city walls.

Blackstone's wondering gaze was snatched here and there as they passed beneath the arches of a massive bridge. He had never seen such activity as the river traffic bustling back and forth under power of sail and oar. From the low-lying river the houses surged into the sky: saw-toothed roofs one after the other. Row upon row of buildings were built on the bridges; shutters opened and scraps of food were tipped into the river. Voices carried, mingling with broken sounds of street music as the barge passed along the river. Monks' solemn, eerie chanting came and went as streets funnelled their echoing voices from whatever church they sang in. Waterwheels creaked and groaned, slapping the water slowly by the half-timbered watermill, whose lower stanchions were green from sitting in river slime. Beyond them spires and turrets stood arrogantly proclaiming their dominance over the cramped city streets. The bargeman steered his boat towards sloping banks that reached down to the river from a broad square where houses built of timber and clay and cut stone overlooked the open space. Places of importance. Grain barges, bigger than other vessels, took up most of the strand as smaller boats bobbed and weaved for a berth.

Cut timber, stacked higher than a man, lined the shore; sacks and barrels were checked by merchants' officers and municipal officials as fruit baskets and caged livestock were hauled from barges.

The boatman used the current to bring his vessel to the riverbank, calling out to others whose vessels jostled for a mooring. As the boat was steered into position curses flew as easily as greetings between men who knew each other from a lifetime on the river. The boatman had been instructed by his master to deliver his unknown passenger safely to Paris, past the unsuspecting eyes of the guards on the bridges – the bustling wharfside served as the perfect means for him to discharge this duty.

The boat eased alongside and men jumped ashore, well practised in securing their boat.

'You!' the bargeman called to Blackstone. 'When we dock you take one of the sacks and follow the other men. Do as they do.'

Blackstone nodded and as the boat was tied off the crew began to heave the sacks of grain and walk with ease across the unstable plank that joined boat and shore. The bargeman stood watching each man as he laboured under the weight of his load as Blackstone waited his turn to go ashore.

'This is no place for a man from a village where he knows his neighbour. There are leagues and brotherhoods in this city, guildsmen sworn to protect each other. You'd be wise not to trust anyone,' he said to Blackstone.

'I'll remember that,' he answered.

'Aye, well, you look to be the sort who wouldn't do much trusting anyway. But a warning won't be amiss if word reaches my master that I gave it.'

'He'll hear of it.'

'Good. He'll press silver into my hand and that feeds a family in these hard times.' He turned his face back in the direction they had come from. 'Stay away from the Châtelet over by that bridge there,' he said, pointing to an unseen place beyond the last bridge they had sailed beneath. 'You get put in the cells there and like as not you'll stay there.'

'And why would I end up in a cell?' Blackstone asked, hoping the man did not know his true identity.

'Because you seem to be a man who can look after himself – a brawler. And back there are the butchers' and tanners' quarters and they're hard men. Vicious bastards at the best of times. If there's a riot to be had you can bet your last sou that they'll be in the front rank with their cleavers and hooks. So if they take a dislike to you – and you don't appear to be the kind to walk away from a fight – if they don't kill you then the cells is where you'll end up. And the stench! That's where the blood and shit is sluiced through the sewers into the river from the slaughtered beasts.'

'Where am I now?' said Blackstone, needing a sense of direction.

'Up there,' the bargeman said, looking towards the broad square that lay above the riverbank, 'that's the Place de Grève, and that fancy stone building is the House of Pillars.' He paused, knowing the name meant nothing to the stranger. 'The merchants' house,' he added, and then with a knowing inflection: 'There are always Provost's police around there. If a man wanted to avoid being questioned because he wandered around like a lamb in a slaughterhouse then he should skirt the square and get into those narrow lanes. Crowds swallow strangers.'

It was Blackstone's turn to heave a sack onto his shoulder and follow the others. The bargeman watched him go, wary of his passenger being accosted after he dropped the sack and melted into the square's bustling crowd. He did not want anyone ashore to connect the two of them. Blackstone was soon out of sight and the boatman's part was done. Whatever happened to his human cargo was of no concern to him now.

CHAPTER 16

Paris seethed. The right bank of the Seine had expanded beyond the city's old walls, where trade flourished, unlike the less-populated area on the opposite bank that was dominated by the university, scribes and clerks. Blackstone had never seen such a jostling mass of people. Traffic jammed the streets while touts beckoned customers inside their master's shops, and merchants called out for passing trade. Stalls were pitched close enough to nudge each other. There was a clamouring of voices from butchers, cloth sellers, cheesemongers and pastry cooks. The dripping quarters of meat attracted flies as the fat was scooped and spread on slices of hard round rye bread cut from the stacked tiers of loaves. Honeycombs of bleached cows' stomach – tripe favoured as a speciality – were spread on wooden frames like a washerwoman's drying shirts. River fish glistened, laid out on reed mats, while jugglers entertained at street corners and dice players squatted in doorways as women with trays of vegetables slowed the crowds, showing ankle and cleavage to encourage buyers. Mendicant monks rattled their begging bowls and chanted prayers as the lame and blind sat like bundles of discarded rags in any corner they could find.

Shopkeepers beckoned customers to view the wares on their tables, although the law forbade them from doing so until the buyers had left the neighbouring shop. The hubbub of these raised voices chattered all about Blackstone as the pressing crowds forced him to wind his way like a fish upstream. As desperate as he was to trace Christiana's whereabouts the vibrant city's atmosphere caught him in its net as each corner he turned offered him more sights and sounds. To visit Paris had always been a secret desire, but the bounty on his head ensured that the gates of the city stayed closed to him. Hundreds of unnamed streets and alleyways crisscrossed in a bewildering tangle and within a couple of hours he knew that he would never find Christiana among what was said to be more than a hundred thousand souls who populated the French capital. He had to find the apartments where the nobility lodged in the city. Horses and mules forced the throng aside as muleteers yelled and whipped the beasts of burden through the narrow gaps between the half-timbered houses, each floor cantilevered over the one below, restricting the light that reached the streets. Memories clawed at him as he was jostled this way and that by the impatient crowd. The last time he had been in such a labyrinth was at Caen a decade before, when he had fought his way from one corner to the next, searching for another loved one, his brother, in the turmoil of street fighting as Edward's army flayed the city of its defenders.

The stench of human waste mingled with that of laundry women's steaming cauldrons and the unmistakable smell from soap makers and bakers who vied for the very air itself against fishmongers who hacked and gutted the day's catch. The aroma of baked wheat sprinkled with sugar and angelica made a mouth-watering temptation. Despite the cacophony Blackstone heard dogs howling at the sound of a clanging handbell and a raised voice that carried from a nearby square. He brushed aside the grasping fingers of a stallholder trying to pull him into a shop and, as he broke through into the square, he caught a glimpse of a man standing on a stone plinth in front of a fountain. His clothes denoted his authority as he rang the bell in front of the gathering crowd.

'What's going on?' Blackstone asked one of the onlookers.

The man glanced at him. 'You don't know *that*, then you're not from here.' He gave Blackstone more serious consideration. 'Hang onto your purse, stranger. We've more purse cutters on these streets than the King has devalued coin in the mint.' He grinned with a nervous sneer. 'Unless you're a King's man snooping.'

'No, I'm a stranger here,' Blackstone assured him, aware that not only his size made him stand out among the crowd but also his ignorance.

'Aye, your accent's not from here – that's obvious.' He looked Blackstone up and down. 'We get plenty of foreigners at the university. You're too old for that though, I'd say, and looking at your clothes and hands I'd reckon you were a working man.'

Blackstone had kept the scarred side of his face behind his hood, concealed from the man's inquisitive gaze. 'I'm a stonemason.'

The man nodded as if accepting Blackstone's explanation and gestured towards the square. 'That's the Master Crier. He has all the news of the day. Takes it across the city so each quarter gets told what it must. Not that there's much to tell unless we're to have another bastard tax raised.'

The Master Crier bellowed above the clanging bell: 'Pray for the souls of the dead and for your own sins as this bell tolls,' he called as the clanging went on a moment longer. He was flanked by half a dozen assistants who carried small scrolls that they handed to him in turn; he then pronounced each decree, his voice carrying across the crowds. There was to be the funeral of a grain trader and the two houses he owned would be put up for sale. A child he described by name and age had gone missing from its neighbourhood. A fair was to be held two weeks hence and three children were to be baptised that Sunday.

As the Master Crier moved away to take his news to another square, jugglers and musicians quickly took advantage of the vacated space and tried to keep the attention of the ready-made audience. The man next to Blackstone turned away but Blackstone caught hold of his tunic. 'Friend, I need some help.' The man tugged free. He had no desire to befriend a stranger in a crowd, not one as dangerous-looking as this one, whose weather-beaten face he could now see. Blackstone quickly pulled the cowl back over his head. 'If I was to look for a gentlewoman—'

Before he could utter another word the man guffawed. 'You what!'

The shout caused others to stop and stare. The last thing Blackstone wanted. He turned away, stooping his shoulders, trying to make himself less obvious.

'He's after a whore who can pretend she's a gentlewoman!' the man shouted to the amusement of those around him.

'No, not a whore,' Blackstone quickly insisted. There was little choice now but to brazen out the confrontation.

'The bathhouse two squares from here!' one of the men shouted, biting into an apple and grab-bing his crotch. 'Forbidden fruit, stranger. There're rumours that noblewomen visit to have the pleasure of a working man!'

'My wife . . . she's an embroiderer, and she's here somewhere. She works for a gentlewoman is what I meant.'

The apple chewer laughed, mouth open, pulped apple blanketing his tongue. Thuggish-looking, he had the air of a man who could handle himself in a fight. 'You need good money for Parisienne whores, my friend. How much you got then? I'll take you where you want to go. But it'll cost you.' Spittle mixed with apple sprayed his front. The man seemed more foolish than brave to challenge Blackstone, but he noticed four others like him who stayed a few paces back. They were obviously a street gang and strangers were easy prey no matter how tall they stood.

The first man Blackstone had spoken to became aware of the gathering threat. 'Leave him be. He's looking for his wife is all.'

The thug grunted an unintelligible response but Blackstone saw his sleight of hand easily enough. A quick stabbing of the Samaritan would cause sufficient uproar for the street gang to seize a stranger's purse. It didn't have to be a killing. A distraction would be enough. The thug's hand now held the blade low beside his leg, ready to rip upwards without being seen. Blackstone took a stride forward and quickly eased the intended victim aside. His other fist came up swiftly and caught the knifeman like a mallet beneath his chin. What had been a grin became a mangled, choking gasp as shattered teeth tore into his tongue. Before the man fell back into the crowd Blackstone had already kicked the fallen knife away and turned, hoping the panic would cover his retreat. The man he had saved brushed past him. 'This way! The Provost's men will be on us.'

The crowd engulfed them as Blackstone, keeping pace with his guide, weaved his way from the square into a side alley, and then turned again into another. The dank shadows quickly hid them. By the time they had moved several streets away, the turmoil in the square had subsided. Finally the man stopped and ushered Blackstone into a doorway, looking back cautiously the way they had come.

'You're the kind of man who brings trouble with him. I thank you for saving me from injury. No women are allowed in the bathhouses, or vagabonds, so keep yourself clear of them. Stay on this street until you see the sign of the tooth puller and then listen for the crier's bell again. Across that square is where the embroiderers work, next to the hatters; that's where they ply their trade. Godspeed, stranger.' And with that his guide ducked away into another alley.

Blackstone soon found the square the man had described and, as the Master Crier repeated his news, Blackstone moved quickly around the edge of the crowd and into the streets on the far side. Small enclaves of women sat in various doorways, or at tables, examples of their skill laid tenderly on washed hessian, beneath a canopy that offered some protection from dust and showers of rain. Some of the pouches and linen cloths were stitched with muted autumnal dyed threads, others with veins of colour. There were costs involved in buying the materials and, despite their skills, these women relied on work from noblewomen as well as street selling. As he walked along he tried to think who might have sold Christiana's piece of linen, the piece that Blackstone well knew was more likely stolen from her without her knowing it.

He went from one group of women to another. Most ignored the dirty-looking labourer; others shook their heads when the questions were asked. After an hour of edging down the street, going from stall to stall, he realized that this last group of embroiderers were all that remained between him and the next row of shopkeepers who had bolts of cloth and swathes of multi-coloured material on sale. He stepped closer to the women who, with outstretched hands holding their cherished work, called for him to buy. Others, like those before them, took one look at his shabby clothing and made no effort. They huddled and whispered, slyly glancing at him. A man as rough as he would barely have a penny to his name, let alone enough money to buy a delicate piece of stitched beauty for a woman. A whore's man, no doubt. His bristles barely hid the wicked scar that was etched from forehead to chin down his grimy face.

'Don't let him put his filthy hands on that, Mathilde!' one of the women cried to another who had offered her work to Blackstone. 'Mind your purse! He's a wicked look about him.'

Blackstone stopped as the woman called Mathilde kept her nerve and her offering.

'Even a common man can know beauty when he sees it,' she said to him. 'Look, sir, look. See my skill? A man could not fail to win a woman's heart with such a gift, wouldn't you say?'

Blackstone looked at the simple but elegant depiction of a rosebud and the skill required to embroider the creeper that entwined itself around its stem like a lover's arms.

'I would,' answered Blackstone.

'Then—'

'I'll buy it from you, if you can help me,' he said, interrupting her sales patter.

'Count your fingers, Mathilde. If you let him take that from your hand, there'll be some missing!' her friend warned again.

Blackstone saw the woman was losing her nerve.

'I'll take it,' he said.

'But . . . you have not asked the price,' the woman spluttered, barely able to conceal her joy at snaring a country bumpkin. 'Five deniers . . .' she said.

'No. I will give you three, though you know it's worth two,' answered Blackstone. 'You have already more than doubled the price because you think me a fool,' he told her and dropped the coins into her outstretched hands, but made no attempt to take the cloth and its embroidered pattern.

It was a good profit. Her fist closed over coins and material as the thought of keeping both went through her mind. At worst this rough-looking man would call the Provost's men, an argument would take place and the other women would back her story that the man tried to take the cloth without paying. Except for one of them – Isabeau. She would always find a way to stab her in the back, jealous of her skills. Old bitch. Her hand unclasped and passed the cloth to Blackstone. She grumbled as she untied her purse and dropped in the coins. 'That's a good piece of silk thread you have there. At a good price.'

'It's a piece taken from a lady, cut from a bolt, likely without her knowing; someone you sell work to,' Blackstone told her and saw that he was probably right about the theft. He showed her Christiana's stained needlework. 'Have you seen this before?'

She took it reluctantly from him. 'An amateur's hand, I can tell you that – but a good one,' she conceded. 'The futaine is of good enough quality,' she told him, her finger tracing the few strands of cotton mixed with silk. 'A coarse linen to stitch. Not a noblewoman, that's for certain. And she's no guild member, either.' She handed it back. 'I've never seen it before.'

'And if it were offered would you buy it? In order to sell it on.'

'We have our own to sell. Superior work, as you can see,' she said defiantly.

He ignored her self-regard. 'And no person, man or woman, has come here and shown such an embroidered cloth to any of you and asked the same question?'

The piece of cloth passed through the women's hands as they all looked at Christiana's embroidery.

The old woman at the end of the stalls barely glanced his way. 'You want to sell that get yourself over to the whores by the riverbank. They'll buy a piece of cloth even though it's not fancy,' she said.

'He's not trying to sell it, Isabeau! Merciful Mother of God, you witter like an old crone,' Mathilde rebuked her, and glanced warily at Blackstone. 'This is little more than an old bloodstained rag. Not even a whore would want it,' she said.

Blackstone showed no sign of displeasure. He simply nodded and tucked the cloth away. 'How do I get to the noblemen's quarter? There's a grand street somewhere, isn't there?'

'Ha! You'll get short shrift knocking on their doors. If their dogs don't have you the constables will,' said one of the women.

The women murmured amused agreement among themselves.

'Find your way north, and you'll start to see the big houses, big windows and courtyards,' said Mathilde, relenting because he had paid her well. 'Up past the market and graveyard towards the Porte Saint-Denis.'

The woman called Isabeau chirped in from the end of the table. 'You'll not get there before dark, so you'll spend the night in a doorway with the beggars and get yourself a good kicking from the night-watchmen,' she said.

Blackstone knew he needed no issue with anyone official. 'Is there a tavern nearby that might not steal a man's boots in the night?' he asked.

'Take your pick. They'll only take your boots once your throat's been slit,' Mathilde answered as the other women laughed with her.

'Get yourself to the Half Wheel. There's no bed, but there's food and a hearth,' Isabeau told him. 'Across a dozen streets, up that way. You'll see their sign. As big as a nobleman's door, it is.'

Their blank stares told him there was nothing more to be got from them. But it confirmed that Christiana had not yet reached these stallholders and, to his mind, that someone had used an unsuspecting Joanne de Ruymont to draw Christiana into the city. And to make him follow. As he turned into the crowd the woman who had given him the name of the tavern gathered her pieces into a broad cloth, which she tied off in a neat bundle.

'Isabeau!' one of the embroiderers called. 'You're packing up so early?'

'I'm cold and I'm hungry. There's no trade today, and it's almost gone anyway,' the woman answered.

'Some of us have sold fine pieces at a good price,' the embroiderer teased. 'Your fingers are too bent and crippled for fine stitching. Perhaps it's time you went over to the bakers' quarter and started making meat pies with hands like those! You'll starve to death otherwise.'

The other women laughed and bent their heads back to the work beneath their fingers. Old age was coming to them all, and sooner or later they would end up like poor old Isabeau, and when that day came they could only hope for a rich woman's charity that might allow them to stitch hems on undershirts before being cast into the street. Such was any woman's life. Better to be a baker's wife; at least they wouldn't starve.

Blackstone eased his way through the crowds. Paris was a confusing jumble of alleyways, dead ends and thoroughfares. Only a few doorways had any distinguishing marks above them, and most likely they were occupied by someone with money or who held some kind of minor status. He was a long way from the merchants' houses, but women from all walks of life bustled around him dressed in bright colours, some with their wimples fastened to plaited hair, surcoats trimmed with fine embroidery, as they sought out bolts of cloth or silks. A number of the women had a maid-servant accompanying them carrying a basket of bought items. Any one of these women could have been Christiana, who always wore a simple coif instead of an elaborate or fashionable wimple to conceal her auburn hair.

The city had every possession and enticement anyone could desire. Paris was like a kept whore that could provide pleasures on demand. It was a far cry from the stillness of the countryside where strangers were noticed and homes provided their own food and entertainment.

Blanche had explained that the Grand'Rue that led to the city's northern gate housed the nobility and those who, through their commercial success, aspired to be part of them, and it would be there that de Ruymont would rent rooms. Fearful for Christiana's safety, Blanche had wanted to accompany him but he and Jean convinced her that it was foolish to draw more friends into jeopardy at a time when the Norman lords were playing their own dangerous game. Christiana had been in Paris for only two days with Guy and Joanne and Blackstone and Jean agreed that there was little reason for King John and his Savage Priest to strike against any Norman lord in the city if Blackstone's suspicions of a trap were well founded. They would let the deception play out so that Blackstone would be drawn to her. She would, Blackstone thought, be safe while she attempted to trace the whereabouts of her father. Those who hunted him would be waiting in the shadows.

Despite his reasoning Blackstone still felt the pull of two conflicting objectives. As much as the need to find her and escape home pressed him, he also wanted to discover who had sold the piece of cloth to Joanne de Ruymont. If this was a trap to seize him then he had to find who had sold the bait. Like a snag on a piece of linen, the unravelling thread would lead him to them. Then, when he exposed the deception to Christiana, she would accept that her father had died years before.

And Blackstone's secret would remain buried with him.

★   ★   ★

As Blackstone moved away from the embroiderers through the alleyways, the old woman Isabeau scurried towards one of the bathhouses. She loitered at the corner of the building waiting for the boy to appear, then grew impatient and beckoned a man going in to bathe.

'There's a boy inside who helps with the water. Send him out to me.'

The man knocked aside her outstretched hand. 'I'm not here to do your bidding, old woman.'

He was a common man, no different from any other who went through the bathhouse doors, and she knew that if there was a chance of saving a coin in his purse then he would.

'You'll not pay for the water if you do as I ask,' she told him. 'The boy will see to that.'

The man considered for a moment, and then without agreement went inside. By the time the old woman had settled on the steps Raoul had appeared from the bathhouse.

'You have the money?' she asked the urchin.

The boy watched, his feral instincts twitching like a rat's whiskers. If the old woman had brought him news of a stranger asking about a certain piece of cloth, then he would be rewarded again by the man who had snatched him at the execution. They had beaten him and thrown him into a shit-fouled dungeon in the Châtelet until the Norman's men had hauled him out weeks later. From a shadowed doorway they pointed out a noblewoman who shopped among the cloth sellers. Be the beggar you

256

are, they told him, and sell this embroidery to the woman. Take whatever she offers, they ordered, and when she asks, as she surely would, tell her it was sold to you by an old man who lives among the poor and begs near the cemetery and at Les Halles. It made no sense to Raoul, a fairy tale to lure a lady to the marketplace, next to a graveyard where the dead were buried in vast trenches. If it was rape they were after they could have picked a less severe-faced woman. In fact he could have pointed them in the right direction for any of their carnal desires. They had slapped him, drawing blood from a split lip, and making his ears ring from the blow. Did he understand? He did. And when he had done as ordered, then he was to go back to his wretched life. Wretched it might be, but the street stench never smelled sweeter. There was no chance to abscond with the coins they had given him with the promise of more when he did their bidding, because Raoul was a shit collector who was known to most. And he was cunning enough to know how the streets worked. Betray a man of status and wealth and they would dig him out as a dog would a rat. It was an offer that would give him a way out of the stinking streets.

'Two deniers, as promised,' he answered the old woman.

She nodded and held out her hand. She wouldn't try to squeeze more from him, because she knew that if she did it would not be long before the bastard child would have someone step from an alleyway and slip a knife into her ribs. Or do it himself. Where the boy got the money from she had no idea, but he spent all his days now helping at the bathhouse, he no longer cleared human waste from doorways. He had placed word with some of the women on the stalls for information. And for once luck had blessed her. No, she wouldn't take anything more from this one, she decided; there was another way to make money from this.

'He's a big man with a scar down his face. He carries his left arm slightly bent like a broken wing. He stands taller than most. I sent him to the Half Wheel. He'll be there before the Angelus. He doesn't look the kind of ruffian who'd want to be questioned by the constables after dark.'

Raoul pressed the reward into Isabeau's hands. It was too late to run to the Norman lord who had paid – and threatened – him. It was likely he would be on his knees at vespers. So he would wait until morning and then, as the faithful were summoned to prayer, he would count each bell strike as that of a tinkling coin falling into the palm of his hand. And then he would try his luck on the Grand Pont and use his skills as a cut-purse on those who frequented the money changers and silver- and goldsmiths who traded there. Misfortune would be sidestepped like a dollop of shit in the street.

CHAPTER 17

There were no linen sheets on a feather mattress or pewter plates to eat from in the Half Wheel tavern. The straw-covered floor and the burning grate was as much comfort as any traveller with a few coins in his pocket could expect. Blackstone ordered food and drink and found a table in a half-lit corner. Easing himself onto the bench he sat with his back against the wall. The main entrance to the tavern was clearly in view and a side door, nearer to him, would make a convenient escape. It would be impossible for those hunting him to find him in the seething mass of this part of the city. But a chance encounter with the Provost Marshal's men might expose him. It was always better to have caution as a travelling companion. His urgency had bypassed his hunger but now he felt ravenous. He ate a plate of rough milled bread and sausage, and ordered ale rather than wine. He spoiled the tavern's undernourished cur with its bowed ribs and fed it tidbits. As darkness fell the tavern became choked with men seeking shelter for the night. No one made any approach to him and the men he watched showed no sign of violence or bad temper. As the evening lengthened and the Angelus bell rang, the ale and cheap wine, its grapes picked too late making it a sour and cloudy drink rejected by better hostelries, soon played their part and eased the tavern into a melancholy hum of muted voices and snoring men. Blackstone claimed the dark corner as his own and lay down, pressing his back into the security of the wall. The dog whimpered and crawled nervously the few feet to him on its belly. Blackstone laid a hand on its neck, soothing it. Like all dogs grateful for not being kicked away it gave Blackstone its trust and lay close to him.

Stroking the dog's ear evoked a memory of home and the pleasure of his own dogs sprawled at his feet by the fire as Christiana sat opposite while she read or embroidered, despite the poor light offered by the flickering candles. They were long, slow evenings that teased them both into passion. But there were nights when each time the needle pierced the cloth his conscience felt its stab. Never look back, he would remind himself. The past was over and done with. It did not exist. Only its ghosts lingered in the present. And some would never be laid to rest, another voice persisted. His secret would die with him, but how could he ever hope to track down Christiana in the vastness of the city? He brought Arianrhod to his lips and asked the goddess to guide him to her. No soothing answer came from his request, but with a simple act of faith that she would lead him to the mother of his children, he allowed himself to drift into sleep as church bells chimed – guardians to his dreams.

The city was in darkness; only the crossroads and the great squares were lit by burning torches. Isabeau huddled in the cold doorway and wrapped her shawl tighter around her. The wind was picking up off the river and the spluttering torches made the buildings' shadows move. She had promised a beggar half her profit from the information given to Raoul and sent his undernourished frame across the darkened street to the Half Wheel tavern. If he did as she instructed it was an investment that she would recoup many times over.

The side door creaked but was little more than the sound of a man turning in his sleep on the wooden floorboards. The night candle flickered from the breath of air that followed the man through the door. He stood for a moment and let his eyes become accustomed to the dimness. A dozen men lay on benches or were slumped across the tables; another three or four had found space on the floor. He saw the tavern dog to one side and the big man who lay behind it with an arm resting across its chest. The dog lazily raised its head and with dreamy eyes lowered it back to the floor, uninterested in yet another who sought a night's sleep.

The intruder raised the candle, searching out

whom he had come for. It was clear that there were few who matched the size of the man described by the old woman. Only the man with the dog seemed to fit the description. He stepped carefully over sleeping bodies and eased himself down onto one knee, extending the back of his hand to allow the dog to sniff him without raising the alarm. In that moment a hand snatched his wrist and he found himself staring at the wide-awake man who now held a knife at his throat. The dog squirmed away, disturbing a sleeping man who grunted as it jumped over him.

Blackstone said nothing, his eyes holding the man's frightened gaze. His slight build had allowed him to tread silently across the floorboards but now he trembled like a leaf. The whispered words were barely audible as he delivered his message.

'I mean no harm. I was sent to warn you.'

Without releasing the man's wrist or lowering the knife Blackstone got swiftly to his feet. A few men stirred but none awoke and the dog had moved to the hearth, whose dying embers still gave some warmth. Blackstone loosened his grip and nodded. The nervous messenger held the quivering candle and led them through the sleeping tavern to the side door. Once outside Blackstone pressed the man against the wall and eased the candle from his hand.

'Sir,' the man said, his voice strangling now that he could see the scar-faced man more clearly. 'Across the street is an old woman who has information for you.'

'Which couldn't wait until morning?'

'A question I asked myself. By then it will be too late.'

Blackstone stayed silent, listening for any footfall, or sound of exhaled breath in the cold air that might be a warning of an ambush.

'Take me to her,' he said, and blew out the candle flame.

Isabeau paid the frightened man and watched as he slipped away into the shadows, his silhouette briefly caught by the crossroads' torchlight.

Blackstone stood over her. 'Who are you?'

'I'm one of the women from the embroiderers' stalls. Will you pay me for the information I have? I'm already out of pocket by paying that beggar.'

'Why wouldn't I put a knife to your scrawny throat to find out what you know?'

'Because you couldn't be certain if the fear made me lie or not. Besides, you paid Mathilde more than her stitching was worth. No labourer would do that, so you have some honour – you're more than you appear to be. You're searching for someone and it has to do with that piece of cloth you carry.'

'My wife,' Blackstone told her. 'What could you know of her?'

'Nothing. But there are others who share your interest.'

Blackstone's pulse quickened but his voice remained calm. 'How much do you want?'

Isabeau had considered what her information might be worth, but her grasp of wealth was limited to what her embroidery sold for. She had earned pennies, and now she was failed by her ignorance. Her toothless mouth opened and closed with uncertainty. 'What's it worth?'

'What is the night air worth? You've told me nothing.' He realized she had no idea what to ask for. 'If your information is what I need then I'll give you ten silver crowns.'

He heard her gasp. Such an amount would normally lie beyond her grasp. Her bent fingers could rest from the work that became more demanding each cold winter.

'If it is not then you shall have nothing other than your life,' said Blackstone.

'My life is forfeit if the people who are out for your skin discover my part in this.' She hesitated. 'You have that kind of money? The purse on your belt looks too light.'

Blackstone eased another pouch from inside his leather tunic, its generous weight confirming it contained enough coin to settle a debt such as this.

First light would soon wake the city, so if there was danger approaching he needed to know about it. He sensed her nod in the shadow.

'A street urchin who has bettered himself promised payment if a man searched out information on that embroidered cloth you carry. He works at a bathhouse, so he's paid by someone else. I told

264

him you had visited the stall and that I had sent you to the Half Wheel. Whoever pays him will come for you by dawn.'

It was what he feared. The trap was for him and they had used Christiana as the bait.

'Hold out your hand,' he told her, and fingered coins into her palm.

She clawed the money and stuffed it into her purse, then clambered to her feet. Blackstone pulled her back down into the doorway.

'You stay here until these men arrive. For all I know you would betray me again to them.'

'It's too dangerous for me to stay. What if they should see me?'

'Then they'll kill you. So best to stay still and think about spending that money.'

They came swiftly and silently. The woman flinched but Blackstone shielded her with his arm, afraid she might panic and bolt. Her ragged breathing rasped like the wind across the rough stone walls. He saw a street urchin lead a dozen or more armed men to the tavern's door. The poor light prevented Blackstone from identifying the man who led them, the black cloak and clothing he wore masking his features.

Half the men pushed through the main entrance, the others into the alleyway to secure the side door. Blackstone knew he'd been lucky; he would have been trapped like a rat. There were shouts and cries of alarm from inside the Half Wheel.

'That's the boy I told you about,' the old woman said.

'Who's the man wearing the black cloak?' he asked, his voice barely loud enough for the woman to hear.

She shook her head. 'I don't know the others.'

Blackstone knew this was his chance to run, but the urge to identify the black-clothed man held him.

'What churches are there where the noblemen live?'

She shrugged. 'How would I know?'

'You embroider for the ladies. You've been there. What churches?'

'The Holy Sepulchre . . . no, they're still building . . . Saint Catherine, and the . . . I don't know. The monks at Saint Catherine are responsible for the travellers who die on the road. Are those you seek alive or dead?'

'Where else?' Blackstone insisted.

Isabeau thought for a moment. 'I don't know, I swear. The only other place nearby is the parish church. Saint-Leu–Saint-Gilles.'

'Where?'

'Far side of the Innocents.'

She saw that he did not understand.

'The cemetery. You can't miss it. Halfway between the river and the north gate.'

It was as good a chance as he was likely to get. If Joanne de Ruymont stayed true to her prayers she would be on her knees somewhere at this time of day, and Christiana would be praying with her, begging for guidance to find her father.

They watched as the men kept a firm hand on the boy who led them and then dragged him inside. He resisted, but his cry of pain reached them as his arm was twisted.

'You have escaped, but they'll kill him,' Isabeau whispered.

The stench of urine caught his nostrils; the old woman's bladder had given way. He lowered his arm. If she ran now she would not be seen. She needed no more invitation than that: she scuttled away into the next alley.

Blackstone also moved, quickly finding another alley corner from which to observe the tavern raid and in time to see men tumbling out, chased by the soldiers, and hear the sound of furniture being thrown and the dog's yelping echoing across the street. The bell for matins rang, doors were being opened, shutters pushed back and night pots tipped into the street. Three of the armed men grappled with one of the customers. He was a thick-set man and tall, though not as tall as Blackstone, and it seemed that he could have been mistaken for him.

'My Lord de Marcy!' the armed man called, forcing their victim to his knees.

Blackstone tensed. The man who had ambushed William de Fossat was here. Blackstone slowed his breath, his hand already gripping the knife at his belt. He slowed his breath and focused on the black-cloaked figure who emerged from the tavern. De Marcy grabbed a handful of the man's hair, pulling his face back so he could be seen more clearly. It took only a moment for the Savage Priest to discount him from being the one he sought. His hand loosed the man's hair and his henchmen gave him a kick to see him on his way.

Blackstone half crouched, ready to run into the throng of men. De Marcy should be killed there and then, but there was no chance of that when he had a dozen men at his side. He restrained the urge to use the buildings as cover and get close and then to scatter them with an unexpected attack. One man with a knife wreaking a sudden vengeance. Strike, kill and run. It was a foolish thought and he knew it. Christiana was in more danger now because these men who hunted him knew he was in the city and that they had missed capturing him.

Raoul had made a mistake and he knew it. He had waited too long to report to the place where the Norman lord had instructed him to go when there was news of anyone asking about the scrap of cloth. He had expected him to be there, readying for prayers, his rich ermine-trimmed cloak pulled up against the night chill and a gloved hand prepared to untie his weighted purse in reward. Instead he found a group of rough-looking men in the outer rooms of the house – cold dank rooms that were used as their quarters – and when he was ushered into the presence of the sallow-faced man who gazed at him with eyes as black as river pebbles it put the fear of Christ into him despite the crucifix that hung from the man's neck. In his few years of life the street urchin had known violence and threat, but cunning and feral caution had kept him alive. When this man spoke his words were weighted with an accent that came from further south. Raoul had heard it before, belonging to wagoners from outside the city, places he had never heard of, but whose descriptions were of another great river and a countryside rich in fruit and crops. It had been of no interest to him as he had watched them drink away their misery in the taverns while he waited to relieve them of their purses. This man was someone of authority. The sword and knife were expensive; the cloth he wore was of a fine weave that would keep all but the most wicked wind from penetrating it. And the black garments made him look as big and threatening as a winter storm cloud.

He reported everything Isabeau had told him and without a question being asked the man suddenly leapt to his feet and shouted orders to his henchmen. Raoul protested that his reward was due, but they cuffed his head and grabbed his arm and hauled him to the Half Wheel. Payment would be his only when the man they hunted was found. He knew better than to argue. And prayed for Christ's mother to protect him.

★   ★   ★

269

The tavern owner's protests were met with threats that his flea pit would be closed down by the city authorities if he dared to intervene. When questioned he confirmed that such a man as described had been in the tavern, but had left before dawn. It was not a satisfactory answer for the Savage Priest and the men inside the tavern were hauled to their feet; those who resisted were roughly handled by the henchmen. Raoul was held as de Marcy gazed into the men's faces. One had a scar that splintered his face from hairline to ear, but he was not as tall as the man they sought. But a man's legend could put a foot in height on him, so he was pushed outside for a closer examination.

The cries of alarm and protest soon drew a crowd and hecklers began cursing the armed men for their violence. It made no difference that they formed a half-circle and drew knives and swords; a Paris mob could swarm quickly and Blackstone saw from where he hid that the raiders were being threatened by the increasing numbers in the street. The black-cloaked figure shouted above the crowd's rising anger and Blackstone heard the words 'King's business'. And that enraged the crowd even more. The unpopular King was already resented and to have men raid a tavern as the city awoke and its citizens made their way to church or work was a stinging rebuke to the Provost of Merchants and the guilds of the city who were essential for King

John to sustain taxes and authority. The Savage Priest, Blackstone realized, had just overplayed his hand.

Raoul cowered in the corner as the tavern owner backed away from the figure who re-entered, momentarily blocking the light from the doorway, strode across the room, knife in hand, and tried to snatch the boy, who jigged behind upturned tables and benches. He screamed for his life, crying in terror as de Marcy lunged and caught him by the hair.

The boy wriggled and screamed as the tavern owner stepped back further still in the empty room but he found the courage to yell at the top of his voice. 'Murder! Murder! Foul murder here!'

The alarm caught the Savage Priest by surprise; Raoul twisted, sacrificed a handful of hair and ducked, bleeding, into the street with the Savage Priest at his heels. Raoul was known to many of the crowd and they gave a collective gasp and cry when they saw the boy, bloodied and terrified, pursued from the tavern by the black-cloaked knifeman. There was sudden turmoil as the onlookers parted, allowing Raoul to escape, and then bodies jostled back and forth as another group of men pushed through from the back, shouting commands to give way. The Provost's men had been alerted and twenty of them, led by a deputy with a cleric at his shoulder, quickly took control and demanded the armed men lower their weapons.

For a moment the standoff looked to turn more violent, but the Savage Priest told his men to do as ordered. He faced the deputy and said something that Blackstone could not hear – only one word rose above the hubbub: Englishman. The deputy seemed uncertain for a moment, but then took a more decisive tone and commanded his men to clear a path and escort the raiders away.

Insults flew from the crowd, and then Raoul suddenly reappeared and hurled a handful of dung at the man who had tried to kill him. The crowd's mood quickly turned to derision and laughter as the foul mess splattered his cloak and the boy ducked and weaved away, escaping into an alleyway.

If the words the brigand's leader had uttered about being on the King's business were true then Blackstone knew there would be little time before they resumed their search – and with more authority – as the court officials would instruct the Provost's men to help.

To hunt an Englishman was a sport worth joining. To catch him was worth the King's favour.

CHAPTER 18

Christiana had the comfort of Joanne de Ruymont's friendship, but the pious woman's insistence of praying four times a day and once more before retiring was a trial she had to endure. However, she was in Joanne's debt for telling her about the embroidered token that she had come across in Paris. The long-suffering Guy de Ruymont refused to join his wife for each session of her prayer. Belief in the Almighty strengthened every knight's backbone, but to spend hours a day on his knees in a cold, dank chapel was not why Guy agreed to accompany them to Paris. Christiana suspected that the noblewoman had always thought that by marrying Thomas Blackstone she had sold her soul to the devil and that these sessions of prayer, though silent except for the clicking of her rosary beads, had much to do with asking the good Lord to forgive Christiana for it.

Their rooms in the merchant house were spacious, with windows on both sides so that the light reached across the broad planks of dark chestnut floors. The servants saw to it that the stone fireplace was well stocked with wood and that a fire burned throughout the day. There were two rooms and a privy, and Christiana slept on the bed in the main room. The apartment on the top floor of the double-storey house gave them views of the distant countryside and large private gardens that reached out from the rear of the property – space that was becoming a rarity as the city grew and landowners sold them for development. Two of the city's gates were less than half a mile to the north and west and Christiana was conscious of their encirclement. She was held in the embrace of the city ruled by her husband's enemy.

Each day she awoke her first thoughts were for her children and how long she could stay away from Castle de Harcourt. The slender evidence that her father was alive could be explored for only a few days, because by then Blackstone would return from his attack on those who held William de Fossat. She had to be home before then, having broken her vow to him. Her anxiety of being parted from her children and the fear of being in Paris was soothed by her sense of self-willed righteousness. Thomas had promised her there would be no more campaigns that year, that he would stay and do what he could to find her beloved father. If he could abandon a promise then she could use his absence to take matters into her own hands. The thought of her father, an old, frail man, lost in a fog of distorted memory, gave her the same wilful determination to act alone that had given her the strength to marry Blackstone.

She was up before first light and took it upon herself to feed the fire and ensure she was washed and dressed before the de Ruymonts came through from their bedchamber for breakfast.

'Today, perhaps,' Joanne smiled. 'We will pray and then we will search. God will guide us. You'll see.' She made the same comment each morning with a calm confidence that Christiana could only envy. Guy fidgeted and casually went from window to window, his eyes searching out those below, both on the street and tending the vegetable garden, as if looking for anyone out of place. When Joanne left the room to prepare for the day and scold a servant Christiana waited until her friend's voice told her she was far enough away not to step back into the room.

'I am responsible for your anxiety, Guy. I'm sorry.'

Guy de Ruymont was known for his charm and good manners, as well as for his occasional and unexpected ill-tempered outbursts to a wife who voiced her pinched-faced displeasures on an all-too-regular basis.

'Many people visit the city, Christiana,' he said, smiling to reassure her. 'There's little danger for us. And no need for you to worry as long as I am here.'

She remembered the first time she had come across the Norman lord's gentle reassurances, years ago when Blackstone had survived his wounds and been forced to attend a Christmas feast at Harcourt. It was Guy who had saved him from embarrassment when Joanne, bitter at losing members of her family at Crécy, had tried to expose the archer's lack of social graces in front of the gathered nobility. Guy's was an act of kindness that had extended over the years and brought the two families closer.

'My presence here might jeopardize your own safety if it becomes known that Thomas Blackstone's wife is in the capital.'

'And among all the rich merchants and those at court, not to mention other knights, barons and estate owners, who come and go along the grand streets and swarm in the side alleys, you think a humble Norman lord will be noticed?' he said self-mockingly.

She smiled. 'You think we women don't know how the times are, Guy? You and Jean and the others talking to Navarre? It's dangerous.'

'Not yet,' he said comfortingly. For a brief second she saw what she took to be fear in his eyes. 'Now, if Joanne spent less time on her knees and more time helping you search for your father, then our time in the city might be halved,' he told her.

Today would be no different from any other when they left the comfort of the rooms. Guy would accompany them as they searched the area around the Church of the Innocents and the marketplace for any old beggar who might be Christiana's father.

'And when we pray, Guy, you are left to do what? Wander the streets?'

'There's some falconry to be had and a gossip or two about the price of winter wheat. The marketplace gives me snippets of information. I make no complaint of being abandoned while Joanne prays for all our souls. You forget, Christiana. Men enjoy their own company.'

'I know that only too well,' she answered – too quickly – immediately regretting her show of irritation yet unable to resist the impulse: 'I am Thomas Blackstone's wife.'

Blackstone walked as quickly as he could, desperately wanting to run towards the church he sought but knowing that to do so would draw attention to him now that the city was awakening. It was still barely light enough to see doorways or those who slept in them, but he caught the smell of something sweet on the air and a pang of hunger mingled with the anxiety he felt for Christiana. By now those who wished to trap him would know he had slipped through their net. Would they risk arresting a Norman lord and his wife in order to snare Christiana, forcing him to surrender himself? The Normans had already lost d'Aubriet by the King's hand, and de Fossat to torture and death by the Savage Priest. If they arrested Guy de Ruymont on any trumped-up charge, Normandy would surely declare openly for Navarre and the English. His thoughts moved as quickly as his feet across the pavement. Christiana's father had fought against the English, but that would not save her now she was married to Blackstone. The protection afforded her by Guy de Ruymont and the King's desire to secure Norman loyalty was a contest that would end in only one way: her capture and his surrender to save her.

The alleyways twisted left and right and as one joined another he lost his sense of direction. He cursed the confines of the city and by the time his instincts and good luck brought him to a main thoroughfare he realized he had missed the church and was forced to backtrack. Raucous shouts from across the way made him falter and he edged cautiously towards the broad street. It was not those who hunted him, but stallholders shouting to each other as they laid out their wares under the covered market. A breakfast of ale, bread and cheese was being shared by the men and women gathered around a brazier, warming the cold night's stiffness from their aching bodies. Beggars, some crippled, others blind and led by children, began to seep from the darkened doorways like wraiths in tattered clothing, little better than rags bound by string. The church was a few hundred paces beyond the walled cemetery. Blackstone's eyes searched the people on the street for any sign of recognition, fearful that the citizen volunteers from the Provost's office had already been sent to search for him. The man he saw at the tavern was the Savage Priest, and by now he would have convinced the authorities of his status. It was unlikely they would issue a hue and cry, something that could soon get out of control and become a riot. There were enough men with battle scars to be suspect, but it would cause chaos to have volunteers on the rampage pulling aside every man with a scar. It was more likely the Savage Priest would control events and send the Provost's men to do their own search for Blackstone. He and his men, once they were released from questioning, would change their tactics and seize Christiana now that they had failed to snatch their prize at the Half Wheel.

Blackstone pushed through the church door and stepped into its cold darkness. A bird fluttered, high up, seeking its freedom; other than that there was little sound in the church, except for a whisper of prayer that came from a hunched figure whose black cowl covered his head. Had his enemy already discovered him? Perhaps Isabeau had been captured. Blackstone's hand was already reaching for his knife when the figure rose, knelt before the altar and then turned so that the candlelight showed him to be a priest. The man was startled when he saw Blackstone standing beyond the benches.

'You offer no humility to God, my son?' he asked. 'A bended knee is little to ask.'

'I need answers that God cannot give me in

prayer. I'm looking for a woman, probably with a companion, who might come here each day to pray.'

The priest looked at the roughly dressed man whose demeanour seemed to challenge not only his own authority but that of the Church. There were many men like this in the city, some had been hanged for going into a place of worship and dragging out their victims to kill them in the street. A church's sanctuary was inviolable to most, but those who chose to ignore the law of God would find their punishment could not be avoided.

'Those who pray here have the protection of the Almighty,' he said carefully, trusting that, by offering no direct challenge, he would be spared any injury.

'If the Almighty wishes these women to come to no harm then you can see me as his instrument for their protection. There are those close by who would seize them. Tell me if you know where they may be.'

No threat had been made against him and the priest knew that such a man who stood before him could easily have reached out and squeezed the life from him.

'Two women pray here during the day. They are pious and generous with their alms. One is older than the other and seems to be her chaperone. I suspect they don't travel far from the safety of this place, which means they stay in the nearby streets close to the cemetery and the marketplace. If I see them again today shall I give them a message?'

'Yes. Tell them to stay here because of the danger that seeks them out.'

Blackstone turned for the door, the light and noise from the street cutting into the silent gloom. The priest felt uncertainty grip his chest and prayed his instincts had been right to send the man to the nearby streets. The bird in the rafters found a broken tile and its freedom. Once again the silence settled.

The Innocents was the city's graveyard, its ten-foot walls enclosing trenches a hundred paces long, dug for mass burials, there being no space for individual graves. Old skulls and thighbones, clean and dull white, were stacked in a few of the archways, a charnel house for those who had been buried over the years and whose place in the ground was needed by others. Handcarts carrying the dead, led by priests or monks, formed an almost constant flow of traffic, wheeling in through the crowds on the busy street. Beggars extended bowls and cupped hands, hoping the sight of the dead might remind the mourners that a small act of charity could help pave the way to heaven when their own time came.

Standing in the entrance he loitered, as did others, watching the carnival of death unfold. Street urchins drank from the fountain as market workers drew water and then carried their buckets away, avoiding itinerant bric-a-brac sellers with their makeshift trays. There were men and women in the cloistered archways, some of the women selling themselves and some of the men buying. Surely he would be able to see Christiana as he scanned the beggars and those too drunk to raise themselves from the stupor of the previous night's drinking. He picked his way around the high walls. They were well built; a craftsman's hand had cut and laid the stone and it had been done many years ago. He silently acknowledged the mason's skill and wished his own life had given him the chance to lay down a monument that had his name cut into the cornerstone. He bypassed the grave diggers shovelling dirt over linen-wrapped corpses, and avoided the tearful women who made their way back to the street. One of them screamed in torment. Perhaps a child had been laid to rest, he couldn't tell, but a man, possibly her husband, tried to calm her and when that failed, slapped her hard, stunning her. Her knees sagged and she rested in the dirt, leaning on one arm until he bent down and dragged her to her feet.

Blackstone wished he had asked Jean de Harcourt where the Norman Lord de Graville prayed during his frequent trips to the city because he would have approached him and sought protection. Testing him. Wanting to see if de Graville was meeting anyone from the court and passing on information – because to betray Blackstone in Paris would secure the King's blessing. Who had informed on William de Fossat and found the means to lure Christiana to the city? But time was now too short. An old man being guided towards a corner of the cemetery by a woman caught his eye. He had shoulder-length white hair and carried himself in a dignified manner. As would an old poverty-stricken knight who had only ever had his pride to help keep him upright. He must have poor eyesight, by the way the woman eased him between the obstacles towards two figures who waited in the lee of the wall, an archway shielding their faces. Blackstone made his way towards them as one of the women stepped forward and reached up, cupping his whiskered face in her hands. Another step closer. The morning light fell on her face and the look of disappointment etched on it.

Christiana.

Blackstone was about to call her name when a commotion at the entrance made him turn. The priest from the church was being held by some of the men he had seen raiding the Half Wheel and voices around them were raised in angry protest. One of the men gripped the priest's hood, twisting it for purchase, forcing him to scan the crowd. They had somehow discovered the church and forced the priest onto the streets to see if he could identify Blackstone. The crowd might have set upon the men – some of those nearest had challenged them for their behaviour – but the priest pacified them, stopping them from taking any action that might cause bloodshed. Moments later a half-dozen Provost's men appeared, adding authority to those menacing the priest, who shook his head as if answering the men's questions, obviously indicating that he did not recognize anyone as they pushed him deeper into the cemetery. Time and again the priest shook his head as the men guided him through the enclosure. Blackstone had gone down on one knee, as if in prayer at the open trench, obscured by the grave diggers and mourners, but the men moved closer to the archway where Christiana and Joanne stood. It was obvious the priest had seen them but he turned his back, not wishing to draw attention to them. He had believed the stranger who had come into his church looking for the gentlewomen to warn them of danger. His instincts had been proven correct. These rough-looking men seemed intent on violence and the Provost's men lent them their authority. No woman, of gentle birth or otherwise, should be surrendered to such men. It might well have ended there had it not been for Joanne's Norman arrogance and sense of outrage. She gathered her skirts and pushed through those standing in her way.

'Stop what you are doing!' she cried, loud enough to scare a flock of pigeons from the walls.

The men turned back to face her, and Blackstone saw the look of anguish on the priest's face. Despite his brave efforts, the woman he sought to protect had revealed herself.

'This is a priest of God! You do not manhandle

284

him like a drunken sot. Whoever you are, be warned that you will be punished by the King's officers. Release him!'

Blackstone moved further around the crowd of onlookers who were now drawn to the noblewoman's outburst. Her command did not fall on deaf ears, because her rank was obvious by her manner and dress – which reflected a woman of maturity, her hair styled in ram's horn fashion, plaited over her ears and covered by her pinned wimple. One of the mercenaries spat in contempt.

'He has information,' said the brigand.

'Priest or no priest,' another added. There was little respect to be had from men who served their savage master with the power of the King behind him.

The Provost's men quickly showed deference before the noblewoman's anger caused problems for them all. Dipping his head respectfully, one of them placed a restraining hand on the brigand who held the priest. 'And you are, my lady?'

'It makes no difference who I am! You are committing an act that will be punished,' Joanne insisted arrogantly, and Blackstone had to admit that in that moment he warmed to the woman's defiance.

'My lady, we seek a fugitive, an English spy and assassin,' the man answered. 'And this priest can identify his wife. If we seize her, he will surrender.'

Blackstone moved closer to Christiana, who had stepped further back against the sanctuary of the wall, her attention riveted on the confrontation. She had no means of escape if the men came any closer. Joanne de Ruymont's face barely registered the shock but she had the presence of mind not to turn and look towards Christiana, for which Blackstone felt a surge of gratitude.

Joanne stepped closer to the armed men. 'No Englishman's wife would be in this place. Why should she be?'

'Because she believes her father lives when the poor old bastard lies dead in a Norman field these past ten years,' one of the Savage Priest's tavern men taunted, grinning.

Blackstone was within twenty strides of Christiana when he saw her sag and raise a hand to her lips. Yet she did not fall. She was strong enough not to succumb to the emotions that swept over her about the truth of her father, made more dreadful by the knowledge that she was responsible for drawing in Blackstone. If these men sought her husband then he must be in the city.

Blackstone looked for an escape route. There was none. If the entrance was guarded they were trapped within the ten-foot walls. He scanned the enclosure: there was only one thing he could do and that was to tip a handcart against the wall and take Christiana across it, then lower her down the other side and run through the marketplace of Les Halles. The covered stalls would be as congested as the alleyways and that would give them their best chance.

Joanne de Ruymont placed her hand on that of the armed man and addressed the Provost's officers. 'This humble priest hears many confessions of the King's subjects; those who need forgiveness. By forcing him to this place you deprive these loyal people, especially the common men like these around us, of having that burden lifted from their souls.'

Blackstone was grateful for the pious speech as others in the crowd voiced their support. 'Now, let us return him to where he can do most good,' Joanne de Ruymont said with the kind of authority that only a woman of privileged rank could muster, a command that sounded like an invitation to those around her. Those close enough to have heard the exchange cheered Joanne, who remained stoically unafraid and bravely eased the priest free from the men's grip. The Provost's men relented, argued briefly with de Marcy's men, but then exerted their authority and flanked Joanne as she escorted the parish priest through the crowd towards the entrance.

Christiana seized the moment and turned away. There seemed to be no escape from the cemetery, but instinct had taken over. Blackstone stepped from behind a pillar and quickly grabbed her. There was barely time for her to struggle for within a moment she knew who it was that embraced her, and let him smother her into his chest.

'Thomas! I must have led them . . . here . . .

to trap you,' she gasped, words and thoughts fighting each other.

He was already guiding her away. 'Joanne has led them away; we must follow,' he said urgently, seeing the opportunity that presented itself.

'Thomas, I don't . . . understand . . . You found me . . . How . . .?'

'Not now, Christiana. We'll slip behind that crowd.' Without waiting for her to say anything he tugged her away and joined the gaggle of people following Joanne. As they went through the entrance they saw Guy de Ruymont standing in the street talking to more of the Savage Priest's men, his attention taken by the sight of his wife leading the priest to his freedom. For a moment Blackstone was uncertain why his friend was there and then realized he must have been waiting for his wife and Christiana as they spent time in the cemetery. And then the Provost's men had come upon the very place where the women thought Christiana's father might be found. De Ruymont saw Blackstone with Christiana and the shock registered on his face. Joanne had knelt in the street and kissed the priest's hand, an act of humility that smothered the crowd's chatter and kept everyone's attention on her.

De Ruymont was the only one who was not watching his wife. Instead, with a quick nervous look about him, he nodded in a direction away from the crowded street.

'He means for us to go to our rooms,' Christiana

said and pulled Blackstone behind her as de Ruymont went forward and brought his wife from her knees.

Christiana led Blackstone northwards from the broad thoroughfare and within minutes was passing the doors of the great houses. Blackstone glanced over his shoulder and saw Guy and Joanne following at a distance. Christiana pushed open a tall, studded oak door.

'It's here,' she said.

Blackstone followed her down a passageway. Some of the houses' doors opened directly into the living areas, others had narrow passages between them which led to a small yard at the rear where merchants could deliver fuel. This passage led to such a yard and a set of steps which went up to the storeys above. Christiana held onto Blackstone's hand as she led the way. By the time they reached the end of the passage and stepped into the yard Blackstone heard the heavy door open and close behind them again. Beyond the yard the passage continued through outbuildings and the vegetable garden beyond. Christiana was already on the stairs when Blackstone looked up to the windows above: light reflected against the uneven glass. If they went into those rooms there would be no escape should the Savage Priest's men realize where they were. If Joanne's behaviour had aroused suspicion and they were being followed then Blackstone would be trapped inside.

'Wait!' said Blackstone.

He heard shuffling feet following down the passageway. Guy de Ruymont emerged with Joanne behind him.

'Thomas! My God! That you are here! Hurry, up into the rooms, we'll be safe there, and then we'll find a way of getting you out of the city,' he said and embraced Christiana. 'It all happened so quickly I had no chance to warn you when I saw the Provost's men and those others going to the cemetery.'

Joanne's face was flushed from the exertion of getting to the house and finally accepting how fearful the situation had been.

'Guy, the house is a death trap if they know you're here,' said Blackstone, and then turned to Joanne. 'My lady, I'm in your debt for what you did this morning.'

'Yes,' added Christiana, hugging her friend. 'I have never seen such cool courage as you showed us today, Joanne. You saved me.'

Joanne de Ruymont kissed Christiana's forehead, and then looked directly at Blackstone. 'I could not let them take you,' she said.

Blackstone realized her long-standing enmity towards him had never cooled and that what she had done, she did for Christiana. 'Where does that lead to?' he asked, looking towards the ongoing passage.

'A garden, and then fields,' de Ruymont answered.

'And the city walls?'

'Three, four hundred yards. The north gate at

Porte Saint-Denis is heavily guarded; it's flanked by towers for crossbowmen. There's no escape, Thomas. You must stay until we make a plan,' he urged, 'And then—'

Joanne de Ruymont surprised her husband by interrupting him. 'And then it will be too late, Guy. I was tricked by someone who knew of my connection to Christiana. They will find us here. Thomas, there is a place before the north gate which is being rebuilt; they use it to gain access to the new earthworks beyond the city. You might be able to pass through the wall there. I have seen it from the rooms upstairs. Beyond that is the abbey—'

'Wasteland!' de Ruymont insisted, cutting his wife short. 'It's where the undesirables live. A stinking marsh where they dump the city's shit! There's a damned leper colony there.'

Blackstone saw the look of fear on Christiana's face. 'All right. We won't go that way,' he said. 'Can we cut back to Les Halles from the fields?'

'Yes.'

'Then we'll go through the market and back to the river. That's how I came here.'

'Thomas,' de Ruymont said quickly, 'wait for us and we'll meet you there. I'll rent a barge and then we can get you both out.'

Blackstone shook his head. 'I have money. You and Joanne must stay a few more days in Paris. You can't risk being connected to me. Act normally; go about your business. You and Jean and the others must not be drawn into my affairs.'

De Ruymont was about to object but a shuffling of feet and scraping of the door at the street end of the passage alerted them.

Without another word Blackstone turned and pulled Christiana with him.

'I'll delay them!' de Ruymont called.

CHAPTER 19

Blackstone and Christiana ran through the vegetable plots at the back of the house. As they moved through the barren potager Blackstone snatched servants' clothes drying on a wicker fence. There was no sound of pursuit behind them and by the time they had made their way around the palisades that filled the gaps between ancient hedgerows, they were clear of the houses. Blackstone checked that no one had come beyond the outbuildings and gave the clothes to Christiana.

'Get changed. You can't be seen dressed like that running across the fields.'

Christiana's fingers fumbled nervously with the ties on her gown, hampered by the buttoned skin-tight sleeves. There was no time; Blackstone ripped it free and shoved it out of sight beneath the bushes as she pulled on the plain clothes over her shift.

'Thomas, forgive me. I'm sorry I came here without telling you.'

He stopped looking across the fields and gardens for any signs of pursuit and kissed her.

'You sought someone you loved; I can't hold that against you,' he said. 'And I wasn't at home as I promised.'

She nodded in gratitude and joy. He understood why she had broken her promise and had risked everything to save her. 'You had good cause to try to help William. Is he well?'

'The same man who hunted you on these streets tortured and killed him,' he told her and watched as the blood drained from her face. 'Listen to me, Christiana. We've gone through worse together. Right now they're searching the streets for us, but we'll be home in a few days, once we're through the wall and across the marsh.'

'But the river . . . you told Guy.'

'No, we'll go across country. They'll have the barges watched and if they make any connection between Guy and us then it won't take much to get information from him.'

She realized he had thought it through and that if anyone could get them home it would be her husband. They had once forded a swollen river pursued by horsemen determined to kill them, but they had clung to each other and survived.

'I'm ready,' she said.

A work party of thirty men were encamped at a section of the north-west wall. Women cooked over open fires, mortar was mixed and there were piles of rubble that would be sorted and handed to the masons. Blackstone recognized these men,

294

who wore the same apron and tools that he had once carried as a young man. Guards were sitting on the rubble in the broken gap as Blackstone and Christiana edged closer, approaching from behind the canopied work places where men cut and shaped the stone as labourers laid them into hods.

'They will have alerted the main gates from the city,' Blackstone said, 'but those two guards won't have been told yet, I'm sure of it. This work party is too far from the main thoroughfares.'

'You!' a voice challenged from beside one of the tented areas. 'What's your business?'

Blackstone took the man to be a works official of some kind. 'I'm a mason. The Provost of Merchants' office sent me here to work.'

'And your tools?' said the man suspiciously. There were always men trying to be paid for work who lacked the proper skills.

'Stolen last night. We were set upon when we slept.'

The man eyed them both. It was not unusual for itinerant workers to bring their women into the city to wash and cook, and sometimes to help carry the loads of stone.

'Colard!' he shouted to a mason who was working beneath an awning twenty paces away. 'Come here!'

The dust-covered man approached them and looked Blackstone up and down.

'Says he's a mason,' said the official. 'Had his tools filched.'

The man seemed indifferent and took Blackstone's hands in his own, turning and feeling the callouses and ridges of rough skin with his own coarse hands. 'Could be. God knows we could use more men.'

Blackstone waited subserviently, letting the man make his judgement.

'What tools?' asked the mason.

'Half a dozen chisels, lump hammer and mallet,' Blackstone answered.

The man grunted. 'This way,' he said and turned back to where he had been working. A set of tools lay across a bench. 'You'll have your arse kicked from here to the Châtelet if you're wasting my time,' he said and pointed at one of the chisels. 'This?'

'Punch chisel,' Blackstone answered.

The mason's finger went down the row, and Blackstone answered each time.

'Claw – straight – pitcher.'

'Make your mark,' the mason said, indicating a flat slab of stone. A genuine mason would not hesitate to pick up the straight chisel and mallet and etch his initials or mark to show the work he had done. Blackstone chose a name at random and notched the stone with expert ease.

'T.B.?' said the official.

'Tassart Bazin,' answered Blackstone. He gave a knowing look to Christiana, who averted her eyes. Thomas Blackstone had left his mark in Paris.

'Good enough,' the mason said. 'He'll do,' he said to the official. 'We'll scrounge tools for him.'

The mason ignored them and went back to his work.

'What guild?'

'Rouen,' Blackstone lied, that being the nearest city to his home.

The official nodded. 'You'll be put on my work roster. Find yourself a place to sleep.'

Blackstone bowed his head, cupping his hands in gratitude, as did Christiana. 'Our deepest thanks, M'sieu . . .?'

'Rancé,' the official answered and turned his back on another grateful stonecutter who could always have his earnings squeezed for the favour of employment.

Blackstone straightened and stepped towards a vacant mason's work area. A plan lay spread across the worktop. Blackstone lifted the two stones that held it and let it roll into his hand.

'Thomas?' said Christiana.

'I'm not here to build a wall, but one day I'll tear it down if I have the chance,' he said and guided her towards the breach in the wall where the guards stood their watch.

'Keep walking. They might not stop us,' he told Christiana.

As they were about to pass through the gap in the wall, one of the guards called out. 'And where do you think you're going?'

Blackstone behaved as if he belonged on the

building site. 'The earthworks. The foundations for the new wall over there. I'm a specialist mason,' he said, tapping the rolled-up drawings.

'On whose authority?'

'M'sieu Rancé,' Blackstone answered.

The two soldiers looked at each other; the one shrugged and the other waved him through. 'And who's she?' the sentry asked.

'Oh, she's my assistant,' Blackstone said, and smiled. 'She's there to hold my mallet,' he added suggestively.

The men laughed as Christiana lowered her head in feigned embarrassment. They made a crude suggestion between themselves, and then ignored the man whose capture would have brought them a King's ransom. Blackstone gripped her arm, his strength soothing her trembling limbs. 'We get across these fields to those hills and we'll be safe,' he assured her.

There was mist gathering in the distance to his left and he sensed the river lay in that direction. The gallows he saw when he came upriver would be close to the bend in the Seine and they stood at the base of the plain that now faced them. Over his right shoulder he could see the abbey that de Ruymont had spoken of, but the vast open space lying before them would prove the most dangerous for them to cross. How long could it be before word reached every city perimeter guard post? He needed to find sanctuary in the forests on the hills. Stray swirls of smoke curled in the breeze from campfires belonging to itinerants who were forced to settle on this inhospitable plain beyond the city walls.

The marshland stench came from more than the fetid bog. The stream that ran through it was an open sewer. They struggled across the plain, but too slowly for Blackstone's liking. The city walls seemed not to diminish no matter how hard they pressed on. Christiana stumbled again, and he could see she would not be able to continue much longer. Her dress was soaked and stank of the foul water. Strands of matted hair clung to her face where the coif had fallen free. He wrapped an arm around her waist and took much of her weight, and cleared the hair away.

'We have to keep going. They'll see us soon enough.'

'I'm all right,' she said bravely with gasping breath.

He knew she wouldn't last the distance and turned towards the road that led from the city's northern gate into the distance. If they could make firm ground without being seen then there was a chance they could pay a wagoner returning from the city to carry them into the forests. Clouds were coming from the sea, as if guided by the twisting river, and would soon shroud the city rooftops. The rain they carried would help obscure their movement, but it would also make the going harder, and its chill would stiffen muscles. They were racing the storm and by the time they reached the roadway the first splashes of rain were swept in by the strengthening breeze. Christiana grunted with effort as Blackstone encouraged her to keep going. To stop would make it more difficult to start again.

'You can't rest, you must keep going,' he urged her. The city gates were plainly in sight and when traffic came through they would be seen. They needed to make another three or four hundred paces along this road before they could stop and take refuge in the huts that spread out from the road.

The going was easier now and she staggered as fast as she could towards the low-roofed hovels. Smoke seeped through the houses' thatched roofs, but there was little sign of life. Without warning Blackstone pulled her down into the mud behind a chicken house as two riders clattered down the road towards the city gates. They were soldiers, perhaps returning from a patrol, but they slowed their horses from a canter to a trot when they passed by. Blackstone gauged the distance between himself and them, preparing for action should they stop. If he could kill them quickly enough he could seize their horses. The decision was taken out of his hands as the men spurred their mounts away.

'I think they saw us,' he told her. 'We have to run.'

He hauled her to her feet, dragging her between the hovels and back onto the road. Blackstone forced the pace, his long strides making her punish her body to keep going. Looking back he saw that the rain squall had obscured most of the walls, but the men on horseback were shouting to others on the wall. And then they turned their horses back onto the road. They had been told of the fugitives. The rain chased Thomas and Christiana faster than the horsemen and she fell headlong, her legs finally giving way. He gathered her in his arms and carried her between the houses, searching for a place to hide. A hunched figure, a woman whose face was half covered by a veil of cloth, stood back from the entrance of one of the huts. She made no gesture of welcome or invitation to enter the house, but by standing aside she seemed to convey that they should.

The gloomy interior was lit only by the fire's embers, and the sodden reed flooring did little to keep the mud from squelching beneath his feet. He laid Christiana down next to the doorway, and let his eyes adjust to the inside of the hut. The woman entered and moved to the fire, whose bed of embers were confined by river stones that supported a cooking pot. She bent over and dropped in a handful of what looked to be herbs into the steam. Blackstone realized that, hunched against the far wall, there were others similarly clothed. Blackstone glanced outside at the sound of horses on the road and saw that the riders had reined them in near the chicken house where he had first sheltered. There were others running from the city gate, but the horsemen seemed reluctant to bring their

301

mounts among the houses. Blackstone looked back at those huddled in the hut. The stench of rotting flesh finally overcame that of his fouled clothing. They were lepers. That explained his pursuers' reluctance to come into the settlement. Christiana opened her eyes and Blackstone laid a restraining hand on her.

'There are men outside,' he told her quietly. 'Don't be afraid, but we have stumbled into the leper colony.'

Christiana was shivering, fear and exhaustion mixing their own apothecary's brew. She crossed herself, eyes widening in horror.

'If we run from this place they'll have us. If we stay until they give up the search we can be on our way,' he told her, and took her trembling hands in his own. 'These people are the living dead, but they can save us.'

She looked up at him and nodded, holding her hand across her mouth and nostrils to filter some of the smell from those confined within the hut. Blackstone watched the soldiers milling on the road, going up and down looking towards the leper colony, not daring to venture within. He heard someone shout a command, ordering the soldiers to spread out into the marshland and see if those they hunted had sought shelter among the itiner-ants' camps. No one in their right mind would go into a leper colony. Half a dozen formed a picket line along the road with twenty paces between each man, as the others spread out in an extended line and made their way towards the campfires in the marshland. The rain became more persistent, forcing the men to hunch up against the water trickling down their necks. These were not the Savage Priest's men; they were garrison soldiers reluctantly carrying out their orders to search for whoever had been seen running across the open plain and hiding behind a chicken hutch. There was no certainty that it was the fugitives. Blackstone guessed they would do as much as they were obliged to, and then get back to the shelter beneath the city walls.

No one in the hut spoke and no one made any approach towards Blackstone and Christiana, who still shivered despite Blackstone covering her with his jerkin. All they could do was wait until the men in the picket line moved away and the search was called off. The abbey's bells rang in the distance; Blackstone guessed it was mid-afternoon and daylight would soon be fading. Cold and hungry, they would be unable to travel on a moonless night, but the thought of the alternative – spending the night in the lepers' hut – made him even more uneasy. The huddled lepers wore rough, black cloaks and hoods over their clothes, all were shod in leather shoes and, as desperately poor as the room appeared to be, Blackstone could see that each had a cot and bedding. All carried a wooden clapper hung by a cord around their necks. No leper was allowed to get close to the public without signalling their approach. The old woman moved towards them and Blackstone felt Christiana flinch, but the leper kept her distance and extended her diseased and disfigured hands towards them. She was offering a bowl of broth from the pot Blackstone had seen her drop the herbs into. He felt an involuntary gag at the back of his throat at the thought of the leper's hands touching the food. He eased himself forward and took the bowl from the woman's hands. He could see that the last thing Christiana wanted to do was drink from it, but the hot broth would give them strength. Blackstone lifted the bowl to his lips; the vegetables in the watery liquid and another smell of some kind of herb made the tasting easier, as it took away the odour in the hut. As he swallowed the broth he felt its warmth seep into his muscles. Then he held the bowl for Christiana and nodded that she should drink from it.

'They have nothing to give, but they've shared this with us,' he told her.

There was the slightest movement of her head as she refused.

'Drink from where I put my lips,' he said gently. 'You need food.'

Reluctantly she took the bowl from his hands and did as he ordered. After swallowing the first mouthfuls she paused and looked to the old woman. 'Thank you,' she said and then finished drinking. Her trembling eased as she trusted her fate to a leper's good will.

Blackstone took the empty bowl from her and put it back into the woman's hands. And in it he placed a purse. The woman made a muffled sound and shrank back to the others where he heard the sound of coins being spilled from the leather pouch. Two men separated from those who huddled and came forward; their clothes were tattered and hid their disfigurement but Blackstone saw their eyes looking at him and after a brief pause the men stepped outside into the rain. Blackstone could not see where they went, but saw the soldiers making their way back across the marshland, the two horsemen already riding towards the city. A voice carried from the ragged formation of men in the distance and the picket line turned for the gates.

'The soldiers are leaving,' he told Christiana. 'We'll wait until they're back inside the walls and then try again. Can you go on?'

She smiled and drew his hands to her lips. 'I want to see my children again, Thomas. Take me to them.'

A shadow fell across the entrance as one of the lepers came back inside with a tied bundle and dropped it at their feet. His face was obscured by his hood from where his broken voice whispered. 'Clothes,' he said. 'Charity from the church. We have not worn them. They are clean. For the woman.' He gestured with the stump of a hand towards Christiana.

She leaned forward and untied the cord, unwrapping an almost threadbare woollen bodice and a cloak. Without hesitation she looked up to the man and began dressing. 'I am grateful,' she said. And then as she pulled the warmth of the old cloak around her, she stood and addressed the shadows in the back of the hut beyond the fireplace. 'We are not criminals and have done no wrong. And you help return a mother to her children. I will pray for you all in gratitude. God bless you and may He ease your suffering.' And she crossed herself. Blackstone saw the others do the same and heard what he took to be a murmur of appreciation for her words.

The rain and mist swept in across the plain, diminishing the great walled city as Blackstone and Christiana followed the man outside to where the other leper stood holding the rope halter of an emaciated palfrey. The undernourished horse might have ten or twenty miles left in him if he bore no weight and was not asked to do anything more than a walking pace. Blackstone lifted Christiana up onto the animal's back and took the halter the leper had let drop. Blackstone hesitated, and then extended his hand in thanks, but the leper took a pace backwards and bowed in gratitude for Blackstone's gesture.

'Monsieur, I was once a man of the law, who was accorded dignity and respect. You have already shown your courage and compassion,' the man said, his weakness apparent from his faltering voice. 'There is no need for you to take further risk. Five miles from here is a chapel of sanctuary where the monk cares for travellers. You will be safe there tonight.'

Blackstone led the horse onto the road; the further they could get from the city the better and by the next day he would have them both at the far reach of the river. Then, once they reached the sanctuary of the Norman barons' domains, there would be no pursuit.

Blackstone kissed the silver goddess at his throat. She had thrown her mantle of care about him and in the city he had been lucky, something a fighting man was always grateful for. He had gone into the heart of the whore and rescued his wife from those who would have trapped and killed him, and in so doing had laid to rest the uncertainty of her father's death.

The cold, hard rain became a comfort as it washed him free of his secret.

CHAPTER 20

The day was closing in as the Savage Priest waited on the bridge that linked the Royal Palace to the city. Behind him, isolated from the seething streets, the King and his advisers awaited news of Blackstone's capture. The bureaucracy that plagued the King had stifled the mercenaries' raid on the Half Wheel tavern and by the time the Provost's men had been commanded to do everything that the mercenary leader instructed, the opportunity had been lost. Had those men not interfered a cordon in the streets could have seized Blackstone who, de Marcy believed, must still have been close to the tavern. The Englishman could not have been gone more than a few minutes.

Simon Bucy walked past the palace guards, cursing the fact that he was still expected to deal with this loathsome creature. The Savage Priest's men had infiltrated street after street as had the Paris constables, but Thomas Blackstone had disappeared and every effort was now being made to trap him on this, his only escape route.

'De Marcy! The darkness will be upon us soon,'

he said to the black-cloaked figure who had not acknowledged his presence and whose silence smacked of insolence, placing the President of the Parlement in the position of an underling.

The Savage Priest kept his eyes on the riverbank. There were only so many places from which the woman he once desired could escape. When she first came into Paris he had watched her briefly, keeping his presence hidden as he sought out that which once ensnared him. She was as beautiful as he remembered but he could not recapture the feeling he once had for her. The years had burned away that moment. Now he just wanted her, to do as he liked with her and know that his actions would inflict inconsolable pain on Blackstone.

'The river is his means of evasion. His only way out of the city,' said Bucy. 'You have done everything I've instructed?'

More men had been sent into the city, others stationed along the river, mingling with the merchants and the labourers who brought their barges to the banks. When darkness came torches would be lit and patrols sent out; no one would escape by river. Barges were being searched even now, rough-hewn river men forced to allow the King's men to board their vessels. The city gates were closed; extra guards had been posted on the wall and the Provost's patrols doubled. Thomas Blackstone was trapped.

Bucy walked to each side of the bridge. The Seine, the lifeblood of Paris, was going to bleed the King dry of his victory over Blackstone if the Englishman slipped away by boat. 'I should have known better than to allow you to bring your vileness into Paris,' he said, agitated. 'Your thugs damned near caused a riot and allowed him to escape.'

Gilles de Marcy ignored the accusation. His own frustration was a torment. A blood-lust had not been sated. 'I was so close I could smell the bastard,' he muttered to no one in particular.

'And the woman?' Bucy taunted, hugging his cloak tighter about him. The river's mist and its chill competed with the fearful presence of the man next to him. 'Merciful Christ, Blackstone's wife was with Joanne de Ruymont!'

'Then arrest her.'

'We cannot. You know that. Your men had the woman trapped in the cemetery. In plain sight! And your thugs were so stupid they let her escape.'

'They have been dealt with.'

The simple statement caused Bucy a shiver of revulsion. He banished from his thoughts the image of what this man would do to those who failed him. By now, no doubt, what was left of them was being fought over by street dogs.

'There were reports of a man and woman beyond the north wall,' said the Savage Priest.

'A servant and a labourer. The Provost's men searched. It was a false alarm. Itinerants probably,' said Bucy dismissively.

'The Provost's men searched,' de Marcy repeated, as if the statement beggared belief.

'He will leave Paris by the river. There is no other way for him,' insisted the King's adviser.

'If he's not caught by dawn then he has gone. Slipped away somehow,' said the Savage Priest. 'Loose me and my men and burn every hovel that might offer them shelter, and flay every man, woman and child between here and his manor and put the fear of Christ into all those who protect him.'

'No one is to ride through Norman domains and do anything! Least of all you!' Bucy spat. 'You pig-ignorant beast! You have no idea of what the King plans or what is at stake. It's far more than your desire to take all that Blackstone has or your lust for a woman you've never ravaged.'

Gilles de Marcy turned his gaze on Bucy and saw him shuffle back a half-step. 'What drives a man, my lord, *is* lust. Our King for complete authority and power, you for status and wealth, and me to kill my enemy with a ferocious appetite that turns men's bowels to water when they hear of me. I lust for what Blackstone has and I will tear those he loves from him. What I desire has been denied me because you protect a traitor and your Provost's men got in the way,' the Savage Priest answered. 'I will kill Blackstone but I suspect it will not be tonight.'

He walked away from Bucy towards the river-bank, and then turned.

'Tell the King that Thomas Blackstone has escaped. He'll soon be back in one of his lairs. And

311

when his highness is willing to cause havoc among his enemies, tell him I will lead the slaughter.'

Simon Bucy, his mind plagued by the prospect of failure, watched as the black-cloaked figure reached the far bank and disappeared into the warren of alleyways. He would pray until dawn that Blackstone would be captured, but he prepared himself to tell the King that the opportunity to seize the Englishman and weaken the Norman lords had been lost.

The lit torches on the boats moved through the mist glowing like fireflies, and the river went silently by.

It took several days for them to reach safety. Blackstone kept away from main routes that bore traffic to and from the city and, once they crossed the river – paying the ferryman extra for his silence – they made good time on their journey home. They spent their nights holding each other against the cold, lying beneath makeshift shelters that Blackstone made, eating whatever could be snared. The sense of danger never left them, and it drove them together in a passion that was desperate in its intensity. To have come so close to losing the other gave each of them a hunger that could only be satisfied by almost frantic lovemaking. On a clear, bright day they walked free of the forest, still served faithfully by the old horse, and gazed down across the frost-laden meadow to the riders who called them by name.

Guillaume and half a dozen men had spent days riding beyond the edge of his lord's domain waiting for any news or sight of his master. The squire had taken extra mounts with him to carry Blackstone and Christiana on the final leg of their journey home. There was a raucous welcome from the men, their language tempered out of respect for Christiana. Once their questions were answered about his escape and he had been assured that no horsemen had come near his domain, Blackstone instructed one of the men to guide the swayback home at a walking pace. It deserved a reward of oats and fresh fodder, and it would see out its days in the comfort of Blackstone's stables.

Once home extra guards were posted while the other Norman lords followed Jean de Harcourt's example and sent out patrols that covered their territory in case King John chose to strike at them. But no such attack came and by the time the Norman barons' spies reported back from Paris it was obvious that there would be no incursion against them. King John still needed their support in case of war with Edward, and he was prepared to let Blackstone wriggle off the hook.

Christiana's relief and joy at being safely returned to Agnes and Henry helped assuage her guilt at deserting them to pursue the chance of finding her father. Blackstone trod carefully as he watched the tears shed in private give way to acceptance of his death. It was better, he decided, not to attempt to comfort her by praising the old man's

313

loyalty to his sworn lord and his death in service to the French King. The fact that he had died opposing the English invasion could only sharpen her grief, given that she was married to one of those men who had stormed ashore a decade before. The warning voice in his head told him that to try and talk about a soldier's death might cause a slip of the tongue – an old knight leading his men, lying in ambush, outfoxed by his enemy. Within a few words the truth could easily slip out and within a breath she would be asking how he knew these things.

He stayed silent and waited until she settled back into the security of family life before explaining that the man behind William de Fossat's death and their pursuit in Paris was the same man who had once pursued her. She took the news badly and he regretted telling her, but had he not, then someone else would have spoken of the plot to entrap Blackstone that had been brought about by those incidents from her past.

Over the days that followed he comforted and reassured her and saw her fear turned into a resilience and then anger that such a creature could still cast his shadow across her life. When she and Blackstone married he had cut a silver penny in half as a token of his love for her, with the promise that wherever the two halves might be then so too would they. She wore hers as a necklace and his had been embossed into Wolf Sword's pommel. One morning when she returned from prayer she carried his sword and scabbard from where Guillaume burnished and cleaned his lord's weapons and armour and placed it in her husband's hands.

'You must kill this Savage Priest, Thomas. One day, when you have news of him, seek him out and rid us of him. Show him no mercy and cast him into hell,' she told him.

She had once defied her guardians by marrying Blackstone and he had defied his birth.

They were as one again.

There was no complaint from Christiana when Blackstone rode out with his men to patrol the forest tracks that might lead assassins to their door. Blackstone had sent orders for additional vigilance to Meulon and Guinot and the other commanders of his towns and then when two weeks had passed without incident or warning he allowed his men to stand down from their duties and share time with their families – something he was obliged to do himself. It was a time to be grateful as the mood settled into laughter and joy as the children became more boisterous the closer the time drew to celebrate Henry's birthday.

Blackstone and his son walked through the stables and petted the horses, the boy's excitement heightened by Blackstone allowing him to choose which horse he would ride to Harcourt.

'Henry, will you be ready to recite your poem?' Blackstone asked.

'I will, Father,' he said.

'And your knife is kept clean? The Norman lords will be impressed with such a fine weapon and they'll ask you to show it to them.'

Henry eased the blade from its silver scabbard tucked in his belt and laid it across the palm of his hand.

'That's good. Did Guillaume clean it for you, or did you do it yourself?'

'I did it.'

'Good. Keep it sharp and close to you,' he told his son.

Gratified by his praise, Henry reached out to touch the bastard horse's muzzle, then quickly pulled his hand back, avoiding the snap of its teeth.

'Don't trust so easily,' Blackstone told him. 'A man can turn savage in an instant as well. Be watchful of those you deal with. Some snap because it is their temperament, but it doesn't make them less worthy to be your friend.'

'Like Lord de Fossat? Mother told me you were once enemies.'

'We fought and then we sided together. There was a bond between us. He was a very brave fighter – reckless at times, and he had a bite worse than this one,' he said, meaning the horse.

'Can I come with you when you fight again?' asked Henry. 'Guillaume has been training me and I could serve as his page.'

'There's to be no more fighting this year. I gave

your mother my word. And after Lord de Fossat's death I've no cause to go to war. There's work to be done on the house and in the fields. But we have to think about your training. You're getting older now. Don't you think it's time to leave the books behind? You need to learn to fight before the real thing comes along. And trust me, sooner or later you'll be called on.'

The boy fell silent for a moment and considered his answer. 'I would like to study more because then I can be wise as well as brave,' he answered.

There was no denying that the boy was intelligent, but the concern lingered that his only son was still tied to his mother's skirts and a student's desk.

'I have another birthday present for you,' Blackstone said, wishing, as soon as he had spoken, that he had kept the gift until they had reached Castle de Harcourt and the celebrations, but he wanted the boy to feel closer to him. His own father had been softened by his mother; a tenderness had been imparted and something of that had been passed to Blackstone. Was it possible to keep that feeling intact despite the viciousness of war and the pain of loss? He acknowledged the conflict within himself – his own son would be better educated than him – but he still needed to learn the art of war.

'You must go to another knight to be trained, that's the tradition,' he said, and seeing his son's look of uncertainty, added quickly, 'but I will have you as my page.'

The boy's joy was a gift in itself. 'Father! Thank you!'

Henry embraced Blackstone and then stepped back, embarrassed at his behaviour. Blackstone wanted to drag him back into his arms, but the boy beamed with delight.

'My lord, I will serve you,' he said proudly, and a bit stiffly, as if he were a courtier to a king.

'Yes, well, I'm sure you will, but it will be Master Guillaume who will be your tutor first and foremost. Do as he says. Behave well and learn your skills.'

'I will, Father. I will.'

'And don't mention this to your mother. Not yet. I'll tell her after your birthday celebrations. All right? A secret between us? For a short while at least.'

'If the King declares war on the English, will we join the Norman lords?' the boy asked excitedly.

'There's a time for everything, Henry. And this year we keep ourselves to ourselves. There'll be no fighting here; it's all down south, so we won't be getting involved. Now, I'm going to build a wall for your mother's vegetable plot. We'll take down the wattle fencing and make her a proper garden. Will you help me do that? It'll help to give you some muscle for wielding a sword,' said Blackstone, trying to enthuse the boy.

Before Henry could answer Old Hugh entered the stables and dipped his head. 'Sir Thomas, my lady wishes Master Henry back in the house. His lessons await.'

The boy looked at his father. 'Do I have your permission, Father? I am learning about the great King Charlemagne.'

Refusal was on Blackstone's lips. Henry was an Englishman's son and it was time he learnt about England's great leaders. But who would teach him? His own knowledge was scant beyond that of seeing Edward and the Prince of Wales on the battlefield, and his ignorance kept him mute. He nodded his approval.

Henry ran from the stable, eager for his lesson, and Old Hugh bowed again.

Blackstone watched the hunchback crab his way across the yard. Suspicion had sat within him since before the danger in Paris when he learnt that de Graville, at the heart of the Norman conspiracy, spent a great deal of time there on his knees in prayer. And it was he who had sent his ageing servants, Old Hugh and Beatrix, into Blackstone's service. His sense of mistrust was seeping into his blood like an infected wound.

The smell of the stable and the thought of England triggered a rare memory of his homeland. Of a brother and a sworn lord who had taken them both to war, away from their village and the few acres they owned. He yearned to hear his own language again and the irreverent taunts of common Englishmen, who stood their ground against an overwhelming enemy.

It was a feeling of almost unbearable loss.

He shook it free. There was no future in looking back.

Death had sought him out and he had evaded its clutches yet again. Neither King John nor his assassin would dare strike into the heart of Normandy. Not any time soon. But the day would surely come when the Norman lords played out their conspiracy and terror would sweep across the land. He wanted no part in their plans, but he would wait, and watch, and then seek out and kill the Savage Priest.

PART II

TIDE OF WAR

CHAPTER 21

'Mercy, my lord! We beg you!' cried the boy, going down on one knee before the scar-faced knight who stood over him.

Blackstone's voice addressed the ragtag army that now yielded. 'Your surrender comes too late. You were given the opportunity before the battle, but now I'll slaughter everyone. Even the children and dogs will die. And then I will destroy your defences so that no one may ever raise an army and challenge me again. Those are the rules of war.' Blackstone glanced at his squire at his side. 'What do you say, Guillaume? Shall we hang them or have them beheaded?' he asked.

'I think they have learnt their lesson in being defeated at your hands, Sir Thomas,' Guillaume Bourdin replied, sheathing his sword.

Blackstone looked back to the expectant faces. 'You always urge me to show leniency. Why shouldn't I finish these wretched traitors off?' He walked across to the boy who had begged for mercy. 'Give me your sword.'

The boy hesitated.

'The sword or your life,' Blackstone threatened.

He took the proffered weapon. 'Now it is forfeit. You will have to earn the right to have it returned.'

'How will I do that, Father?'

'By being a better soldier. You and the others could have outflanked Guillaume and me when we went through the western gate. We're outnumbered twelve to one. You're lucky it's your birthday party, Henry, or we would have had you and your miserable army thrown to the dogs.' Blackstone smiled and touched his son's face. 'Now, you and the others run down to the stream and see if you can build a bridge across it.'

'Will I get my sword back?' Henry Blackstone asked his father.

'You build the bridge and you'll need this fine wooden sword to fight the enemy. Off with you. Go on!' Henry and his dozen friends who had fought the losing battle ran off.

From within Castle de Harcourt's walls voices raised in anger echoed across the courtyard. Blackstone turned towards the great hall.

'Have Marcel keep an eye on them, he's better with the children than any of us,' he told Guillaume. 'I don't want to face his mother's wrath if he falls in the moat.'

As Blackstone moved into the castle his daughter ran to him. He scooped her up. 'Agnes, where's your mother?'

Before the child could answer, Christiana appeared and took the girl from his arms.

'Thomas, do something,' she said.

'About what?'

'The Countess and Sir Godfrey are arguing with Jean and the others.' The little girl squirmed in her arms. 'Agnes, go and find the other girls,' Christiana ordered.

'Mama, Father promised'

'Don't argue. Go.'

Blackstone's gut wrenched. Had Blanche finally learnt of her young cousin being killed? If she had it would tear the Harcourt family apart. He went down on one knee, and, as she often did, the child traced the scar that ran from his hairline down across his face and disappeared below his jaw into his tunic.

'I have to talk to Uncle Jean. I won't be long,' he said tenderly and kissed her head.

'You've been with Henry all day,' she said, knowing it was her brother's day to have the full attention of her father.

'And you know why, don't you?' Christiana said. Agnes nodded.

'Then kiss your papa and tell him that you love him and whisper that you will wait like a good daughter. And then I will tell you a story as I promised. Is that agreed?'

She nodded, hugged Blackstone, kissed his mutilated face and whispered into his ear.

Agnes ran back into the shadowed passages calling for her friends.

'You spoil her,' Christiana said, though not

disapprovingly. 'Now go and soothe your friends' tempers.'

Blackstone sighed, allowed her to kiss his cheek, and pushed open the doors into the great hall.

Sparks flew from the log pushed into the massive fireplace by Sir Godfrey de Harcourt's boot. 'It's foolish! You take up this invitation by the Dauphin and they have you at their mercy!' the lame knight shouted at his nephew.

Blanche de Harcourt and the half-dozen nobles in the room turned as Blackstone closed the doors behind him. He looked at their faces and instinctively knew that this argument was nothing to do with a tragic death that happened weeks earlier. The Normans were courting the King's son again.

'Thomas! Talk some sense into his piss-pot head!' Sir Godfrey begged.

'We came here to celebrate my son's birthday. I'm not the one to interfere in politics. I don't even know what's happening,' Blackstone answered.

'In God's name you don't!' Sir Godfrey said, worrying the fire again. 'You're as much a part of this household as I am! And your friend here is taking up an invitation to dine with that sallow-faced half-wit of a King's son. At Rouen! They'll slam the city gates closed on him. It's a damned trap if ever I heard of one.'

Blanche de Harcourt's hand rested on her husband's arm. 'Jean, Godfrey is right. You cannot trust the King, you know that.'

'The King won't be there,' Guy de Ruymont said. 'We will be the Dauphin's guests and have his protection. He is the Duke of Normandy and even the King would not violate his son's given word for our protection.'

Blackstone circled the men, watching their faces, noting their determination to sweep aside uncertainty and anxiety. They were gambling on winning the crown of France. To lose meant everything would be forfeit.

'Guy, how many times have you sat at my table and told me that the King's shadow falls across everyone? Have you forgotten so quickly how William was slain and how I was nearly trapped when his men tricked Joanne? Your wife is no fool but she was duped and Christiana used as bait for me. The King has raised his game. Only a week ago he had a Paris merchant butchered for speaking his mind to friends about the monarchy!' said Blackstone, trying to shock the determined men into reality. 'Hanged on a meat-hook and left to die in agony.'

'Jean, listen to Thomas,' Sir Godfrey urged his nephew.

'No. Guy's right,' Jean answered. 'I will be under the Dauphin's roof and have his protection. He needs us, don't forget that. If Normandy pledges him its loyalty and our plans work then he'll become King.' Jean spoke directly to Blackstone, as if urging his friend to support him. 'It's the opportunity we've been looking for.'

Blackstone addressed the conspirators. 'Do you think the King's spies haven't already told him? Jean, listen to Blanche and your uncle. It's a trap,' he said.

Jean de Harcourt paced the room, the weight of opinion threatening his desire to finally dislodge the King of France and create unfettered autonomy for Normandy and an escape from the crippling taxes being imposed on the nobles. 'We would have the support of the Pope. Even the Church is to be taxed,' said Guy de Ruymont.

'And the Prince of Wales raids throughout the south; he has two thousand English and Gascons. Once John raises his army with these new taxes it will be too late. We should make our move now,' Jean de Harcourt urged.

A heavy-set man pushed himself from the fireside bench.

'Thomas? You could act as envoy to King Edward. If he gives you a firm commitment to invade we can do the rest.'

'My Lord de Graville, you overestimate my influence,' Blackstone answered warily, still suspicious of how much time the older man spent in Paris.

De Graville took a step towards him. 'You command more than respect, Thomas, there are what . . . two hundred-odd men of yours scattered across the countryside who would rally to your call?'

The old Norman was right. Blackstone was in

a unique position, not least because those in the great hall had protected him. Itinerant soldiers – English, Germans and Gascons; men who had fought the great battles and needed a leader who could pay for their fighting skills – had followed the English knight whose notoriety often caused opponents to yield without engaging in battle.

Blackstone made no reply. The conspirators needed as many fighting men as they could muster but to become involved in French conspiracies and politics was to walk in a maze of intrigue, betrayal and murder. It was a sport for nobles, not a fighting man.

One of the dogs defecated onto the rush-strewn floor, and yelped when another of the nobles kicked it away. Blanche threw a handful of powder into the flames, a mixture of sulphur, arsenic and antimony, used during the great pestilence against rat fleas as well as for its aroma, to veil the stench.

'Edward *will* invade. Street criers in London have brought in five hundred archers. The English nobles have committed to Edward. This situation is one he's always dreamed of, an attack from the north *and* the south. And this time he will help Navarre become the power behind the Crown,' said de Mainemares, the noble who had kicked the dog. 'Charles of Navarre remains a festering wound in King John's side.'

De Graville lowered his voice, as if the whisper lessened his guilt of conspiracy. 'France's strength will come from the English King's invasion,' he said. 'The Dauphin is a boy. He's weak and debt-ridden.'

'And what then?' Blackstone asked. 'You'll murder him as well as his father? This is more than a King against a King. It's family business. King Edward wants to secure the greatest amount of territory for his children as much as King John wishes to keep France secure for his. It's what we all do. We fight and take what we can for ourselves so that our children have a future.' Blackstone pulled open the heavy chestnut doors. 'I'm going home. Thank you for your hospitality, Blanche. I believe that what my Lord de Mainemares says is true: Edward will invade. But to place your lives under the protection of the Dauphin is foolish. You underestimate your enemy. King John is no fool. He'll have you where he wants you.'

A conspiracy needed guile and sworn secrecy and the Norman barons had the one but not the other. Secrets leaked out like whey through a cheesemaker's cloth.

Jean de Harcourt strode angrily towards him as Blackstone faced him.

'You sell your sword, Thomas!' de Harcourt said.

For a moment Blackstone allowed the Count's grip to stay on his arm. 'And I always choose the paymaster,' he said quietly, and then easily loosened his closest friend's grip.

'Jean!' Sir Godfrey called. 'Thomas is his own man. Always has been.' He limped to the doorway and extended his hand. Blackstone grasped it. 'You were a self-willed and insolent bastard of an archer, Thomas – more than most – but your sword has served this family and your King. You're not a part of this. Go in peace with Christiana and the children. You'll hear no more from us on this matter. I'll go to King Edward. I've sworn my fealty once; I'll do it again. And this time we will give him Normandy and he will give us the France we need.'

The heavy doors closed behind Blackstone, their sullen echo thudding into his heart. It felt as though his friend had been entombed.

It was bad enough that Blackstone and Jean de Harcourt had parted in ill temper; when he gathered his family to return home, a shame-faced Henry stood with Guillaume and confessed to losing his treasured knife.

'You don't deserve the honour!' Blackstone thundered. 'You need to learn when privilege is bestowed on you! You searched the riverbed?' The answer was already obvious when he looked at the boy's wet clothing.

'I did, Father, diligently.'

'But you weren't damned well diligent enough to keep from losing it. Agnes cares more for her cloth doll than you do for a gift of great value. It shames the memory of the brave man who wore it and gave up his life.' He turned away with a dismissive gesture. 'You ride behind the wagon.

Master Guillaume is your squire; he'll suggest a suitable penance.'

As the wagon carrying Christiana and Agnes rocked along the rutted track Christiana stayed silent. A boy's duty would always be harsher than that of a girl's. Guillaume rode with Henry at his side on a gelded palfrey.

'Father's still quiet,' Henry said. 'I've really angered him.'

'He's worried about my Lord de Harcourt. These are dangerous times, Master Henry,' said Guillaume.

'Is he worried about us?'

'Of course. He's your father.'

'Should I ride with Mother and Agnes, do you think?'

'Men-at-arms don't ride in wagons. I've told you that before.'

'Or on a mare,' Henry said, remembering.

'Or on a mare,' Guillaume answered. Henry fell silent because men-at-arms did not chatter like girls either. He hoped his father's anger and concern would settle by the time they reached home.

It was a day's travel with the wagon, though this time it seemed even slower and more ponderous than usual, which had more to do with Blackstone's mood than the well-travelled road. He had always felt the simple joy of going home, to lazy smoke from the cooking fires drifting above the broad expanse of the valley and wooded hills that contrasted with the high, shadowed walls of Harcourt. But this time he could not dispel the incessant voice urging him to go back and do more to convince Jean not to travel to Rouen for the planned meeting with the King's son.

As they turned towards the hamlet where his villagers went about their work, they stopped whatever they were doing and bowed their heads in honour of their lord who passed by.

They and their master could not know on that cold morning in late March as they welcomed Sir Thomas Blackstone home, that violence more savage than anything they had thought possible would soon descend upon them.

The rider appeared four days later.

Old Hugh took the mud-splattered man from Castle de Harcourt to his mistress and she in turn called Blackstone.

'Marcel?'

'My lord.'

'You're soaked. No, no, don't stand. Stay seated at the fire.'

The old man gratefully accepted Blackstone's charity to stay on the fireside stool, but he seemed close to tears.

'What's wrong?' Blackstone asked Christiana.

'The nobles went to Rouen and Blanche has gone after them. She's armed herself, she's convinced Jean is going to be killed,' she told him.

'Why would the Dauphin kill Jean? Whatever

they're planning they're in it together,' Blackstone said.

Christiana turned to the old man. 'Tell Sir Thomas what happened.'

'A messenger arrived late last night, after my Lord de Harcourt had left for Rouen. I overheard what it was not my privilege to hear. Two weeks ago the King was to attend a wedding outside of Paris, but a plot was discovered to capture and imprison him and the Dauphin. The King changed his plans and evaded his attackers.'

'Then your master would have known of this,' Blackstone said.

The old man shook his head. 'Those who plotted do not know they were betrayed, and my master was not involved. It was the King's son-in-law who planned it.'

'Navarre would kill to get the crown,' Blackstone said. 'He's the one who's convinced Jean and the others. Who warned the King?'

'My lady believes it was one of the Count's friends,' the old man answered.

Blackstone felt the alarm squeeze his chest. If Jean had been betrayed then it was by one of the men, all friends, in the great hall that day.

'Did she take anyone with her? Soldiers? A squire?' Blackstone asked the steward.

'No, my lord,' the servant said. 'She went alone. I didn't know what to do.'

'What about Sir Godfrey?' Blackstone asked.

'To England,' the servant replied.

Blackstone refrained from allowing his irritation at Blanche's action to show. The old man had been a servant since childhood at Castle de Harcourt. Blackstone knew him as a trusted retainer, a man who had helped ease his own broken body in his first faltering steps to recovery. He nodded at the servant. 'You were correct in coming to me. Go to the kitchen and tell Beatrix to feed you and that you are to sleep near the fire. Tomorrow, return to Harcourt and wait for news from me or Guillaume.'

The steward bowed and turned away.

'Thomas, you have to go after her,' Christiana said.

'And do what? If she's so determined to interfere in her husband's affairs, what right do I have to stop her? I don't want to get caught up in their plans. My duty is to you and the children and my people here.'

'Thomas! She cared for you!'

'*You* cared for me!' he shouted. It was a mess, a god-awful dung heap of a mess and he was being dragged into it.

'Help them, Thomas. She'll fight tooth and claw to stop Jean from being hurt or dishonoured. They gave us shelter when we were both abandoned in the world.'

'As a favour to the King of England!'

'Shame on you! They weren't duty-bound to offer their friendship! Nor was Jean to accept you as a man-at-arms. Their obligation ended when you were strong enough to leave their household. Blanche will kill any man who tries to hurt Jean, just as I would for you.'

Blackstone felt her stinging rebuke. No matter how much he argued to the contrary, his wife's love for him would settle any dispute. It was easier to lay siege to a fortified town than scale the heights of her determination.

Her voice softened. 'Blanche is my lady and my friend. Help her, Thomas. For me. She tried to stop me going to Paris.' She leaned into his chest. Blackstone kissed her hair.

'If my men saw how easily I yielded to you, I'd have a mutiny on my hands,' he said.

'I didn't have to convince you. I could read your thoughts all the way home. You just needed to know it was all right to leave me and the children. And your men would never dare question your decisions.'

'Unlike my wife,' he said.

'They don't know the Thomas Blackstone that I know,' she answered, bravely ignoring the fear that lodged in her heart whenever he left her to confront danger.

In the hours before first light Guillaume saddled his master's horse and fastened his shield and Wolf Sword to the pommel. The younger man's loyalty and fighting skills had been proven over the years at Blackstone's side and his master had no hesitation in leaving the safety of his family in the squire's keeping.

'You'll stay here for a day and a night,' Blackstone told him. 'If I'm not back by then, or you have not heard from Castle de Harcourt, you will take Christiana and the children down to Chaulion and stay behind the walls. Tell Guinot to hold against any attack. Have men on the road between here and Harcourt and others on the road to Rouen. If the King sends armed men on either of these roads it will mean I've run into trouble. Escape while you can. He won't harm the people here. Tell them to deny me and swear their allegiance to him. Make them understand that the King will not harm his subjects, especially if they have been under threat from a war lord like me.'

'They won't turn their backs on you, Sir Thomas,' Guillaume said.

'They'll have to. Those are my orders,' Blackstone said.

Blackstone left his horse outside the city walls in the care of a blacksmith known to him, so that the great beast and his coat of arms would not raise curiosity or attract unwanted attention. One of the stalls held Blanche's chestnut mare. She was here, then, and had taken the same precaution as him.

Blackstone had walked through Rouen's narrow streets years before when Jean de Harcourt had taken him into the great castle to see for himself the Duchy of Normandy's seat of power. Now that the King's son had been given that title and responsibility for the region, in the hope of bringing the Norman barons and landowners under the King's control and making them more receptive to the increase in salt and hearth taxes, there were more soldiers than Blackstone had seen before. They moved through the alleyways and market stalls making random checks and searches of people in the streets. When Blackstone was an English archer riding with Sir Gilbert and Godfrey de Harcourt, they had gazed down onto the city's battlements and seen the banners of the French army and its nobility that had gathered days before the battle at Crécy. It had always been a wonder to him how so many thousands of men could be accommodated within the confines of the city's walls. Now as he walked the labyrinthine streets it was not difficult to imagine men quartered in every house and stinking alleyway. The streets were wide enough for two carts to pass side by side, but the throngs of people moved laboriously, shuffling between street and alley as overburdened pack donkeys were whipped and cajoled, jostling for passage past street vendors and their trays. Men and women, bent double from the loads of firewood and charcoal on their backs, shouted obscenities to those moving too slowly. The stench of urine and excrement wafted from narrow side streets where men and women squatted to relieve themselves. The cacophony of voices rose and fell, competing with the tavern signs clanging in the wind that funnelled into the constricted streets.

Blackstone's mail and surcoat were concealed beneath his cloak, and he kept its cowl pulled over his scarred face. It was not likely that common men and women in the streets of the great Norman capital would recognize him, but he did not wish to risk drawing the attention of the soldiers. Only when he reached the entrance of the great castle and the guards that stood before them did he show his face.

'I have a message for the Countess de Harcourt et Ponthieu. Is she here?'

The men did not step aside in deference to his rank.

'No one's allowed inside. And there's no woman come through these doors, whether it's a countess or a whore.' The soldiers grinned, their manner almost a taunt to Blackstone. The guard's impertinence signalled that the Dauphin's soldiers carried their lord's authority in this troublesome duchy. Perhaps they would welcome a challenge so that a local knight could be thrown into the dungeon. Anything to teach the Normans a lesson, and in their ignorance they took him to be Norman. Blackstone knew that confrontation would serve no purpose.

'Then you will have your captain take my message to the Count himself,' Blackstone said.

'I doubt it. The Dauphin is hosting a banquet in the great hall. The mayor's there, and the nobles; not even the captain is allowed to disturb them. Best be on your way, sir knight. It's by invitation only,' the man sneered.

Blackstone turned away. He had the information he needed; now all he had to do was to find a way into the great hall.

The courtyard heaved with horses – tethered, fed and groomed by stablehands – who cared little about a nobleman striding across their yard. Blackstone recognized Jean's horse. He went through the stables, climbed over the baled hay and onto the low wall that separated the courtyard from the kitchens. The yard on the other side of the wall was closed off by a heavy gate; guards would be posted on the street side, but the yard itself was empty except for two supply carts loaded with barrels and caged poultry and animals for slaughter. He dropped down and ran up the steps into the steam and heat of the castle's kitchen. Servants and cooks scurried back and forth as platters of food were ferried from the griddles and fires where carcasses were turned and basted on spits. A steward shouted commands at children who carried the trays of food through a passage doorway. The man looked startled when he saw Blackstone, unsettled by the scar, unable to take his eyes from it.

'My lord?'

'Is everything under control? I am the Dauphin's

taster,' Blackstone said, looking quickly at a servant using iron hooks to haul boiled meat from a cauldron.

'T-t-taster?' the man stuttered in confusion.

'You were not expecting me?'

'No, I—'

Blackstone grabbed a knife and quickly stabbed the meat. Blood tipped the blade and Blackstone wiped it clean across the distressed man's chest. 'It must fall from the bone. And the Dauphin will not tolerate gristle. You were told that?'

The steward momentarily lost his authority in the kitchen. 'I was not given specific instructions, but—'

'You have them now,' Blackstone interrupted.

The steward rebuked the servant. 'Put it back! Boil it longer!'

By the time he turned to ingratiate himself with the scarred knight, he saw only Blackstone's cloak disappearing into the darkened passage. Relief from further interrogation eased any uncertainty he might have felt about how the man had gained access from the gated yard.

Servants moved aside as Blackstone strode along the dimly lit passage. Voices could be heard from the great hall behind the wood-panelled wall. There was no way for him to see into the room unless he entered through the main double doors, one of which was open for serving food and which afforded him a glimpse of the hunched shoulders of men eating from heaped platters. Further along, the passage steps led down from the flagstone floor for two rises, but then, before they descended further, another staircase turned and spiralled up. The twenty-eight twisting steps took him across a darkened passageway and then out to an empty minstrels' gallery. Below him thirty or so ermine-robed barons and city officials were gathered. Two long trestle tables, their white cloths covered with platters of food, were set along two sides of the room connected at one end by a dais for the main table. The sallow-faced eighteen-year-old Dauphin, with weasel eyes and a narrow, pinched nose above thin lips, was flanked by Jean de Harcourt and another man who, by the quality of his clothing and jewellery, Blackstone took to be Charles of Navarre. There was no sign of Blanche. Only Sir Godfrey was absent from the same men who had argued their case at Castle de Harcourt and were now seated at the Dauphin's table. The future power of Normandy and France ate and drank as if the kingdom was already theirs.

Which of these men had betrayed his friend, Jean de Harcourt? And if this was a trap, were the Savage Priest and his killers lying in wait?

CHAPTER 22

At first light that same morning, Guillaume killed Marcel, the Harcourts' trusted servant.

Fear had driven the old man away from the comfort and food the kitchen offered but Guillaume caught up with him two miles from the village. As the servant heard the hoof beats behind him he twisted in the saddle. His pursuer saw the etched panic on his face. The man's nag had an ungainly gait, and as Marcel had turned, the horse stumbled from the shifting of his weight. The old man tumbled from the saddle and fell heavily, the wind knocked out of him. By the time he regained his breath Guillaume stood over him. Marcel scrambled to his knees, arms raised in supplication to the man he had known since he was a boy given sanctuary by Countess Blanche, who hid him in the passageway with his wounded master. Now the young squire waited, sword in hand, his dispassionate gaze signalling impending violence.

'No servant runs from a warm hearth and food. You were given sanctuary. Speak to me, Marcel.

How much do you really know of what has happened at Harcourt?' Guillaume said quietly.

Words failed the old man. His lungs fought for air, his eyes clung to the face of Sir Thomas's young warrior. The boy whose master he had once nursed with care and devotion. To beg was not beneath his dignity; he had none. To plead years of loyalty and faithful service might save him. He sobbed and told Guillaume everything.

Guillaume touched the servant's head. 'I'll spare you,' he said quietly.

The old man, who only days before had watched over Blackstone's son playing at the river, bowed his head in gratitude.

Mercy was allowing the old man to believe he was being spared. Guillaume drove the sword down through Marcel's spine.

He wiped the blade on the servant's tunic and turned back to where Christiana and the children would still be sleeping, unaware of the betrayal or of the violence soon to befall them.

The King had planned his incursion well. Had he arrived in the streets of Rouen the packed thorough-fares would be alerted and de Harcourt and the others might have escaped. King John's determination to root out the malcontents was the first step towards bringing Normandy to heel. Secrecy was a rare commodity in these times, which was why he had spent the previous night in a village near the city. The King and his men had entered

Rouen's great castle from a cellar door left open by one of the Norman knights who had betrayed the rebels' cause.

Blackstone heard a muted cry of alarm from the passageways below. He took a stride to the edge of the gallery, ready to shout his warning, but it was too late – armoured men scuffed their way from the lower staircase into the great hall.

Blackstone stepped back a pace. The soldiers were accompanied by a marshal of France and the King himself, who wore armour and helmet as if ready for battle. More soldiers swarmed into the room and the doors slammed shut as servants were herded and beaten into other rooms.

'Stay where you are! Anyone who moves from the King's presence will die!' the marshal commanded the nobles. The King reached across the table and grabbed Charles of Navarre by his tunic and threw him against the wall. It looked as though the King was about to kill his son-in-law. Blackstone could see the terror in Charles's eyes as he stumbled back. His squire pulled a knife and pressed it into the King's chest. Even Jean de Harcourt looked shocked at the direct assault on the King. King John stood his ground and calmly commanded his men to disarm the traitorous squire. Within seconds soldiers had brutally struck him to the ground and his breaking arm could be heard even from where Blackstone stood, still concealed, his back pressed against the wall.

The Dauphin tried to stand up to his father. 'My lord, I beg you, do not inflict violence on these men, they are my guests. They are under my protection. This is my honour you trample on.'

King John pointed at Charles of Navarre. 'My treacherous cousin, the man who married into my family and who wishes to take my crown, conspired with these men' – he gestured to the shocked faces of the men from the Castle de Harcourt – 'to have me killed. Do you think they would let you rule? Are you such an ass that you could not see their scheme? You're my son! Behave like a king even though you cannot think like one!'

Blackstone watched the Dauphin. The boy's face drained of what little colour it had. He tried to speak but the words choked in his throat.

'Charles of Navarre, you are to be imprisoned. These men are to die. Take them away,' the King ordered.

The conspirators were roughly manhandled, but Jean de Harcourt did not go quietly.

'We have a right to a trial,' he demanded. 'You kill us without one and every Norman will rise up against you. The English will be welcomed by your enemies because you show yourself to be impulsive and unjust. You are not fit to rule!'

A soldier clubbed him to his knees, and as they dragged him to his feet his face turned upwards and he saw Blackstone draw his sword. His friend was going to try and save him. The men's eyes locked for a moment. De Harcourt shook his head.

His lips silently formed the word *Blanche*. The room was cleared, some men being dragged away and others herded into side passages and rooms so the King could determine the degree of their involvement in the conspiracy. Men's voices tumbled through the narrow passageways as others' cried out in panic and pain. The marshal bellowed the King's orders and Blackstone heard a surge of movement in the corridors below.

'Close the city gates! A curfew is declared!'

Blackstone could not escape by the same route that he had entered, and the main entrance would be heavily guarded by the King's soldiers. He moved cautiously down the staircase but as he reached the cross-passageway the darkness shifted. He felt the air move as the attacker's exertion expelled breath. Blackstone stepped aside and raised an arm in defence as a knife cut across his cloak and scraped against his mail. The dagger clattered away as his weight parried the blow, throwing the assassin off balance. Blackstone grappled in the darkness. His attacker was smaller, lithe, twisting like a coiled snake, and as silent, but Blackstone threw him down and went in for the kill, his own knife drawn, ready to plunge into the unguarded throat beneath his grip. The strangled whisper for mercy came a breath before the subtle fragrance of crushed lavender touched his senses.

Blanche! Fear cut through him like steel. He had been a moment away from killing her. He dragged her clear of the passage and onto the gallery. Blanche de Harcourt wore a breastplate beneath her cloak, a velvet cap had fallen in the tussle and a trickle of blood ran down her forehead from where Blackstone had slammed her into the wall. Her bruised cheekbone and scraped skin were caked with grime. He held her until her eyes opened. Her alarm quickly gave way to uncertainty.

'Thomas?' she whispered.

Strident voices carried from below as men were ordered to move here and there. He placed a finger on her lips, then made sure she was clear-headed enough to understand.

'How did you get here?' he asked.

'The council called for their squires before the Dauphin went into the great hall for the banquet. I came in with them and hid myself. Why are you here?'

'Marcel came to us.'

She hesitated. Fear still swept through the castle as men's voices carried along the passageways. Armour and mail rattled against the narrow stone walls and torchlight flickered as shadowy figures moved to seize anyone suspected of conspiring against the King.

'There's a way out at the bottom of the staircase,' Blackstone told her.

She pushed away from him. 'No!'

Her determination to save her husband could betray them both. Blackstone spoke gently, trying to ease her anger. 'Jean and the others are lost. The King will take them to Paris. There were more than a hundred men with him in the hall, there'll be even more outside.'

The threat of discovery forced her voice into a whisper. 'You would abandon him?'

'I came here to save you, Blanche. I saw Jean when they arrested him. He looked right at me and he said one word, and that was your name.'

'Then I'll go myself. I'll find men who will help me rescue him.'

'I'll follow them to Paris, but you have to return to Harcourt. The King will sweep up everyone connected with this mess. He'll take your children and seize the castle. You have to go back now. Guillaume will take you south. There's no time to lose.'

He watched as the reality of the situation seeped into her thoughts. Blanche de Harcourt was about to lose everything except her own inherited title.

'The King won't dare condemn Jean and the others without a trial. It would turn so many against him. His own councils would oppose it. There's still time,' she said hopefully.

'I'll do what I can,' he said, knowing there would be no trial, only summary execution.

Despite the desperate situation, Blanche de Harcourt did not show her fear. 'How do we get out?' she said.

With Blanche's hand on his shoulder Blackstone stepped down into the darkness, waited as the cross-passage fell silent, and within fifteen careful paces saw light showing around a planked door. He yanked the cast-iron handle and they stepped into the lush wetness of meadow. They were outside the city walls and, within the hour, back to the blacksmith where he and Blanche had left their horses.

'Ride hard and take anything of value. You'll need money. Tell Guillaume not to wait. There's no time. He knows where to take you,' Blackstone told her.

'But you're not telling me where, Thomas,' she said.

Blackstone said nothing. She understood. She climbed into the saddle.

'In case I'm captured I won't be able to betray them. Your family needs my ignorance. I would do the same.'

'Only until you get to Christiana. You know that Guillaume values your life more than his own. Take the forest track. It's less travelled,' he said.

She tightened the reins, holding back the horse. 'I will raise a thousand men of my own and make this King wish he had never laid a hand on my lord and husband. If they kill Jean promise me you will avenge him,' she said desperately. 'Swear to me!' she insisted. 'Your word!'

'My word,' Blackstone said and slapped the horse's rump with his gauntlet.

The situation was hopeless. He hawked and spat and watched Blanche's horse kick up turf as it

galloped away. A part of him craved the companionship of his long-dead brother and the men he
served with at Crécy, in a time when shared fear
made him braver, when life was simpler and
others took the decisions that committed men to
kill or be killed. But at that moment, watching
the cold mist cling to the treetops he accepted
that his was now a solitary life of leadership. The
actions of others had placed the King of France
firmly against him. His would be guilt by
association.

'I need another three horses,' he said to the man
shovelling dung from the stalls.

'I've only got swayback rounceys, my lord,
nothing worthy. Meat is what I was keeping them
for.'

Blackstone spilled coins into the man's grimy
hands. 'Buy yourself mutton instead.'

Four men stood caged in the jolting cart that
laboured along the Abbeville road on the way to
Paris. Stripped of warm clothing and clad only in
their linen shirts, Jean de Harcourt, de Graville,
Colin Doublet – Navarre's squire, who had threatened the King – and de Mainemares endured the
misery of the King's pleasure. The cold air humiliated the men further, their shivering unmistakable
as their guards taunted them, sneering that they
trembled from fear. The gibbet, where common
criminals were executed, lay a short distance from
the city's walls. A peasant, his wrists chained like

those prisoners in the cart, was forced to stumble alongside on the uneven road, his flesh chafed and bleeding from the tug on his manacles. Lord de Graville's face was ash-grey. He was a ringleader but he was not the traitor Blackstone had thought him to be.

Blackstone eased his horse slowly through the forest, shadowing the King's retinue. The thick leaf mould muffled the sound of his progress as the column moved along the route towards Abbeville, the road along which King John's father had retreated when English archers had slaughtered his army and made history for themselves. Perhaps it was the memory of this dishonour that made King John stop at the turn of the road on the heights above Rouen.

'De Ruymont. Here!' Blackstone heard him command. Realization knifed into Blackstone's chest as the Norman lord spurred his horse forward to the front of the column. Disbelief held a heartbeat and then anger set it free. Guy de Ruymont, whom both de Harcourt and Thomas Blackstone called friend, was the traitor.

The marshal gestured the soldiers to release the peasant. 'You were condemned to hang for murder, but you will be pardoned for the duty you will perform.'

The man bowed and his chains were released. One of the soldiers handed him a falchion, a curved short sword, little more than a lengthened billhook and favoured by common soldier and man-at-arms for close-quarter battle. It was a hacking blade.

The condemned men were dragged from the cart. Doublet fought despite his broken arm, but the guards heaved him screaming in agony onto the ground where he wept pitifully. Ignoring his injury, soldiers took hold of the chains attached to his wrists and pulled them wide.

'Your bodies will be hung by these chains until they rot. Your heads will be impaled on pikes so that every person passing this place will know of your treachery,' the marshal told the condemned men. 'Get to it, you scum!' he ordered the peasant.

The amateur executioner hacked at the writhing Doublet. After three or four vicious yet clumsy blows the head fell into the grass. The sickening act of butchery tore at the condemned men's courage.

De Mainemares was next. He could barely walk; incoherent prayer spluttered from his lips. The terror finally took his legs from under him, but the soldiers spread him across a fallen tree stump and the falchion fell as if wielded by a hedge-layer attacking a sapling.

Blackstone knew he could do nothing to save his friend, but he readied the horses as he saw Jean kneel in the mud and pray.

De Graville cried for mercy. 'Sire! I beg you! It was Navarre who wanted you dead! We wanted only a fair hearing with my lord the Dauphin. No harm was planned. None.'

His cries were ignored as soldiers dragged him to the field. 'A priest, sire! At least let us have the sacrament of penance,' pleaded the Norman, bereft of a confessor.

The blood-splattered executioner went to work on the man's neck. De Graville grunted as the bone took the blade's bite, but the muscles hardened from years of warfare yielded less easily. The peasant swore and sweated until the head fell.

Jean de Harcourt got to his feet. The tremor had left him. 'Guy de Ruymont! You were a trusted friend and God will not forgive you for what you have done to us all!'

They began to drag de Harcourt to the blood-soaked grass. De Ruymont looked away.

'Look at him!' the King commanded. 'You betrayed him as surely as you condemn his wife and his children.'

The King's words struck de Harcourt. He surged against his captors. 'Sire!' de Harcourt cried. 'My family are innocent of my crime.'

'There will be no mercy for those you cherish. It will all end here, today,' the King replied, and pushed his baton beneath de Ruymont's chin. 'Watch him die! Or I will forget our agreement and have you butchered with the others!'

Guy de Ruymont had no choice but to watch his friend being dragged away, arms stretched by the chains, and then pulled to his knees.

In the forest's shadows Blackstone struck his sword blade across the horses' rumps. The cut to each was superficial but they whinnied in panic and their terror alarmed the soldiers as they tore through the undergrowth.

'Stand to!' the marshal cried. 'The King!' A body of knights and squires quickly formed around King John. The moments of uncertainty gave Blackstone his chance as the bolting horses broke cover and careered towards the column, scaring their mounts.

Confusion gripped the men as a figure emerged at full gallop from the clinging mist. An open helmet exposed his scarred face, and a blood-red shield bore the device of a gauntlet gripping a sword. The King heard his marshal swear in recognition; then he shielded his lord's body from the attacker as Blackstone silently bore down on the startled men.

He had guessed the instinctive reaction of those closest to the King, and his charge angled across the field, bypassing the bodyguard. Changing direction, he pulled up the horse a hundred paces away and faced his friend as men rode from the ranks to attack him, infantry at their heels. The executioner and the men holding Jean de Harcourt froze in uncertainty. His friend had no chance of escaping death, but he would die knowing two things.

'She's safe!' Blackstone said clearly, looking directly at the condemned man, and saw the understanding on Jean's face. 'And your family are under my protection!'

Jean de Harcourt's eyes spilled tears. Blackstone's stature on the wild horse, controlling its power beneath him as men-at-arms galloped and foot soldiers ran to attack him, proclaimed his fearless contempt for them.

When the armed men were sixty paces away, Blackstone nodded a final farewell to his friend and kissed Wolf Sword's blade in salute.

'God is with you, Thomas!' de Harcourt cried out. And then laughed as Blackstone called out to the King, boxed in by the marshal and his knights.

'You're a craven bastard of a king! Dog shit sweetens the air better than your presence on this field of cruel injustice. Know this, John of Valois, I am Sir Thomas Blackstone, I slaughtered your army at Crécy, I seized your towns in Normandy and Gascony, and I will stand at King Edward's side and see you defeated. You are my enemy. I will come for you for the harm you have done this day.'

Then his knee pressed the stallion's flank, turning it directly into the advancing men, arcing Wolf Sword down in slashing blows that split helmets and skulls. Spears jabbed but his shield took the low-angled thrusts and the horse's iron-shod hooves trampled the attackers. He had drawn the men from the column, a feint to shatter the line. The horse turned again and within a dozen strides bore down on Guy de Ruymont. Blackstone's eyes held those of the terrified man.

'Mercy, Thomas. My family . . .' he said helplessly.

Without remorse, and ignoring the momentary image of the man's children playing with his own, he sliced the blade across de Ruymont's throat, severing head from body. The torso plumed blood, its hands still gripping the horse's reins, staying upright long enough for the horse to gallop wildly into the flanks of the men protecting their King.

And long enough for Blackstone to raise the sword above his head in a final farewell towards Jean de Harcourt. The executioner's blade fell onto his friend's neck as the men-at-arms gave chase, but Blackstone was already beyond their reach, galloping across the open meadow known as the Field of Mercy.

Blackstone rode hard towards home until darkness smothered the forest track. There would be no pursuit or likelihood of ambush until morning. And then he and Christiana and the children would run for safety further south. Had Guillaume already taken them to Chaulion? When daybreak came King John's men would be at Harcourt and hours there-after at Blackstone's hamlet. He loosened the reins and let his horse's instinct find its own way through the night towards home. But at the first lifting of darkness the breeze warned him of disaster – the acrid smell of burnt timber and smouldering thatch. And when he came across Marcel's slaughtered body on the track his worst fears were realized. He waited in the trees above the old fortified house, the surrounding barns and peasants' homes – burnt-out;

ghosts of smoke drifted from the blackened timbers. He stayed motionless, searching the devastation for any sign of life or of those who had taken it. As the smoke parted he could make out the bodies of villagers dangling at the end of ropes. His horse threw up its head, nostrils flaring as the stench of death reached them. He spurred it down the hillside and with sword in hand eased his way through the tortured village. Nothing had survived. Dogs lay hacked and speared alongside men, women and children. Farm animals had been taken, except for the cows that lay beside the gore of their own spilled entrails. The blackened doors to the manor house lay open and as his horse's hooves echoed across the threshold into the courtyard he saw his servants' bodies, their blood already congealed. The raiders must have struck before nightfall the previous day, when he was at Rouen.

'Christiana!' he called, waiting, hoping that she had hidden before the attack had reached the home. His horse stood steady amid the carnage. Trained for battle, it awaited its master's command. Blackstone dismounted. The enemy was long gone, or they would have attacked in the confines of the courtyard. He ran up the steps, calling out her name and those of his children and of Guillaume, their protector.

Tables and benches were overturned; his three hunting dogs lay dead on the reed floor of the great room. The blackened remains of burnt tapestries clung to the stone walls, but his gaze was taken to the fireplace and the huge chestnut beam that lay across the broad grate. The naked body of Old Hugh, dried blood on his face and a gash in his chest where his heart had once beaten, stood in grotesque welcome to his master's homecoming. Each hand was nailed into the beam. The attackers had crucified and then tortured him. Crudely written words on a piece of cloth hung from the servant's already cold body. Blackstone pulled the stained linen free. The words chilled him. *I believe in a cruel God. I am his wickedness expressed in anger.* The cloth was from one of Christiana's dresses.

An avenging horde had fallen upon them. King John was devout; these were the sentiments of a man possessed by evil intent. It was true that the French King lived in fear of conspiracy; he had already shown that he would strike at the heart of those against him, but he would not twist his devotion to God in such crude terms. He was king by divine will; he would not perceive himself as the hand of wickedness. No, Blackstone realized, this attack was committed against him by the Savage Priest, sent by the beleaguered King to rid himself of those who plotted, or those who knew the intentions of the conspirators. A purge of violence would sweep across Normandy, just as Prince Edward's *chevauchée* scoured the south.

A reckoning was at hand.

Blackstone felt a stab of fear. Where were his family and Guillaume?

CHAPTER 23

Blackstone stepped over the bodies of his servants. The attackers had taken all the food from the kitchen and slaughtered his people where they stood, or cowered. Beatrix lay, eyes glazed in death, a meat cleaver loose in her fingers and a dead mercenary with a slashed neck a couple of paces away. Amidst the carnage he found a half-eaten ham and an unbroken bottle of wine; after feeding his horse, he ate and drank his fill. His pursuit might take days and he did not know when he would eat again.

The heavy clouds moving in from the west told him there would be more rain later that day. The stiffening breeze played across the treetops, leaving the stillness of the ruins below to taunt him. Where once had been the sound of children's laughter, a woman's shout to her husband, a man's voice raised in answer, was now silence. The bodies lay where they had been killed. The wild boars would soon emerge from the forests and gorge on the corpses. This was no time for sentiment or sorrow at the destruction of his home and the slaughter of the people he had vowed to protect. The bodies of his wife and children were not among the slain.

There was hope.

There were three tracks that led in and out of the hamlet, wide enough for a wagon, but there was no sign of any fresh wheel marks. That meant Guillaume might have left in good time on horse-back. If he had followed Blackstone's orders and waited the day and night as instructed, the raiders would have them. Now that the King had decided to kill or capture those he thought were against him, Sir Thomas Blackstone's family would make a prize catch. And he who held his family held Blackstone.

All the horses were gone, most likely taken by the raiders. Only the old swayback that had brought them from Paris had been slaughtered. Blackstone rode around the smouldering village; the torn earth meant the horsemen had come in from the Harcourt road. He wondered if the Countess had escaped in good time. The pitted track suggested there must have been fifty or more riders. Blackstone rode slowly for the first two miles; then he found a blood trail on the road towards Chaulion. He found the bodies at the side of the road. One man lay sprawled, partly covered by the tall ferns. Another lay twenty yards further on, his body half on the road, half in the trampled foliage. A running battle had taken place. Flies buzzed and crows flapped stiffly away as he moved through the wet ferns and found more bodies, swords by their sides and blood splattered on the nearby leaves. Four were Blackstone's men, the others he did not recognize. It looked as though they had fought a rearguard action. There was no fair-haired boy, no ringletted daughter showing among tangled stems. No embroidered dress, the same warm colour as her hair, that Christiana wore when riding. Blackstone caught his own sense of desperation and acknowledged his heart's entrapment by his family.

If Guillaume had had some warning of the attack and disobeyed Blackstone's orders, his family would be safe behind Chaulion's town walls. The men who had done this were unlikely to lay siege to a walled town held by fifty of Blackstone's men.

He urged his horse on in fear for his family and a deepening hatred for Jean le Bon – King John 'the Good' – who had executed his friend so cruelly and sent killers to his home. It could be no other than the Savage Priest who did the King's bidding. The man Christiana had urged him to kill.

Guillaume had killed Marcel and then turned back to the village. Panic gripped him until the galloping horse's urgency focused his mind into an iron-strong determination to do as Blackstone had commanded. Save his lord's family. Marcel's confession of betrayal laid bare King John's trap. Jean de Harcourt and his conspirators would be snared at Rouen at the Dauphin's feast. Guillaume realized King John had played his hand well. When Guy de Ruymont leaked the information to Blanche he knew she would ride to warn her husband, and that the trusted servant Marcel would be used to draw Blackstone away from his home and his family. The favoured servant had been bought by de Ruymont over the months. A lifetime of sleeping on cold floors and endless hours of labour could render the most loyal susceptible. Marcel had been offered more silver coin than he had ever seen and promised a more exalted position in de Ruymont's own service. Slowly, as a creeping sickness sucks life from the body, his loyalty had been bled from him. Old age would be soothed with comfort and status. And if the servant had failed and Blackstone had chosen to stay with his family then King John's killers would already be on the road. Either way Blackstone would be caught in the net.

Christiana refused Guillaume's demand to leave immediately and seek refuge at Chaulion as Blackstone had ordered. She argued, demanding he ride after Blackstone and warn him.

Guillaume's love for his master and his family was as deep-rooted as the memory of the terrifying fear those ten years ago, when Blackstone the English archer had pulled aside the curtain of the boy's hiding place in the castle at Noyelles. Blackstone had given him life and honour. Fear was something to be overcome, spat out like the poison it was, and Christiana's fear could throw them to the wolves. He grabbed her, risking rebuke at his disrespect for her status. Countess Blanche de Harcourt might already be taken at Rouen because of her own desperation to warn her husband. Sir Thomas would do what he could, but he would not sacrifice his life needlessly. Now Christiana had to make a decision. She could ride to Rouen, blinded by emotion, and play into the King's hands, or she could submit to her husband's command and allow Guillaume to take her family to safety. The King's mercenaries would be here soon after first light. Would she abandon her trust in Sir Thomas's skills as a knight? For a moment it seemed that she would strike Guillaume, but she relented and obeyed the man entrusted with her family's safety.

Guillaume picked out three of the best horses: coursers – big, powerful hunters that would carry them far and fast. Christiana had gathered bedrolls for the children and packed food and drink. Fearful servants were calmed; they would come to no harm providing they declared their loyalty to the King and their denial of Blackstone. Guillaume redistributed the provisions between the three horses and threw down the bedrolls. No unnecessary weight would be taken on their escape. He told Christiana to dress the children warmly.

Guillaume took Henry into the stables. As simply as he could he explained the bare truth. His father was in danger and would return to them, but men were coming to the village to seize him, his mother and sister.

'What will they do to you?' the boy asked.

'I'm your father's sworn man. They'll kill me.'

The boy thought for a moment. 'What do you want me to do if that happens?'

Guillaume tucked his sheathed dagger into the boy's belt. 'This was mine when I was your age. I once threatened your father with it because I was trying to protect someone. I want you to protect your mother and sister if anything happens to me. Can you do that?'

The boy nodded, uncertainty clouding his thoughts for a moment. 'Yes,' he said decisively, knowing he would push the knife into anyone who threatened his mother and sister.

Guillaume had Henry take one of the horses from the stall. The boy had only ridden palfreys – reliable but less spirited horses than the big courser he would now have to manage, the one his father rode when not using his destrier. Holding the reins the boy gazed up at the flaring nostrils. Guillaume watched him raise his arm and let the horse snuffle his hand. It shifted its weight unexpectedly; this stranger was not the usual stable-hand who groomed and fed him, or the tall man who could command him.

'Come,' Henry said calmly to the horse, 'we have to go a long way. You'll be all right. You'll run faster than any of them with me on your back.' Henry allowed the horse a moment to listen to his voice and then gently but firmly tugged the reins. Blackstone's son would do well, Guillaume decided.

They would be forced to ride hard. Christiana would have no choice but to carry Agnes, held close to her.

Guillaume picked half a dozen armed men to ride with them for protection; then he summoned the villagers. He offered assurances and told them the King's men sought Sir Thomas and that their lord's orders had been made clear. Defame and deny the man who had protected them these past years. A few called back asking why danger was suddenly upon them. There was no time to explain – he urged them to do everything the King's men demanded. Their lives were in their own hands. John's men would soon be there and they were to obey Sir Thomas's command.

At first Henry struggled with the horse's power, slowing the party to a canter. Guillaume rode close, one hand ready to snatch at the reins, but the boy's determination kept him in the saddle. They were barely three miles from the house when one of Guillaume's men cried out a warning. Guillaume turned in the saddle and less than half a mile back five horsemen gave chase. He realized they were probably scouts for the main party. As the track rose up he could see beyond the trees and the smoke already filling the sky from the burning village. There would be no mercy given to Blackstone's people.

'Stay on the road, Henry! I'll follow!' he shouted to the boy. 'Hang onto his mane! Gallop, boy!'

There was no time to wait for an answer, or to

offer any soothing comfort to the frightened boy. Guillaume turned the horse and spurred back to join his men. Agnes was bound to her mother by a broad swathe of embroidered linen and Christiana spurred the horse upwards to crest the hill. Life or death was moments away. Guillaume's sword was already drawn as he shouted commands to the rearguard. The men turned to meet the attack head-on and Guillaume led them. Seven to five, the advantage was theirs. The men clashed. Sweat-streaked horses whinnied, men bellowed curses, striking each other in desperation. Guillaume parried a blow with his shield and thrust his blade beneath his attacker's exposed armpit. He wheeled the horse and slashed the back of the skull of another man who was besting one of his own men. The horsemen were common hobelars; they wore no coat of arms, had no colours of the King, or of a lord. They were hired men – and they were as fierce as Guillaume's, who held their own for only moments longer. Two defenders were already down, unhorsed, one of them trampled and killed; the other ran for the safety of the forest through waist-high ferns. Guillaume called to the man, but he was already being pursued and seconds from death. Guillaume took a fierce blow and reeled in the saddle. Two men attacked him simul-taneously and as one beat savagely against his shield the other swung a cutting blow across his body. Guillaume pressed tight with his left leg and kicked his horse around with his right; the momentum pushed back the shield attacker and allowed him to parry a sword strike from the other. The swordsman was committed, the momentum of his horse carrying him past Guillaume, who struck down across the man's exposed neck. Guillaume's horse churned the ground as it wheeled to his command and he fought off the second man, who made a mistake in his panic at seeing his companion's death, and allowed Guillaume to lunge beneath his guard. Blood seeped below the man's jerkin onto his legs from a stomach wound and as his head lowered in disbelief at the pain that suddenly gripped his guts, Guillaume slashed again. The man rolled like a drunk from the saddle and lay unmoving. The remaining attacker in the ferns turned and galloped back towards Blackstone's village.

Others would soon be in pursuit, and it would be a far greater force than the few men they had just fought. Four of his men lay dead; two remained unharmed. The men gazed wildly at the spiralling smoke. They were soldiers who had fought for years and finally settled under the protection of their Lord Blackstone. They had married their whores and borne children and their families were back in the village.

'No further for us, Master Guillaume, if you please,' one of them said, the horse beneath him skittish from the scent of blood.

Guillaume nodded. Life was precious, but a point came when something more was demanded.

'Good luck to you,' Guillaume said, granting them leave to turn back.

'And you,' the second man answered. Then both men wheeled their horses and headed back to the devastation that surely awaited them.

Guillaume watched them for a moment longer: drink-rotted soldiers who would kill without conscience sacrificing themselves at last for something that had some meaning in their lives.

He urged his horse on; there were those he had sworn to protect.

Blackstone skirted the crossroads at Chaulion's monastery. The walls were manned by more men than usual. Blackstone held off, keeping to the safety of the forest. He waited until a cloud slipped across the face of the sun, so that the men's faces were less shadowed. There wasn't a man he did not recognize. He was safe unless the raiders had breached the walls he and his men had built, and his men had joined the enemy. Trust was a currency in short supply. Blackstone had weeded out most of the scum from the men who looked to him for command, but there was always a risk. He rode forward.

When the defenders of Chaulion monastery recognized the rider, the gates opened and armed men gathered.

'Perinne!' Blackstone called as the long-serving soldier pushed his way through the men. 'All's well?'

'Aye, m'lord. There's been scum sniffing their way around the crossroads.'

'Did they approach?'

'Not here,' said Perinne, one of the first defenders and wall builders at the monastery who had fought with Blackstone over the last decade. 'They rode back and forth along the road; they could see they had no choice with the town and us held firm.'

'Good. Keep the men alert. There's a war coming our way and I'll need you.'

A murmur of anticipation went through the men.

'We'll be ready, Sir Thomas.'

'Was there any sign of my family with those men?'

'None. Have they been taken, lord?' Perinne asked; the men in the towns knew Blackstone's family from the time they spent with them.

'It's not clear yet,' he said, turning the horse. 'I'll ride to the town. Wait until Guinot sends my orders.'

He did not wait for a reply but spurred his horse down to what had been his and Christiana's first home together when he had fought for and won Chaulion.

There were five such towns spread across the countryside, unofficial outposts held by Blackstone for the English King, each garrisoned by fifty or more of his men. Each town controlled the immediate area around it, which meant the roads and trading routes could be restricted or harassed. The strongholds provided buffer zones between the mostly undefended villages that lay scattered across the countryside. The English held Brittany and Gascony and Blackstone's men held towns across Lower Normandy, some as far as the Périgord. Bastions of French noble houses were everywhere between, but offered no serious threat to the superior numbers holding the towns.

As he galloped down the road between town and monastery he kept his eyes on the forest ridge but there was no sign of raiders. Sentries called out his approach as horse and rider were recognized.

A thickset man with cropped grey hair and a face like worn leather grasped his master's hand in greeting. Another defender led Blackstone's horse to water.

'What news, Guinot?' Blackstone asked, relieved to see his commander again. His eyes scanned the walls, checking that each man was in his place, that the town was properly defended.

'A trader came through and told us he'd heard Évreux and the citadel at Pont-Audemer are under siege by the King John's troops. Lisieux may already have fallen. What's happening?'

'He's striking at the Norman barons. He wants retribution, among other things.'

'And you, Sir Thomas. He's looking hard for you.'

'You've seen men here?'

'Aye, a hundred or more of 'em. They travelled

the road between here and the monastery but they could see we held the advantage. They stayed through the day and most of the night. They made no attempt to attack. They asked for you. They demanded you go out to them or your family would be killed.'

'Did they have my family?' Blackstone asked.

The man shook his head. 'If they had, Sir Thomas, they would have shown them to us. They were bluffing, but more riders joined them. I've kept extra men on the walls just in case the bastards come back.'

Blackstone nodded. Guillaume must have got his family away, but been unable to find a way to reach the safety of the town.

'I'll have men ready themselves to join you, my lord.'

'No, hold the town, Guinot. King John will scourge the countryside. He doesn't have an army in the field yet, so he won't lay siege to towns far from Paris. That's why he's attacked the more strategic places. He'll want a buffer between him and Brittany.'

The man grinned. 'A war, m'lord? If King Edward returns that's where he'll come from – the west.'

'Or through Calais, so John will have enough to do without tying up his men on my towns. That's why we hold. If Edward comes he'll need a line of defences in place.'

'And that's us,' Guinot said, his despondency apparent.

Blackstone put a hand on the man's shoulder. Fighting men profited from war, and to restrain them in peace needed a leader who could rein them in. Blackstone raised his voice so all the men could hear him. He told them what had happened at Rouen and the destruction of his own fortified house and village.

'War will come and you will be needed. Stand fast and be ready for when I send for you.'

The Gascon held the horse's bridle as Blackstone climbed into the saddle. He knew there was little point in suggesting Blackstone take rest and food, but that there was great danger was apparent.

'Reconsider, Sir Thomas. You need men with you. Let me put some horsemen on the road as escort. If you're being hunted you'll need help.'

Blackstone shook his head. 'I'll be less noticed and can move faster on my own. Guillaume and my family won't go any further to the east. If these roads were blocked by King John's men then he'll know he can't get through to any of the other towns. He'll be in hiding or he'll push south. The further he goes the better chance he has of meeting up with the vanguard of Prince Edward's army.'

'They're hundreds of miles away,' the man said. 'More than a week's hard riding.'

'Hope is spurred by desperation,' Blackstone

373

answered. 'Send word to Meulon and Gaillard; let them know that the lord they once served, Count de Harcourt, has been butchered by the King. Have the men in the towns ready for my orders. The killing has only just begun.'

CHAPTER 24

Blackstone rode for three days and nights and on the fourth day crossed a high ridge as he watched a hundred horsemen or more on the road in the valley below. They were routiers and when they reached a crossroads they separated into groups of half a dozen or more men. They were widening their search. Whichever way he went he was going to run into some of the widely scattered enemy who hunted him. He gazed across the horizon searching out anything that might help him decide on which direction to take next.

He could see reflected light from a river several miles away and remembered journeys he and Christiana had taken across these limestone mountains far from home. There were few towns or villages west of where he stood. Christiana might have remembered and taken the children away from the dense woodlands. There was greater safety in the chestnut forests, but his family's speed of escape would be hampered and they'd need food and shelter. If she and Guillaume had gone down onto the plains they could seek safety from a nobleman who shared the same animosity towards the French King. There were many small towns and bastides, held by independent captains in allegiance to King Edward, whose walls might offer protection, but there were also as many garrisons held by those loyal to the French Crown. Would Guillaume have risked travelling through disputed territory or would he seek out a stronghold that might withstand an assault from rapacious routiers who would have no siege weapons, preferring to attack less defensible villages? Blackstone remembered a monastery that stood on a rocky outcrop overlooking a river. Perhaps the half-dozen men who rode towards the river knew of it, and would lie in wait for anyone approaching it. Blackstone's options were getting fewer by the day and, unless good fortune continued to favour him, the scattered groups of men might sooner or later stumble upon him or his family. Blackstone touched the silver image of the goddess at his neck and asked for her protection. And then he asked God as well.

He occasionally lost sight of the men he followed as he was forced to change his route across the jagged gorges, but their movement gave them away and he waited patiently, silently watching as they stopped to eat and drink, hearing only voices being carried faintly on the wind. He heard no mention of his family or what the men's intentions were. They rode on without diversion, neither searching forest trails that were little more than animal tracks, nor turning off from the route that would eventually bring them to the crossroads that commanded the roads into the monastery. The day wore on until murky twilight settled and the men finally rode through a forest of alder and ash, close to the river's edge, and disappeared from view once more.

Blackstone eased his horse off the track into the soft undergrowth. As he reached the forest edge he dismounted and tied the reins. He waited, his stillness reassuring the horse, and his hand across its muzzle ensuring its silence. Then, stepping quietly and slowly, he eased through copses of alder saplings, his footfalls muffled by the rustling trees and swaying bulrushes.

The six men gathered around a smoking fire, squatting upwind from the drifting smoke, their backs to their tethered horses. Thirty yards away, his image broken by trees, Blackstone eased through the smoke's veil, its movement blurring his own. The horses would not pick up his scent, and the men, one or two already unsteady from drink, were gazing into the fire, fussing and worrying it. As the breeze funnelled down the river it veered into the bank and swirled for a moment before continuing its journey. The men swore as smoke smothered them. They edged around to change position and paid no attention to a whinnying horse that finally caught the smell of the stranger who was now only a few yards away, using the twisting, choking smoke to hide his attack.

Blackstone ran forward and swung Wolf Sword. Two men died before they saw their silent attacker. Sudden cries of alarm gave impetus to the others' desperate scramble. A third stumbled in his haste to draw his sword from the scabbard; a distant memory of being told to abandon a scabbard when going into battle flashed through Blackstone's mind. But these men were caught completely unawares. For them there was no threat and no expectation that a single man, the hunted, would become the hunter. The man fell beneath Blackstone's sword stroke and for a moment he was disadvantaged, withdrawing the blade as the others found their weapons and attacked. Their grunting curses spurred them on, but Blackstone easily sidestepped the first man, who stumbled past him and sprawled across the fire. He plunged the blade into the other, turned to the one who had stumbled and kicked him hard in the face, feeling the man's cheekbones break. As the man rolled away in agony Blackstone drew the blade across the back of the man's legs, hamstringing him. There would be no escape from the vengeance. The last of the men hesitated, turned to run, tripped and lost his sword. He scrambled to his feet with the scar-faced knight only paces behind him. He got as far as the shallows, but the power of his pursuer meant he had only seconds to live. He half turned, about to beg for mercy, but the blade swung down and a bloodied pool seeped down into the marsh as the broken bulrush stems caught his body.

Blackstone walked back to the half-conscious man who was trying to hold his shattered jaw in place. Blackstone knelt next to him and grabbed a handful of hair. 'Who leads you? Who is the King paying?'

The man, his mouth filled with blood, tried to splutter an answer. The force of Blackstone's blow had rendered him incapable of speech. But a single whispered word was forming through the broken teeth. Blackstone twisted the man's hair into a tighter grip and lowered his face to hear more clearly. It sounded like the word *priest*. Then the man laughed and spat blood into his face. Blackstone killed him quickly.

Tiredness and hunger were beginning to take their toll. Blackstone brought his horse forward, then separated the dead men's horses, tying them in pairs around the perimeter of where he would spend the night. No matter from what direction anyone might approach, the horses would raise the alarm. He kept his own horse close to him. He rebuilt the fire and pushed river stones closer into the ash bed. The men had enough food in their packs, so he ate and drank, and then lay, sword in hand, with his back to the warm boulders. Tomorrow, he promised himself, he would find his family.

The rustling leaves taunted him with their ghostly whispers until he finally surrendered to a fitful sleep.

He awoke before dawn, stiff from the damp night. Mist smothered the land in an eerie half-light, dressing the stiffened bodies in gossamer shrouds. The horse raised its head as he approached. It would be a long, slow day's ride with the added danger of meeting more horsemen without warning. Once he had cut the dead men's horses loose, he oriented himself, trying to keep the unseen river to one side, letting his memory guide him. Years earlier he and Christiana had travelled these forests and valleys. There were many places where the limestone mountains were cut by gorges. They had swum naked in cool pools and made love beneath the shade of the broad-leafed trees. He knew the river meandered to the sea and that the monastery was built up on the edge of the escarpment at a place where the waterway's deep waters curved gently. The monks had been there for centuries, the river serving them for trade. If Guillaume had been forced to travel this far south Christiana might have remembered the monastery and sought sanctuary within its stout walls. Where else could they hide for days without food and water? The scattered villages and bastides of the area were loyal to King John, and they in turn would give shelter to the killers. If Blackstone's family attempted to reach one of the fortified towns garrisoned by loyal Gascons they would be hard pressed to get through those hamlets without being seen. The forests and mountains offered their greatest chance of concealment, but also the greatest danger of stumbling upon King John's marauders.

The day wore on at an agonizingly slow pace, but he could still smell the salt tang drifting from the brackish water of the distant river. The freshening breeze swirled the fog and, as the road turned up into the foothills, he soon lost his bearings. The midday sun burned the high ground free of the mist and he caught glimpses of trees, their tips piercing the stubborn blanket that still lay across the low ground. He reined in the horse frequently and sat listening for the jingle of a bridle or the creak of a saddle. He thought the other groups would, like the men he had killed the previous night, be camped, waiting for the wind to clear the mist. They would not search for him or his family until they could see the lie of the land. There seemed no respite from the clinging damp – and then he heard men's laughter and sensed that they were close: a hundred paces or less, he thought. However, there was no smell of a fire and no movement from horses. Six or sixty men might be paces from him. The scuff of a hoof might be enough to tempt the killers from their camp, so he eased his horse away, climbing higher across the sound-deadening bracken. The old wounds in his left arm complained and, as they often did, turned his thoughts back to the slaughter of Crécy, and those final minutes of rage and terror in the mêlée of battle. During the past ten years there had seldom been a day when his mind did not see or hear his brother's death. There were nights when Christiana backed away in fear, rousing him from the nightmare. He had struck out once and hurt her and had never forgiven himself. Since then they had not spoken of the incident or the pain of his brother's death-cries that haunted him. And now a vile King had butchered an enemy who had become his friend, sending a twisted creature to torture and kill. That same taste of bile he had known back then soured his mouth now.

Blackstone ignored the cold night air and, although the mist had lifted slightly, he remained wary. The road ahead disappeared into a narrow passageway between twenty-foot walls of rock where trees' talon roots clung to its flanks and their spreading boughs overhung the track like vultures' wings. It seemed a place of evil, and if men were encamped further along in the under-growth, a fallen tree across the narrow path would give them the perfect ambush. Night creatures of this world and the next crept and scuttled through the tangled undergrowth. Blackstone eased the horse backwards, keeping his eyes on the malig-nant passage that surely led to the devil's lair. He made the sign of the cross, then brought Arianrhod to his lips – superstition and instinctive fear should never be denied. Then a movement caught his eye. Had it not been for the darkened road ahead he might never have seen the brief flicker of light high in the rocky outcrops; it was a smudge of red bleeding into the soft veil that crept across the mountainside. He let his gaze settle and waited, and once again saw the blood-spot of light. It was as if someone had opened and closed a door, shielding a fire. Perhaps it was a woodcutter's hovel, or a shepherd's hut. If it were horsemen camped for the night then there must have been another path further back that he had missed. He dismounted and led the horse upwards, sweating from the strenuous climb and grateful for the coolness of the night. Rain fell, blurring his vision, but it made no difference; there was no further sign of firelight. He was five hundred paces from where he believed the camp to be, but no matter how intently he stared into the darkness, there was no further glimmer, or any sign of men. Tethering his horse he picked his way through the rocks, looking back every ten paces to remember his route. Along the hillside a great shoulder of rock jutted out; it would be there that anyone wishing to shelter would be. A narrow animal track cut through fern and bracken and he followed its twisting route until he could step behind the slab of rock and ease himself around to the dark passage where the light flickered dimly. It was a cave entrance covered in a makeshift willow gate, laid with cut ferns. The caves were large enough for men and horses, and he reasoned there might even be tunnels offering another way in and out. There was no sound. No sentry. The men would be sleeping, secure in their mountain lair. A sudden, unexpected attack would kill at least half a dozen of them. If escape was needed he could retreat around the jagged shoulder, down the track and back into the trees. He had a clear picture in his mind of his approach, which would serve him just as well on his return. His left hand guided him along the rock face, his sword held ready to strike. Smoke seeped from behind the dense screen. The men inside would need to shift the wicker now and again to let the smoke escape. That was why he had seen the brief glimpse of fire glow. At least one man would be awake inside. As his hand reached out to rip the screen away the deep shadow moved in the fissure he had just passed. Too late, he felt the trickle of blood from the point of a sword blade at his neck. The men were better prepared than he had given them credit for.

'Who are you?' a voice whispered, wary that there might be more than one man.

Blackstone felt a shock of recognition. 'I am your patron and sworn lord,' he answered.

Guillaume closed the screen after them and they stepped into the firelight that set the shadows dancing across the cave wall. Huddled in the corner, Christiana and the children looked gaunt and dirt-streaked, their matted hair and mud-caked clothes testament to days spent living rough on the road. Christiana held Agnes beneath her cloak, concealing her child from the intruder. She had a knife in her hand, as did Henry, who stood in front of his mother ready to protect her as Guillaume had asked him. Disbelief, then joy swept over them as Blackstone held them to him. Henry had stayed back a pace, allowing his mother and sister the affectionate embrace. Blackstone kissed his daughter's tears away and wiped the grime from her cheek. He turned to his son, who waited expectantly.

'I've seen that knife before,' Blackstone said. 'It's not the first time it's been pointed at me.'

'I'm sorry, Father. I didn't know it was you,' Henry said, uncertain if the words were meant as a rebuke.

Blackstone felt a desperate need to reach out and hug the boy to him, but by the way his son stood, eyes raised to meet his father's, Thomas could see that he was no longer a child. Instead he reached out and gripped the boy's shoulder.

'You have served your mother and sister well. I'm very proud of you, Henry,' he said gently. And he could see that earning his father's praise meant more than any gift he could have bestowed on the boy.

There was little food, but enough to stave off hunger. The cave stretched back forty feet or more into darkness, where the horses were herded into a makeshift corral of broken branches. Blackstone's trust in Guillaume had been more than rewarded. He had brought them this far without injury, ensuring they had shelter, food and warmth. The squire's own comforts had been denied and he was gaunt from fatigue and the strain of responsibility. The man's intelligence had pre-empted the attack on their home, and his insistence on their escaping had saved Blackstone's family. The walls of the limestone cave held the heat from the fire, and Blackstone instructed Guillaume to let it die down. Once there were only embers and the warmth of the rocks around the ash they would have no need to stand guard. Guillaume was reluctant, but Blackstone had seen the approach and without the threat of firelight no one would dare stumble their way through broken ground without an objective in sight. Guillaume nodded gratefully and accepted his master's command. He moved to a place opposite the entrance and sat back against the wall, sword at his side, finally yielding to his exhaustion. Blackstone found what comfort he could and held Christiana to him, covered with her cloak, while Agnes snuggled beneath his sword arm. The warmth of the horses' bodies and the relief that they were all unharmed allowed them to sleep.

The following day they travelled along goat tracks, buffeted by a changeable wind that brought cold, stinging rain. Blackstone led the way and Guillaume brought up the rear, with Henry, Christiana and

Agnes between them. They had seen no sign of horsemen and, as they descended into the forest, the monastery's slate-roofed stone bell tower came into view, perched on its escarpment. It looked to have been reinforced by boulders and river stones, and might in some past time have offered defenders a final refuge.

Christiana rode up alongside him. 'Thomas,' she said, easing aside her cloak to show Agnes cradled in the crook of her arm. Blackstone looked at his daughter's flushed face. She was sleeping, but her damp curls were plastered to her head by fever rather than rain. He reached out and laid his hand on her face. He nodded. 'The monks have medicine. We'll be there by dark.'

He guided them to the approach road to the monastery, and then held them in the shelter of some rocks.

'We must ride in,' Christiana insisted.

Blackstone calmed her. 'I have to make sure it's safe.'

Christiana's anguish was obvious, but she held back the rebuke that rose to her lips. Blackstone moved forward, careful to keep himself away from the skyline. From his vantage point he could see the layout of the monastery and grounds of the Abbaye de Saint-Antoine-de-la-Rivière. Black-robed monks went about their duties. Each area served its purpose for their daily life, enabling them to live independent of the outside world. Stables, wood yard, vegetable plots – each walled enclosure had three or four monks working in it. On one side of the path that led to the arched entrance and then to the church and cloisters, goats, sheep and cows were penned. Half a dozen two-storey buildings ran along one side of the church, and the granary, bakery and workshops on the other. Thirty or more monks and an abbot would be living in the monastery, sustained by their own labour and prayer.

Guillaume moved next to him.

'There's a warren of passageways inside. They'd hinder anyone trying to make an escape. I don't want to get caught like a rat in a trap,' Blackstone told him.

'The abbot is obliged to offer sanctuary and shelter. What could harm us?'Blackstone pointed to where a monk led two donkeys into the stalls. 'Monks have no need for those,' he said, meaning the seven strong-looking horses tethered in the open-fronted stalls. 'We wait until dark and see if there are soldiers down there.'

'They might belong to travellers or pilgrims,' Guillaume said, and then paused uncertainly. 'Agnes is worse. I can hear it in her lungs. She needs shelter and food, Sir Thomas. And their medicine.'

Blackstone watched as the monks moved from the walled gardens, the wood yard and the stables, gathering at the fountain house to wash their feet and hands after their labours. Guillaume pointed. Half a dozen men moved out from the dormitorium above the horse stalls. It was where common men were given a place of shelter and a straw mattress.

'Hobelars,' said Guillaume. 'And there can't be more than six of them. There are no other horses.'

'Where's the seventh man? He's not with them.'

'Did you wound any of the men you fought? Others might have brought him here.'

'I killed them all,' said Blackstone, watching the men move towards the chapel to join the monks. 'And brigands would have these monks at sword point. No, they're soldiers.'

'English or French?' Guillaume asked.

Blackstone could hear his daughter's shallow, rasping breath.

'Let's find out,' he said.

The priest, seated by the fire in the monastery's library, gazed into the curling flames. He had seen paintings of men being cast down into hell and there was no doubt in his mind that when the dark shadow of death suffocated mankind most would feel Lucifer's embrace. Except for him. For not only did he do God's work but also served his temporal master with devotion. He scratched a louse from his head. This interminable waiting would try the patience of Saint Benedict himself, under whose auspices this monastery had been built and whose abbot now offered him shelter. He did not stand in full agreement with the Benedictines, who stole hours from the day to work as common men. Their black habits conjured images of busy crows pecking at a field, grubbing for food. A hierarchy should be maintained, which was why his own order kept the lay monks for manual work while the clergy attended to the liturgy and the spiritual well-being of all men. Or in his case the nobility.

He had read what was available in the poorly stocked library; its manuscripts were dated, and the light too poor to read in comfort from the constant gloom of low cloud that tired his eyes. Boredom and impatience were beginning to chafe like a penitent's sackcloth shirt. His mission was of the utmost importance, but the foul weather had closed in and made it impossible to travel the treacherous roads. Hidden enemies could ambush them from the cover of the fog and, no matter how skilled the soldiers who rode with him, a surprise attack would give assailants the upper hand. He could not risk being captured. Death or ransom was not an option.

Sandalled feet shuffled through the passageways of the dimly lit monastery. The movement told him it was almost time for vespers. The bell rang. He sighed in resignation and gathered his pale-coloured habit. It was a sacrifice to leave the warmth of the library for the penetrating cold of the abbey's chapel and submit his aching knees to the unyielding floor. The chimes rang out. These Benedictines were never satisfied. Had they not already added an extra mass during the day? Was it an indulgence to spoil oneself in additional prayer? His stomach growled; it would be some time yet before his hunger would be satisfied. A modicum of suffering might make God take pity and reward him with a seaborne breeze to clear the mist and let him be on his way. There was more at stake than religious devotion. A war was at hand and he needed one of God's small miracles to turn defeat into victory. He turned his back on the fire's warmth and realized that a small miracle might not be enough.

It was dark by the time Blackstone reached the monastery doors. Guillaume beat on the studded doors with his sword's pommel. They were drenched and shivering. No sound came from the inner rooms, the windows stayed shuttered, no one ventured into the foul night. Guillaume beat on the door again, and then they heard the sound of a shuffling step and saw the faint glow from a tallow candle as the pedestrian gate was opened. A monk, looking as ancient as the stones themselves, stood uncertainly as he gazed at the two men, one still with a sword in his hand.

'Sir Thomas Blackstone and his family seek shelter,' Guillaume told him. 'We have a sick child.'

The monk's gaze had already moved to Christiana and Henry, and he could see the unconscious child held by her mother. He stepped back and ushered Blackstone and Christiana inside. Blackstone turned to Henry.

'Stay with Guillaume and the horses. Someone will come.'

The soaked and trembling boy looked wretched, but made no complaint and nodded at his father's command.

For one so aged the gatekeeper monk moved quickly into the monastery, touching his candle flame to cresset lamps that lit the way. Another door was opened and they were ushered into a bare room with a boarded cubbyhole that served as a bed and a small partition as a prayer niche. The gatekeeper lit two more wall lamps and gestured for them to wait. The monks spoke only after the midday prayers, when the day's manual labour began. The monastery fell silent as the bell ceased its ringing.

The monk stepped away and Blackstone reached out and took Agnes from Christiana. Her breathing was shallow and laboured as he laid her on the straw mattress. There was nothing to do but wait. Minutes later an older man bearing a crozier, the abbot's symbol of office, came into the room with three other monks. They barely gave Blackstone and Christiana a glance and went directly to Agnes. The abbot nodded and as one lifted the ailing child, carrying her from the room, the other held a candle to light their way through darkened passageways. Before Christiana could object the old man spoke calmly, a soft kindness to his voice, as if breaking the silence should be done with the least intrusion: 'Your daughter will be taken to the infirmatorium. We have no brothers with sickness or injury so you can be with your daughter. Go with Brother Gerard.'

Christiana followed the wavering shadows cast by the retreating monk's candlelight. The old man turned to Blackstone. 'I am Abbot Pierre. You are welcome to share my house. We have a place for pilgrims and paupers, but these quarters here are kept for those of rank, such as your squire and page. The room next door is yours. Are these accommodations suitable, my lord?'

'My squire and my son travel with me. This room is more than adequate. I'm grateful for your hospitality. But you have soldiers here.'

'They need not concern you, Sir Thomas. They travel as escort for a brother priest.'

Blackstone remembered the word of the dying routier he had killed at the river. *Priest*. Was there a connection between these soldiers and the paid killers after all?

The abbot moved to the door. 'I will arrange food and drink for your companions and extend the invitation for you to dine with me and my other guest in my quarters. We have hot water should you wish to bathe. I will ensure you have clean linen. Your horses are being stabled. Brother Tobias here will take you to the refectory and we will have food prepared for your lady. You will say mass with us?' the abbot said, having glanced at the pagan token at Blackstone's neck.

'I have already interrupted vespers. Forgive me, but there was an urgency with my daughter.'

The abbot made a small deprecating gesture.

'We will attend mass,' Blackstone said, determined not to create ill feeling.

The answer was satisfactory. There were fighting men who would have declined the invitation. 'Then I shall have one of the brothers come for you. Please inform your companions that they are obliged to stay out of the conclave.'

Blackstone was as unfamiliar as most with the inner rituals and disciplines of a monastery. The abbot saw his uncertainty.

'The brothers' living quarters, the cloister and gardens. I have already extended dispensation for your lady and your daughter to be cared for in the infirmatorium.'

'And we will gladly respect your wishes, Brother Pierre.'

The abbot nodded and turned to leave.

'Would you care for a bath, Sir Thomas?'

The subtle question was not lost on Blackstone. He had been in the saddle a long time.

'I would welcome it,' he said, and guessed that his host shared the same feeling.

Guillaume and Henry unsaddled the horses. Evening prayer was still in progress and the second of four psalms to be sung lilted across the darkened cloisters. They rubbed down the horses with straw, barely able to see by the candle that flickered in its beaten metal holder. By the time the litany was chanted, Henry had slumped exhausted into the hay. Guillaume let the boy sleep and attended to Blackstone's intransigent horse. A monk arrived and helped him dry off and feed the remaining horses.

As the man pitched hay Guillaume shielded a candle and went down the stalls looking at the mounts belonging to the soldiers. They were better horses than most hobelars would ride, strong of limb and well shod – the kind of mount a nobleman might keep for favoured men, men who might have to ride long and hard and then fight.

The abbot's guest, the priest, said another quiet prayer in thanks for having the authority and responsibility of his office. Were he a common monk he would be sleeping in the dormitorium, sharing the latrines with thirty others, and most likely fed little more than pulses and bread. The obligation of hospitality towards those of import- ance and rank meant a more plentiful offering of meat and poultry would be served with undiluted wine. He waited for the abbot who, no doubt, would be late in attending his own dinner. He seemed an amiable ambassador of Christ, but distracted by everyday responsibilities, which, no doubt, made the old man forgetful. Dear Lord, where *was* the abbot? The priest's stomach cramped in its desire for nourishment. At last he heard someone moving in the corridor. The door opened and a monk gestured for someone behind him to step into the room. A tall, broad shouldered man-at-arms stepped through the doorway and the priest's hunger was immediately forgotten. The scar-faced man waited at the door, expecting to see Abbot Pierre but found, instead, a priest staring at him. He was clearly someone of import-ance by the look of the rings he wore.

The flickering cresset lamps showed that the monastery was a draughty place, but the priest did not shiver from the cool air, it was the sight of the man standing before him as shadows wavered across his face. He was struck by God's miracle that had answered his prayer. The way ahead was now clear. He made the sign of the cross and kissed the crucifix at his neck.

'I am Father Niccolò Torellini,' he said.

'Sir Thomas Blackstone,' the priest heard the man-at-arms say as he stepped forward, taking the big man's hands into his own.

'I know,' he said. 'I held you in my arms on the battlefield at Crécy.'

CHAPTER 25

A door into a passage leading to Blackstone's past had been opened and, like the darkened corridors around him, light did not show its end so clearly in his mind. Godfrey de Harcourt had told him, while he was recovering from his wounds, that the Prince of Wales had called for a priest to give the badly wounded young man the last rites. And now that priest stood before him relating the same story. Blackstone had only the memory of a burning crucifix and warrior angels awaiting his journey across the divide.

'I did not know that you had survived, Sir Thomas,' Father Niccolò said. 'I feel God has blessed me in bringing you here.'

Blackstone offered no explanation of what had happened to him over the past ten years. Men of God saw miracles where an ordinary man would see good or bad fortune unfold. God's will was unfathomable. Prayers in battle often went unheeded. Perhaps the Almighty was deafened by the clash of armour and the screams of men. This priest was an echo from that time. It was a coincidence, that was all. Nothing miraculous should be read into it. Blackstone had sought refuge at the monastery and the priest had done the same.

'I must see my wife and daughter,' Blackstone said, eager to leave; he was troubled by the priest's hold on his soul.

Torellini nodded. 'You are not permitted, but I will go. Listen to me, I beg you. I serve the Florentine banker, Rodolfo Bardi, who has much interest in the welfare of the King of England and his son the Prince of Wales, whose life you once saved, and who is now in grave danger. I have been sent by King Edward as his messenger. Wait here and when I return I will explain further.'

The priest believed the fragment of information would keep Blackstone waiting for his return, but the moment he left the refectory Blackstone took a lamp and found his way to the stables. The monks were at compline, their final prayers for the night, so the dormitorium was empty except for the snoring soldiers. Blackstone kicked the nearest man awake. Instinctively the hobelar reached for the sword at the side of his palliasse. Blackstone stamped on the blade and tipped the man off the bed. He had the advantage, despite the others being already on their feet and reaching for their weapons.

Blackstone stepped back, offering no threat, the action asserting his rank, letting the man recover, which he did quickly, gripping his sword. One of the men stepped forward. 'I'm the sergeant of these men. What is it you want, my lord?'

The men looked to be battle-hardened veterans.

They had recovered from their sleep quickly, ready to strike any intruder. They would make good bodyguards for an unarmed priest travelling on a vital mission.

'I am Sir Thomas Blackstone,' he said. The sergeant's eyes registered his recognition. He lowered his sword and the other men followed his lead.

'I know of you, my lord. I fought at Cobham's side at Blanchetaque. I was wounded at the river – we were glad of the archers that day. I am John Jacob; how can we be of service to you?'

'You ride as escort for the Italian priest. Why are you here?'

'We were to sail to Bordeaux and meet up with Prince Edward's army. But the weather came down on us before we could get any further south. We were blown ashore. We lost four men in the storm. We've been here two days waiting for the fog to lift. The priest is nervous.'

Blackstone addressed the men. 'He has good cause to be. King John has men everywhere, mostly routiers, and he holds many of the villages and towns. You'd be hard pressed to find the Prince.'

'Be that as it may, my lord, if the priest says we have to find him then that's the way it is. We're on the King's business.'

'Do you know what news is to be delivered?'

'Only Father Niccolò knows that,' the sergeant answered. 'You'll ride with us?' he asked with

399

undisguised hope in his voice. A knight of Blackstone's reputation and fighting skill was worth having on what seemed to be a fool's errand. No good could come of wet-nursing a priest in hostile territory.

Blackstone shook his head. 'I've other business to attend to. I'll speak to you before I leave. I know the lie of the land.'

'We're obliged, my lord.'

Blackstone nodded and turned away. Was it so long ago that he had slept rough with coarse archers, who fought as sworn men for a knight? A life shared with Christiana and the Harcourts had softened his manners, but seeing these Englishmen stand-to, belligerent and ready to fight, kindled a memory. He missed the comradeship denied him by being a commander of such men.

The gloomy passageways felt oppressive as Blackstone waited for the priest's return. The still air, clammy from the fog outside, made his undershirt stick to his skin, making him wish he could be free of the confined space. Now that his family was safe he would rather be taking the fight to his enemy. His daughter's illness had held sway over his emotions. The thought of Christiana and the children falling into enemy hands had hardened an already resolute determination, but now the girl lay still and helpless in the grip of fever, and he was angered by his inability to protect her. He watched Father Niccolò moving towards him, a cloak of good English cloth edged with fur over his white habit blurring the image of a humble man of God. Blackstone distrusted those who professed humility and vows of poverty. Mendicant friars lived from a begging bowl; others in the clergy seemed secure in self-sufficiency and interest. He had seldom seen common men attend church services. It seemed that worship and blessings were attended mostly by the nobility and the rich. Perhaps heaven was similarly divided. Blackstone tried to put a face to the English King's banker, Bardi. His name had been mentioned when they first invaded Normandy and Blackstone had crept into the ceremony when the Prince of Wales was knighted in that small Norman church, but the moment had been filled by the King's presence. He could not remember ever seeing this priest, or his master, but the delicately featured Torellini, with the hands of a woman, had been entrusted with a mission by the King of England – that alone commanded respect.

'Your daughter still sleeps. The monks have attended to her and your lady stays by her side,' Father Niccolò told him. Then, in an unexpected gesture of compassion, he touched Blackstone's arm. 'They say that if she survives until dawn, she will recover. Now, let us leave her in God's hands so that we may talk.'

'Bring her here,' Blackstone said abruptly.

'What?'

'If she is close to death then she and her mother

401

will need her family's comfort. Have the monks bring them to my room. They can attend to her there. If she survives the night then I'll listen to what you have to say. If she does not, we will mourn her death and then you will continue on your journey and I on mine. Everything seems to be in God's hands.'

Father Niccolò could see no alternative but to do as Blackstone demanded. He turned back towards the infirmary. There was need for more prayer. His knees would be aching by morning.

Guillaume and Henry slept in the first cell-like chamber while Blackstone and Christiana stayed together with Agnes, who was settled on the bed that had been provided for Blackstone. The silent monks came and went every half-hour through the night. Exhausted, Christiana finally fell asleep and Blackstone covered her with a blanket, then went back to nursing his child. He dabbed water on her lips and kept the wet cloths, brought by the monks from the fountain house, on her body. At each visit the monk would bring another herbal potion and, as Blackstone cradled his child, her lips were eased apart and drops administered on her tongue.

As the hours passed by the night was disturbed by the bells that called the monks to their midnight prayers. No one in the two rooms awoke, so Blackstone kept a lone vigil. The haunting cadence of the monks' hymns and plainsongs offered an unexpected comfort to him. The night wore on, but two hours after the one period of prayer ended, another bell rang, taking the monks from their beds back to the church. Blackstone had not moved the whole night and when the bell rang for matins as the dull morning light eased through the window, he saw that Agnes's fever had broken. The child turned in her sleep; Blackstone softly stroked the curls back from her forehead and felt the tiny life under his hands respond to his touch. The morning prayers ended, and once again the infirmary monk returned to check on his patient. Blackstone allowed the man his examination, and the monk nodded and smiled, then made the sign of the cross. God had guided his hand to administer life-saving potions.

Blackstone woke Christiana and allowed her the tears a mother sheds at the news of her child's survival; then he kissed his sleeping daughter and left the room. He had made an agreement to meet with the Italian priest.

As God's breath had soothed away Agnes's fever, so too had the wind blown away the fog. Blackstone found the priest trailing the monks who were leaving the morning service. Knowing Torellini had seen him he walked around the animal pens and waited on the cliff top, from which he could now see the river that ran through the landscape below. On the horizon a brief ray of warmth slipped like a gold sword blade between earth and sky, only to be hidden almost immediately by the lowering clouds.

'Tell me what it is King Edward has charged you with,' he said.

Torellini nodded in answer to his own thoughts. Destiny, guided by the hand of God, had seen fit to deliver the child from death and Blackstone back into the King's service.

'The Prince's army is fewer than six thousand men; they are weary from months of raiding across France, but they expect the King to invade through Normandy and intend to meet him at the Loire. The Duke of Lancaster has landed in Brittany with two thousand men. The French army would be caught and crushed between the three English forces. This is the great battle to secure France that Edward has always dreamed of.'

Blackstone sensed the closeness of victory over the French, just as King Edward would have done.

'Godfrey de Harcourt went to Edward to pledge Normandy. The King now has strongholds across the north. There couldn't be a better time for him to invade.'

'Then you have not heard of Godfrey's death?' said Father Niccolò.

Blackstone felt the hollow pit of his stomach contract. The old lame knight was dead? 'What happened?'

'King Edward accepted his allegiance; he returned to his castle in Normandy and was ambushed. They cut him down.'

Ambushed. Was it the same vicious killers who had swept into Blackstone's home? Did it make a difference who killed you? Perhaps it did, if they took pleasure in making a man die slowly.

'Do we know anything more?'

'No. But King Edward fears for the Prince. He has had prayers said for him.' Torellini let the information sink in. For a King to engage chaplains to pray for his family was a rare show of anxiety.

It could only be bad news that Torellini carried.

'Then what news is it that's so important?' Blackstone asked.

'Enemy ships are in the Channel. The King cannot come. The Prince is alone with only Lancaster as reinforcement. It is the King of France who has the advantage. Everything the English have fought for over all these years could be lost.'

The French King had made promises to protect his people from the ravages of the English raids that had swept through the south-west. Taxes had to be raised, and for the King not to finally strike out at the marauding English would signal the disintegration of his country. King John had the northern army gathered at the Loire; the Count of Poitiers held the southern army to the west.

Father Niccolò spread his hands, a gesture of hopelessness. 'King Edward has many influences from Italy. Italian art adorns his palaces, our doctors serve him, he buys our armour, and English cloth is on our weavers' looms.' He looked almost apologetically at Blackstone. 'We commit money to the English throne. We have been loyal over the years, even when times were difficult and debts were not repaid.'

'War is a risk,' said Blackstone.

'Victory benefits us all,' the priest answered.

Blackstone knew it was a simple statement of fact. The common soldier pillaged at the point of a sword for his profit; the bankers weighed the odds and backed those they thought could win. The more blood spilled on the battlefield, the greater the profit to the bankers.

'Ride and warn him that he stands alone against the French. His only escape is to retreat south to Bordeaux. In time a fleet can be sent,' Father Niccolò said.

'When?'

The priest shrugged.

'His retreat might already be cut off,' Blackstone said.

'Quite so.'

'Then what?'

'The French Pope would do all he can to favour the French King. His cardinals will try to sue for peace. The Prince has plundered great wealth; he will be anxious to keep it because his army is so weak. The French could extract favourable terms.'

'You believe the Prince'll agree to peace?' Blackstone said.

Father Niccolò nodded. 'Of course. His army is

in no condition to fight a major battle and his father does not want his son killed or captured and ransomed. Prince Edward must make the best of it. You must relay the King's wishes.'

Blackstone looked out across the swathes of forest that blanketed the hills. He had no idea how far away the Prince's army might be. A messenger would have to travel quickly through those forests and hope not to be seen by French scouts or brigands. King John was making a final, desperate attempt to regain stature in the eyes of his people. He was bankrupt. Taxes could be raised only if the people were safe from raids by the barbaric English, whose depredations laid waste the countryside. Crushing the English would secure the people's loyalty and silence his critics. The retribution wreaked against the conspirators in support of Charles of Navarre was almost complete. Only Blackstone remained alive.

Torellini related what informers in the French court had reported. It was the French King's time for victory. The anxious King who suspected betrayal at every corner could finally restore France to her rightful place as the greatest kingdom in Christendom. Even royal astrologers had predicted a great shift of power for France. Encouraged by all the signs of potential victory John had forced an agreement with the thousands of French noblemen, who would bring their knights and soldiers to fight, that they would no longer have the baronial right to quit the field of battle when it suited them. For the first time, they could leave only when victory was complete or when the King allowed it. It was a binding agreement with a nobility driven by their sense of personal status and obligations of honour. It was what gave them their undeniable courage. Blackstone had witnessed enough evidence of that when the French knights kept advancing into the storm of English arrows at Crécy.

'So,' Torellini asked, 'will you ride to save your Prince?'

Blackstone knew his family would be safe under Torellini's protection – he represented not only the power of the Church but the wealth of Florence. Blackstone nodded. 'I will – but Prince Edward won't surrender,' he said. He knew the lion Prince that he had once saved loved war, but suing for peace with booty and honour intact was a temptation for any fighting man. Blackstone had fought for his King and suffered loss and injury but something of his own father's spirit had always held him close: a belligerent and unyielding duty to be honour-bound to those who deserved such loyalty. His father was once an archer loyal to his sworn lord as Blackstone had been to Sir Gilbert when they invaded Normandy all those years before. Loyalty to one another was what Killbere believed in. Men fighting side by side. The King had honoured Blackstone at Crécy and the Prince had awarded him his coat of arms at Calais. Blackstone held his towns in the King's name. He was an Englishman whose forebears stood at his back: ghosts of fighting men who denied him any choice other than to be what he was. There was no simple explanation to what lay in Blackstone's heart; he knew it was a cat's cradle of emotions that entwined his sworn lords – the King and his son – his family, friendship, and the abiding affection he held towards his men. Whatever name could be put on it, it had to be honoured. Retribution would be inflicted on those who caused any of them harm.

Edward must not retreat. The priest had offered him a means to seek his own revenge against the French monarch and his assassin – and to do that he needed a battle.

'The Prince won't surrender,' he said again.

All Agnes needed now was sleep and nourishment. Christiana bathed and fed her, then opened the shutters and looked out across the monastery's grounds. Guillaume and Henry were not in the adjoining room. Satisfied that Agnes was asleep and no longer needed constant vigilance, she pulled her cloak around her and went out into the chill wind that now blew from the north. Guests' movements within the grounds were restricted, so she could not imagine where Guillaume and Henry had gone, or why her husband had not returned. Her thoughts flew beyond the monastery walls. It was urgent that they leave once Agnes had recovered sufficiently to travel. But where would the family go? Their home had been destroyed and she had no idea of Blanche de Harcourt's fate since her escape from Rouen. How many had survived the King's revenge? All she knew was that the life they once had – all they had built – had been destroyed.

By the time she had examined the options for the family's well-being she had reached the stables. Guillaume had saddled and prepared her husband's war horse, and Henry was making final adjustments to the bridles on the two coursers. Guillaume turned to face her, but said nothing. He already knew there would be conflict between his master and Henry's mother.

'Where is Sir Thomas?' Christiana asked.

'He's talking to the priest, my lady,' the squire answered, securing Blackstone's cleaned and honed sword to the pommel.

Christiana's eyes followed the movement. Her husband was leaving her and going off to fight.

'Where are they?' she demanded.

'I don't know,' he answered. 'Somewhere in the monastery.'

Christiana saw Henry avert his eyes and fiddle needlessly with his horse's stirrup.

'Henry, are you riding with Guillaume and your father?'

'Yes, Mother,' the boy answered reluctantly, torn between affection for his mother and obedience to his father.

Christiana turned away. Her husband could not abandon her and her child at such a time.

Father Niccolò Torellini eased a ring from his finger and handed it to Blackstone. 'Take this and use it as proof that you speak on my behalf and at the command of the King. In today's world it is a matter of trust. Men can be bought and a King's messenger could be murdered,' he said.

Blackstone's fingers were all too thick to accept the gold band with its blood-red stone. Torellini smiled and offered a small drawstring pouch. 'Here, use this.'

'Offering this as a token means nothing. I could have killed you on the road and taken it,' said Blackstone.

'True, but when you see the Prince, tell him that he was present when his father gave it to me and that the chapel where we prayed that day bore the sign of St Peter. Then he will know I have sent you.'

'I might ride for days without finding Prince Edward. I may already be too late,' Blackstone said. 'No matter what happens, I need your word that my wife and daughter will be kept safe at Avignon.'

'You have it,' said the priest and grasped his arm. 'When you lay before me at Crécy I saw the body of a boy torn apart by war – not even the physicians thought you would live. Now, here is the man made whole by a generous God and given

411

great strength to serve his King. God be with you, Sir Thomas. I shall see you at Avignon.'

Blackstone caught a movement in the corner of his eye. The auburn-haired woman, her full dress pushed against her body by the freshening breeze, walked out of the stables and turned to face him. There were a hundred paces between them, but he could see the glimmer of anger in her green eyes.

'Father, I have another hurdle to clear before I leave.'

Torellini saw her and nodded. 'Good luck.'

'With my wife or in finding the Prince?'

'Whichever you perceive as the greater challenge, my son,' he said.

Christiana saw Blackstone walking towards her accompanied by a cleric dressed in a white habit. He was not of the same order as those in the monastery, who were now about their daily labour. His complexion was smooth, like that of the Spanish people. He took two steps to every one of Blackstone's, his busy hands punctuating his words. When Blackstone saw her from a distance he stopped. The priest nodded in response to something Blackstone said and moved away towards the abbey. Blackstone continued until he reached her.

'Is Agnes all right?' he asked, concerned.

'She's sleeping. They say she'll be well enough to travel in two or three days. When were you going to tell me you were leaving? Do you intend to abandon us now?'

He guided her away from the building, not wanting his explanation to be given within the walls of the portal, nor their voices to carry. The abbey had offered sanctuary, but travellers came and went, and should strangers appear in the next few days he did not want his plans whispered by gossiping monks who might wish to relieve the monotony of chanting their prayers.

'I was coming to the room to speak to you,' he said. 'There's been much to arrange since morning prayers.'

He told her what Father Niccolò had related to him.

'One man cannot save an army,' she told him after listening patiently. 'You tried to save Jean and the others, but matters are out of your hands now. Your English Prince has to defend himself with the help of others, not you. You must find a place of safety for your family, there's no other duty for you right now. We've been blessed that Agnes has survived; are you prepared to risk her life again?'

'I've struck a bargain with the Italian priest,' he said. 'I'll ride to warn Prince Edward, and Father Niccolò and his escort will take you to safety.'

'I'm in a place of safety. Do you intend us to be taken to a convent? Do you think those men who hunt you would respect undefended nuns? Thomas, there's nothing more you can do to avenge Jean and the others. We'll find a new home together, we'll start again, your name alone will bring men to serve with you,' Christiana said, trying to keep herself from pleading with him.

Blackstone turned back to look at the monastery walls. Above the arched tympanum of the sanctuary's entrance were carved images of the Last Judgement. Angels blew horns above the figure of Christ offering an open hand in blessing. Was he welcoming the righteous, or giving a warning to guard against the evil that consumed men? The blessed gathered next to Christ's right hand, while below His feet the bared jaws of a creature swallowed the damned. Carvings of man-like creatures crowded together in suffocating closeness, mouths gaping in terror of being eaten alive by the devil, stared back at him.

Paradise or hell.

He would risk one for the other.

'The Duke of Lancaster is on the north side of the Loire. He'll never get across to join Edward,' he told her.

How many times had he ridden with the Harcourts across those northern plains and stood in wonder at one of nature's great defensive barriers? The Loire's swirling eddies and currents could drag man and horse down. English forces had struggled to find a crossing all those years ago before Crécy, but now it would be impossible.

'What the Prince doesn't realize is that the river will be flooded from the heavy rains. He has no

414

reinforcements. And if he surrenders to King John, then our family will never know peace.'

'This is not about saving Edward, it's to quench your anger.' She fell silent for a moment, knowing it was useless trying to convince him to stay. 'What would you have us do?'

'There's a bargeman who will take you and the priest, with his escort, downstream. You'll make good time, and it will take you far enough south to avoid the men who hunt us. Then they'll take you by road to Avignon.'

'Avignon! The French Pope?'

'You'll be safe there. The Italian has influence. I'll join you when matters are settled.'

She looked up into his face, searching for what hidden meaning lay behind his eyes.

'I want the man who tortured and slaughtered our people,' he told her. 'You want him dead. I promised you that.'

'No, it's more than that. We are too far south for de Marcy's men to find us. He will be raiding elsewhere.'

'Or rides with the King to fight Edward.'

He was using de Marcy's name to convince her but she saw through him. She caught her breath. How well she knew him.

'No, Thomas. It's the King you really want. And they will kill you before you even get close to him.'

'He butchered Jean, hacked him to death, gave him no confessor. My friend deserved a better death and I swore to avenge him. This bastard

French King set loose the Savage Priest who flayed William and crucified Old Hugh and slaughtered our people. My people! I want them both feeling Wolf Sword through their heart.'

'You cannot abandon us now. Damn you,' she whispered, 'damn you. We have everything we need as long as we are together with the children. You're a fool, Thomas. There's no glory left to fight for. Only us.' She waited for him to say something, to rebuke her for challenging him. But he stayed silent and let his gaze stay on her. She touched the scar on his face. 'You have tested God's patience too many times. You've bargained with Him once too often. He'll take you this time. You'll widow me and I shall be left to beg on the strength of your name.'

'Then you will never starve,' he said, bitter that she had stepped away from him when he needed her embrace.

'You'll not take Henry,' she bargained.

'You had him for seven years. You taught him to read and write, you gave him what a child needed . . .'

'He's still a child!'

'Only to you! He's in his ninth year! He has to learn about war, Christiana. I've already broken tradition by keeping him with me. By now he should have been with another family serving as a page. He has to learn. Better he does it under my protection.'

'No. He stays with me and Agnes. He's proved

his courage already. He stays with us, Thomas, I mean it. I won't have him dragged to the slaughter, there'll be enough killing to come in his life, but I won't have him sacrificed for your vengeance.'

Blackstone smothered the rising anger that threatened to inflame their argument. Tears of defiance welled in Christiana's eyes.

'We part on bad terms, Christiana. I don't want that.'

'Then leave Henry with me.'

'You blackmail me.'

'Only because my love is not enough.'

There, in that moment, she broke down his resistance. 'You use a velvet glove to wield a mace. I always give in to you,' he said.

'Only when you know I'm right.'

'Which seems to be more often than not.' He nodded. 'The boy can stay.'

She stepped up to him and he embraced her. He smelled the fragrance of rosemary soap she had used to wash her hair, and felt the warmth of her soft skin as he laid his lips on her neck.

Paradise or hell.

When the bells sounded at sext, the midday sun was only a promising glow behind the cloud. Blackstone and Guillaume rode down the escarpment to the edge of the forest. Guillaume looked back towards the monastery, where, for at least a short while, they had been safe. Blackstone had spoken to the English soldiers who escorted the

Italian priest and offered them silver coin for their ongoing protection of Christiana and the children.

'We are on the King's business, Sir Thomas,' the sergeant had said. 'And our orders were to deliver the priest to Prince Edward. There's nothing in 'em that says we have to go to Avignon. You can see how this makes it difficult for us to honour your request.'

'I have agreed to relieve Father Niccolò of his responsibility so I'll be riding to the Prince, and the information I have for him is vital. The priest will deliver my family to the Pope. No one will strike at them there. If I leave this monastery and go my own way, you'll be dead by nightfall. The forest and valleys crawl with Frenchmen and those they pay to hunt and kill us. You'll stumble like blind men in the battle. This way, you'll reach safety and have the pleasure of the whores at Avignon.' Blackstone had tossed the bag of coins to the sergeant, who felt its weight in his hand. He looked at the others.

'Take the money,' one of his men said. 'The King's business will still be attended to. It makes no difference who takes the message to the Prince. It's a fair bargain.'

'When you reach Avignon, Father Niccolò will reward you with another payment. And I will be in your debt,' Blackstone told them.

One of the soldiers snorted and spat. 'My lord, if what you say is true, there's as much chance of you living as a rat in a dog pit.'

His sergeant rounded on him. 'Quiet, Rudd. Sir Thomas is right. One man who knows the lie of the land could get through better'n us riding with the Italian. And if there's a wager to be made, my money is on him.' He tossed the coins back to Blackstone. 'We'll take the payment from the priest, Sir Thomas. Havin' your bond is worth more'n a few coins.'

Rudd snarled: 'It's us as well! It's not for you to say! Take his money!'

Without warning the sergeant struck the man down. 'You'll do as I command, you whore's son, or I'll cut your hamstrings and leave you in the forest to fend for yourself!' He faced Blackstone. 'You leave the priest and your family to us. And when you reach Avignon you'll know where to find us.'

Blackstone looked to the others. They nodded. The fallen man got to his feet.

The agreement had been made.

Guillaume faced the road ahead. Blackstone had not given even a backward glance.

They parted several miles to the north. Blackstone sketched a map into the dirt.

'Send word to the towns. Leave half the men, those with women and children – they'll have more to fight for – and gather the rest. Meet me somewhere about here,' he said, pointing at a scrape that served as the river that ran north of Poitiers's walled city. 'The Count of Poitiers has his army to the west and he'll move south with King John. I have to catch up with Edward. If they get behind him he has nowhere to go and the French will crush him. His only chance of escape would be surrender.'

'The English will be hard pressed to move at speed. Their wagons are loaded with months of plunder. How long before they're trapped?' said Guillaume.

'Probably no more than two or three days.'

'And if you aren't there, what do I do?' Guillaume asked.

Blackstone climbed into the saddle. 'Serve the Prince, then ride to Avignon. I'll be dead.'

CHAPTER 26

Blackstone found his way through the countryside from memory. Landmarks were few and far between, but the lie of the land and the prevailing winds helped him gauge direction. By the end of the first day he had crisscrossed forest trails and negotiated his way across a fast-flowing river. By nightfall, soaked through and numb with cold, he rode as far as the dwindling light would permit, then curled the reins round his fist and slept with his back against a tree and his shield across his body. He awoke before first light when the breeze shifted and brought the smell of woodsmoke into the trees. Men had moved into the forest during the night, but there was little smoke, which meant the men would be some distance away. He listened, but there was no sound: no disgruntled voices complaining of the cold or of the hard ground where they slept.

He led the horse, feeling his way forward in the darkness with the length of his sword, tapping the trees like a blind beggar. By the time he reached the open ground he could see distant pinpricks of light from a half-dozen fires scattered across the landscape, small speckles of red, giving off wispy smoke in the still, predawn air.

He wondered if Guillaume could make it as far as the towns where his men awaited their orders. If the French had scouting parties scattered across the land, neither he nor his squire would get through unless the gods smiled or Arianrhod covered his journey with her gossamer wings. At a time when a morning mist was most wanted, the land was clear from the fresh breeze that allowed men to see for miles.

The fires to the east were the most distant, and the broken ground and gorges between him and those men offered a buffer. But those who were closer – whose fire he could smell in the damp air but could not see – they were the most dangerous. How long could he ride before they came upon him? Men's limbs would be stiff, and they would be slow to react, still groggy from a night's sleep. Now was the time for risk. He gathered the reins and spurred the horse. To ride slowly and with caution could invite a sudden, unexpected attack. If he rode hard the horse's hoof beats would probably alert some of the men, but at least he would have the momentum to outdistance anyone in pursuit.

There was no track across the broad meadows and no sign of men labouring in the fields. He knew there were villagers scattered across the hills, but they had either been frightened by marauding brigands or word had reached them from travellers on the road to and from Poitiers that the English were close. Most in this area were loyal to King John, so Blackstone knew he would be given no shelter.

Once Blackstone had raced across the open plain, he eased his horse into the edge of another forest. Dismounting, he walked the horse through the dense woodland, then tethered it and made his way back to the forest's edge. He had a clear view across the open valley into the foothills and the woodland he had travelled through. It did not take long for him to see the distant riders – half a dozen or more – making their way down onto the track and then cantering as they followed one man who scouted ahead of the group. This man halted them and pointed to Blackstone's tracks. The galloping horseman they had heard meant the rider sought no comfort from a campfire. And who might risk avoiding them? An English messenger might, and he would be a valuable prize. The horsemen looked towards the forest, where Blackstone unconsciously took a step further back into the undergrowth. One of the riders, who appeared to be in charge, raised himself in the stirrups and swung his sword arm in a broad arc, evidently a signal. There must be another group of men on Blackstone's side of the valley. The riders turned their horses onto the meadow and made their way towards him.

Blackstone pushed through the trees. Branches

clawed out from the lower trunks – they would rip a man's face off if he tried to ride through them. He led the horse and cleared the path with his sword until he was deeper still into the forest. With luck the men would be slowed by the same problem, but he had to make headway before they entered the woods and heard the slashing of his blade. He redoubled his efforts, desperate not to be entrapped in such a confined fighting area. Shafts of sunlight suddenly penetrated the canopy. The wind had cleared the morning cloud and showed him the way to a track made by wood-cutters and charcoal burners from one of the nearby villages. Blackstone climbed into the saddle and listened. There was the crack of dry wood beneath horses' hooves, and muted cursing. They had not yet dismounted and fought their way through the labyrinth.

No sooner had he felt the brief comfort of advantage than he heard an excited cry. One of the men was already on the track a few hundred paces behind him. Some of them must have found an easier way through the forest. The man called out again, telling the others that he had found their quarry.

Blackstone spurred his horse along the track. Within half a league it became wider, with grass verges and wildflowers mixed with a tangle of new saplings. His horse smashed through easily as he pulled it off the track and plunged back into the forest. Men had been at work in this part of the woodland, which was less dense, allowing him to manoeuvre the horse through it. He needed another woodcutter's trail before they surrounded him. If there were crossbowmen among them they could have him down and at their mercy.

Now voices carried back and forth in the forests behind and to one side. The men had spread themselves out in their search for him and called so their sweep was broad and thorough. Whoever came across Blackstone first would soon summon the rest. He listened to the sound of their progress around him. They were close. He eased forward in the saddle and rested his hand on his horse's face. Stay calm, stay calm, he whispered in his mind. One man appeared thirty paces to his left, bending over his pommel as he ducked below a low branch.

The man's eyes looked right at him for a second or more, but did not see any movement so the glance yielded nothing and the man pushed on forwards. Blackstone turned at the sound of another approaching horseman. He was making his way through the trees, jinking left and right as he avoided branches and fallen boughs; his head was down, looking to see how to guide his horse through the fetlock-snapping undergrowth on the forest floor. He was within ten paces; if he looked up now he would see Blackstone. Another voice cried out beyond the man, and the rider turned in that direction, away from Blackstone's position.

The voices fell silent and only a faint crushing of undergrowth could be heard. Blackstone eased the big horse forward, though he knew that the sound of its passage must be heard by the searchers. He hoped they would think horsemen moving so close to them must be one of their own. The trees thinned, a narrow track presented itself and he urged the horse forward.

A few hundred yards further on Blackstone lost his advantage. The track broadened out into a clearing – a disused woodcutters' encampment containing several old fire pits.

Blackstone reined in his horse. The shadows of the forest moved from the trees into the clearing. It was the second group of horsemen. The men-at-arms urged their mounts forwards and then stopped. Behind him the same movement told him he was surrounded. He glanced back. Ten men waited, their nervous mounts sensing their riders' anxiety: wanting to kill him, but hesitating. Ten behind, ten to the front. No crossbowmen. Some wore pieces of armour, others mail, a few nothing more than a hobelar's jerkin. Twenty men. A scouting party for the bigger force? Which was where? Or were they brigands – roaming bands of looters? Had these been the men who had attacked his home and slaughtered his people? Blackstone did not move. If they struck at him with urgency he would not survive. Their manner indicated they were overconfident, convinced that one man could not harm them.

The track ahead, his way out beyond the clearing, was barred by six of the men, three behind three. The others' formation had been determined by the space between the trees. He felt his horse's muscled bulk fight against the rein, its hooves back-stepping, gathering energy, waiting for its rider's command.

To his right, beyond the men, the forest offered a tantalizing refuge, but by the time he could forge past the swordsmen and blunder through the low branches he would be more vulnerable than safe – and that was provided he could hack his way through sufficient numbers of the men.

There was a better way. He would feint to the right, draw the men from the front rank off the track, and attack the three in the rear. These men rode poor quality mounts, rounceys and palfreys; his horse's strength would give him the advantage of momentum. Those who encircled him would hesitate long enough for him to kill at least two of them and then the track ahead would be clear. He could outrun them.

He gathered the reins, held Wolf Sword low, ready for a slashing cut to the unguarded neck of the first man's horse. Blackstone followed a simple rule in battle: inflict the most violence on the enemy in the shortest time. Striking fear into opponents was as potent a weapon as a sword thrust.

He gathered the horse's strength below him.

'We've spent many a cold night looking for you.

We found the others by the river,' one of the men to his front called.

Blackstone made no answer.

'You seek the man who ordered the slaughter at your manor?' the man asked.

Blackstone eased the pressure from his knees, the horse moving skittishly on the spot. He calmed it.

'You were there?' Blackstone demanded.

'We were,' the man answered, looking at the others, a decayed grin confirming the pleasure they'd had. 'The peasants said you ruled them with fear. That they had no choice but to obey you on pain of death. Well, we gave them that. It made no difference. We weren't interested in them. It was you or your family we wanted.'

'And now you've found me.' Blackstone waited. The men had not advanced, still cautious because of who he was. 'You butchered them. Killing was not enough – was that King John's command?'

'King John wanted you dead, and his payment was generous, but Lord de Marcy is our master and he wanted to inflict a greater pain.' The man hesitated; then his voice took on a meaner edge. 'Your reputation rides ahead of you, Sir Thomas, and we think he would pay more if we took you alive and he had the pleasure of torturing you himself. He likes value for his money.'

Routiers. Mercenaries. English, Germans, Gascons – men of various ranks, all ex-soldiers, all taking their pay from an experienced captain

428

promising booty and rape. No different from half the scum Blackstone had paid when seizing citadels in the name of Edward, King of England, and in the name of Thomas Blackstone, except he would not allow the killing of women and children. It was a decree often enforced by brutal punishment of those who disobeyed.

'So he could crucify me?' Blackstone said.

The man laughed. 'Good sport was had with your old hunchback, my lord. He screamed like a pig when we castrated him. Your balls alone would be a prize worth having. What shall it be? A chance of life? A gelded stallion still has its use.'

'Twenty men against one. I have no choice,' Blackstone answered.

He had manoeuvred his horse so that it angled against the block of six men. He would drive a wedge between them and this maggot-mouthed bastard would be the first to feel the agony of Wolf Sword's bite.

And then Blackstone realized he was trapped.

He had a good view of the track. Arrow-straight it cut through the forest for five hundred yards but now in the distance he could see other men running forward, and behind them, a horseman. His escape route was blocked.

The advancing men on the track did so at a fast pace and then stopped three hundred yards away. The men behind Blackstone rose up in their stirrups. One raised his sword arm in salute.

'We have him!' he cried.

Blackstone watched the sky flicker as a dozen dark missiles curved against the clouds. He knew the whispering sigh would follow and that he dare not move. He was not the target. Those were English archers on the track. Eight men fell; horses screamed as arrows plunged into them. Confusion and disbelief broke the men's ranks.

Blackstone spurred his horse three strides forward and swept his blade across his antagonist's thigh. The force of the blow and the sword's sharpness cut through muscle and bone. It was a deliberate stroke to disable the man. He had information that Blackstone needed. The man fell heavily; his body spasmed as he clutched what remained of his leg with both hands. His screams drove rooks and crows from the branches into a cacophony of a devil's choir.

Blackstone barged his horse against another whose rider fell before he could deliver a blow; a third routier, panic spoiling his aim, caught Blackstone's shoulder with the tip of his blade. Blackstone's mail took the cut. He yanked his reins to face his assailant. Before another blow fell a yard-long arrow punched through the man's chest. The men on the track had moved nearer. The unknown knight on the track galloped closer, his sword raised to kill one of Blackstone's attackers whose horse had bolted into the path of the advancing men. The surviving routiers plunged into the forest to escape the arrows.

Blackstone's victim lay on the stained ground,

shivering from loss of blood, desperately trying to tie off his half-severed leg and staunch the blood with his jerkin's belt. He had vomited, but the stench and foulness made no impression on Blackstone, who dismounted and laid the blade against the man's throat.

'Where is de Marcy?'

'Save me, Lord Blackstone. Seal the wound. Heat the blade and seal the wound. I beg you.'

The horseman pulled up and watched Blackstone standing over the injured man. The knight's visor was still closed, his weathered shield smothered in dents from years of battle obscuring even more of his coat of arms. Blackstone barely gave him a glance as the bowmen ran into the clearing. They, too, offered no threat to Blackstone.

'Tell me where he is and I'll have a fire lit and sear the wound. You'll have a chance to live,' he said to the gasping man.

'Your word?'

'You have my word.'

'He rides with King John's army. Close to the King himself.'

Blackstone was unaware that the French army was already this far south.

'How do I recognize him?'

'He has a dead man's face. His eyes black like fire pits, as black as his shield and pennon. Half a finger missing.'

An incomplete memory flickered in Blackstone's mind. When he was an archer, Caen had fallen and he searched the bloodied streets for his brother when he caught a priest who robbed the dead. Blackstone had pinned him to a church door, their faces close enough to smell the other's breath. In the struggle he had severed one of the priest's fingers. The same priest? The gods of war played cruel jests.

'He's a man of the cloth?'

The man nodded. 'Once. They call him "le Prêtre sanguinaire".'

Blackstone rammed the sword into the man's throat.

The horseman steadied his mount as the man writhed. 'That's what your word means, does it?' he said.

Blackstone pulled the sword free and grabbed the horse's reins ready to face a possible challenge. 'It depends who you give it to. Murderous scum deserve what they get.'

The knight pushed up his visor. Blackstone took a pace back.

'You're a scar-faced, bull-pit mongrel, Thomas, and you fight like one. Sweet Jesus on the Cross! I never thought to see you again. You should have been dead years ago at Crécy,' said Sir Gilbert Killbere and leapt down to embrace Blackstone.

Killbere's was a scouting group, looking for French forces. Prince Edward was desperate to know the direction of King John's army's approach, but Sir Gilbert had found only scattered pockets of soldiers, who fled into the forests when they saw the archers. Once the bowmen had recovered their mounts Killbere led the group across country. It would take three hours to reach Prince Edward's main force. Blackstone spoke briefly of his mission to reach the Prince, but made no mention of the message he had to deliver.

'You don't trust me?' Killbere grunted with annoyance. 'Me? Mother of God, Thomas, I took you under my wing!'

'It'll wait, my lord.'

'My lord? Thomas, we're equals now, man, at least address me by my name! Share your burden. What's the message? If your horse stumbles and you break your neck I'll need to know.'

'This horse never stumbles, my lord.' Blackstone smiled, pleased that after all these years he could ride by Killbere's side in friendship as an equal, and annoy the old fighter without falling victim to a cuff across the head.

'You're as stubborn as you are broad!' Killbere fumed. 'A pig's arse makes better conversation when it farts.'

Blackstone settled the matter by telling Sir Gilbert of his own life's events since Crécy and, mollified, the usually reticent Killbere recounted to Blackstone all he could not know of the previous ten years in England. Lord Marldon was dead, Chandler the overseer took Blackstone's land as he had vowed, but months after Crécy was found, as Killbere had once predicted, outside a tavern with his throat cut.

'Lord Marldon never forgot those who betrayed him, as Chandler had when he turned your brother in to the sheriff,' Sir Gilbert told him.

Blackstone shook his head. 'I can barely remember any of it. I was a boy. We laughed a lot in those days.'

'Laughter can still be had with tavern ale and a whore's hand on your crotch. Sweet Jesus, who remembers anything any more? We fight for a King and the purse he offers. Life is simple, Thomas. I always said you think too much. A soldier needs luck when he fights. And you, you've God's hand on your shoulder, you lucky bastard. Look at you!'

Blackstone touched the silver medallion of his protector at his neck. 'I'm being hunted. And my family. Jean de Harcourt and his friends went under the axe. They were betrayed.'

'You know who?'

Blackstone nodded. 'I killed him.'

'Then an Englishman's sword is still God's avenging angel.'

'You've found religion?'

'It found me. Underneath that damned war horse at Crécy. I challenged God to let me live with the promise that I'd kill all those who went against my divine King. It seemed a good bargain for the Lord and for me. Edward has plenty of enemies.'

Blackstone remembered the blurred tumult of conflict and Sir Gilbert falling beneath a French knight's war horse.

'I always thought you had died that day.'

'The rain and blood-soaked ground saved me,' Sir Gilbert told him. 'The French horses churned that field better than yoked oxen. I broke my leg and some ribs, but they dragged me unconscious from under the beast. I had two knights ransomed and the King bought them from me.' He spat and swallowed wine from a skin. 'How long can a man keep money in the world today? I bought a small estate close to Lord Marldon's, but I got bored with beating peasants for not tilling my land. I'm no landowner, I'm a soldier. Besides, I lost it all gambling.'

'The others?' Blackstone asked.

'Elfred lives. He made enough money from the plunder to buy his own men. Will Longdon's with him. Elfred's a captain now with a hundred archers under his command.'

Blackstone's memory of his old comrades who served as bowmen was rekindled. 'Are they close by?'

'He serves Prince Edward – has done since the raiding started here. I swear Edward's more ferocious than his father. We've burned and pillaged every damned town and village in our path for almost a year. I wager he'd drag our arses around France for the next ten years if the King wanted it, but he can't – not any longer. King John's tail is up. He's given chase. We're on the run. Thank God Lancaster is coming.'

Blackstone remained silent. An exhausted army

needed hope and his message was about to rip that from them as surely as that bastard priest had torn the heart from his servant in Normandy. Blackstone's past had caught up with him. There was no such thing as chance; it was destiny that had brought him back to the English. Now a creature from a brief moment in his past, who was then little more than a shadow on the streets of an embattled city, a common priest cutting fingers from men for their rings, had grown in stature and power and fed his cruelty a rich diet of inflicted pain. And he rode with the French.

So be it. Blackstone would embrace his fate and wreak vengeance on a King who had butchered his friend and unleashed one of God's fallen on his family. He would slay them both and put an end to destiny's torment.

CHAPTER 27

The English army sprawled across the land-scape, exhausted from months of fighting and indiscriminate killing on their mighty *chevauchée* across France. They rested, short of water and with their food supplies dwindling, around the stone fortress outside the town of Montbazon. Prince Edward stood in the great hall with his most able commanders – the Earls of Suffolk, Warwick, Oxford and Salisbury – in attendance. The most able war leaders of King Edward's kingdom looked as grubby and spent as the men they led. Prince Edward turned Father Niccolò's ring in his fingers.

'We know the provenance of this ring, Sir Thomas, as we know yours. Your name was often spoken in our father's court. Blackstone the knight in France who took towns in his name, Blackstone the man who put to death those who opposed him, Blackstone . . . the boy archer we ennobled for the life you saved. We do not doubt your word, Thomas.'

'Still, my lord, I am to tell you that it was given to the Italian at the chapel that bore the sign of St Peter,' said Blackstone.

'So it was. We remember.' He handed the ring back to Blackstone. 'You'll see it is returned to its owner. It was given in generosity for service to the Crown.'

'I will, my lord.'

Prince Edward was agitated. 'And you say Lancaster cannot come, and neither can the King.'

'No, sire.'

'The Italians are keen to see their investments safe; they don't care about what we do to serve their debt.'

'The King cares more for your safety,' said Blackstone.

Killbere was included in the group of commanders. 'The routiers were keen to take him, sire. He could have stayed out of sight for his own safety and then his message would have come too late.' Killbere looked to where three papal representatives were ushered into an antechamber. Their red hats flopped across their purple robes as they sat on looted gold-encrusted chairs provided for their comfort by the English Prince. 'Those poisonous toadstools'd have us roll over like beaten dogs with our belly and balls for the whole of Christendom to see.'

'And they may yet see them. King John's army is less than ten miles behind us on our left flank,' said the Prince. 'Do you think we could make Bordeaux before the French catch us, Thomas?'

There was a Roman road south-east of Poitiers,

which ran across undulating pastures and woodland. If it could be reached in time it would allow
the English to move more rapidly with their
loaded wagons. It was also the route King John
would take if Edward refused to surrender. The
English would be caught in the open, running
like hares from the hounds.

'Do you know how many have answered the
arrière-ban?' Blackstone asked, ignoring the question as he tried to formulate an answer.

The Earl of Suffolk flicked his head towards
what lay unseen beyond the Périgord forests: 'Our
scouts counted over eighty banners. Sixteen to
twenty thousand, perhaps fewer.'

Prince Edward stood and paced the room. His
original force had been increased with Gascon
troops, but that was months ago. He looked out
of a window that showed him the ragged state of
his army sprawled below.

'We've near enough six thousand,' the Prince
said, a worried frown suddenly creasing his face.

'The French'll not leave the field, sire, not unless
King John orders it. Father Niccolò has spies in
the French court. Their nobles are obliged to see
you defeated,' Blackstone said and looked to the
flanks where the archers gathered to eat what food
they had left. 'How many archers?'

'Less than two thousand, and they have too few
arrows. You'll speak to them for us, Thomas. Hey,
Oxford?' he queried the man who would command
elements of the English and Welsh bowmen.

'Aye, let him speak to them, my lord, his presence will lift their spirits.'

The men fell silent. Blackstone could see they were tense. Killbere could barely restrain himself from commenting on the lack of a decision. Blackstone was under no such restraint.

'You wish to surrender, my lord?'

Blackstone had done what no one else had dared: to question the Prince of Wales and with a tone that hinted of derision. And the Prince knew it.

'Be mindful, Thomas,' said Salisbury. 'Mindful.'

Blackstone stared at the Prince of Wales, the man who had elevated his status and who believed Thomas Blackstone had cut through a horde of French knights to save his life, nearly sacrificing his own. It was a debt that could never be forgotten, even by a prince. And the Prince would never know the truth.

'They'll surround us and starve us out. And then we have lost everything and I am ransomed,' Edward answered.

'Then make ready and fight,' said Blackstone.

The Prince's voice rasped with irritation. 'In the name of God! Can the army run far and fast enough? You know this place! Tell me!'

'Run, sire? Women and dogs run.'

'Blackstone!' Warwick shouted, taking a stride towards him, but the Prince was already ahead of him, a restraining arm halting him.

'There are so few of us! Our men are exhausted and we have no water! And you accuse me of cowardice!'

Blackstone had not flinched. The two men were of equal height. Their strength was comparable, only one had rank's greater stature.

Blackstone did not yield. He spoke plainly in a measured tone that bore an inflection that could leave no doubt in the Prince's mind.

'You have scorched this country from head to toe. You've slaughtered men, women and children in a vicious manner that will always be remembered and defame your name. You have wallowed in victory over the innocent and the poor and you have raped and pillaged until France weeps blood. You are not the boy Prince who fought at Crécy until battered to his knees; you are the Prince who ripped this land to shreds without contest and with disgrace! What kind of honour is that?'

The stunned silence was broken by Salisbury and Warwick grabbing Blackstone's arms in fear that his disregard would lead him to strike Edward. Blackstone offered no resistance. He had taunted the heir to the throne and could lose his life for it.

The Prince of Wales hesitated, and then turned on his heel and headed for the cardinals. The Earls followed after looking uncomprehendingly at the rogue knight.

Killbere paused before turning from the pavilion. 'Sweet Jesus, Thomas – still defiant unto death!'

Blackstone watched the men approach the cardinals, ready to discuss the terms of surrender. The huge oak doors closed on them. He had done as he had promised Father Niccolò, but had omitted the King's orders that the Prince should sign a truce and return safely home.

Blackstone rode bareheaded along the ranks. Some men called him by name; others ignored him, unaware of who the scar-faced, dirt-caked knight was. He looked almost too poor to afford the habergeon of mail beneath his grimy surcoat and padded leather jerkin that lay across the saddle's pommel. A knight without armour, squire or page was a beggar on the battlefield.

Blackstone went in search of the English and Welsh archers and found the green-and-white-clad men away from the others as they lit their fires and cooked what little pottage was left to them. Many of the faces from ten years ago were not there, but the type of man had not changed, and they looked just like those with whom Blackstone had served. Thick-muscled men and boys brought on from childhood to use the mighty war bow. But this was not the army of ten years ago; these archers might sting the enemy and kill a few hundred, but the Prince was right: they had too few archers and too few arrows. Arrow bags were less than half full, like the men who sat slumped; dispirited from the gruelling *chevauchée*. And this was bad news for Prince Edward. The English needed their archers to win their wars.

For the first time Blackstone noticed the grizzled

stubble that clung to etched features. The men looked exhausted. Their wind-burnished faces could not disguise the hollow tiredness beneath their eyes. Blackstone looked around him. All the men had that same haunted look. They were not fit to fight a major battle. And Prince Edward was no fool.

'That old nag could serve the army better if we put it on a spit, sir knight,' said a voice from somewhere back among the archers.

Blackstone reined the horse to a halt. He searched for the man who had spoken. Once again the voice called: 'And you'd be better with a bow in your hand – better'n that German's sword you stole when he wasn't looking.'

Blackstone dismounted and pushed his way through the men until he came to one whose back refused to turn from his cooking pot. Blackstone kicked him gently, pushing him to the ground.

'You never did have any respect for authority, Will Longdon,' Blackstone said as he extended his arm to help raise the archer to his feet.

The men embraced, and laughed with the joy of seeing each other again.

'And you've not lost your common touch, Thomas, or the strength in your boot. So – you missed your old comrades so much after all these years that you came all the way down here to see us. What? You miss sixpence a day and all the misery you can bear?'

Will Longdon led the way through the men, up

a short incline and into the fringe of a forest. A man emerged from the treeline.

'I found this knight wandering lost,' said Longdon.

Elfred grinned and clasped Blackstone to him. 'Still don't know which way the enemy is coming from then, Thomas? Sweet Mother of God, it was a fine surgeon that stopped half your face falling onto your shoulder,' he said, looking up into the leathered face and the white scar that travelled across it.

'I begged the surgeon not to let me end up like Will here. His face would make a dog's arse on a moonlit night look a thing of beauty.'

Elfred pulled him to a group of archers who shared a cooking pot.

'Give us space, lads, if you please,' he told them. Elfred's archers moved away, leaving the three men to settle and take a share of the food. Blackstone declined.

'There's enough,' Elfred insisted.

'No, there isn't. A blind man could see that. Keep it for your men. I'll eat with Sir Gilbert later.'

Elfred passed the pot to Longdon, who took a spoonful and passed it back.

'Here!' Elfred called to one of his men who squatted with others sharing a meagre pot.

'Master Elfred?' a boy answered.

Elfred gave the boy the pot. 'Share it out as I told you.'

The boy returned to the others.

Elfred sighed. 'He's fourteen. Lied about his age. But he's a born archer, Thomas. Just as you were.'

'I had an archer's eye; no more, no less, Elfred. And good men who taught me how to fight. Just as you did.'

As with all soldiers, the rights and wrongs of the campaign were soon bemoaned. The exaggerations were trimmed and the reality of their situation was obvious to everyone. Between the stories and the memories of past days, of who had died and who had not on that historic day at Crécy, Blackstone told his own story.

'The Savage Priest?' Elfred said in answer to Blackstone's question. 'Never heard of him. Will?'

'I stay away from clergy, be they savage or otherwise,' the archer answered.

'You know where to find this black-hearted creature?' Elfred asked.

'I need a battle to get to him,' said Blackstone.

His companions fell silent. 'Thomas,' Elfred said, 'we're finished here. We're laden and we want to get home. When the King lands, and Lancaster gets to us, then that might be different. Some fresh muscle is what we need, then maybe we can give this French King a thrashing. We tried to kill his father at Crécy. He took an arrow in the face – I like to think it was mine – but if the French army come at us now, I tell you he'll have us like rats in a sack.'

Blackstone accepted a wineskin offered by one

of the men. The rough red wine caught his throat, and he coughed.

'The years of soft living and fine wines have spoiled a good archer,' Longdon said. The men laughed, but the archer raised a hand to silence them. 'You new lads have had an easy time of it. You've heard me talk about Thomas Blackstone and his brother. We came ashore in Normandy and we saw real fighting, not raiding these country towns and taking what we wanted; no, we fought like tomcats to stop the French castrating us, and we bled and we died together. Only then did we take our plunder.'

'Sir Gilbert will tell you what a liar Will Longdon is,' Blackstone told them. The men laughed and gibed. 'I'm no longer an archer,' he said, holding up his bent arm. 'You might have guessed that already. But I still fight like one. You can break an archer's war bow, and you can cut the draw fingers from his hand and even take the arm, but unless you cut out his heart and set it on a pike, then you can never kill the way an archer fights.'

The men roared with approval. Blackstone's presence would race through the companies of archers like a heathland fire in summer and his words would be told again and again; embellished each time in the telling; confirming an archer's belief in his own prowess and filling each man's heart with pride in who he was and the glory of past deeds. An empty belly could be endured, but a soldier needed a blood-gorged heart to keep fighting.

Blackstone stood. 'I'd best get back. I'll bring you what news there is.'

The men embraced again. 'God rides at your shoulder, Thomas. If you can survive everything that's befallen you, then there's hope for us all.'

'You cling to that, Elfred. And sharpen your knives. The King and Lancaster are not coming.'

CHAPTER 28

Prince Edward and his commanders watched the Cardinal and his entourage turn their donkeys and ride back to the French King and his army, a dozen miles away, where they waited for news of whether Prince Edward accepted the Cardinal's peace proposals. King John was intemperate, but had enough sense to know when a papal legation could serve his purpose. Keep the English Prince talking long enough and he would further exhaust his supplies. Time bought would allow even more French reinforcements to join the army.

The Prince spoke quickly, flourishing a document: 'Relinquish all that we have taken. Surrender all conquests in France from the past three years, pay two hundred thousand nobles in recompense, repair all that we have damaged and they will let Navarre out of prison.'

'My lord,' Suffolk asked, 'are you of a mind to accept?'

'Would you deny us betrothal to a daughter of the King? It's what's promised if we agree. She would bring us the county of Angoulême as her dowry. Good lands, Suffolk. Another foothold for the King. Can you deny us that? A good match, Sir Gilbert, would you say?'

'A fine dowry, my lord, but I'll wager this daughter has teats like crab apples, a face like a rat and the breath of a dog.'

No one could restrain their laughter, except the Prince himself, whose silence cut them short. Prince Edward faced him. 'You offend a royal house, Sir Gilbert.'

'Only if they are French, my lord,' Sir Gilbert answered simply.

The Prince smiled, crumpling the peace proposal. 'Prepare to move,' he told his commanders. 'We use the time the Cardinal takes to explain his proposals to King John to get ourselves closer to Bordeaux. Let them think we are considering their offer.'

'Do we find ground and fight, sire?' Killbere asked.

'We run as hard and fast as we can, Sir Gilbert, and pray the Cardinal convinces King John that we have no wish to confront him. Now, where's that insolent Blackstone?'

Killbere pointed across the meadows to where the mounted knight turned away from the companies of archers. Their cheer could be heard within the walls of the stone fortress.

'He's a war leader, my lord,' Killbere said simply.

Edward turned from the room. 'Then there's

the pity. Because there's no damned war for him to fight!' retorted the Prince.

Within the hour Prince Edward led an English army that pulled itself along like a crippled soldier. Sir Gilbert and Blackstone were summoned, and rode alongside him.

'We will not be shamed into battle. You will not speak to your Prince with such insolence ever again. It is not for you to know what lies in our mind, Blackstone,' he said.

'I apologize, sire, but it's not only France that will be lost should you surrender, but the glory of England. There's no country in the world that doesn't know of our King's greatness. The heart needs to spur a man's mind,' Blackstone answered.

'You're a common man, Thomas. You behave as a base archer who would cut a man's throat to see how long it took for him to die. You offend your rank if you believe that you were knighted so you could hurl insult and abuse at your King's Prince. Had he been here he would have had a rope around your neck for such insolence.'

'That you did not, sire, shows an understanding greater than that of even his highness, and I mean no disrespect to my sovereign lord.'

'I wonder, Thomas. Do you respect anything or anyone?'

'I respect a man who makes a necessary and difficult decision when an easier option is offered,'

Blackstone said carefully. He wasn't yet free of any charge of impertinence.

Edward rode on in silence for another minute.

'You want revenge, Thomas, and you wish to use me to secure it,' the Prince said finally. 'I know what happened to de Harcourt. Our father also has his spies in the French court. Do not deny it.'

'I do not, my lord.'

'And Father Torellini's message from the King? Was I to surrender?'

'The King wishes that you return safely, unharmed and without ransom. The decision to yield should be yours,' Blackstone admitted.

Prince Edward turned to look at Blackstone. 'Don't ever lie to your Prince again. Not even by omission.'

Blackstone held his gaze. 'Everything I said was true, my lord. We should not leave this country with dishonour.'

Prince Edward knew Blackstone would not recant his accusation of the brutal campaign he had led across France these several months. It had been bloody and merciless. It had been necessary. Scouring a man's skin to the bone while no one tried to defend him was no different from John the Good standing aside while his country was put to the torch. The dishonour lay with the French King.

'The French King's army grows stronger by the hour; we need to know how long we have before finding a suitable place to make our stand,' the Prince told him. 'You and Sir Gilbert will ride ahead with thirty men and find me such a place. We've a day – two at best.'

'You'll fight then, my lord?' Killbere asked.

The Prince stared ahead to a road that led to an uncertain future.

'It was always our intention to do so,' he said. A glint flashed in his eyes. A smile barely curved his mouth. A great battle and a chance for victory over the French King could not be denied.

Blackstone and Killbere urged their horses on as Salisbury spurred his horse to take their place.

'I'd have had him staked out and flogged and sent back to his French whore tied backwards on a donkey,' the old warrior said.

Edward smiled. 'No, William, you would not. You value him as much as we do. He will die to see justice done. You cannot ask more of a man than that.' Prince Edward raised a flask to his lips and swilled the dryness from his throat. 'And his wife is no French whore. She's a Norman whose father died defending his land against us. We should thank God that Blackstone still fights on the side of the English.'

Blackstone and Killbere searched the skyline for French forces and bands of routiers. The English army needed to gain ground if they were to stay ahead of their enemy. If de Marcy's routiers were riding with the regulars they were most likely acting as their scouts. Killbere's outriders reported that French pennons could be seen beyond the hills.

'They've outmanoeuvred us,' Killbere said. 'Bastard French whoreson wasn't listening to any parley; he's covering his arse with steel-plated breeches.'

'He can move faster than us. He'll be close to the Roman road at Poitiers. We can worry him enough to let Edward bring the main body forward. We have to get men up here with us.'

Killbere sent riders back to the Prince with the message that the French were close to cutting off his route to Bordeaux.

'Whether Edward had played for time or not,' Killbere told Blackstone, 'he's no choice now but to fight!'

But Edward sent no troops. He force-marched his army south as Blackstone rode tirelessly back and forth from the scouts, reporting everything they had seen. If the English had not been slowed by the lumbering baggage carts they might well have stumbled into the rear echelons of the French before they made their river crossing to the south of Edward's march.

The River Vienne separated the forest from the southern route of the French army. 'Here, my lord,' Blackstone said, as he drew a line in the dirt. 'Here is a bridge at Chauvigny; King John would turn his army across the bridge and reach the Roman road south of Poitiers cutting you off. If he gets there before you, there is no escape. If we can hold him – push him away from that route – then you can keep moving around Poitiers towards Bordeaux until you choose to fight. Give Sir Gilbert and me two or three hundred men-at-arms and mounted archers and we'll attack their rearguard. You keep the army moving through the forest and get to the road. King John won't know how close we are. Push hard, sire. We can hurt him.'

'It can't be done, my lord,' Warwick said. 'We've already covered twenty miles today. We won't make it in time.'

'And even if we could, we'd be in no fit state to fight,' Salisbury added. 'We're desperate for water.'

'Give him the men,' Oxford argued. His battle-hardened knights Richard Cobham and James Audley would take the fight down the enemy's throat. 'Cobham and Audley can hamstring the bastards from their rear and Blackstone and Killbere can go at their flanks. We can wound him. Blackstone is right; it will break their marching order or at least put the fear of Christ into them.'

Blackstone stayed silent as the commanders argued and considered their options.

'No,' Edward said finally. 'We'll not split our forces. Find a place that gives us an advantage, Blackstone. Find it so we can choose when we fight.'

★   ★   ★

454

Blackstone and Killbere, who took some time to cease from cursing Edward's decision, shadowed the French army. They were out of sight behind the low hills, but the air held the murmur of armoured men, horses and equipment moving relentlessly.

The two men, with the few soldiers who remained with them, rode on in silence, pushing further south through the forest, when Blackstone suddenly gestured them to halt. They had stumbled within sight of a considerable number of men-at-arms, the French rearguard, their image broken in the distance by two hundred yards of trees. Blackstone held back the men, all nervous of their presence being betrayed by the neighing of a horse or a movement an observant French knight might see. Blackstone gauged the number of riders. Each block of French men-at-arms that passed through the gap in the trees numbered at least seventy. It took little time to realize that there were several hundred of them.

'Jesus, Thomas,' Killbere whispered with only the slightest movement of his head. 'We've stumbled into a hornet's nest.'

Blackstone turned and followed his gaze. Horsemen were also on their flank, making their way through the forest, turning and twisting, finding the tracks for their horses. They were too far into the trees to identify, but there was no doubt that they were routiers, and if they stayed on their present course they would ride right onto the Englishmen.

Blackstone slowly drew his sword, as did Killbere and the men. They would have to fight their way clear. Anticipation shortened Blackstone's breathing, his fist gripped his sword until his knuckles ached. It was the same before every combat – the blurred vision that swam briefly before changing to the clarity of a raptor that saw every movement and nuance of battle. When fear gave way to exultation.

Before Killbere could stop him, Blackstone eased his horse aside and rode towards the flanking men. To ride against an enemy alone was suicidal. Killbere held fast, still in the forest's cover, waiting to attack as Blackstone halted his horse on a broad track, twenty yards wide, leaving him completely exposed to the approaching men. Five, then ten, twenty and thirty men, filtered from the forest, followed by even more, and not one of them raised his voice in challenge or his sword in anger.

Blackstone turned in the saddle and called back quietly: 'They're my men.'

The French rearguard had no time to organize a defence. As they cleared the forest and moved into the open Blackstone and Sir Gilbert swept out of the trees with Guillaume and more than a hundred horsemen. Panic-stricken horses careered into each other as knights shouted and cursed in confusion, trying to strike back at their attackers. Guillaume led men onto their flank, as Killbere's swept right, hacking and slicing the outer riders who had nowhere to run – turmoil at their backs, the English and Gascons at their front. Blackstone and the men behind him rode into the heart of the mêlée, the force of their charge carrying them deep into the Frenchmen who lumbered helplessly into each other as they attempted to turn their horses. It was a slaughter.

Within the hour more than two hundred French lay dead; others, captured by the Gascons, would fetch ransoms. The survivors galloped for safety, pursued by Blackstone's men.

The blood-splattered Guinot, Chaulion's garrison commander, reined in with Perinne and Meulon with Gaillard at his side. 'I can't stop them, my lord. They've been sitting behind a town's walls too long.'

'Let them be!' Blackstone ordered. 'Meulon, Gaillard, regroup your men and cover our flanks in case there are others in the forest. Perinne, you stay with Guinot, take our wounded from the field.'

The men wheeled their horses to carry out his commands. Beyond the escaping French another group of riders had appeared on the crest of a hill. Armoured knights, their banners catching the late afternoon sun, stood motionless watching the debacle. Blackstone could not make out the coat of arms. He spurred his horse.

Killbere saw Guillaume give chase and went after them. The two horsemen caught up with

Blackstone as he crested the hill, but the French knights had already gone. Killbere pulled his helmet free and tousled his sweat-soaked hair. 'We hurt the bastards, but it's little more than a sting. Where in God's name is King John?'

The three men could see no sign of the French army.

'I don't know, but I saw their scouts on this ridge. They're close – couple of miles, maybe – hidden by those hills. If Edward comes out of that forest he'll have no battle formation and if the French are drawn up he'll have no choice but to fight on their terms. Gilbert, ride back, take Guillaume and the others, warn him to stay in the trees, guide him to as far as we reached.'

'I'll stay with you, my lord,' Guillaume said.

'No, ride as Sir Gilbert's escort. Take Guinot and as many of the others who still remain. There might be French scouts between you and the Prince. Avoid them.'

Blackstone didn't wait for their answer and urged his horse down the hillside.

The forests drank in the remains of the day's light, the setting sun emptying the landscape of men's hope. Blackstone eased the horse forward, letting it find its own way over the patchy ground. He turned in the saddle to look back towards the forest where several thousand men would be stumbling, exhausted. There was no water to be had in that dense woodland, and if the French army blocked the roads south, the English would be hard-pressed to gain any relief before battle commenced. Blackstone knew there was a smaller river that lay south of the Poitiers road, but if the French were already there the English could be easily surrounded and starved into submission. There seemed to be nowhere suitable for them to stand their ground. And then Blackstone saw the tall stone tower of a Benedictine abbey. The narrow river lay just below it, and he could see across the village rooftops to the hillside beyond. That ground was the best place to make a stand. The holy tower was a beacon. Perhaps God *was* on Edward's side after all.

The abbey was a sharp reminder that Blackstone's family had left a similar monastery days earlier. As the bells rang out for vespers, Blackstone allowed himself a prayer for their safety. They would be well away by now, ever closer to Avignon, where the Italian priest would ensure their safety. Once this battle was over and his sworn revenge satisfied, they would be reunited.

He turned the horse back towards the forest. Prince Edward now had his place of battle and Blackstone had the opportunity he had waited for – to kill the French King and the Savage Priest.

Christiana and the children lay huddled on the barge's wet deck. They and Father Niccolò, with the sergeant, two other men and three tethered and snaffled horses, had glided downriver for four days. A second barge with the other hobelars and horses followed the broad-beamed boat, its tiller embraced by a bargeman. By the next day they would disembark and be within a few days' ride of Avignon. The priest had shown kindness, telling Christiana and the children stories of his home, where God's sunshine blessed the food and powerful city-states ruled. There was no King to obey, and trade was made in all manner of goods. Medicine and art flourished, children were educated and gold coin was minted. As they were swept across eddies and currents, he told Christiana that he had been witness to Blackstone's wounds ten years ago at Crécy. His injuries were their common link, for soon after that his broken body had been given refuge by the de Harcourts, where Christiana had nursed him. And loved him.

Their food aboard was sparse after the first two days, and the curtains of rain and river mist, between the occasional sunshine, soaked and chilled them, exposed as they were on the open deck. Agnes had recovered enough to travel, the monks' herbal remedies restraining the fever, but the child slept more than she was awake, held close to Christiana, whose cloak kept the worst of the rain from her. Cold and wet they may have been, but they were safe. Two days earlier there had been a brief glimpse of armed men ashore who had followed the meandering riverbank for a few hours. The river was, however, too wide for horsemen to ford, and the bargemen stayed in mid-stream until the men were forced away from the water's edge when the track ran out.

They had been blessed with a warm day; the sun's rays eased aching limbs and dried wet clothing. It was now only a few hours until daylight, before the bargemen would ease the barges ashore to unload their human cargo. Glimpses of moonlight showed the pastured hills lying downstream. The gentle creaking of seasoned timbers and softly lapping water lulled those aboard into a cradling sleep, all except for the bargeman and the soldier, Rudd, who stood his watch.

The bargeman held the tiller and gazed above the baled cargo, watching the night tide, mindful of sandbanks and shifting water that told him where shale beds lurked below the surface. Midstream was deep and fast-flowing, requiring a lifetime's experience of navigation on the river, but still demanding vigilance as they moved into layers of surface-hugging mist. The bargeman, his attention fixed on his work, did not notice the soldier who made his way forward, knife in hand.

Christiana's breathing was slow and steady, her sleep deep enough to dream but shallow enough to rise to the surface if the barge groaned from the river god's threat. The soldier knelt next to her, swallowing the spittle that filled his mouth from the excitement of his lust. She lay on her back, her cloak open, exposing her dress that had snagged halfway up her leg. The girl child was next to her, close to her face, soothed, perhaps, by her mother's breath. Rudd turned to look behind him; the bargeman was hidden behind the bales, the other two men still slept and, as the mist thickened, their forms became even less visible. He waited a moment longer. No one stirred. Blackstone's brat was curled against the bulkhead cocooned in a blanket, his back to his mother.

Rudd edged closer so he could straddle her in a single movement, his breeches already undone. His hand clamped her mouth and as she bucked and gagged, startled into wakefulness, he had his weight across her, holding the knife point below her eye, moving it away to lead her gaze to Agnes, inches from her. Rudd held the blade beneath the child's chin, his meaning clear.

She nodded, and followed his sign to pull her dress higher, his hand moving from her mouth to her breast. His knees forced her legs apart, his eyes never wavering from hers until she turned her face away and looked at Agnes, terrified that the child would wake and scream. Even as he forced his way into her, she kept her eyes open, watching the knife blade waver near the child's throat. Christiana's pain intensified as his muffled grunts increased. The scream, when it came, was not from the vulnerable child but from Rudd himself.

Henry awoke as the boat groaned in its efforts to stay on course and saw Rudd raping his mother.

He plunged Guillaume's dagger into the man's bare buttocks, then fell back from the sweeping arc of the man's blow. Rudd cursed, Christiana twisted, and the man fell away. But his reactions were immediate, the pain and the smothering blood across his hand spurring him to lunge at her with his knife. He was half up, his breeches catching his knees, slowing his momentum, but already swinging the blade down in his blind rage.

A fist snatched a handful of his hair, yanked back his head and exposed his neck to a blade that cut his throat to the spine. Rudd gurgled blood, lungs rasping, hands whirling in his final moments, trying to reach those that held him. His eyes rolled into his head and the sergeant cast him to one side.

'My lady,' he said gently, bending quickly and tugging her dress down; the sight of Rudd's death had ousted all thought of modesty. She trembled, and then clutched her clothes, nodding, pulling a waking Agnes to her. By then the second soldier had joined the sergeant and heaved Rudd's body away from her.

'Father,' Sergeant Jacob called, beckoning the sleep-groggy priest from the back of the boat. 'Lady Christiana needs you.' Jacob turned to the soldier: 'Finn, get a bucket and swill this blood and shit away.' Then he knelt to help Christiana. 'Come away from here, my lady. We'll make a better place for you and the child.'

'Thank you,' she said, accepting the help of his

strength; then, looking into his face as the moon-light thankfully slid away behind clouds: 'Nothing happened.'

'I know,' he answered, sharing the lie.

She looked at Henry, who stood with his back against the boat's side. Before she could utter a word, Jacob turned her away. 'He's all right. I'll look after him,' he told her, and let a stoic Father Niccolò guide her back towards the stern of the barge.

Jacob bent down and retrieved the dagger, fat and blood slimy on its blade. He dipped it in the bucket and then wiped it on his sleeve. Henry had not moved, frozen at the sight of Rudd's head being nearly severed.

'Master Henry,' the sergeant said. The boy did not respond, so Jacob touched the lad's face, and guided it to look at him. 'You saved your mother. Do you understand?' he said quietly, his voice barely above a whisper.

Henry began to tremble.

Sergeant Jacob gripped the boy's shoulder, sliding the dagger back into its scabbard in the boy's belt. 'Be brave, lad,' he urged, but Henry's face turned to the dark sky, his mouth wide open, his lungs desperate to scream, but no sound came; he was rigid.

The sergeant slapped him hard, the calloused hand raising a welt across the boy's face. Henry's head snapped back, his eyes glared, but his hand reaching for the dagger was quickly stopped by Jacob.

'All right, lad, all right. You're all right now, aren't you, boy?'

Henry's body relaxed. He nodded. 'Yes, sir.'

'Now, the job's not yet finished, is it?' And he turned to look at Rudd's half-naked body, crumpled against the bulkhead. 'Can you help us finish it, Master Henry?' he asked, knowing the boy needed to see through the gruesome task if he were ever to face death again.

Henry nodded again and followed the lead of Jacob and the other soldier, Finn, grabbing hold of the body to heave it overboard. Rudd's gaping throat yawned, his eyes a curse in death, but Henry stared right back into the lifeless eyes and knew that he was glad, deep into his heart, that this man was dead. He also knew that the love he had for his mother had been stolen by the darkness.

Rudd's body barely made a splash as the current dragged it below the fast-moving barge. Water sluiced across the deck as the soldier swilled it down. Sergeant Jacob offered Henry a bottle of gut-ripping cider. The boy pulled on the neck, winced and coughed, but then took another mouthful, the rich bite of its aroma cleansing the stench of Rudd's loosened bowels from his nostrils.

'Now, best you go back to your mother and sister,' Jacob said.

Henry shook his head. 'No. I'll stay with you.'

★　★　★

Prince Edward kept his army in the trees. They were without water, and had little food. No fires were permitted to offer any comfort from the dank forest, and the men stayed dressed for battle. The army had barely a few hours' rest before Blackstone and Guillaume led them from the trees before sunrise. He guided them down the valley beneath the walls of the abbey and onto the hillside at the northern end of a wood known as the Bois de Nouaillé.

'The men are tired and hungry, my lord,' said Guillaume as Blackstone watched the soldiers prepare themselves to defend the rising ground.

'Then they will be more bad-tempered than usual,' Blackstone said. 'Pity the well-fed French, Guillaume, their breakfast will soon be vomited on this field.'

Guillaume handed Blackstone what little water was left. 'You have hardly taken anything yourself, my lord.'

Blackstone could not deny the young squire his concern. He swallowed the water, and watched the exhausted army. 'Fate chases me. I'll settle matters in this battle.'

'My lord?' Guillaume asked, not understanding what Blackstone meant.

Blackstone wiped the sweat and grime from his face. 'Ten years ago I fought across Normandy with the King. There was bitter fighting when we took Caen and one night I searched for my brother in the streets. The fallen were everywhere and I came across a priest in the shadows who was desecrating the dead. I almost killed him but he escaped. My knife took his finger. And when Sir Gilbert came upon me in the forest I questioned a routier who told me this Savage Priest has a finger missing.'

He dismounted and handed the reins to his squire. 'This man flayed William de Fossat alive, destroyed my home and tortured and killed my people. He threatens my wife and children. When you attend mass pray that fate has not deceived me. I'll kill him on sight.'

Blackstone strode towards Killbere, who had returned with a scouting party. His broad grin told Blackstone he must have had sight of the French army in all its glory.

Killbere reported directly to the Prince and the commanders. 'The French are about a mile away, my lord.'

The Prince looked across the undulating land and his weary men still trudging across the hillside. 'If the French are that close, we'll be hard pressed to form up for battle. Let's pray the cardinals come back again. We need time. Where?'

'They're hidden behind that ridge. They're ready.'

'As many as we believed?' the Prince asked.

'Like fleas on a dog's back, my lord. Banners as thick as an invasion fleet's sails,' Killbere said. 'Ten or twelve thousand fighting men, right enough, my lord. They haven't gone home yet.'

The men laughed. French courage was never in doubt, but French noblemen had always made their own decisions when to leave the battlefield.

'No, not this time,' the Prince said with good humour. 'If Blackstone's information is correct then King John holds them to their word to fight.'

'Then we'll make them wish they had not,' Killbere said, bringing a murmur of agreement from the others.

'You'll not make any further progress, my lord,' Killbere continued. 'Blackstone has chosen the best place to defend. You face north-west and have a commanding view of the plateau in front of you when they come over that hill. Their cavalry is in the front division. Five hundred or more.'

He paused letting what he had said sink in to the commanders.

'It won't be the first time they've tried to put us under their hooves,' said the Earl of Salisbury.

'They'll want our archers first,' said the Prince. 'They're no fools; their scouts will have seen how few we have.'

Killbere scratched more lines in the dirt. 'Well, my Prince, the three divisions who will follow have abandoned their horses. They fight on the ground. Like us.'

The commanders looked from one to the other. Was this gross folly on the French King's part or had he realized the terrain was best assaulted on foot?

'Crush us with the cavalry and swarm through us,' said the Earl of Warwick. 'He learns from us.'

The Prince of Wales shook his head. 'But he makes a grave mistake. We are in defence and when he comes on foot he must labour uphill and through his dead. My lords, with God's help we shall win this day. Tell us more, Gilbert. We are heavily outnumbered but we are already cheered.'

Killbere pointed out the lie of the land. The folding hillside supported a vineyard yielding to the marshland below; thickets lined the southern slopes where the English defensive line would stand and a broad hawthorn hedge ran across the face of the gentle hill.

'They cannot outflank us, not with the forest at our back and the valley and marshland below us on our left flank. There are two gaps in that hedgerow, barely enough for a half dozen horses to get through. If they broke through there, then the fox'll be among the chickens. They would get behind our lines. I'll hold it, sire. Give me men-at-arms and a company of archers, and we'll stop the bastards where they stand.'

'William,' the Prince said.

'My lord.' The Earl of Salisbury stepped forward.

'You and Sir Gilbert hold the ground behind that hedgerow. Blackstone?'

Blackstone stepped closer to the inner sanctum of commanders.

'You have served us well. Go to your archers

469

and tell them they must hold their line. They must not falter, or the French will get behind us.'

'They're not my archers. They fall under the command of my Lords Oxford and Warwick,' Blackstone answered, respectfully aware of the great Earls of England.

'No matter. Say what must be said,' the Prince told him. 'And say it in language they understand.'

Blackstone bowed his head slightly. 'And then? Where would you wish me to fight?'

'Choose your own place. Keep what men you have with you. Strengthen our weaknesses. If there's a breach, fill it.'

'I will, my lord.'

Prince Edward stepped closer to the man who should have died from his wounds ten years earlier. 'History makes us brothers, Thomas. Your common heart is more noble than most. Ride out as our champion and challenge the French to their faces. Let them know that a man of low birth can rise up by the grace of our King and be honoured for uncommon courage.'

Elfred and Will Longdon ran with their men into position along the slippery banks that rose up from the narrow river's marshlands. Other captains and sergeants did the same until the mud-covered archers settled onto their haunches gasping for breath, waiting for final orders from their commanders. Their mouths were already parched from the lack of water, for the marshland offered no comfort to slake their thirst. Blackstone and Guillaume rode down the hill to where the men waited.

'Thomas, what can you tell us? Are the French close? Do we attack or hold?' Elfred asked.

Guillaume held the horses' bridles as Blackstone went among the men.

'Hold,' Blackstone answered.

'Sweet Jesus, we should be running for Bordeaux,' one of the archers said. 'I'd leave my plunder and good riddance to it. Plate and jewels are no good to me if I'm dead.'

'Enough of that!' Will Longdon shouted. 'You were brave enough slitting throats in noblemen's houses; well, now you earn your pay.'

Elfred swept a curve with his bow across the front of the gathered men. 'And you'll know it when them horses come galloping. You'll piss your breeches and smell the stench of the man next to you, but you'll stand your ground as archers have always done.'

'You saw the lie of the land,' Blackstone said. 'We hold the high ground. They'll come up from the far side of the plateau five hundred yards away. Then they'll charge downhill and up to us. The hawthorn hedgerow across our position is where they'll try and breach.'

'Aye. Pray it'll slow the bastards' advance,' Elfred said.

'Salisbury is digging in his archers behind it, which means you have to hold here. When the

French charge, our left flank is the weakest. They'll pour through here and you have to stop them, or they'll be at our backs. I'll reinforce the breach.'

'We've barely arrows to take but a few assaults, Thomas,' said Elfred. 'This needs to be over with before too long or we'll have nothing.'

'And I don't even have enough spit to insult them before they kill me,' Longdon said.

'I'll make sure they're insulted before any of us die. Don't break the line to take prisoners. Will, Elfred, you've to keep the men here. The French have a thirty-foot hill to crest; we'll take them then. The moment the charge comes through, hold them as long as you can, and then run down this line here,' Blackstone said, pointing out the route he wanted them to take across the river's marshland onto the opposite side. 'You'll strike the horses more easily where they're less protected from their armour; bring the men down, finish them with whatever you have: knives, swords – beat the bastards to death with river stones if you have to. Just kill them.' Blackstone climbed back into the saddle so his voice would carry.

'The Prince has commanded me to champion the army! I'll face them as a common man, no different from any archer, and they'll know our Prince insults them!'

The archers raised a cheer for one who came from their own ranks.

'I'll taunt the bastard! I'll curse like a tavern

whore and let him know that English and Welsh bowmen are waiting to kill him and every arrogant arse-wipe of a nobleman!'

The archers roared their approval.

Blackstone steadied his horse's impatience. 'They have a short memory, these French. They forget English archers have slaughtered them before, and will slaughter them again. And then the world will know that there is no greater army, no better men, none that can be defeated. Shall I tell him?' he called.

Men shouted back, arms raised, teeth bared, as the blood surge lifted their voices in raucous chorus: 'Aye! Aye!'

'Let them come!'

'Piss on him!'

'We'll make ten thousand widows today, Sir Thomas!'

Blackstone looked at the exhausted, ill-fed men. They were as ragged an army as he had ever seen. They would need guts and desperation to survive and win this day. He wheeled the horse, a final nod of acknowledgement to Elfred and Will Longdon: 'Remember Crécy. We left too many friends rotting in those killing fields. Let's punish these bastards once and for all.'

Blackstone rode out across the open ground as each army sent a champion to challenge anyone who would accept. It was a traditional formality before battle, a moment when men of both sides could gather their courage for the carnage that awaited them.

Guillaume watched his sworn lord ride towards the French army. The squire looked at the men gathered from the towns held by Blackstone as they sharpened their weapons, waiting for the chance to kill. Meulon and Gaillard, ferocious in looks as well as fighting, waited stoically. They turned to look at Guillaume and raised their spears. They and their men were ready. There would be plunder from the killing that could keep a man for the rest of his life. A third or more of the men were missing from those who had attacked the French rearguard. As so often with mercenaries, many had chased the wealth that fleeing noblemen represented.

'Sir Thomas told me the archers have insufficient arrows. They won't be able to stop the French this time. How many of our men remain?' Guillaume asked.

'Less than a hundred, Master Boudin,' Guinot answered. 'It's enough. We can reinforce where we must.'

'There's no plunder till it's over, Guinot. The marshals have already proclaimed the ordinance; no man must break the line. Make sure they understand.'

'Aye, they understand. They're keen for the killing to start. The quicker they kill the sooner they get to those worth something.'

★　　★　　★

474

The French champion sat astride his magnificent armoured war horse, covered in a gold and red decorated trapper that flapped gently in the morning breeze. The glorious figure that was the cream of French knighthood wore fitted armour and an emblazoned hawk on a crimson surcoat. He lifted the war helm from his head so he might be heard more clearly as the horse snuffled at the bit and its hooves pawed the ground. The French – even their horses seemed impatient to fight.

He was a knight of high rank, of that the English, Welsh and Gascons were left in no doubt. He raised his voice and extolled the virtue of his King's cause, the glory that was France – that the day was already won – and that he as champion would strike the first blow. The first of many. And then his eloquence was drowned by a raucous jeering from the English ranks. He continued a moment longer, and then, as if realizing he faced a barbarian race, he replaced his helm and eased the great beast back into the front line.

Blackstone rode the bastard horse the breadth of the French ranks. It bore no fine trapper, its cinder-burnt coat speckled from hell's fire; its misshapen head was lowered as if ready to charge into the brilliantly coloured ranks. To French eyes it bore a plain-clothed common knight, despised and feared, whose appearance as champion added insult and disrespect. To be goaded by such a lowly knight would lash French pride.

As always, Blackstone wore an open-faced bascinet so his enemy could see the scars of battle and readily identify him, whose shield bore the gripped sword: *Defiant unto Death*.

He was also gauging the enemy's strength, looking at the three divisions formed up one behind the other and whose numerous banners told him who commanded them. As he rode at a canter his eyes sought out the King's standard in the third division; the fleur-de-lys was unfurled next to the fork-tongued Oriflamme. The French would be merciless and take no prisoners, they would not seek ransom, and the only life spared would be that of Prince Edward so that his humiliation, and that of the King of England, would be complete.

The undulating land rose and fell like ocean swells, giving the French some higher ground, but their advance would first take them downhill and then force them up the slopes to meet their enemy. Edward would not attack. The English were past masters of holding advantageous ground. They had learnt from years of fighting that if they waited long enough, refusing to be drawn, French arrogance and honour would destroy their opponents' patience. Blackstone had no need to seek out the French marshals' banners. Beneath them were armour-clad destriers – and as his eye swept across their numbers he gauged there to be nearly five hundred knights who would be used to smash the archers. He turned and looked back to the pitifully small army that clung to the hillside less than a mile away, its pennons so few in number compared to the French. Men-at-arms and common soldiers stood together, archers in a saw-toothed formation between the ranks, horses held in the rear, the fighting to be done on foot. He could see the gap in the hawthorn hedgerow where Killbere and Warwick would face a near-impossible task trying to stop the weight of a charge.

He faced the French. The royal standard fluttered next to the Oriflamme, the place where Blackstone must reach to kill the King, and the instrument of his torture, the Savage Priest.

Horses whinnied; men's mail creaked in their leather strappings; the stiff breeze fluttered embroidered banners, making them crackle. Blackstone was close enough to see the eyes of the footsoldiers and whiskered faces of the marshal's knights with visors raised, lances ready to tilt. He raised his voice so it would carry across the closed ranks.

'King John! You hide behind men who will die for an unjust King. Remember my words at the Field of Mercy, where you butchered Jean de Harcourt, when I slew the traitor Guy de Ruymont? You are an ignoble king, a turd on the heel of an Englishman's boot, and we will wipe our arses with your royal standard! Now I confirm my pledge: I will kill you and the twisted creature Gilles de Marcy you set against me and my family.

Common men will slaughter your nobility and you will be condemned in disgrace. Today is when France dies with you. Send him to me! Send that whoreson to me and see how I kill him. And when he is butchered I will come for you!'

He wheeled his horse and galloped back to the English lines.

Behind him trumpets blared, French voices roared defiance and the thunder of iron-shod hooves rumbled across the hillside.

CHAPTER 29

Two pageboys, no older than Henry, their brows creased in anxiety, ran forward to take his horse to the rear but it took another older man to help them bring the bastard horse under any sort of control. The French marshals' charge was only a few hundred paces from the line.

Blackstone ran to Killbere, both men securing their sword's blood knot onto their wrist.

'Armoured horses! You won't stop them. Do what you can. Listen for my command. Give way when I tell you!'

Killbere nodded, passing on the command as Blackstone took his place with Guillaume at his shoulder. Behind them Guinot waited with the men. Fifty paces to each side Meulon and Gaillard readied their men as the ground trembled. The mighty war horses thundered forwards, a terrifying assault that could break the resolve of the bravest men. French tactics had changed. Blocks of mounted knights, five hundred strong, charged the lines to shatter the vulnerable archers and then behind them ranks of soldiers on foot would march forward, their overwhelming odds crushing the English.

The earth shuddered beneath the weight of the charge, rippling through men's bodies, reaching for their hearts. No matter their rank or birth, men snarled and cursed, prayed and swallowed their fear in anticipation of the shockwave that would strike them.

Perinne threw wide his arms and bellowed at the advancing horse: 'Bastard French whoresons! Come on! Come on!' Men raised their voices and jeered at the terrifying sight that came ever closer. He lifted his sword arm and gathered his shield, bracing his body, knowing that Blackstone would feint to one side and that he would then strike at the horseman's blind side. Rolling thunder from the pounding hooves muted the trumpets and cries of command as a gathering rage tore from the Englishmen's throats. Louder and louder they bellowed, forcing courage and hatred to pump strength into their arms.

The stench of horse sweat and men's fear mingled. Blackstone stood ready, seeing in his mind's eye Elfred's commands to his archers. Arrows nocked, backs bent like bow staves, loosing the murderous flight of arrows through the air. In that moment he was standing with them, feeling the strain and discomfort of muscles hauling back the cord that few men could master. His brother would have been at his side, his friends sharing the same eagerness to bring down swathes of enemy before they could reach the lightly armed archers. It came back to him in a rush of memory – the blurred desperation of fighting forward to save his brother, the slashing desperation, ignoring injury and pain.

'Stand ready!' Killbere shouted, snatching Blackstone back to the thundering present.

The first volley of arrows shivered and fell from the sky. The horses kept coming, the armour deflecting the force of the yard-long missiles. Through their narrow visors French knights caught glimpses of upturned faces, teeth bared, screaming abuse, sword, lance and axe ready to strike.

And then they were upon them.

The first wave of wild-eyed horses faltered, reins hauled back by their riders as the men on the ground ducked and weaved, slashed and stabbed. Soldiers raised lances, three to a lance, bristling like a sapling copse, heaving their weight behind the steel-tipped ash poles. Horses screamed, their own body weight forcing them onto the razor-sharp blades. Guillaume sidestepped, half turned and brought his sword around in a low, savage sweep, catching the back of a horse's leading leg. It screamed and lost its footing; the knight cursed and jabbed spurs into its flanks, but the weight of its armour and the severed tendon meant it could barely stumble a few more paces.

Man and horse fell. Guillaume quickly returned to Blackstone's side as Gaillard rammed his spear into the Frenchman's visor.

481

'The horse!' he screamed, wanting his men to butcher the beast to slow the advancing knights.

Men fell on the helpless creature, dancing clear of its thrashing hooves, and hacked through its neck armour. Blood pumped from severed arteries as Meulon swung an axe and severed the straps that held the saddle; and then the blade eviscerated the dying animal. The stench of blood and the animal's final screams served to unsettle the war horses coming up the hill.

'Gilbert!' Blackstone yelled.

Killbere was hacking at a fallen French knight who had miraculously raised himself to his knees under the weight of his armour – and that was as far as he got, as Killbere used both hands to swing his blade left and right, severing the man's raised arm and then butchering him. Killbere heard the shout above the roar and saw Blackstone run diagonally across the assault towards the saw-tooth positions of the archers.

The French charge had one desperate goal: slay the lightly armed men whose arrows could bring so many of their knights down. Some of the Gascons who protected the archers' flank had been trampled, left floundering and broken. Horses pounded them underfoot, French lances rammed into them as the crushing weight of their charge broke the line.

Killbere ran forward to fill the gap left by Blackstone, who had skirmished forward to where Elfred was trying to reposition his men in a desperate attempt to retreat behind the next group of besieged English men-at-arms. The zigzag line that gave the archers protection also meant they were vulnerable if their protective flanks were broken. Easy killing for the French horsemen.

'To me!' Blackstone shouted above the cries and screams. Guinot had lumbered behind him, desperately sucking air, sweat blinding him, but still only yards behind. A horseman yanked his reins, hauling the strength of his horse into a sudden change of direction. Blackstone was barged down and moments away from being smashed by its iron-shod hooves. Guillaume threw himself at the knight, who swept down a chained flail that hit the squire's back with a cruel impact. He fell, winded, twisting away as Guinot seized the off-balance knight. Grabbing his arm and belt, he hauled the cursing Frenchman to the ground, almost crushing himself as the knight fell half onto him. Guinot swore and bucked, but the man's weight was too much. A raised mailed fist was about to smash into his unprotected face when Guillaume came behind the horseman, wrenched his visor free and stabbed his knife repeatedly into the void. The man's gurgling scream was cut off suddenly by the squire's savage attack.

Guinot rolled onto his knees as Guillaume twisted away and darted forward, looking for Blackstone in the swarming field of colour and noise. Blurred images engaged in desperate fights to the death, sword pommels used as hammers, spiked maces piercing helmets and skulls, men kicking wildly in their death throes as other soldiers and horses trampled them. And all the time bellows of fear and threat as the trumpets blared their commands. Thirty of Blackstone's men had followed him into the breach and, like a broadhead arrow, formed up around him. Fallen lances were raised, shield walls locked by half a dozen men at a time, shoulders tight, hunched, heads bowed, spears bristling, as men-at-arms wielded sword and axe at the head of the phalanx. Blackstone and Guillaume felt Guinot and Meulon behind them, bull-strong fighters there to push into the desperate attack.

The line held.

A rising tide of men suddenly appeared beyond Blackstone. The Earl of Suffolk's archers had remained concealed in trenches and now rose to shoot into the trapped, desperate Frenchmen. Blackstone hunched onto one knee, shield high; others followed as a flight of arrows swarmed a hundred yards above their heads and smashed into armour and flesh.

The Gascons re-formed, surged past Blackstone and went in for the kill.

Blackstone spat, wiped blood from his eyes, turned to his men and looked across a jumbled field of hand-to-hand fighting. Lungs raw from effort he spat again, saw his men were still with him, fire burning behind their eyes. Elfred raised an arm in acknowledgement as the sixty-year-old

Suffolk rode across their ranks, urging his men to re-form. Blackstone's actions had saved him and his archers. The veteran knight called out to Blackstone and gestured wildly with his sword. Blackstone turned his men. The French King's son had launched an attack against the hedgerow held by Killbere. Men gathered their strength, knowing that so far they had fought only a small detachment of the French army.

Despite the slaughter the French horsemen had held their own, their remarkable courage inspiring the following ranks who advanced in extended line on foot to the beat of drums and blaring trumpets. Fear sustained the Dauphin's determination – not of cowardice, despite this being his first battle – but a fear of failing to prove himself to his father. Spurred on by the man at his shoulder, who saw where a bloodied Thomas Blackstone ran back and forth to seal any breach, he kept pace. Exhaustion must surely claim the English soon. Hours of hand-to-hand battle would weary the strongest defenders, but the Englishmen fought savagely. Some of their archers had barely any arrows left to shoot, but they ran into the fray with sword and knife.

Death strode at the Dauphin's side – the dark disciple commanded by the French King to protect his son with his own life if necessary – a penance for allowing Blackstone to slip through their grasp in Paris. Protect the Dauphin. See he comes to no harm. See that he leaves the field with honour. And take whatever opportunity presents itself to kill the Englishman. Killing Blackstone could still yield riches and land, but de Marcy had no intention of sacrificing himself for a pimpled youth.

The Savage Priest urged on the eighteen year-old heir to the throne. 'Blackstone is there, sire! He defends the hedgerow!'

The Dauphin recognized the pennons of Salisbury and Suffolk – the veteran Englishmen were as renowned as the great French marshals – but the Dauphin could see no flag bearing Blackstone's coat of arms. Whatever the vile creature sent by his father wanted from this battle was of no concern to the Dauphin. The man had a demonic hatred within him. The boy was sweating, his lower lip trembled, the cacophony of war and the mayhem of slaughter making him cast about nervously this way and that as the narrow slit of his visor revealed the horror and butchery on the hillside before him. Sweat stung his eyes; his heart's drumbeat competed with his rasping breath. Men of rank formed around him, praying to God that the boy did not falter and bring shame on them all.

'He's there! In their midst! We have him!' de Marcy roared to his men around him.

He and the Dauphin would not be the first wave of men to breach the hedgerow, but the reward and good favour that would come from killing Thomas Blackstone would fire the blood of de

Marcy's routiers. Kill the scourge of France and claim glory and reward.

'No mercy, sire! Remember that! *Pas de quartier!*' yelled the Savage Priest, the spittle of desire thick on his tongue.

The Dauphin nodded vigorously, found his courage and was swept along as they surged forward, caught in the wave of killing, ready to believe that God favoured only them. Men-at-arms funnelled into the gap; the clash of steel and cries of *Saint George!* were matched by the full-blooded determination of the French, who countered the English and Gascons with triumphant roars of *Saint Denis!* The hedgerow's gap funnelled men as they forced their way through, but the weight of the French attack was bolstered by a determination to reclaim lost honour and rid themselves of the English forever. Defeat the English on this field of battle and Gascony would be seized; capture the Prince of Wales and surrender and humiliation would be complete. Not even these barbaric Englishmen could outfight such odds that favoured the French.

And for those who served the Savage Priest, Blackstone's head on a pole guaranteed them wealth and all the towns he held. And de Marcy would wear the mantle of legend.

The assault surged uphill and began to push through into Killbere's ranks. He steeled himself, bracing for the charge as men-at-arms supported him, spears raised and lances ready to impale those who poured through the gap. Frenchmen went down but their armour snapped most of the shafts and the sheer weight of numbers began to smother the defenders.

Killbere slashed upwards at a French knight, vicious cuts that wounded and maimed, then ducked from shield and lance as men bent low to hack the fetlocks of those horses that still survived. Tumbling horses screamed, French knights were crushed or beaten by poleaxe and mace, but it was a tide that could not be stopped.

Blackstone and his men stood their ground fifty paces back, ready to take the assault head on once Killbere pulled back. 'Give way, Killbere!' he shouted. 'Yield ground! Let them come to us!'

But the clamour of battle drowned his voice. Before he could shout another warning, Guillaume ran forward to carry his master's command, cutting at men until he reached Killbere's shoulder. Blackstone felt a sudden grip of panic: the sight of his squire fighting forward stabbed at his conscience, reminding him of a lost brother in the chaos of another battle.

He saw Guillaume's head tilt, unheard words screamed at Sir Gilbert, who gave one final slashing arc with his sword that severed a Frenchman's arm. The man's shock carried him forward until another drove a battleaxe with such force it cut through his armour. So deep was the strike the Englishman could not extricate his axe, and his attempt to do so cost him his life as a French sword pierced his throat.

The hedge's gap funnelled the armoured knights as English swords and axes struck into the heaving mass. The English could not withstand the weight of the attack. Blackstone whirled, slashing at the first of the knights, who lost control of his panic-stricken horse. Guinot lunged at the horse's eyes with his sword, blinding it. Impervious to its screams, he and Blackstone jumped clear of the lashing hooves. A wounded horse served the defenders as it ran in agony back among the French. Guinot ground his sword into the knight's shoulder between his armour, forcing it through bone and flesh, and heaved his weight onto the man's chest to stop him writhing, as Blackstone kicked the man's visor and thrust his sword into his face.

Too many! They were far outnumbered by men on foot and horse. The swirling mass surged this way and that. Men spat broken teeth and clung to severed limbs. Time slowed down – moments of intensity swallowed hours and men's lives. Somewhere amidst the bobbing helmets Blackstone saw the Dauphin's shield raised in defence and for a heart-clutching moment thought he saw the figure of the Savage Priest, a brief flash of light that showed men gasping for breath behind the jostling mêlée. A visor raised, air sucked into burning lungs – and then the visors closed, shoulders bent to the task of forging a gap through. There was a shield of men around the Dauphin, but some were breaking forward, fighting ferociously.

Blackstone and his men held the ground. They needed a stronger defensive line. The English sold their lives dearly, leaving the dead and dying to slow the stumbling French knights. Lungs heaving, Blackstone and the others readied themselves to stand fast against the armoured men who snarled and roared their way forward. French drummers hammered out a throbbing rhythm driving on their soldiers as trumpets blared a discordant cacophony.

Blackstone's men braced for the impact, crouched, shields forward, sword and axe half-raised, eyes intent on the man each would kill first. The French faltered as they struggled across the dead and dying but then gained momentum as more of them poured through the breached hedge's gap. They half wheeled, as if on command, and came directly towards Blackstone and his beleaguered men. In that moment he knew their defence could not hold. He looked at the blood-streaked men at his side – Guillaume, Killbere, Meulon, Gaillard, Guinot, Perinne, his sword arm low ready to strike up and geld the first knight to reach his blade – each of them with eyes locked onto their enemy, teeth bared, intent to slaughter.

Blackstone turned to face the bristling surge of colour, ready to die, as surely they must against these fresh troops. And then, in the midst of the attackers, Blackstone saw the Dauphin's standard and next to it the Savage Priest's black-tongued pennon. Blackstone's shock quickly passed, flushed away by the urge to kill. De Marcy had come for him!

Raising Wolf Sword he hurled himself forward.

A heartbeat behind him the line of men followed. In the bellowing noise of attack a battle cry soared above the tumult and was quickly taken up.

Défiant à la mort! Défiant à la mort!
Defiant unto Death!
Defiant!

The Savage Priest barged and hacked his way towards the gap. Fleeting glimpses of his men before him showed where Blackstone might be. Blood-splattered coats of arms – griffin, eagle, dove and flower – swarmed across his narrow vision. He helped kill those who fell within the protected circle that enveloped the Dauphin. It would be suicide to strike out alone from the royal bodyguard. He was as protected as the Dauphin. He had sworn to the King to use his mercenaries to carve a path forward – but the closer he stayed to the Dauphin's shoulder, the less risk there was to his own safety. His men made progress as they clambered over writhing Englishmen – gaining ground towards Blackstone, who stood shoulder to shoulder with others as they took the fight to their enemy. De Marcy's strength coursed through him. Blackstone! His blood-red shields held the English line.

'Push on! Forward! We have him! Keep on!' he yelled, his determination carrying the Dauphin with him.

French men-at-arms sucked the strength from the English defenders as the French mounted knights gained ground, but then God's curse shattered de Marcy's hope as their own horsemen jostled the French aside. Men stumbled and were barged out of the way.

Blackstone and his men fought closer together, Killbere and Gaillard, Meulon and Perinne side by side. Guinot had found an old tree stump and pressed his back into it for support. Axe and shield fought mace and sword. Like a heaving bull Guinot stood his ground. Defence was his strength and he would yield no further. Blackstone heard someone muttering a constant litany: *God is mercy! God is mercy!*

Guillaume shielded Blackstone as his sworn lord half turned. They had clawed back the lost ground and held the breach, but the situation was desperate; the Dauphin's attack was gaining ground and there were still thousands of fresh troops waiting under the French King's command.

Blackstone looked back to the narrow riverbank. Elfred and his archers had moved across the marsh as they had been instructed. There were still enough arrows left to seek out the horses' unprotected rumps. Now the animals were struck time and again, their back legs faltering, giving way to pain and injury and throwing their riders onto

English and Gascon swords. Blackstone's men went at their enemy, their savagery fuelled by fear and charged with lust.

The Savage Priest was a visceral creature who felt the tide of events turn. They were being slowed by the Englishmen's renewed efforts and the Dauphin was tiring. Blackstone was still too far back to be reached. Thirty or more of de Marcy's men had gone down beneath the English blades and the horsemen still hindered the attack. The English shuffled and then strode downhill, forcing the advance to falter. Brawling, cursing men closed in, hampering the French knights that had broken through. Wounded horses created confusion, scattering men, trampling fallen knights underfoot.

The Savage Priest grabbed the Dauphin's arm, wrestled with the boy's uncertainty as he tried to twist free, but the killer's strength was the greater.

'Back, sire! They'll take you! Back!' de Marcy insisted. He would find no sanctuary if he failed to bring the King's son out of harm's way. If Blackstone survived the fight and the English won there was no gain for de Marcy. He yelled again at the Dauphin. Greater and nobler knights heard the cry and pushed de Marcy aside as they hustled the boy away.

Blackstone saw the retreat. De Marcy was escaping! Killbere and Salisbury's men fought at the breach. Blackstone and his men closed it with a relentless savagery. Those who had broken through were trapped behind the English lines, caught in the marshlands and slaughtered by English arrows. Blackstone soon lost sight of the Dauphin's pennon. He knew the opportunity was lost.

The defence held and the archers dug in behind the screen loosed their final volleys into the French lines. The hedgerow served the English better than another thousand men. The French had been forced to fight their way through to grapple with the Englishmen, and those who were not killed by arrows fought the English who stood in ranks trading blows, toe to toe, with an overwhelming enemy who could gain no further ground. Axe and mace smashed bone and tore limbs. Men were eviscerated and lay in cloying mud as others trampled their entrails. Blackstone reached Killbere and the two men fought side by side, each covering the other, while Guillaume and Guinot formed the flanks of a fighting wedge that thrust like a spear into the body of attacking Frenchmen. The battle was fought by pockets of men fighting hand to hand. Each victory pushed beaten attackers down into the mud as the English held.

When Blackstone went down again beneath a flurry of powerful blows, covered by his battered shield, Guillaume and Guinot and a dozen others forced their way forward to encircle his body in defence. Killbere reached down, heaved Blackstone to his feet and the fighting went on relentlessly. Blackstone and Killbere's men finally closed the breach. Along the English front line the dead lay heaped and the wounded writhed, but no one stepped forward to end their suffering.

And then, mercifully, after hours of slaughter, the French advance faltered.

Killbere raised his visor, gasping for air. Blackstone sucked lungfuls into his heaving chest. Both, like those around them, were soaked in sweat and blood. It was a strange, unsettling near-silence that lay across them. Distant shouts and muted cries were as clear as bird calls.

'We need water,' Guillaume said, pulling free his bascinet, wiping a blood-smeared hand across his face, his body trembling from exhaustion.

'There is none. Not here,' Blackstone said. He pointed with his sword towards the enemy. 'They've got the water. If we want it, that's where we have to go.'

'Merciful God,' Killbere said. 'We've stopped them. We stopped the bastards.' He laughed and looked at the survivors around him; most were on their knees, exhausted by the combat. Killbere stayed upright, leaning on his sword. French trumpets sounded across the narrow valley. In the distance they could see there were banners leaving the field.

'The Dauphin,' Blackstone said.

'Bastard's taking his men . . .' said Killbere, watching the King's eldest son disappear behind the massed troops of the other French divisions.

'No . . . King's taking him out of harm's way . . .' said Blackstone, his parched mouth making it difficult to speak. His eyes searching for the man he thought he had seen.

'No! Look! Goddammit, Thomas, they're running for home!'

Other banners and pennons followed the Dauphin's. 'The Duke of Orléans takes Poitiers and Anjou with him! Their whole second line has gone!' Killbere grinned and roared with others as the sense of victory swept the English lines. Hundreds of men broke ranks and ran forward, knifing the badly wounded, pulling knights' jewel-encrusted belts from their bodies, scavenging for plunder among the fallen. Voices of command went up and down the line.

'Stand fast! Stand fast. Commanders!'

Blackstone added his voice: 'Men! Back in line. They're not finished yet.'

Meulon and Perinne grabbed men's tunics, hauling them back into line as Gaillard prodded others with the blunt end of his spear shaft. The respite they felt was quickly dashed.

The trumpets' cacophony blared again, this time to a different sound. The English had fought only a small segment of the French army. The King himself now advanced, bringing thousands of fresh troops with him.

Blackstone's gaze settled on the wall of pavisers, the huge shields protecting the Genoese cross-bowmen that came behind them.

'Sweet Jesus, Thomas. I fear it's the end,' said Killbere.

The Oriflamme advanced, wavering above the mass of bodies, bringing the promise of death without mercy ever closer to the English ranks, whose resolve began to falter as the fresh troops steadily came on, their drums and trumpets heralding victory.

'Killbere, say something. Speak to the men,' Blackstone said wearily.

'I'm too damned tired,' Killbere admitted.

The moment was saved by Prince Edward, his mail coif pulled free from his fair hair as he rode bareheaded along the lines, his royal standard flying so all would know him, and with it the billowing cross of Saint George. The lions of England and the lilies of France emblazoned on shield and surcoat smudged the grey sky as the war horse bore him across the ranks of his beleaguered men. Edward raised his sword and miraculously the French trumpets fell silent for a few moments and in that eerie peace the Prince's voice carried clearly across the hillside.

'Yet still they offer themselves for slaughter. They march onto our swords. We must grant them their desire. Let the river take their blood to the sea so that if God ever gives fish the power of speech – they will speak in French!'

Men's laughter broke the spell of exhaustion.

'They will have no victory while I am alive! I do not command cowards! We are a nation of men who cannot be conquered by these French. They are already broken, they already flee – it is their final act of desperation. Stand fast and be ready for victory!'

Blackstone and Killbere were no different from the thousands of men who raised their weapons and gave voice in answer to their Prince's command. And the closer the fleur-de-lys came, the sooner Blackstone could have his revenge. The French trumpets called the advance for the great swathe of men to move forward.

And the French King whom Blackstone had sworn to kill, marched with them.

English and Welsh archers shot their final volleys into the French flanks, but their lack of arrows meant the enemy came ever closer until finally they reached the English lines. For the first time the archers could not kill enough of their enemy to stop a full assault.

Cries of '*Pas de quartier!* No mercy! No mercy!' echoed across the French ranks as the English went down beneath the weight of their assault, butchered where they fell. The Oriflamme would burn their souls in hell. No prisoners were taken. Every man who opposed the King of France would die.

'Elfred! Will! Here! With me!' Blackstone screamed. The French were upon them. Their sheaves empty, archers threw down their bows and armed themselves with sword and dagger and threw themselves forward. Some hurled stones and then wrestled the French to the ground where, like a pack of wolves, they savaged their victims to death. The horror showed no sign of ending.

English defiance took hold and broke the French into fragmented groups so that they were attacked and killed from all sides. And they in turn were granted no mercy. Meulon and Gaillard formed shield walls – a few men standing shoulder to shoulder – to deflect attacks on the archers. Guillaume was swallowed by the thrashing blows around him, but Blackstone was helpless to reach him, constrained by the weight of men eager to lay claim to killing the scar-faced knight. Killbere and Guinot smashed their way through and then Guillaume was once again on his feet. Brief, unnatural lulls as men died, retreated or, through exhaustion, simply stopped fighting, gave vital moments of rest. Blackstone could see the French King's standard still flying, but there were hundreds of men between him and the man he had vowed to kill.

'Sir Thomas!' Perinne shouted, pointing across the tangled conflict. The flag of Saint George was being carried around the French left flank. They were English horsemen. Edward had sent Jean de Grailly and a mounted unit to outflank the French and attack their rear. Now a different fear gripped Blackstone. No matter how few the horsemen, they could cut through French ranks and reach the King. Blackstone's prize could be taken from him. He turned back. In the distance behind his own lines he saw English banners where other men-at-arms ran for their horses. Prince Edward was gambling on the outcome of the battle by taking men from the line for a mounted attack.

Blackstone ran for his horse. Guinot was with him, both men's lungs heaving from the effort.

'Stay with the shield wall!' Blackstone yelled at him.

'Never, Sir Thomas! Not today! Not now!' The old soldier glared, daring his sworn lord to deny him a chance to strike at the heart of the enemy. Blackstone had promised him a fight and he meant to have his day.

Blackstone knew it too. He nodded. English trumpets sounded, sending the Prince's defiance rolling like a thunderstorm through the forest.

Men stayed locked in the death struggles of the battle; others were galloping down the hill's contour. Blackstone and Guinot led a group of men who caught up with them, and they in turn joined others. A gathering wave of violence swept downhill as men-at-arms hurtled pell-mell into the French. The attack struck their rear and flanks, and as English and Gascon infantry surged against them, they began to break. The French army fought for every inch of blood-soaked ground. English knights were pulled from the saddle, French lances, cut to five-foot lengths for ground fighting, speared men and horses.

Blackstone's bastard horse trampled men underfoot, its adrenaline giving it irresistible power. He abandoned any hope of restraining it; lathered in sweat, teeth bared and nostrils flared, it smashed anyone in its path – a path that led to the French King's standard. Blackstone brandished Wolf Sword. The banner was sixty yards away, surrounded by knights fighting hard to keep it aloft. Where was the King? A bodyguard of men wearing black armour and white surcoats marked with fleurs-de-lys surrounded the flags. The King was hidden among these men, wearing the same surcoat. They yielded to no one and no English knight could break their position. One French knight fought ferociously with a battleaxe.

Blackstone heard Guinot's voice rise over the noise of the fighting. 'The standard! Seize it! Take it down!'

He was too far ahead for Blackstone to guard him and Guinot was unhorsed; he swept aside lesser men and plunged forward on foot towards the King's standard and the Oriflamme. His mace struck the helmet from the axeman's head. It was the King. The blow rocked him, but he steadied himself as the bodyguard of black-armoured men rallied and slew the aggressor. Blackstone watched helplessly as Guinot went down under a flurry of blows, beaten and stabbed to death, not knowing that he had almost slain the French King. The bareheaded monarch bled from a head wound, but still swung the axe, scything a deadly arc.

Two Frenchmen ran at Blackstone, their lances ramming his shield. The force of his own horse's forward momentum threw him from the saddle. In an instant his back slammed down, but luck was with him. He fell onto bodies that broke his fall, and the men who tried to press home their attack stumbled on the corpses. Blackstone's shield took the first blow, its impact lessened by their poor footing. He rammed the first man with the shield's rim, catching his chin and seeing the jaw shatter and teeth vomit through the blood. The second man was already too close to turn his blade against so he bore the pain of the mace that glanced from helmet to shoulder and back-handed him with Wolf Sword's pommel. It crunched against the man's temple, which dented like a cracking egg. His eyes rolled, his knees buckled, and Blackstone knew he was already dead.

An opening appeared before him in a broken line of fighting men. Thirty paces away the bare-headed axeman turned and gazed directly at him. The King of France recognized the man sworn to kill him. Ranks closed, but the English were there in force. The knight grasping the Oriflamme went down under a vicious attack he had no hope of countering. The sacred battle flag toppled. Blackstone was clawing his way forward, heart pounding, ears deafened by screams and shouts, his eyes locked on his prey. Snared in the scattered sounds an Englishman's voice called: *Yield! Yield, sire! Yield! The day is ours!*

French knights lowered their weapons.

Twenty paces.

The King had one hand on a young man's shoulder: his youngest son. There was no need for him to die. King John's courage could not be questioned. He had fought to the end.

Ten paces.

He turned and saw Blackstone pushing his way forward, then offered his gauntlet to a knight.

The King had surrendered.

Five.

Englishmen turned and faced a grunting, scar-faced knight, sword raised, ready to strike. The old warrior Cobham was at the King's side with Warwick. He yelled to Blackstone, sword arm gesturing, a look of panic on his face – but the words could not penetrate Blackstone's rage. The King of France took a step backward, a protective arm around his son, as several English knights grappled with Thomas Blackstone, throwing him to the ground, pressing him into the blood-drenched soil. Blackstone could do no more. He offered no further resistance. His blood-smeared blade lay next to his face, still held by the blood knot on his wrist, and the swordsmith's mark, the running wolf, etched on his soul as indelibly as it was on the hardened steel.

In the distance the abbey's bells rang out the midday call to prayer. The battle had lasted more than seven hours.

CHAPTER 30

Men left the field to treat their wounds, to find food and water and then sleep away the fatigue that the battle had exacted upon them all. Scavengers from nearby villagers went among the fallen and stripped whatever of value they could find. The thousands of soldiers and men-at-arms who lay dead were left to rot. Only the noblemen's bodies were recovered and laid to rest in nearby cemeteries. The English Prince and the King of France dined in the royal pavilion as others haggled over the ransoms to be paid by the captured nobles. The prisoners would have to be kept at their captor's expense until the money was paid, and that could take years. Better that a price was agreed and the Frenchman released with the promise not to bear arms until his debt was paid. The fortunate few who had captured men of great rank sold their prisoners to the Prince, who would make a handsome profit when the ransoms were eventually settled.

Killbere trudged back to where Blackstone waited. His horse had been injured, but he had sewn its wound and dressed it with salve and, provided the beast was not asked to ride hard for a few days, it would heal. A war horse was a great expense and its well-being was vital for a knight left with nothing but that and his skill as a fighter. The only glimmer of satisfaction Blackstone could rescue from his failure was that he and his horse had survived.

Killbere made his way through the lines to the marshlands where Blackstone sat using the shallow water to bathe the deep bruises and welts from the blows he had taken. Guillaume smeared the same horse salve across his master's back where wounds had broken the skin.

Killbere slumped and splashed water onto his face. It would take time for the dried blood to be completely scrubbed away. 'Edward won't see you,' he said finally. 'You will not be allowed to question John.'

'I need an answer, Gilbert, that's all,' Blackstone said.

'You've caused embarrassment and displeasure to a Prince of the realm. He'll forgive you in time, but for Christ's sake, Thomas, you tried to kill the King of France after he'd surrendered. Cobham and Warwick think you should be flogged, hanged and left out there to rot with the rest of them.'

'I almost had him,' Blackstone said. 'But I need to know where de Marcy is. That at least.'

Elfred and Will Longdon squelched across the soggy ground to where Killbere and Blackstone sat. Meulon and Gaillard carried baskets of food and wine.

'Sir Thomas,' Longdon said, handing a wineskin to Blackstone and dropping an armful of food seized from the French camp. 'They had more food than they could eat. And I'll wager that wine won't scour your bowels.'

Blackstone drank deeply and passed it to Killbere. 'You should be gathering clothing and valuables,' Blackstone said.

'Most of it's gone,' Longdon said, his mouth full, gratefully accepting the wineskin from Guillaume, swilling away the food in his overfilled mouth. 'Bastard peasant French robbing their own. We should go and burn the whoresons out of their villages. Need this first . . .' he said, pointing to the next mouthful of food being ripped between his teeth.

'Where's Perinne?' Blackstone asked.

'Attending to Guinot's body. We said we'd keep whatever booty and food we found for him to share,' Meulon said, and slumped onto the ground, pulling back his sweat-soaked mail from his head.

Elfred cut a thick slice of bread for each man. 'They nearly finished us, Thomas,' he said.

'And if the Dauphin and Orléans had not left the field they would have done,' said Killbere. 'Mad bastards couldn't see that. God knows why they went.'

'Perhaps they missed the comfort of their beds and the softness of their whores,' Will Longdon grinned. 'I care not. We beat them.'

The men fell silent as they drank and ate, their

506

exhaustion sobering their thoughts. Recounting in their mind's eye what they saw, where a false step or unlucky blow could have brought any of them down.

'If the French had not dismounted they'd have worn us down,' said Meulon. 'They thought to fight like us.'

'None can fight like us,' said Will Longdon. 'We gave 'em a lesson this time, by God. They won't forget this one, Thomas. We'll drink and whore on stories of this day for years to come.'

Elfred showed no sign of sharing his archer's enthusiasm. 'Most of my men were killed. God knows how many English and Gascons lie out there. It was close-run. Our Prince will need to supply us with more arrows next time.'

Blackstone stood and pulled on his leather jerkin. 'There'll be no next time, Elfred. The King is taken. France is finished. There'll be no more war. Better get used to the idea of being a peasant swineherd.' Swallowing a final mouthful of wine he stepped away. 'Stay with my horse,' he instructed Guillaume.

'Thomas?' Killbere called. 'Where are you going?'

'I told you. I need an answer,' Blackstone said as Meulon and Gaillard got up to accompany him but he gestured them to stay, and made his way towards the royal pavilion.

Killbere groaned. 'Sweet Jesus, he'll find himself at the end of a rope if he doesn't show some respect.'

Longdon shoved a wedge of food into his mouth. 'Best get the rope ready then, Sir Gilbert,' he said as a weary Killbere got to his feet to follow Blackstone.

The captured nobles were in Prince Edward's custody. There was no need for them to be guarded, their word was their bond, but an English picket was in place to protect them from further theft of their possessions by light-fingered Englishmen.

Killbere caught up with Blackstone, who squatted, watching the sentries. 'I feared you would end the day on a gibbet,' he said. 'So I came to help.'

'Then you would be guilty by association,' Blackstone answered.

'But I wouldn't do anything to antagonize my King or Prince,' Killbere said, his gaze challenging Blackstone.

Blackstone pointed to the pavilion of scarlet silk where the King's young son was kept.

'Would those sentries know you?'

'The whole army knows me,' Killbere said, but then relented and looked towards the men. 'Perhaps not. They're Oxford's men.'

'Then you won't be involved with me if you go and tell them that the King's servants are commanded to attend him at the Prince's pavilion.'

Killbere's discomfort was obvious. 'John's lad? He's a fourteen-year-old boy. You can't hold him responsible for his father's deeds. Thomas, I'll not be party to murder.'

'And I would not ask it of you. Trust me.'

Killbere sighed, his indecision brief, then without any further questioning went forward to the sentry.

There were four servants attending to the boy who duly left the pavilion once the guard had delivered Killbere's message. By then Blackstone had already slipped between the silken folds and waited. There was no one else, other than the boy Prince and a clergyman, to raise the alarm. The King's son had been bathed and dressed; a table was laden with food, some half-eaten on a gold plate. The boy knelt in prayer on a richly woven rug, the priest next to him. Low murmurs of entreaty escaped the old man's lips. It was unlikely his creaking joints would allow him to stand quickly and raise the alarm.

Blackstone spoke softly; Wolf Sword hovered at the boy's chin. 'Do we share the same God, you and I?'

Their eyes opened and the boy recoiled, but Blackstone kept the sword's point steady. 'You'll stay on your knees, priest, and go back to your prayer. Now.'

The priest's bony hands quivered, but he clasped them together and squeezed his eyes shut. The boy hadn't flinched despite his fear.

'I saw you, sir knight. On the battlefield.'

'And I you, my lord,' said Blackstone. 'You called out a warning to your father at each blow aimed by our men-at-arms.'

'Do you kill me now?' the boy asked.

'Can a French Prince be trusted to keep his word and remain silent?'

'I am Philip and I give you my word.'

Blackstone read the boy's eyes, and then lowered his sword.

'I want to know where Gilles de Marcy is and why he was not with your father when we took the battle.'

'Why is he important?'

'This is not a discussion, young Prince,' Blackstone answered and then relented. 'But he professes that God is cruel and that he acts as the hand of God.'

The priest opened his eyes. 'He is an abomination. De Marcy's soul hovers between earth and hell.'

The boy looked at Blackstone. 'None the less, he was trusted by my father. If I do not tell you, will you kill me?'

'No,' said Blackstone. 'I didn't come here to cause you harm.'

'And do I have *your* word, sir knight?'

'I am Thomas Blackstone, my lord, and I give it. So there's no reason now why you shouldn't call the guards.'

'Except we are bound by our honour,' said the boy.

Blackstone waited. The young Prince got to his feet. 'Very well. Gilles de Marcy was instructed to take my older brother from the field. For his safety.'

'Where was the Dauphin taken?'

'I don't know. But de Marcy was released from the King's service. A bargain was struck. He escorted the Dauphin to safety rather than stay on the field. Brutal cowards are easily bought, Sir Thomas. He has almost five hundred men with him. Routiers. He is his own man now.'

Blackstone nodded, realizing that was all the information he could expect. He eased away to look through the folds of silk, checking that the alarm had not yet been raised. As he was about to make his escape the boy knelt once again in prayer and said: 'May merciful God grant our father forgiveness for any wrongdoing, Sir Thomas.'

Blackstone hesitated. 'Then it's a good thing God never sleeps, because the list is long.'

'De Marcy rides south to Provence,' the boy said, closing his eyes and bowing his head. 'There is nothing left here to plunder.'

Blackstone stepped out of the tent but his way was blocked by a sergeant-at-arms and an escort of ten men.

'Sir Thomas,' the sergeant said, 'you will surrender your weapons. On my Prince's command, you're under arrest.'

Blackstone stood before the marshals of the army in Edward's pavilion. The Prince had bathed and changed; his armour was laid to one side, a table prepared for his meal. No one spoke as the Prince ran a hand carefully along the flat surface of

Blackstone's sword. His sullen mood belied the great victory he had just achieved.

'Your violence is well regarded, Thomas, we value your skills in battle, and our gratitude has been generous, has it not?'

'It has, my lord,' Blackstone answered.

'We have tolerated much, enduring your impudence with good humour and grace as befits our father's son. And yet you persist in your disrespect. You defy a King's surrender, you threaten his son who is under *our* protection and hospitality! You defy us!' Prince Edward's temper broke and he rammed the sword into the ground at Blackstone's feet. 'You are still a common man, Thomas, and ever will be. We will not hang you for your disrespect. But we will not tolerate you any further. Our battle is won. The towns you hold in our father's name will no longer be yours, your plunder from this great victory will be forfeit and you are banished from our King's realm and our territories in France. Our debt to you from those years ago is paid in full. Take your sword and your defiance elsewhere.'

Guillaume laid his master's habergeon across the war horse's pommel. The mail had been scrubbed clean, as had his jupon, of bloodstains. A day wearing only a linen shirt beneath his leather jerkin would keep the iron links from rasping against the wounds on Blackstone's back.

Blackstone fixed his spurs as Killbere blew snot

from his nose and then drank more of the wine looted by Will Longdon. 'A servant saw you go into the boy's pavilion. We're getting careless, Thomas.'

'It was a long day, Gilbert, but you're right, I should have seen him.'

'God spared a King and robbed you of your vengeance. It cannot be argued that Jean le Bon is not favoured – not to win a fight but to live on.'

'Perhaps he's saved for another day. Revenge is never discarded, Gilbert.' He looked at his old mentor; words barely necessary. 'I'll bide my time,' said Blackstone with a chilling edge to his voice.

Killbere's face creased. What if Blackstone took it upon himself to defy the Prince again and wait for darkness to try and strike at the French King?

'Now, Thomas, let the bastard go. We are fighting men not skulking assassins.' He grinned and grasped Blackstone's arm. A restraint behind his meaning, lightness in his words. 'Ah, what difference does it make now? You never got to de Marcy, Thomas. And you didn't kill the King. And now both are beyond your reach.'

'De Marcy will cross my path again.'

Killbere saw that Blackstone was not to be convinced otherwise. 'It's a pitiful state of affairs, Thomas. You lost most of your men in the fight; others have looted enough to return to their whores and children. You've less than when you started. Serving England has its cost.'

It was a bitter truth. Blackstone's hard-won

gains over the past ten years had been snatched away by a wave of belligerent defiance. He cared little for the loss of hearth and home – but exile and the death of those loyal to him cut deeply. Comfort now lay in the love of his family and the knowledge that he still had the strength to wield Wolf Sword.

'I've a few men left. They can go their own way if they choose. I'll put it to them. You've men-at-arms to ransom, though,' Blackstone said.

'Hardly worth a piss in a pot. Half these Frenchies claim penury. It'll take years to get anything out of them. Either that or they'll die from their injuries.'

'We were lucky in the fight though, Gilbert.'

'That we were. Lucky and quicker on our feet. I'll give Edward that. He took a risk going on the attack. God, but that was a fight, was it not? A fight to end all fights. A good way to end. A good way.' Killbere gazed across the field of slaughter. 'We'll need to move before the wind shifts.'

Blackstone eased into the saddle. 'Edward's for Bordeaux now. He's sailing for Plymouth, taking back the prize of prizes,' he said as he took up the reins, the bastard horse fighting the bit.

'And you're for Provence?' said Killbere.

'Yes, Avignon. My family,' Blackstone said, easing the reins through his fingers. 'I need to see to their welfare now.'

'Aye. South. A good thought. De Marcy is south,' Killbere said.

Blackstone stayed silent. His eyes shifted across to the horizon. The Savage Priest was out there somewhere and there would only be justice when he was found and killed. But first he must attend to Christiana and the children. 'And you?'

'I was thinking of Lombardy,' Killbere said. 'There are those who offer good contracts for the likes of me. They need soldiers. Lots of small wars. This town hates that town; this city wants that city. Nothing too dangerous. Good money. So I'm told by a Frenchman who went across the Alps and did some work there. Bought himself an estate from it. Warmer there too. And good wine. I think their women smell but they say it's a pleasant odour and makes a man salivate with desire.'

'You'll travel past Avignon, then.'

'So I was thinking.'

Blackstone smiled and nodded, then turned and looked at his men who still followed him: Guillaume, Meulon, Gaillard and Perinne, their wounds dressed, their weapons cleaned. There was no question of them being anywhere other than where their sworn lord led. Blackstone urged the horse forward.

'It was good to see you again, Thomas,' Killbere called.

'And you,' Blackstone answered.

As Blackstone and his men skirted the battlefield, monks were loading the bodies of fallen knights for burial in the abbey's cemetery. Elfred and Will Longdon, along with a dozen archers, pulled arrows from the dead that still lay in their thousands. Bundles of bloodied, damaged shafts were gathered like sheaves of wheat on the back of a cart.

'Did you call the roll of your men, Elfred?'

Elfred wiped his bloodied hands across his jerkin. 'Aye, I lost damned near eighty of 'em. Half of those that are left won't see the winter through. I'm paying them off so they can feed themselves and their families. I've a dozen good men left. Except for him, mind,' he said looking at Will Longdon.

Longdon grinned: 'They were good lads Master Elfred lost, but it's a greater share of the plunder for the rest of us.'

Blackstone looked at the arrows. 'You'll salvage maybe half of those, Elfred. Most did their work too well to be saved.'

'We'll repair 'em,' Longdon said. 'We'll need 'em if Sir Gilbert's plan is a good'un.'

'You're going with him?' Blackstone asked.

'We've no choice, Thomas, if we're to earn a crust,' Elfred said. 'You was right in what you said. France is finished now and I've no desire to go back home and be a poor man again. Aye, we'll follow the mad bastard awhile; see what becomes of us.'

'You lost your lieutenant – whatsisname – the Gascon,' Longdon said.

'Guinot. Yes. He went down at the end,' Blackstone answered.

'Aye, him. Your men said as much,' Longdon said, tilting his head towards a group of horsemen who waited a few hundred yards away in the trees.

'You've forty-odd men who've nowhere to go, Thomas, except wherever it is you're going. They've a mind to stay with you,' Elfred said.

'You know more about my business than I do,' Blackstone answered.

'Fighting men talk to each other. Worse'n gossipin' washerwomen, some of them,' Elfred said.

Blackstone turned in the saddle and looked back to the distant figure of Killbere walking his horse towards them. 'You'll be following on then,' Blackstone said.

'Dare say we will,' Elfred answered.

'You know where?' Blackstone asked.

'Our route takes us past Avignon,' said Will Longdon – and grinned.

PART III

CRUEL JUSTICE

CHAPTER 31

The Savage Priest had escaped just in time. He rode south-east from the battlefield leaving the Dauphin and his uncle, the Duke of Orléans, to make their way back to Paris. It was not a lack of courage that lost the French the battle, but that King John had been a fool for entrusting his troops to his bewildered and uncertain son and his own brother, Orléans. The English could have been defeated. When the Dauphin's standard had fallen and it seemed that his battalion would be slaughtered, de Marcy had realized that the King's son and his brother, who commanded the forward battalions, had ignored the experienced marshals' advice. The English had moved quickly, their trumpets and flags signalling their troops to reinforce each other. And Edward had more competent commanders. The Prince's raids had obviously not inflamed God's anger otherwise he would have lost.

The Savage Priest had tried to kill the Englishman, but the fates seemed always on the scar-faced knight's side. They should have slain him when the lone knight rode out and challenged the King.

De Marcy had urged John to strike him down there and then. He had refused, clinging to the honour demanded in battle that a champion was there to challenge the enemy's army, not to be slain. To John's fury, de Marcy had had the impudence to curse the King's naivety. The Savage Priest had waited with the standard and the Oriflamme as Thomas Blackstone rode back to the English lines with the French armoured cavalry at his heels. By the time the Dauphin's attack had failed, de Marcy knew the English would prevail. The King had seen the danger of his inexperienced son falling to the English and Gascon army and ordered him from the field. Perhaps there was still a use for the Savage Priest. The killer had shielded his son when they had reached the English lines and struck forward to try and slay Thomas Blackstone.

'Take my son to safety and you'll be paid in gold,' John cried above the tumult.

De Marcy seized the opportunity. The offer allowed him to run. A worthless King offering money he did not have.

'No payment, sire,' he said, wheeling his horse. Let the King of France make his desperate bid to subdue the English; de Marcy would benefit by forgiving the debt and gain the gratitude of the Dauphin. Sooner or later the feeble son would become King and remember de Marcy's service to the Crown. The benefit was twofold: as France bled to death on its own soil there would be no force capable of stopping de Marcy's routiers. Towards the southern coast, the rivers and the ports bustled with Mediterranean trade. The towns and monasteries would be fat with plunder. It was time to take the killing further south.

More than twenty years before either Blackstone or de Marcy was born a conflict of authority arose between King Philip of France and the Italian Pope, whom he accused of heresy, sodomy and consorting with a pet demon. The Pope threatened him with excommunication, whereupon the King tried to kidnap the Holy Father. Italian outrage increased when, after the assault, the Pope suffered a fatal heart attack and a Frenchman was, through the King's influence, elected as his successor. Fear of Italian reprisals convinced the Pope to move his See to Avignon, which, although a fiefdom of the Kingdom of Naples, was within the French sphere of influence.

The following six French Popes built not only fortress-like walls at Avignon but a profitable business selling church offices. It became a financial empire. Pardons, indulgences and absolution were to be had for a price – everything was for sale. The papacy took a percentage of every offering made at every altar, but one of the most lucrative sources of papal income was the selling of benefices. Several hundred bishops' sees and hundreds of thousands of lower offices were sold. And forgiveness for heinous crimes was granted – at a price.

The most extreme measure the Church could command – the threat of excommunication – was used to squeeze further income into the coffers. A sliding scale of fees was in place and the vast wealth was handled by Italian bankers. Travellers told how counting coin, raked like ears of wheat, was a common sight in the papal palace at Avignon. That which was spiritual became temporal – and venal. It was this place of power and authority that would offer sanctuary to Blackstone's family.

The bargeman brought Christiana's party ashore after four days. They travelled across country until they crested the high ground that revealed the mighty River Rhône curving beneath the fortified city of Avignon, its walls built on the cliffs that rose up from the riverbank. The sergeant had never been this far south before and was dependent upon the priest to guide them through the city towards the jumble of crenellated walls, formidable but still meagre compared to the soaring towers and battlements of the papal palace that rose behind them. As they rode closer he could see that although the fifteen-foot-thick walls would make a strong fortification against assault, other parts of the walls were in disrepair and being rebuilt. Any defence was only as strong as its weakest part. The rock face would give enough purchase for men to clamber and escalade ladders would take attackers across those first low ramparts. His soldier's instincts told him that, if he were assaulting this city, that was where he would put the main force. Once inside the walls the townsmen would die in their homes, and the Pope, for all his power, would succumb to fire and slaughter.

Narrow twisting streets, crammed with buildings, trapped the fetid air that rose from the teeming humanity confined in the labyrinth. It was a spectacle none of the riders other than Father Niccolò had witnessed before. He barely gave a glance to the heaving crowds who infested the alleyways and passages. Merchants jostled each other; artisans plied their trades; astrologers' painted boards with moons and stars swung from poles as prostitutes loitered outside Italian banking houses. Circus-like sideshows gathered crowds; an armless woman showed how she could sew and spin wool, and toss a ball and throw dice with her toes. The babble of human voices – shouting, talking, enticing – echoed up the stone buildings. Beggars stretched out filthy hands to the riders, but Torellini used a switch to strike them away from his robes. The soldiers ignored them, or turned an ankle, raking those too slow to move with a spur.

Sergeant Jacob raised his voice to clear the way. When the iron-shod hooves clattered onto cobblestones the press of bodies in the narrow streets was forced to part – those that could not move aside were pushed and crushed by the weight of the horses, as boats pushed aside the water.

A large public square was blocked on the far side by massive gates that led into the papal palace.

It was a place where the faithful could gather to view His Holiness Pope Innocent VI crossing in hypocritical humility on a white donkey, as his gold-embroidered robes were lifted from the dirt by retainers. He rode beneath a canopy followed by equerries carrying the white wool band worn by the pontiff on his shoulders as a symbol of authority and might. Father Niccolò slowed their advance as a procession of cardinals in their wide red hats walked without haste, accompanied by servants, across the vast square, parading as if they were royalty.

He approached the guards at the palace gates, and then returned to John Jacob. 'You and your men will not be allowed to travel any further into the city. I will see that Lady Christiana and the children are held safely until Sir Thomas arrives.' He handed Jacob a purse of gold coin. 'As agreed,' he said.

'Can't they come with us?' Christiana asked. She had barely spoken since the assault on the barge. Henry had stayed with the men, listening to Sergeant Jacob tell stories about England, his village, the wars he had fought – and about Henry's father and those who would follow him if his cause was their persuasion, or if the purse was large enough. Christiana had stayed silent and held Agnes close to her for the final days of their journey. She maintained a quiet dignity despite her features being more drawn and sallow, but her mask of bravery hid the greater shame of the rape

526

and the despair of knowing that her son had witnessed it. How long would it be before Blackstone found them and father and son spoke of the journey to Avignon?

Father Niccolò offered her reassurance. 'My lady, I have property behind these walls. There are gardens with cool fountains and fragrant herbs that please the air. My benefactor Rodolfo Bardi owns them, and they are at your disposal. But common soldiers armed for war are not permitted. Sergeant Jacob and his men have fulfilled their duty both to their King and to your husband.'

'Go with him, my lady,' Jacob told her. 'I'll wait with my men in one of the taverns until we hear of what's happened to Prince Edward. That's as much as I can do to give you peace of mind.'

Torellini saw sense in the sergeant and his men staying for a few more days. The political intrigues of the papal city might force the expulsion of Blackstone's family if Prince Edward were triumphant against King John. A banker considers the risks, and a priest calls upon God, but Father Niccolò was close to both. If Blackstone had not reached the Prince in time and been told that he could sue for peace if that meant his safe return to England, then the English might have been defeated and Edward held for ransom. That would enforce the Pope's strength across Europe and ensure the authority that King John had vested in him. The gates swung open.

'Look for the sign of the three horseshoes.

They'll stable the horses in their yard and offer beds and food. You've money enough,' Father Niccolò told Jacob.

'Aye, we've been well paid, and we'll sell Rudd's horse,' Jacob answered, and then turned to Christiana, whose expression was that of someone on a drifting boat in a fast-flowing river. 'We're close by, my lady, and Sir Thomas will come for you,' he told her.

The priest led Christiana and the children through the gates into the shadowed streets of the papal city. The sharp smell of incense wafted through the air, as if blessing the clinking gold coin being loaded into sacks.

Blackstone and Guillaume rode slowly, trailing a pack horse carrying what booty could be taken from the battlefield. Blackstone had stripped a fallen French knight of some fine armour to replace his own that was lost when de Marcy burned his manor house. Some of the daggers and swords of the fallen had jewelled hilts and grips. They had bundled twenty such weapons together, to use for barter or to dig out the stones and sell them. Food and clothing were also tied across the pack animal; there would be little to scavenge as they rode across a landscape already scoured by roving bands of men making their way home.

Hours later as they rested they saw parties of knights, some wounded, and others being dragged on stretchers, as they filtered away from the conflict.

Many would die on the road home, even those of nobility and wealth, who had given their pledge to pay ransom. Three thousand Frenchmen lay dead on the field at Poitiers, and another three thousand had surrendered. Word of the English victory travelled rapidly.

Blackstone pulled their horses off the track where three French knights and their squires rested. One of them was mortally wounded and they had slowed their journey to accommodate his injuries. Blackstone had his men give them water and food and heard how villagers, enraged by learning how many had surrendered, had attacked them and their wounded comrade – whom they considered cowards – with stones, pitchforks and axes. Vanquished French knights would obtain neither food nor comfort from the towns and villages they passed through on their way home.

Two miles behind Blackstone's forty hobelars, Killbere travelled with Will Longdon and Elfred's archers alongside a wagon loaded with plunder. Wherever Blackstone looked across the landscape the French were drifting away, some alone, others in small groups of five or six – men who had fought side by side as kinsmen or friends, their skills and courage no longer required. The mortally wounded knight died before Killbere's men reached them.

'There's a monastery you can take your friend to and have him buried,' Blackstone told them.

'Sir Thomas,' answered the knight, a man from

the first French battalion who had seen the heaviest of the fighting against the English, 'the graveyard will be full; would you and your men ride with us to the nearest village so he may be buried in the churchyard there?'

Blackstone agreed and the band of men rode on with the knight's body. As they reached the next village a church bell rang out in warning of the approaching men. Villages had blocked the entrance with hay carts, and ditches had been built weeks before to stop brigands attacking at night. Blackstone and his men held off as one of the Frenchmen went ahead seeking permission to bury their comrade in the cemetery. But he was refused. Blackstone went forward, and dismounted. It was an uncommon action for a knight to dismount to address peasants, and the men pressed back a few paces as he stepped forward to speak to them.

'This knight is far from home, but he came to fight the English Prince who tore apart your land. Would you deny him a Christian burial?'

The throng of men, armed with axes and scythes, shouted angrily, but Blackstone stood his ground. 'You see men behind me, more than enough to ride through your hovels and burn them to the ground, and yet you still defy us.'

'We have nothing!' one of their leaders shouted. 'And these base knights ran from the conflict, leaving us alone to defend ourselves! Where were they when the English and Gascons pillaged and burned? Where? On their arses eating tender meats and drinking fine wines. And now they ask for compassion from those they themselves trampled on! Damn them! They've abandoned France and us! We won't have them buried here – and if you force us we'll dig the bastard up and feed him to the dogs.'

The speech met with a roar of approval.

'Then you'd rather die,' Blackstone asked, glancing back to his armed men.

'If we must! We have nothing left but our lives and what good is a life without crops, or stored food? They took everything. Our children already die!'

Killbere and the others caught up.

'Thomas, kill the bastards and teach them a lesson. God knows I've no love for the French,' he said, glancing towards the French knights, 'but a decent burial from your own kind isn't much to ask. Peasant scum are the same everywhere.'

'I used to be peasant scum under the law of Lord Marldon, if you remember.'

'What you were and what you've become are different matters, Thomas. Sweet Jesus! Torch them, bury the Frenchie and let's be on our way.'

Blackstone called to Elfred: 'Get me two sacks of flour and a bag of coin.'

Killbere sighed. 'Thomas, you're as soft as a milkmaid's tit and as brainless.'

'So you've said before, Gilbert,' Blackstone said and smiled.

Blackstone had the flour and money handed over to the villagers. 'There's been enough slaughter. Feed your children and buy what you can from the towns.'

The men seemed momentarily perplexed, but the act of generosity made them lower their weapons.

'You have a priest at the end of that bellpull?' Blackstone asked.

'We do. We should put it round his neck for all the good he's done us. But purgatory awaits anyone who murders a priest.'

'Then fetch him and let's bury this man and ask God to cast his benevolence on us all.'

The French men-at-arms expressed their gratitude to Blackstone, whose gesture was more appreciated by them than the English. Once the burial had taken place the knights asked if they could join him.

'I'm going south to get my family,' he told them, 'and then no further.' He nodded towards Killbere. 'He's taking the men into Lombardy. You'd be welcome.'

'Sir Gilbert?' a Frenchman asked, seeking approval.

'There's nothing like inviting strangers to a private banquet, Thomas,' Killbere grumbled.

'We must choose our friends now, Gilbert. We've been cast adrift by circumstance. If we find fighting men who'll stand at our shoulder there's a chance that some of us might live a while longer.

There are tavern whores in Italy who've yet to enjoy your charms.'

'By God, that's a truth. Aye, join us,' he told the Frenchman. 'We'll find ourselves another battle and be better paid for it.'

By the time the victors of Poitiers were within three days of Avignon, Killbere had accepted fifty-seven more men whose lives were adrift, within two days another seventy, and each time stragglers joined they knew of the scar-faced knight who rode at their head. The resurrection of the boy archer who had saved the life of a Prince at Crécy, been honoured with knighthood and fought to kill a King at Poitiers was already folklore. Sir Thomas Blackstone was a talisman.

Blackstone left the men on a forested hilltop that gave a clear view of the fortress city of Avignon rising up from the cliffs on a broad reach of the Rhone.

'We'll rest and make our plans for a day or two,' Killbere had told him.

'And wait for me?'

'What else? I know you, Thomas, better than you know yourself. You haven't brought these men at your back to abandon them here. You may think otherwise, but there's nothing left for you and your family. And you're no farmer. We'll wait a while. Not too long, mind, so don't you become a damned monk down there.'

'They'll be looking for whores, Gilbert,' Blackstone said, looking at the unkempt men.

Killbere glanced at those now under his command. 'If I can keep them back long enough I will. I can't let them loose down there. They'd be like rats in a sewer; I'd never get them back. There are other towns.'

Blackstone ordered his Gascon hobelars and the new men to obey Sir Gilbert. Then, with a brief farewell to Meulon and Gaillard, he made his way down towards the city.

'Sir Gilbert?' Elfred said as they watched Blackstone and Guillaume ride away. 'You think he'll come back?'

'He's done his duty for Edward and now he's to see to his family. You can't deny a man that. But where else can he go afterwards? He'll be back.'

Within the walls of the papal city Blackstone felt like a country squire who'd been looking at the back end of a horse for too long. He stood head and shoulders above those who filled the corridors, which were more ornate than those in any nobleman's house he had ever seen. Courtiers, messengers, bankers and visitors gathered in groups, speaking in a variety of languages and tones, dressed in rich colours of fine cloth, beaver-skin hats and ermine-edged robes. Silk merchants argued with bankers, who made deals with spice traders, who sold their precious commodities to middlemen. The Papal See was open for business.

Blackstone doubted that even King Edward's palace could be so richly adorned. Walls lined with religious frescoes swept colour through corridor and chamber. While one wall extolled the glory of hunting and religious men dressed in splendid clothing, another eulogized the Virgin Mary, while yet others showed the Saviour dying for the sins of the world. Another bragged of fine castles and tranquil countryside, expressing the desires of those who commissioned the paintings. Floors tiled in patterns of flowers and heraldic beasts led to offices of the Curia; courtyards with arches that soared to windows of inner corridors bustled with pilgrims hoping for the pontiff's blessing. Women in brocades and furs, their stewards scurrying behind attendant knights, glided down the passageways.

Niccolò Torellini ushered Blackstone through a gilded door into an antechamber, which in turn led to a scented garden. A small fountain trickled water over stone troughs into a pond. The buzz of voices faded as the doors closed behind him and the stillness of the walled sanctuary shut out the urgency of the heaving corridors. Agnes leaned across the low wall, her fingers dipping into the water as she talked to the fish that rose to the surface thinking she was offering food. Father Niccolò touched Blackstone's arm.

'I will find your wife and son,' he said quietly.

He moved through another door that led to the rooms at the banker's house.

Blackstone walked towards his daughter, listening to her voice as she played in a make-believe world. He stopped a few paces away from her. The warmth of the sun trapped in this courtyard garden and the fragrance of roses and lavender embraced him like a victor's garland. A moment of peace and tranquillity, an image of simple beauty he wished he could somehow preserve.

'Agnes,' he said gently.

The child whirled, eyes bright with expectation. 'Papa!' she said and ran into his arms. He held her tightly, the scent of her skin and the touch of her small body flooding him with tenderness and gratitude. She brushed hair from his forehead and traced the scar. 'Did you fight a big battle?' she asked.

He nodded. 'How did you know?'

'Henry told me. I didn't believe him but Father Niccolò said it was true. You want to see the fish? I've given them names.'

He settled her down on the pond's wall and sat next to her as she began pointing out the dark gold and brown flashes that skirted beneath the surface.

'That one's called the Pope's Hat, there's Aloise and Bernard, but the big one is called Master Jacob because he swims around the others and keeps them under control.'

'So Master Jacob looked after you just like your fish does with his charges,' Blackstone asked.

'Oh yes, he looked after Mama and Henry and me. And he told Henry stories about you.'

'Were they nice stories?'

She shrugged. 'I don't know. Henry said they were, but he might have made them up himself.'

Blackstone kissed the top of her head and heard one of the doors into the courtyard open. Christiana stepped into the garden as Agnes ran to her. 'Mama, Mama, Papa is here. He's come back.'

Agnes clung to her mother's skirts, but as Blackstone gazed at his wife's face he felt a tinge of fear. The smile that gave him no chance of victory in an argument seemed subdued. Something had happened. They embraced. He felt her cling to him with quiet desperation.

'I feared for you,' he whispered into her hair.

She nodded, keeping her face buried into his chest. 'And I you.'

He wiped the tears from her cheek.

'And Guillaume? Does he live?' she asked.

'Yes. He fought well. He's at an inn in the city. I've stabled the horses and stored some plunder there. We'll have some money now.'

She nodded, as if distracted. He had expected some sign of relief at knowing that the squire who had brought them through so much danger was alive and close by. There was joy missing from her eyes.

'Has something happened to Henry?' he said, his instincts outweighing his desire for her.

She seemed surprised at the question. 'Henry is well.'

'Then where is he?' Blackstone asked, trying to ease whatever was disturbing her. What troubled her: had he left her alone once too often to worry that he might not return?

'Henry goes where he should not. He slips out of these apartments and mingles with the merchants and their retainers in the corridors. He hears gossip and agreements being made. It intrigues him. I scold him but he disobeys me.'

'He's a boy. Perhaps these walls confine his natural curiosity.'

'Is that reason enough to disobey his mother, Thomas?'

He saw it again, a downward glance that hid something more.

'No, it isn't. I'll speak to him.'

She stood on tiptoe and kissed his cheek; then she grasped his hand. 'I'm so happy that you've returned unharmed. Don't leave us again, Thomas.' She looked at him. 'Promise,' she said, and then ran ahead with Agnes, laughing as they brushed their hands across the lavender bushes and then cupped the fragrance to their faces – as if no such promise was expected.

Blackstone bathed and then ate the food served by Torellini's servants. Christiana told him about their river journey and how one of the soldiers had drawn a knife and threatened her, and how Sergeant Jacob had killed the man. She made no mention of the assault on her. Blackstone knew she had sufficient strength and willpower to endure hardship and fear, but perhaps the incident with Rudd in the confines of the barge had placed her too close to the killing. Blackstone held back from telling her of his own journey and the battle at Poitiers.

'I'm going to find Henry,' he said.

She reached out for his hand. 'Does King John still live?'

He nodded.

'Then no good came of it. You should have stayed with us,' she said in answer to his failure.

Father Niccolò guided him through the corridors of the papal city. It was only when the groups of men moved from their path that some glanced up at the tall knight and reacted to his scarred face.

'Have you spoken to my son while he's been under your protection, Father?' Blackstone asked as the priest ushered him into an alcove, where the dim light subdued his presence.

'He keeps much to himself,' the priest told him, 'but he is brave and strong, and he studies hard the books I give him. His Latin is good, and I am teaching him Tuscan, which is the more pleasing of our dialects. You should be proud of him. Sir Thomas, there are rumours racing through the corridors about what is happening to France now that the English have been victorious. We should talk. I have a proposal for you. It would benefit you and your family.'

Blackstone had kept his gaze on the crowded

corridors, searching for his son. When he turned his attention back to the priest it was to seek the truth of the matter: 'What has happened to my wife?'

The priest shrugged. 'The heart can grow tired through fear,' he answered. Blackstone studied the man's face. It would be impossible to detect a lie from Rodolfo Bardi's personal spiritual adviser, a man whose influence went beyond the pastoral care of others. Niccolò Torellini bargained with the great and the powerful. Inscrutability was his trade.

'And the soldier who was killed?' Blackstone asked.

'I was asleep. I don't know what happened. Sergeant Jacob killed him. That's all I know.' He caught sight of Henry, relieved that it would halt any further questions. 'There he is; I'll fetch him. And we should talk – about other matters.'

Blackstone watched as Father Niccolò bobbed his way through the jostling crowd, a nod here, a smile there, as he acknowledged greetings from those who were obviously rich and influential. Blackstone had seen the same arrogance of nobility and wealth among Norman barons and French lords, men who could wield power without getting blood on their own hands. For that they employed soldiers such as him.

The crowd thinned, allowing the priest to shepherd Henry over. The boy gazed at his father, who smiled, but noticed a shadow flicker across the boy's eyes.

'I knew you would return, Father. I knew you would win,' he said and stood waiting hopefully for his father's embrace. Man and boy stood in silence, neither reaching for the other.

'Welcome your father,' the priest said, bending down to the boy.

Henry stepped closer and extended his hand. 'Welcome home, Father. I'm happy you were not injured.'

Blackstone smiled and grasped his son's hand, and felt that the skin was moist. Fear.

CHAPTER 32

Blackstone's reputation had drawn the men who now waited for orders, but it was Sir Gilbert Killbere whose fearless leadership offered them a chance of wealth that went beyond the usual wages of banditry. He kept the men encamped a couple of miles from Avignon on the forested hilltop. They had waited three days since Blackstone had gone into the papal city, resting and organizing their route into Italy, where they could sell their skills to one of the warring city-states. Travellers had told them of large marauding bands who were burning their way along the eastern bank of the Rhône, to Marseille and beyond. French and English soldiers released from service after the battle of Poitiers had joined marauding groups of Germans and Hungarians in search of plunder. From where Killbere's men were camped they could see columns of smoke more than twenty miles away.

The wayfarers had told Killbere how more than two thousand routiers had attacked Marseille, but the town had been well defended and prepared for the assault, which failed. As the marauders grew in strength their attacks became more widespread and towns and villages fell under their swords.

'Our men are getting restless,' Elfred told Sir Gilbert. 'They think we're losing plunder to these others.'

Killbere was no camp soldier and waiting without a plan of action chafed like a wet saddle. 'Soldiers always whine like brats with colic,' he said, drawing a whetstone along his sword blade. 'They've food and drink; we need to rest. It's a long road ahead.'

In truth, he admitted only to himself, he was uncertain how best to proceed. A battle plan was simple. Men lined up opposite each other and fought to the death. Raiding villages and towns was easier still: slaughter the men, enslave women as whores and take whatever food was available, remembering to donate sufficient gold to the church so that sins might be forgiven. But finding a paymaster who would guarantee employment was beyond his experience. Serving a sworn lord and the Crown had been his life. Loyalty had been the currency he had always dealt in. The great wealth of plunder and ransom from battle had usually gone to the nobility, and to lower-rank knights who knew how to run estates with their newly found fortune while growing weak from lack of combat. Killbere knew himself to be caught between two conflicting needs: gaining wealth and having a sworn lord to serve. Perhaps his chances in the world would be better if he offered his services as a champion, without the baggage of commanding men whose loyalties could turn at the toss of a gold coin. But he was thirty-five years old and feeling the strain of years of hard fighting. Younger, stronger men would have more stamina to stand and trade blows. He needed small wars where the killing was easier.

'Is it serious?' he asked.

'Not yet,' Elfred said, looking across the sprawled camp. 'But there are always troublemakers.'

'And Blackstone's men?'

'The Normans are like knotted rope. Meulon and the other ugly bear would wait until the sun never sets for Sir Thomas. I'll have the sergeants keep an eye on the others.'

'Aye, do that. But those who want to go, let them – they'd be no good to us in the long run – but see they take nothing with them except that which is theirs.'

'They'll want their share of the plunder we have,' Elfred answered.

Killbere wiped his sword blade clean. 'No, they leave with nothing but what they had when they joined us.'

Elfred nodded. If the malcontents had to be confronted, then they would be killing their own and their venture could fail before it got much further. Both men looked beyond the distant hills and the black plumes of smoke. Death was on the march, and it was coming their way.

★   ★   ★

The oil lamps and candles burned late into the night in the heart of the papal city. Pope Innocent VI, like many of the Popes, showed kindness and sympathy to the poor for Christian charity offered an assured place in heaven. Were it not for his guidance the hospitals and almshouses would not exist. On papal instructions a percentage of a merchant's profits were given to the needy. Those who had wealth were obliged to offer something to those who had nothing. On this night, however, the underprivileged were not his concern. The bullion buried in the papal vaults and the vast wealth held by the merchants of the city was at risk. A gaunt and infirm old man, he suffered more than physical ailments; his indecision offered no direction to the politicians and court of the most important city in the region. The Holy See was under threat. Word had reached the Pope of the burning and destruction of the towns that straddled the Rhône. Bands of men, more barbaric than Saracens, threatened the entire region. The room was hot and men's tempers flared as no one, least of all the Pope, could decide on a plan of action. The only directive issued that night was to draft more labour to finish the incomplete walls. It was inconceivable that brigands would attack their great city, but after the defeat of King John, no one was safe. The land was lawless.

Blackstone lay in the cool bedchamber, gazing up into the shadows at the arched ceiling pillars decorated with cherubs garlanded with gold laurel leaves, spilling coins from one hand while holding a horn of plenty in the other. This was a banker's house, ornate with soft furnishings, embroidered bed coverings and fine silk tapestries. Christiana had fallen asleep in his arms, but before she turned her back and he had pressed her body to his, she had flinched when he touched her. They kissed and he once again attempted to caress her, but she put her fingers to his face and lips and asked him to wait – without explanation, other than to say the fear and tiredness from her journey had still not left her. It had been like that for the past three days. No passion had been spent between them, when once neither could resist their lust for each other. He knew that it had been an arduous journey for her and the children and the attack on the barge would have taken its toll.

Blackstone confined himself to the banker's house and garden, enjoying the time with Agnes, allowing Christiana the days of comfort that the refuge offered. Henry absented himself at every opportunity to explore the corridors of power. The boy had changed, there was no doubting it – more confident, but also more withdrawn.

Was that not to be expected? Torellini had asked him when he mentioned it to the priest. A boy defending his mother, a family with fear in their hearts and danger at every corner. The past would slip away.

Torellini handed him documents that secured his

future. Blackstone fingered the folded parchment, the Pope's waxed seal as cold and dry as the desolate past that would haunt him for the rest of his life. A haunting that would always drive him on.

'Your journey is only just beginning. Great wars are behind you but conflict will never be far away. I will care for your family.' Torellini's eyes questioned the Englishman. He knew the answer before asking it. 'You have not yet told Christiana of your plans.'

Blackstone shook his head. There was a time and a place to do battle.

And now was not the time.

He slipped from the bedclothes when he heard muffled voices and scuffling footsteps through the corridors. There was no sign of Father Niccolò. Blackstone went out into the courtyard and saw lamps burning within other rooms. He dressed and slipped his archer's knife into his belt. Guards stood at the far end of the corridor as noblemen and priests were ushered into a great chamber behind closed doors. Blackstone turned a corner, pushed open the door to an outside staircase and went up to one of the lower battlements. He could see beyond the walls and the flickering lights of the city where taverns still plied their trade along with the whores and soldiers and those who travelled with the hope of fortune or the opportunity of a political office – the surest route to wealth and influence. His eyes scanned the dark shapes of the hills. Knife points of light wavered. Killbere and his men were still there. Voices raised in argument drifted up from the lamp-lit chamber below. The words were indistinguishable but he caught their sense of panic. Whatever the cause, it would soon surface. He settled his back against the wall, preferring to sleep in the chill air and to see the dawn rise rather than go back to the ornate chamber and a cold wife.

'Riders,' Will Longdon said as he relieved himself against a tree.

'Watch where you're pointing that,' Elfred cautioned as Longdon changed the direction of his gaze and everything else followed.

'Sir Gilbert,' Elfred called.

'Aye, I see them,' Killbere said as his men gathered at the treeline and looked into the distance where horsemen galloped towards the city gates.

'Two hundred maybe,' Meulon suggested.

'That's not all,' Killbere said, pointing beyond the fields on the other side of the river where a black snake of cavalry writhed through the folds of the hills. 'Elfred?'

'More'n a thousand, I reckon,' Elfred said, his archer's eye gauging the indistinct numbers.

'Our Thomas'd tell you how many hairs they had on the heads if he was here,' Longdon said, wiping his hands dry on his breeches.

'Sir Thomas to you, pisspot,' Killbere grunted. 'Those up front – the knights – they're the envoys. They'll do the talking.'

The men watched in silence as the gates opened and city dignitaries and two cardinals went out in their finery to meet the riders. A dozen of the knights followed the city officials inside.

'What's all that about then?' Will Longdon muttered. 'You think Sir Thomas knows about it?'

'He will soon enough,' Killbere said, glancing around the rising hills. 'Elfred, get the sergeants to send out riders, to keep an eye on our backs.'

Blackstone had left the inner walls as the sounds of chapel bells tumbled across the rooftops. Those who prayed made their way to matins; others, who slumped in doorways, unable to afford a room, stirred and slept on. He found the painted board displaying three horseshoes and made his way through the archways into the yard. The pungent smell of horses mixed with the less savoury stench of human waste. Stable boys dragged soiled straw from the stalls as Blackstone looked at the liveried horses. He recognized three of the horses belonging to the soldiers who had accompanied the Italian priest.

Blackstone moved into the darkened tavern. Men and women slept wherever there was space. He stepped across the prone bodies and made his way up the stairs. John Jacob had been well paid for his mission; if Blackstone had gauged the man correctly he would have paid for a room. There were no doors on the niches that served as sleeping bays. Sergeant Jacob was already awake and sat sharpening his knife. A pitcher of ale was at his feet, the small window open, street sounds rising. Jacob got to his feet as Blackstone stood in the doorway.

'I heard you were back, Sir Thomas. You have anyone else with you?'

'Guillaume. And there are friends outside the city. I thought you'd have struck out for Bordeaux and home. You and your men.'

Jacob made light of it. 'Three of 'em have gone. The climate here suits me, my lord, and besides, I was not at the battle so I gained no plunder. The priest paid us well. I've no complaints.'

'You stayed to offer my wife assurance,' Blackstone said.

Sergeant Jacob nodded, and put away the knife. 'I thought it could do no harm for her to know there was someone close should she need it.'

'I came to thank you,' Blackstone said.

'You've no need, my lord. I did as I said I would, that was all.'

Blackstone sat on the window seat. 'Did my son act well?'

'As you would expect, Sir Thomas,' Jacob answered. The evasiveness barely noticeable.

'On the barge. When you killed Rudd. Did he act well?' Blackstone quietly insisted. 'Did the boy use his knife?'

'Have you spoken to the lad, Sir Thomas?' Jacob asked, still wary of being drawn to explain the exact circumstances. Sir Thomas Blackstone might hold him responsible for the assault.

'Not yet. But I will.' Blackstone took a draught of the ale while waiting for Jacob to answer.

'He did, my lord. He behaved courageously. He stabbed Rudd before I got to him. And then he helped us push his body into the river. He did your name proud.'

The explanation had still omitted the details of the assault. Blackstone had no need to pry any further. It was obvious what had happened.

Blackstone extended his hand and the man grasped it. Sergeant Jacob held Blackstone's gaze. 'Rudd was drunk with a knife in his hand. Your son defended his mother and sister and I finished the job. I can assure you, Sir Thomas, that's all that happened.'

Blackstone pressed no further. John Jacob had protected Christiana and now he shielded her name.

'England has little need for us now, sergeant. The French wars are over,' Blackstone said.

'Then I'll fight the Scots. There's always them to cause trouble.'

'No. That's done with. Edward has imprisoned the Scottish King. Men like us are left to their own devices.'

'Then you'll be doing what exactly, Sir Thomas?'

'That's yet to be decided, but when it is, I could use a good captain at my side, John Jacob.'

'I'm a sergeant, my lord.'

'Captain,' Blackstone answered.

Jacob nodded in acceptance, but before the men

spoke another word the clatter of horses echoed down the street. Blackstone leaned out of the window, but the riders were a couple of streets away; all he could see were their pennons fluttering below the roofs.

Blackstone pushed his way through the corridors to Christiana and the children. 'Stay here,' he told her.

'What's wrong?' she asked

'De Marcy is here. He's inside the city.'

'Here? Why? For us? Does he have men with him?'

Blackstone had moved from the room to the garden and back again. 'A bodyguard, that's all. Where's Henry?'

'He went out to the merchants, as he always does. Thomas, are we in danger?'

'Does he know about de Marcy?'

'What?' she asked, unable to hide her fear.

Blackstone grabbed her arm. 'Does Henry know about the Savage Priest and what he did? Does he know I went to kill him?'

She hesitated, and then nodded. 'Yes, he knows. I told him on the barge. He asked me why you'd left us.'

'Keep the door locked and open it only when I return.'

Blackstone pulled the door closed behind him. He moved as quickly as the crowded corridors would allow and, despite his size and strength, which pushed men aside, the sheer number of people slowed him. His own fear was that Henry would try to prove himself and attack de Marcy. If that happened, no one would stop the Savage Priest from killing the boy.

By the time Blackstone reached the part of the palace where huge doors opened onto a courtyard, servants were holding the intruders' horses and squires stood with the pennons of de Marcy and a lord of Provence. The Pope's welcoming ministers ushered the sallow-faced killer and his entourage into the corridors of power. Papal guards lined the route as de Marcy strode towards the inner chambers where the Holy Father waited to greet him. Fear of what this killer and his routiers could do had forced the Pope to welcome him and hear his demands.

Blackstone pushed through the merchants and traders who had been herded against the walls. There was no sign of his son. Fear crushed him as tightly as the crowd. One of the soldiers half turned to press back the throng and Blackstone saw Henry. The boy was crouched below men's legs, knife in hand, like an animal preparing to spring.

Blackstone pulled and turned people away, and as de Marcy came within five strides of Henry, reached out and grabbed the boy's shoulder. The guard turned, men's voices were briefly raised in alarm, and then subsided into complaint. Blackstone yanked Henry back into the crowd, but the commotion was not lost on de Marcy. His pace faltered, his eyes scanned the huddled men, pressing shoulder to shoulder. It was impossible not to see Blackstone. The doors of time closed and their memories collided. Both knew the other. Their eyes locked, and Blackstone saw the look of triumph on the Savage Priest's face. Neither man could do anything, surrounded as they were by the numerous papal guards.

Blackstone pulled Henry further back into the crowd as the dignitaries and de Marcy went on to the Pope's chambers.

Christiana scolded Henry as she gathered their few possessions together. 'You've exposed us all to danger. Now he knows we're here. If you'd obeyed me we would still be safe.'

'I'm sorry, Mother,' Henry said.

'There's no shame in trying to kill someone as evil as de Marcy, Henry,' Blackstone told him.

'You encourage him?' Christiana said.

'He was trying to succeed where I had failed. But,' he said, turning to Henry, 'they would have killed you. That's the only reason I stopped you. You have to think before you kill.'

'Blessed Mother of God,' Christiana whispered, crossing herself, 'you bring death to the last place of refuge we have.'

There was a rapid knock on the door and Father Niccolò, breathless and sweating, having run from the Pope's chamber, entered and then leaned back against the door, as if the devil himself were pressing from the other side.

'De Marcy threatens the towns that control the routes into Avignon. He would seize all trade and bullion. He demands payment of more than fifty thousand gold florins. And he wants you. You have to leave. Now. The Pope will give you up. He has no choice.'

He looked sympathetically at Christiana. 'I am going back to Florence. There is a boat waiting. My lady, I hope you are convinced that the offer I made Sir Thomas is a good one and is now the best chance you and your family have of escape.'

Christiana looked to Blackstone. 'What offer?'

Father Niccolò winced. He had come between man and wife. He quickly shrugged the moment's awkwardness away. This was no time for protracted family negotiations.

'Thomas. Please. We must leave,' he urged.

'What offer?' Christiana demanded again.

Blackstone hesitated before answering. But answer he must. Time had run out.

'I have a contract to lead forces in Florence.'

'To leave France?' she asked. 'This is my home! I'll not run again!'

'There is no damned France left, Christiana! The King is taken, the Dauphin will struggle to gain power. Charles of Navarre will be released and the killing will start again. Christ, it's all done with here!'

Blackstone gave a brief look of regret at his

blasphemy to Torellini, who nodded and made the sign of the cross.

'Keep the documents I gave you safe. I will take your family; the transalpine Princes will welcome you and your men. I have already sent word.'

'I told you, Father. They aren't my men. They're Sir Gilbert's.'

'Then why are they still waiting in the hills before they make their way into Italy? They wait for you, Sir Thomas.'

Christiana's anger was barely contained. 'You believe de Marcy's men will cross the mountains?'

'Yes,' Torellini said. 'Once his demands are met here, and they will be, he will join forces with the Germans and Hungarians who are already in the north of Italy. They have aligned themselves to the Visconti of Milan against the Pope and the Papal States. My lady, there is nowhere safe now except with me in Florence.'

'I'll not leave my husband again,' she said, with a brief glance at Blackstone.

Blackstone hesitated. She would be safer with Torellini. The priest had kept his word and delivered her and the children to safety. If Henry had not tried to attack de Marcy their presence at Avignon would have gone unnoticed. That, he knew, was not why she was afraid of leaving him. What mattered was that the last time he had left her she had been hurt.

'We'll stay together,' Blackstone said.

★   ★   ★

The threat of excommunication against Gilles de Marcy had no effect on the Savage Priest. Under pressure from the papal politicians the Pope made, some would say, a pact with the devil. He would save the vital trade routes that brought the Holy See its wealth.

And that, as Father Niccolò explained while he led the Blackstone family through labyrinthine passages to safety, was why the Savage Priest had dined with Pope Innocent and was fêted like a prince. The payment would be made, his demands would be met and Blackstone's life was worthless within the confines of the city. Palace guards were already raiding their rooms. But Pope Innocent had played one card that de Marcy did not yet know of. Torellini emphasized the importance of the documents he had given to Blackstone. The Pope, by affixing his great seal to the folded parchments, had endorsed them. They secured arms and payment once Blackstone reached the transalpine Princes whose provinces straddled the border between France and Italy. If he would lead, then others would follow. Father Niccolò had assured His Holiness that Florence would finance the contract to fight the Visconti and those routiers, such as de Marcy, drawn to their wealth and power. With that seal of approval Blackstone's fortunes had changed again.

It gave him the authority and the means to wage war against the Church's enemies.

* * *

Blackstone carried Agnes as the dank passageways, lit by cresset lamps, gave way to a gate below the outside walls of the city. Alerted by Torellini's messengers, Guillaume and John Jacob with his two remaining armed men waited with the horses. Agnes smiled and waved at them both as the protectors greeted Christiana, who seemed reassured by their presence.

Father Niccolò made the sign of the cross and blessed them as Sir Thomas Blackstone knelt and kissed the hand of the priest who had held him in his arms all those years ago.

'I grant you absolution for any previous wrongdoing, Thomas, and pray that you find safe passage through the mountains. I will see you again.'

Blackstone held Agnes in one arm and climbed into the saddle. 'Guillaume, lead the way,' he said.

Hooves clattered across the cobblestones as Torellini waited at the gate, an arm raised in benediction and farewell, but Blackstone never looked back.

Killbere spat in disbelief: 'God's work?'

Blackstone showed him the sealed documents. 'The Vicar of Christ's,' he said.

'As good as! You don't attend mass or go on bended knee enough for the privilege, Thomas. Sweet Jesus! Forgive me, but you're only one step removed from being a heathen.'

'I'll be happy to have Him on our side, Gilbert,

and I'll make sure you get to pray on behalf of us all, seeing that you've already sworn your sword to Him.'

'Aye, but that was a pact to save my own worthless skin! You've been handed the keys to heaven.'

Killbere looked to where Guillaume had fashioned a canopy for Christiana and the children. 'It's a risk having them along,' he said.

'What would you have me do? Abandon them?' Blackstone answered sharply.

Killbere put a placating hand on his friend's arm. 'Thomas, not for us. For them. You've already dragged them across the whole of France with ravenous wolves at their heels. Anyway, no matter; they'll be as safe as anywhere with us. We've nearly two hundred men, but we need more.'

'They'll come,' Blackstone said. 'Gilbert, I gave my men over to you. Now I have to take them back. I want no ill feeling between us.'

'There is none. I'm glad of it. I've been scratching my arse for the last few days thinking how best to go on. Now you've returned the problem is no longer mine. I wish I could tell you you're the answer to my prayers but I can't because no supplication passed my lips.'

Blackstone looked across the river towards the hills. 'We have to get past de Marcy's troops, and reach a safe haven until more men can be found.'

'They're not the only ones we have to worry

about. We stopped merchants yesterday and helped lighten their journey,' he said, and then scowled as Blackstone was about to question him. 'Thomas, it was food and drink and a few bolts of cloth; we didn't cut a throat, I swear. But there are more horsemen, several hundred by all accounts, moving across Provence. From what the merchants said, they're scorching their way along the plains to the north and towards the mountains. We won't stand a chance if we're caught between the two.'

'We're few and we travel fast. And we've always had luck in our killing,' Blackstone answered.

Blackstone presented John Jacob to the Chaulion men as their captain; since losing Guinot at Poitiers, those English and Gascon troops had no one to command them and Perinne who commanded the Chaulion monastery made a better lieutenant – a man who could follow orders and see them carried out. He gave Perinne and the men permission for any man to go his own way, but no one was prepared to leave Blackstone and Perinne, like Sir Gilbert Killbere, knew when it was best to step aside.

'We'll grow in numbers and there are victories to be had. We take what we need when we need it – and pay for it. There'll be no rape, no slaughter of children – my men know me for this – and I'll punish any man who disobeys. We forget our past belligerence towards each other; we're a mix of men as good as can be found, and we'll take our fight into Italy and be paid for it. Turn your backs on France; she has no need of us now. We serve a new cause and we serve each other,' he told them.

Blackstone instructed a bodyguard of men, commanded by Guillaume, to protect his family and then ordered them to strike camp. The Savage Priest would know soon enough that he had slipped away. By nightfall they had made ten miles, with sightings of horsemen on distant ridgelines, but he would not let them stop for rest or food. The cloudless, moonlit night aided the men sent ahead to scout the tracks that meandered through the valleys and climbed into the low, tree-covered hills.

After a week of tiring travel, Blackstone led them into a broad valley where a fortified manor house stood. Its ancient walls, laid centuries ago by a Roman legion, divided field and vineyard from pasture and pens, and looked to be easily assaulted. But the manor house and its courtyard had a greater strength than its walls; it belonged to a kinsman of the transalpine Prince, the Marquis of Montferrat, who had agreed to invite Blackstone's men into Piedmont where they would be hired by the Vicar-General of Italy to fight anti-papal forces. The fortified manor house served as a beacon for one of the routes through the mountains. If harm befell the Seigneur of this territory, then those responsible would find their way ahead blocked, their troops constantly ambushed and a revenge exacted in blood. No money would buy redemption.

Marazin, lord of the manor, greeted Blackstone, who had gone ahead with Killbere to make certain that no trap was about to be sprung. The bearded old man who greeted them looked as noble as a dirt-caked hobelar. A broad belt held a stomach straining against a grease-slicked leather jerkin that bore witness to years of hand-wiping after meals.

'You've a document?' he demanded, standing in the courtyard, unarmed and unafraid, as a couple of dozen crossbowmen on the ramparts levelled their weapons at the two knights.

Blackstone offered one of the sealed documents that vouched for him and which gave assurances of money and indulgences.

'There's little by way of defence, my lord,' Killbere said. 'A whore with a flagon and a knife could breach these walls.'

The man squinted up at the pockmarked knight. 'You'd have experience of such women, then. We've no whores here; we're a God-fearing house, and you'd best not have any such women in your group back in those trees.'

Blackstone let Killbere answer for himself, taking a moment of pleasure as the tavern-loving fighter offered a stumbling apology.

'I meant no offence, my lord. It was a coarse, unbecoming phrase. We are grateful for your pledge of safety.'

The man seemed to have a begrudging spirit. 'I take the Pope's coin, I don't house scum from that

Babylon called Avignon. We honour the holy mass and all times of prayer. You'll have less sleep here than in the saddle. Bring your family and sworn knights in, Sir Thomas Blackstone, and leave your horsemen outside the walls. We've food and drink for three or four days. No more. Then you'll be on your way to my kinsmen at the border.'

He turned his back. Killbere looked crestfallen.

'A sin-free house,' Blackstone said, easing the horse away. 'The power of prayer is something to behold. I feel we've been led here for your salvation.'

Killbere saw no humour in Blackstone's words. 'I'll fight my way to heaven's door, Thomas, not crawl on my knees sober and chaste.' As they rode back to the trees the manor house's chapel bell rang for morning prayers. 'I'll stay outside the walls with the men,' Killbere said.

An agreement was reached with the Seigneur. Christiana and the children, along with Guillaume and all the men, except the sixty that Blackstone would take on ahead, would stay at the manor house. Blackstone and Killbere would take Meulon and Gaillard with John Jacob and secure their next place of rest, almost within sight of the crossing point. Leaving a day ahead of the others would allow them to travel with the lumbering wagon on the uneven tracks. Guillaume and the French knights would bring the remainder of the men and Blackstone's family from the manor house and rendezvous at the chosen place. Until they left Christiana and the children would be safe under the old man's protection, and with the larger part of the force with her she would be able to travel swiftly under their escort to where Blackstone waited for them.

The Seigneur beckoned Blackstone. 'Your well-being is of no concern to me once you leave my protection. I've honoured my part, but my men report that de Marcy and his routiers have left Avignon. They're riding from the south. And there are more horsemen on the northern hills. Hundreds of them. They've destroyed three towns and half a dozen villages, places loyal to King John. Is your Prince still raiding?'

'No, he sailed for England. Are they de Marcy's men?'

The old man shook his head. 'No, another band of brigands. Does it matter? They're worse than the plague; they're insensible to the fear of God.' Even if the Pope had not paid him to offer safe passage to the fearsome-looking Blackstone, he would have done so: his instincts told him that the man was to be aided and trusted. The day would come when his own alliances would not save him and any act of kindness might contribute towards an easier death. 'The Savage Priest is a son of iniquity; his cruelty is unbridled. No church is safe, no village spared. He's drawn even more scum than he had before he sided with John. Bankers take his plunder; lawyers document a town's extorted tributes. He's equipped like a king, with his own surgeons and priests, blacksmiths and whores, so he can't travel fast. You have a chance to outrun him and reach de Montferrat.'

'And the other routiers?'

'There's no bargain to be made with those skinners, no ransom asked. They're looting and killing. God help anyone who ever raised a voice in support of King John. Perhaps he promised them money and didn't pay. Who knows? Landowner and peasant alike are dying because of it. And if these two armies come together, then nothing will stand in their way.'

Blackstone walked with Christiana through the vineyards, knowing he was due to leave her again in a few hours. The gentle warmth of the day and the clear, bright sky seemed to ease her spirits. She spoke of living with the Harcourts and how their two families were entwined following the bloodbath at Crécy, and the joy of the life she had shared with her English archer who had risen in rank and honour. He was the breath of her life.

'I lived with Jean and Blanche as my protectors, Thomas,' she told him. 'That was my home after my mother died and my gentle father placed me in their care. I swore I would never be forced from my home again.'

'I brought that upon you, Christiana, but this war was not of my doing,' he told her gently.

She brought his hand to her lips, and then placed

its rough palm against her cheek, as would a child with a parent. 'You have always fought with honour, Thomas. For your King and your Prince; for Jean and for us – but now we go to another country without cause.'

She trembled in his embrace. The past few weeks had torn France and its people apart, and the savagery that pursued their family had suddenly reappeared and the fear it brought diminished her.

In Blackstone's eyes the girl he first saw, whose hair was the colour of autumn leaves, had never changed, nor had his happiness at being with her. But now, as he listened to her sadness and regret, she seemed as beaten as the country itself. Most men would have already abandoned her to a convent after learning of her rape, but he feigned ignorance of it; the shame seemed more his than hers. He had failed her.

'Forgive me,' he said quietly.

'There is nothing to forgive,' she said, putting her hands across his, her small fingers barely covering his palm. 'Unless you've given your affection to another,' she added, and smiled.

'And who might that be? Do you see any ladies in our company? And Sir Gilbert hasn't one feminine trait worth considering.'

'I shall tell him you said that.'

'Dear God, don't. He'd carve me up. He's been cursing me since I was a boy in my village. I've felt the cuff of his hand more than once.'

'But not recently,' she said, and smiled again.

'No. He's getting old, I think. I've known him a long time. He berated me for going back across the river for you at Blanchetaque.'

'I thought that was Elfred?'

'I forget. It was a lifetime ago. Do you remember when I found you in the village, when the Bohemian cavalry were breathing down our necks?'

'I was terrified, but you made me feel strong. I remember that. And when I clung to you on the back of that horse I remember you smelled. Really stank. Archers stink. It's why we French feared you.'

'I knew I should have let you drown.'

'I thought we would – or that they'd capture us. They nearly did.'

'Nearly. We were young, and we were going to live forever. Nothing was going to deny me having you. That's what I remember.'

She took his arm and leaned into him. The vineyard ran down towards a small river, disappearing from view into the forest, and then reappearing again beyond the hills. Like the lifeline on her palm that lost itself in the creases and valleys of her hand. 'You remember Malisse,' she asked.

'The old hag who was Blanche's chambermaid?'

She nodded, and laughed. 'Godfrey de Harcourt always said she was a witch that should be burned. Slowly. She read my palm once and told me I would marry you.' She hesitated: 'She said we would have three children.'

'Then perhaps we should prove her right,'

Blackstone said, and pulled her face to his lips. In that moment it seemed the Christiana he had always loved returned to him. She eased away tenderly, not wishing to face him.

'It's too late for that,' she said. 'I'm having a child.'

Blackstone had no control over his response. His first thought was that it could not be his. She read the pain in his eyes and in that moment realized he already knew what had happened on the barge.

'Who told you? Jacob? Henry?'

Blackstone tried to clear his mind of the images that refused to go. He shook his head. 'Neither. Jacob defended you, said nothing. Nothing at all, only that you'd been attacked.'

'I didn't fight,' she said, surrendering to the inevitable admission.

'What?'

'He had a knife at Agnes's throat. I didn't struggle. I couldn't.'

Blackstone knew he had lied to himself about the fact that the rape did not matter. She would have fought – he'd always known that. She was Christiana; she would have fought rather than be shamed. But she had not.

'Would you rather Agnes had her throat cut?' she asked calmly.

'No. Of course not. No.' He had convinced himself that the assault did not matter because he had never lost his love for her. The child was not his. It was a bastard child from a rapist. His stomach plunged with the same wrench that he felt before going into battle. He loathed his own reaction and fought it.

'I'll not purge it away, Thomas. The infant cannot be condemned for what happened. Can you understand that?'

'Yes, I understand.'

'Then do I stay with you and my children or shall I seek refuge in a convent and throw myself on the mercy of the Church?'

As the sun's rays glanced across the treetops and caught the copper-leaved vines, he reached out and touched her hair. Who would forgive Thomas Blackstone for the sins he had committed?

'You have no need of mercy or forgiveness from any man. Least of all me. We have been blessed with each other and with our children. The ways of the child are not the way of the father. We'll stay together and see what becomes of us.'

It was the best he could do. A thread of hope for them both, a slender lifeline.

It was not enough, and they both knew it.

CHAPTER 33

Blackstone led sixty men and the laden wagon through the scented pine forests, climbing towards the route indicated by de Montferrat's kinsman at the manor house. When the trees allowed them a view of the sky they could see mountain peaks guarding the valleys that would lead them into Italy. Killbere had said little on the twenty miles travelled, other than to comment on Blackstone's sullenness. He had uttered a reply about being sick of France and wishing for new horizons, but then curtailed his answer to command more outriders to scout ahead. The forest became denser, and gullies and ravines ran like veins down the edge of the track, hidden by tangled undergrowth and fallen boughs, offering opportunity for ambush. De Montferrat's kinsman had warned Blackstone of banditry from villagers who lived on what could be seized from travellers. They made no threat against the kinsman and their raids were infrequent, and for that reason he never ventured into the mountains to exact retribution. Blackstone wondered, when he had been warned, if the man might have been taking tribute from them. It made no difference; he had been warned.

'If they come, they'll come at us from above,' Killbere said, looking at the slopes that swept away into the treeline above the track. 'I'd rather we were on a ridgeline than down here. At least then we'd see the bastards.'

'The old man said the routiers were north of us. There's no horseman going to attack in a place like this,' Blackstone answered, thankful that his mind had been turned away from dark thoughts of Christiana.

They camped on a curved plateau, where the road ran straight for three hundred paces in either direction until it curved from sight. That gave a clear view of anyone using the road. On the other side of the track a wall of rock ran several feet high before the forest's bony roots gripped its crumbling surface. Beyond the rock face the trees grew denser the higher the ground went. The plateau where they settled was covered thinly with trees, and the slope that fell away went down forty feet to a tangled bed of fallen boughs, thorn bushes and wild berries.

As Elfred and Will Longdon's men unhitched the wagon and hobbled the mules, Meulon and Gaillard instructed their sergeants to post sentries at each curve in the road and for others to find an animal track and go into the forest. The sentries were to lay a rope to guide their relief to where they stood guard. Blackstone wanted no one stumbling through the night.

'Safe as anywhere, I suppose,' Killbere said to Blackstone.

'Trouble is, nowhere's safe. Where would you attack a camp like this from?'

'A sudden rush from each end of the road.'

'That's what I thought. We'd have nowhere to run, our backs'd be against this drop. And if they had a few crossbowmen and got them up there in the trees, we'd be like trout in a fish trap.'

'I'll put the men in small groups and each can defend its ground,' Killbere answered.

Blackstone nodded: 'And tell them that if it's a hit-and-run raid to let whoever attacks escape down that end of the track. We don't have enough men for ambush or pursuit at night. And no fires.'

Killbere strode away calling for Jacob and Elfred.

Blackstone looked at the sixty or so men securing their horses, and finding their place to fight should it come. Being adrift in enemy territory in a poorly defendable camp would give few men sleep that night. But exhaustion and cold would take them, and that's when Blackstone, were he to attack a camp like this, would strike – two hours before first light, when men found that half-troubled sleep and they ached from curled bodies desperate for comfort.

Blackstone was wrong.

They came in the depths of darkness. Flickering torches burned like fireflies sweeping down through the forest's steep hill. The killers knew the hillside, could smell the boar and wolf, find the night tracks of badger and fox. And the sentries' throats were slit long before the wild men began their rush downhill. They were silent except for the rushing crackle of foliage.

Gaillard was the first to rise up, woken by what sounded like a storm throwing its weight down through the rustling forest. The movement triggered Blackstone and Killbere. The fug of sleep cleared quickly, but there was still a moment while the glimmering torches caused hesitation. Fireflies were the souls of unbaptized children seized by demons. The same thoughts crossed every man's mind: the ghosts and goblins, the witches and damned were sweeping down out of the blackness to consume their souls.

Blackstone saw his men freeze.

'They're men! Raiders!' Blackstone yelled, breaking the spell.

The moment his voice carried, the attackers gave a mighty roar that struck fear into them all. Wild-looking bearded men, some wrapped in animal skins, others in rough-woven cloth, makeshift armour and helmets, hurled the burning torches into their midst, turning the ground into a hundred fires as they leapt into the clearing wielding axe, spear and sword with a savagery that nearly overwhelmed the defenders. Pockets of Blackstone's men moved quickly into formation as the wild men threw themselves onto the soldiers' blades. As each group of Blackstone's men held their ground, it forced their attackers to manoeuvre around them. Dancing shadows flickered and then darkened as bodies fell across the burning torches. It was as if the great forest had unleashed bears and wolves to consume their prey.

'Shields and advance!' Blackstone heard Killbere command, and from the corner of his eye saw one of the groups huddle and then surge against the wild men. Horsemen galloped from one end of the road and struck at Elfred's men who defended the wagon. They were soon overwhelmed and their attackers threw weapon and food bundles into the arms of the horsemen. The wagon rocked precariously as men clambered and fought, and then a wheel from each axle slipped over the edge. The wagon slewed before settling onto its side as men jumped clear. Blackstone led a group of men towards the wagon's beleaguered defenders, the uncertain torchlight making the fight ever more ferocious.

One of the wild men swung a battleaxe at Blackstone, who took the weight of the blow against his shield, but the size and power of his attacker forced him off balance. His shield was ripped from his arm when the man swung again. Blackstone went down as a paw of a hand gripped his throat, the man straddling him and bearing down with a knee on his sword arm. Blackstone grasped a burning torch and thrust it at the man, who easily reared back his head to avoid the spluttering flames. Blackstone kneed him hard in the crotch, which weakened his stance, and Blackstone rolled clear. They grappled, first one then the other gaining the advantage. The man's stench of stale sweat and pungent animal skin filled Blackstone's nostrils. The battleaxe swung again, the flat side of the blade catching Blackstone's head. Stunned, he felt the man gain extra strength and pin him but as the axeman reared back to deliver the killing blow he hesitated, his eyes startled by the glinting Arianrhod at Blackstone's neck in the torchlight. That hesitation was fatal. Blackstone rammed Wolf Sword up through animal fur, then bone and muscle, its blade forced so hard into lungs and heart its tip broke through the base of the man's neck.

Horsemen galloped away and the wild men ran. The raid was over. They had taken what they could. Sixteen of their own lay dead; others crawled in agony and were despatched. Blackstone's company lost eight dead and as many wounded. A small price to pay against a greater force. Those who could not be saved were killed quickly; the less severely wounded would be treated. Blackstone ordered their dead to be buried. A Christian prayer would be spoken to keep their souls from being stolen from their graves by night demons.

The sudden incursion of the wild men had caught them unawares. Elfred, dried blood from a scalp wound encrusting the side of his face, trudged back with Will Longdon and the archers, as John Jacob brought back the horses that had been scared off by the attacking men. Killbere and some others dragged the enemy bodies to the edge of the hill and rolled them unceremoniously down into the tangled thorns and undergrowth.

'They can feed the birds and berries. Better than night soil, though they stink more,' he said.

'How much did they get?' Blackstone asked as Elfred reached them.

'Damn near half of it. Sweet Jesu, we spilled much blood for that plunder, and there'll be torment due from the devil's own when we die. But I swear to you, Thomas, I'll heap more sins upon my head if I catch those thieving bastards.'

The men made no protest as Killbere ordered them into details to bury their dead and gather what was left of the food and weapons. Then, horses and men straining with effort, they dragged the overturned wagon onto its wheels. By the time they had repacked their cargo it was already two hours after first light.

'We need those weapons and supplies, Elfred,' Blackstone said. 'Captain Jacob, take your best men and find their tracks; we'll be right behind you.' Jacob and a half-dozen men peeled away as Blackstone turned to Will Longdon. 'Take six archers and ten men and return to the others. Bring them on early; travel only in daylight. We'll rendezvous at dusk tomorrow at the Marquis de Montferrat's, and then we pass through the mountains. We'll not arrive as beggars in a Prince's kingdom. There's to be no relying on others until we make our terms.'

Blackstone and Killbere urged their horses down the steep incline, skirted the brambles and fallen boughs, and rode for the distant forest, followed by those already mounted.

'God help them when Sir Thomas and Sir Gilbert get their hands on 'em,' one of the hobelars said.

'God will look the other way when the terror falls upon the scum,' Will Longdon said.

'Don't you get yourself lost!' Elfred called as the wagon and escort started down the track.

'Straight as a yard-long shaft, me!' Longdon called back.

'Aye, I've seen some of them shafts of yours. Like a damned crescent moon, half of 'em.'

Each raised a hand in farewell.

Longdon waited as his column of men filed past and then, as he reined his horse to fall last in line, the breeze caught a scrap of cloth on the bramble thorns below. A flutter of blue, like a snared bird, creased the pale green material. Easing his horse down the slope he reached across the tangled mass with his bow and lifted the embroidered material. The stitching showed a blue swallow curving in flight. For a moment Longdon puzzled over it, then his mind caught the fugitive memory. Of course – it was Sir Thomas's. Folding it neatly he tucked it beneath his jerkin.

★   ★   ★

De Marcy could make no accusation against the Pope for Blackstone's escape. He had been given all that he demanded, as well as absolution for the slaughter he'd inflicted during his lifetime. That the prize of Blackstone had slipped away meant there were those of the inner court who had warned the Englishman. No matter, De Marcy would strike out and join the Visconti of Milan, the Pope's enemy, who had more riches than the King of England. Those with wealth and power needed men like the Savage Priest to impose their will, but his mind was now preoccupied with where Blackstone and his family would run and whether he should search for him or continue with his planned alliance with the German and Hungarian routier company across the border. The temptation to stay longer would not abate. A final act to enhance his reputation had been placed before him if only he could bring down the Englishman. There were knights whose fighting skills were legend, and Blackstone was one of them: a beast on the field of battle, consumed with a rage that swept man and horse aside with a focus on destruction that de Marcy understood. It could take weeks, searching for one man and his family, and yet, he brooded, Blackstone had been right there, at Avignon, placed in full sight for the Savage Priest to seize – God's gift. How far could he have travelled? With bribery and threat he would find out their route. Perhaps it was not too late after all.

* * *

Blackstone, Killbere and their men filtered through the darkening forest. Nightfall was at their heels and, if they were to make the rendezvous the following night, they needed to exact their revenge against the raiders and recover what weapons and plunder they could. They had lost the men's tracks some miles back, but the scouts had fanned out and found the broken ground over which they had travelled. It was only after another five miles that they sighted the men who had swept out of the night.

The area surrounding the village that Blackstone gazed down upon had been fortified with low dry-stone walls, curving and twisting like a writhing snake, making it impossible for riders to strike directly against the village. Sharpened stakes lay between each wall, to maim the horses of anyone foolish enough to attack, leaving their riders vulnerable even if they survived the fall. A high palisade gate was the only way in and out of the village.

'A ratcatcher's worth of peasants. Belligerent bastards by the look of them,' Killbere said.

'Two hundred fighting men, probably the same again that we can't see,' Blackstone answered, keeping his eyes on the hovels, each joined to its neighbour by wicker fences. Fighting through the village, even if they could get into it, would be hard going.

'We don't have enough men to attack,' Killbere said.

'And I can't give you cover because we don't have enough arrows,' Elfred told them.

The villagers had cut back the edge of the forest on their flanks, leaving stumps and tangled brambles. They would have a clear view of anyone trying to approach, and had made it impossible for an assault to breach their defences without taking heavy casualties.

'Well, that's it. We go on. We can't get ourselves trapped in there, especially at night,' Killbere said.

Blackstone's small force would have no chance against the entrenched villagers. He looked across the lowering skyline as clouds hugged the hills. 'Wind's from the south. It'll soon be dark. Elfred, get the men ready.'

'Fight at night?' Elfred asked. 'With respect, Sir Thomas, we're at a disadvantage and night-fighting isn't going to favour us.'

'It favoured them,' Blackstone answered.

Blackstone ordered the men to gather bundles of fallen kindling and dry branches. The villagers had slashed down the undergrowth but had not gathered all of the felled saplings. As blackness covered the valley, men ran forward and laid the tied bundles against wall and palisade. Within minutes the flames from the resinous pine branches began to consume the village gate. With half a dozen fires burning, Blackstone's men threw green branches into the flames, letting dense, choking smoke smother the village. Screams and shouts echoed across the stone walls as the villagers' defensive positions now trapped them. Unable to run between the walls and embedded stakes they funnelled into the only entrance left to them: the flaming gate. As the warriors ran forward in an attempt to push the burning pyres free they were silhouetted against the flames.

A hundred paces into the darkness of each flank Elfred's archers rained down arrows in a lethal crossfire. As men fell, panic gripped the women and children, who turned and ran back into the eye-watering smoke to try and clamber to safety over the village's defences. Blackstone's men waited, clear-eyed, the breeze at their backs. The wind caught embers, and then tinder-dry roofs smouldered and suddenly flared. As the warriors retreated in disarray from the burning gate, Blackstone led his horsemen out of the darkness and into the chaos. As fire jumped from hut to hut and the wind swirled smoke through the narrow gaps between them, the tongues of flame cast the riders' giant shadows.

The villagers were disorganized, but fought as best they could, some running to protect the women and children, others forming ragged lines of defence, but despite their courage they were cut down by the horsemen. Within an hour those fighters who had opposed them lay dead. Smoke still drifted as first light exposed the village's charred remains. Blackstone's attack had killed more than ninety fighters as well as a dozen women whose bodies lay, swords in hand, next to their men. Children had died in the flames and beneath galloping hooves but they were few, which was the only comfort Blackstone could take. The escaping villagers had clambered over the walls, those not caught on the sharpened stakes running into the night, still guarded by the hundred or so fighters who survived the attack.

Hobelars found a wounded man who quickly confessed where the village hid its plunder. Men dug beneath the charred remains of the village leader's house and from the cache pit pulled out caskets of plunder, weapons and food. Once the booty was recovered a hobelar cut the man's throat.

'A good night's work,' Killbere said, grinning, passing a wineskin to Blackstone. 'There's food and wine they'd stored for the winter. Panic took their horses, but if we wait a few hours they might wander back.'

Blackstone guided his horse through the smouldering carnage as the men brought the wagon down from the forest. There would be sufficient food now for their journey across the border and when Guillaume arrived with Christiana and the children his reinforcements would have more weapons than when they started.

'How many did we lose?'

'Only three. A few wounds. Nothing that won't heal.'

'Was there money?' Blackstone asked.

'Not a lot. They raided mostly for weapons and supplies by the look of things,' Killbere said.

'Share it with all the men when they get here.'

'Even those who didn't fight? The others back at the fortress?'

'Everyone gets a share. Have the sergeants keep the men alert, Gilbert. There are still a hundred or more armed men who escaped and they'll have their people with them. They could overwhelm us now there's light.'

He was about to turn his horse when a movement across the valley caught his eye. The long sweeping plain, wide enough for five hundred men to stand shoulder to shoulder, darkened as troops rode into view. It was difficult to see in the faint light what coat of arms fluttered at the vanguard of the approaching army.

'Damn it, Thomas, I hope that's not de Marcy. We'll not outrun him from here,' Killbere said, and then called for the men to form up as Blackstone stared into the dim light from where the armed men edged forward through the smoke that still clung to the trees and ground.

'Keep the men ready, Gilbert. Whoever they are they might lose interest once they know the village is destroyed.'

The slow and steady hoof beats came on, the sound of armour and leather creaking in the quiet dawn. The ranks stopped at six hundred paces, where forty men dismounted and ran forward so that they were no more than three hundred yards from the village roofs. They were crossbowmen.

'Who in God's name are they?' Elfred asked. The few hundred men who waited wore no livery, and were dressed haphazardly in mail, some with armour on their legs and arms.

'They're routiers,' Blackstone said as the crossbowmen levelled their weapons.

'The Priest?' Elfred asked.

'No. It's not him,' Blackstone answered. 'I saw his pennons at Avignon.'

'Thomas, it's the other horde of skinners. Let's get our arses out of here or they'll swarm over us like lice in a tavern whore's bed,' Killbere said.

'And leave what we came for? No, we'll make pretence of joining them if we must. We need to get across the border if we're to have any future.' He turned to look at the men behind him. Dried blood caked their soot-creased faces and hands; they looked vicious enough to take on the heavenly host. 'The devil himself would hire us now.'

The crossbowmen waited as a dozen horsemen advanced from the ranks bearing pennons and banner. The slight figure of the rider who led the men wore fine armour and bascinet, its visor raised. The flag of red and gold horizontal bars fluttered in the wind.

'Ready!' one of the men-at-arms shouted to the crossbowmen, who brought their weapons to bear on Blackstone and his men. The short, fast-flying quarrels would punch through armour, muscle and bone.

'What a poor way to die,' Killbere said, drawing his sword.

About the time that Blackstone found the raiders' village, Will Longdon arrived back at the manor house where Guillaume and the men waited. He explained to the captains what had happened during and after the ambush and that by first light the party were to leave and meet up with Blackstone, ready to cross the border. The men took food and drink; then they found a place to sleep before leading the others back next morning.

Once Henry and Agnes were covered with blankets, Guillaume and the bodyguard formed their own picket around the family. Will Longdon watched from a distance. He wanted the lady's favour. He had known Thomas Blackstone since the knight was a boy archer, but whereas Blackstone had risen in rank, Longdon was still a ventenar in command of a small company of English archers. Although he had gained plunder over the years there had been no betterment in his status and he had remained in the service of the King of England and the Prince of Wales. No common archer would ever sit at a nobleman's table, or be allowed any intimacy of friendship. But Thomas Blackstone, a common man who had fought alongside Longdon and the others, no different from them, had been blessed with the status of rank. To tell Lady Blackstone that he had fought alongside her husband, before she ever knew him, would give Will Longdon a moment of recognition.

Guillaume rested thirty paces away, and as the nearest picket on duty turned his back, Longdon chose his moment. He quickly got to his feet and approached her through the shadows.

'My lady,' he said quietly.

She looked up, momentarily alarmed, but Longdon's shoulders hunched in brief subservience, and he showed his hands were free of any weapon. 'I have something that belongs to Thomas – I beg your pardon, madam – I mean Sir Thomas, your husband.'

Christiana had never lost her fear of the English archers' reputation, and to have one approach so quickly and silently frightened her. She hid her uncertainty; the man had stopped a dozen paces away and gone down on one knee, and quickly took something from beneath his jerkin: a patch of cloth.

'Come closer,' she said. 'Let me see your face.'

Longdon moved into the light of a torch that burned on a stake next to her tent.

'It's me, my lady,' he said. 'Will Longdon.'

He was familiar to her, and she felt reassured. 'What is it? What is it you have that belongs to my husband?'

He extended his hand and gave her the piece of cloth, with the embroidered swallow.

'Sir Thomas dropped it when we were ambushed. I know it's important to him; he's had it since just about the time I've known him.'

She fingered the cloth she had given Blackstone all those years ago. 'Yes, it is important. Thank you.'

Longdon wanted to impress her, hinting at a greater friendship between himself and Blackstone than really existed. 'I was with him that day when he took that trophy, I was. I was right there. I didn't know he'd cut that piece of cloth off the old man's jupon and kept it as his trophy. So it must be important to him.'

Uncertainty furrowed her brow. 'I don't understand,' she said.

'It were his first kill. The crossroads in Normandy. We was going to be ambushed. But Sir Gilbert laid us archers off to the side and we flanked the men waiting for us behind a hedgerow. Thomas took the old knight down. One nice clean shot. He vomited, because it was his first kill, but I'd wager no one would believe that now. Not the way he is. The things he's done. I thought I should give it to you, my lady, because knowing me I'd lose it before I had a chance to give it back to him myself.'

She had turned her gaze away and made no reply. Longdon had expected an acknowledgement – no reward was necessary, but some kind words of appreciation, telling him that her husband was lucky to have people like Will Longdon at his side. She stayed silent. Awkwardly, he turned to leave.

'You were there?' she asked.

'Oh aye, m'lady. Right there. It was a grand shot. Well aimed and true, like I said. Through the man's neck and a yard later out his groin. He was as dead as a stone right enough. There was no plunder to be had, a rusty old sword is all he got if I remember right. But you never forget the first man you kill.'

She squeezed the cloth into her hands, and nodded. 'Thank you for bringing this to me. And for telling me where it came from.' She fumbled for a coin in the pouch at her belt.

'No, no, my lady. There's no need for that. Sir Thomas is my friend. Good night, my lady. We'll have you safely with him by tomorrow night.'

Longdon turned away into the darkness, gratified by her thanks.

Christiana reached out a hand against the rough-hewn wall to steady the tremor that shook her, determined not to let the archer see her distress. Will Longdon could not have known that it was she who gave Blackstone the piece of cloth as a token of her affection at the castle at Noyelles, before the great battle of Crécy. What was certain was that Longdon had been with Blackstone since the English had invaded Normandy. And what could not be denied was that the old knight who died at the crossroads from Thomas Blackstone's arrow had been her father.

How long had Thomas known the truth?

CHAPTER 34

Through the smoke and swirl of soot from the still-burning thatch, Killbere saw Blackstone raise his arm to keep everyone nervously in place.

As Blackstone rode slowly forward, showing he held no weapon, the leader of the routiers signalled to the men-at-arms for restraint.

'Thomas Blackstone, you're alive,' said the leader's familiar voice as Blanche, Countess de Harcourt, spurred her horse forward to meet him.

As the night wore on, and the several hundred men encamped, they shared not only food and wine with Blackstone's men but a mistrust from the mostly French and German mercenaries. Some ease settled among the men as a mutual understanding grew that they all sought plunder, no matter what desires drove their commanders. A scuffle broke out between the French knight, Robert Corval, who had fought at Poitiers for King John, and one of those who had deserted and found their way south to attack his subjects. Blackstone settled the matter with the promise that if either man killed the other, he would kill the survivor. An uneasy truce prevailed.

Blanche de Harcourt told Blackstone how, by the time she had returned from Rouen to Harcourt on that fateful day, the road to Blackstone's home was alive with de Marcy's killers. She turned back, returned to her family estates in Aumale and raised a force to destroy as many of those who supported King John as could be found. She had swept down central France collecting deserters from both armies, itinerant soldiers from Hainault, Bohemia and Hungary, willing to kill for payment. Her *chevauchée* had been as fierce as that perpetrated earlier by Prince Edward.

'I burned every village and town I came across who swore loyalty to King John,' the Countess told Blackstone. 'I gave no mercy. We slaughtered livestock and destroyed crops, denying the King any revenue of taxes, any means to feed his army or call for the *arrière-ban*. Those who have nothing can give nothing, not even themselves.'

Blackstone had always known this woman was a powerful influence on his friend Jean de Harcourt, and he had never underestimated her passion, but hearing of this second band of routiers slaughtering their way down to the Alps served to remind him that ruthless and passionate women were often the backbone of many a Norman noble house.

'This village was as far south as I'd planned to raid,' she said. 'Beyond here the Italians squabble

591

and fight among themselves. I've no interest in them, Thomas. Now, all I want is to go back. The Dauphin will try to rule, but Charles of Navarre will soon stir trouble. I want my family safe.'

'You'll pay off these men?' Blackstone asked her.

'Yes. That's our agreement. I've two hundred of my own, loyal to Jean's memory, but the rest? Well, there's value in them. My God, they're vicious scum, many of them, but with the right leader they would be a force to reckon with,' she answered, knowing his own journey lay across the border.

Blackstone looked out across the hundreds of small fires, a reminder of his first sight of an army on the hills, waiting to cross to Normandy with King Edward. The sight of these rough-hewn men rekindled the memory of the apprehension he had felt as an untried archer when moving among them. Sir Gilbert Killbere had spoken up for him and his brother, and the man's fighting skills and reputation had secured them a mentor that no man would challenge. Now these killers needed a leader who could stand up to them and weld them into a fighting force. His own fighters were disciplined enough to follow him and his captains, but if he could harness Blanche's routiers' greed and temper their viciousness, he would have the small army that Father Niccolò and the merchants and bankers of Florence wished to contract.

'I'll talk to my captains,' he told her. 'Can you hold them here long enough? I need to meet de

Montferrat and bring Guillaume and Christiana with the rest of my men.'

'We'll ride with you. De Montferrat might prove an ally worth having for the future. There's plunder to be divided and gold to be counted, and we can do that across the border. And once we cross, they can decide who they follow. And I'd welcome seeing Christiana and the children before I go back. I may never see them again once you go into Italy.'

For the next few hours Christiana walked and gazed across the dark landscape. There were night creatures in the forests but their screeches and cries were natural to her ears, and preferable to the snores and curses of men who lay out on the stony ground. She had to make a decision before first light. She settled next to the children, covering them with her cloak for extra warmth. Henry lay with his arm across his younger sister, protective even in his sleep. Agnes slept like the innocent she was, still cradling her bedraggled doll.

Thomas Blackstone had left them on many occasions when seizing towns or challenging men-at-arms for their fealty; she had always known that his strength and reputation would see him safely home and that with his presence no ill would befall them. But Blackstone's loyalty extended beyond his family and she began to feel the bitterness that was, she knew, unjust. The fear for her children's safety had been great, and what she had endured to secure it had been cruel but necessary. Now the barbaric reputation of the English at war, something that plagued the French noble houses, had once again struck. The image of her father dying at the hands of the man who became her husband, and of him knowing this, as he must have done once he had learnt of her family, wounded her love for him as surely as if a heated blade had been plunged into her heart. No wonder he had tried to stop her going to Paris. He'd known the truth all along. A part of her mind fought back, telling her that coincidence was God's will, that it was war that had killed her father, and had nearly slain Thomas Blackstone, but these thoughts failed to hold back the flood of her anguish.

She got no closer than ten paces towards the sleeping Guillaume when he rolled clear of his blanket, alerted by her almost silent footfall.

'My lady,' he said.

She knelt next to him, keeping her voice low. 'Guillaume, I want to leave. I want to take the children.'

'But we are leaving, at first light. We'll be through the mountains by nightfall. Sir Thomas will be waiting for us and have the Marquis de Montferrat's protection. And then we will be in Italy.'

'No, Guillaume, there will never be enough protection now. My lord and husband will draw vicious men to him wherever he goes. They'll want the glory of killing him. I want to go home.'

Guillaume's uncertainty silenced him for a moment; everything behind them had been destroyed. There was no life: there was no house, no servants; all had been obliterated. 'There is no home to return to,' he said. 'Sir Thomas is your home, my lady.'

'Take me back to the river near Avignon. I'll find a bargeman to take me north, and from there we can ride back to Normandy. That's where I belong. That's where my children belong. The house of Harcourt will give me the protection my children need.'

'I don't understand. The Harcourts are dead, the house taken by King John's men. Sir Godfrey was slain, and the Dauphin will remember their betrayal. You can't go back.'

'Jean and Godfrey betrayed the King and paid for the treason. But their brother Louis stayed loyal to the family name. He will offer me protection. And the Dauphin will extend his forgiveness to me because my father died fighting the English. If you won't help me, I'll go alone with the children.'

His honour meant everything. It was how a man was measured. It should not have been his concern if a knight's lady decided to disobey her husband. Obedience was a demand made and seldom questioned. But now the woman he had known since childhood, who had, like him, been given refuge by the Harcourt family, needed his protection.

'Sir Thomas charged me with your protection at all times. I can't let you go alone.'

She saw the conflict written on his face, but forced away her compassion for his feelings. She would use any means and anyone necessary to escape the torment that her life had become. She carried a bastard child and the man she loved could barely hide his resentment. Her son had watched his mother's violation and withdrawn from her; and as hard as she tried she could not halt the searing wound from the truth of her father's death.

'We should leave with the others and then go our own way, my lady. I'll take a dozen men with us for escort. We can't travel in darkness and we'll need a pack horse with provisions,' Guillaume said.

'Thank you. We will always be in your debt.'

She left him and went back to the children. Guillaume's conflict was eased by his promise to protect his master's family with his life, but his loyalty still lay with his sworn lord, Sir Thomas Blackstone.

Will Longdon, half drunk, was sprawled on a makeshift bed of straw beneath a blanket. He lay like a child, one arm outstretched as if for comfort across his war bow. He gagged when Guillaume's hand covered his mouth and smothered his snoring. Longdon's strength twisted him around, dragging him from the dark recess of his slumber. As strong as the archer was the young squire easily held him, until his eyes focused and he acknowledged the gesture of silence.

'Master Guillaume, I nearly pissed my breeches,' he said quietly. His immediate fear was that Christiana had laid a complaint against him for having approached her.

Guillaume was kneeling next to him, but looked furtively over his shoulder into the night. 'I only found you because you snort like a pig and smell like one.'

'There's been little time for bathing, Master Guillaume; some of us have been in some hard fighting.'

Guillaume was being slighted, but veteran fighters like Will Longdon were permitted some leeway, providing their superiors allowed it. He thrust a flask of water into Longdon's chest. 'Swill your mouth and freshen your mind. I need you awake to carry a message.'

Longdon did as ordered, rinsed his stale mouth and spat to one side. Then he splashed water onto his face. Guillaume waited, and watched to see that the man was at last alert.

'Can you find your way back to Sir Thomas?'

'Aye, course I can. It's why he sent me, to bring you and the others.'

'By night,' Guillaume said.

The burning torch Guillaume held Longdon's creased face in flickering light, his disbelief unmistakable. 'A fox wouldn't find him. The trails twist like a gutted dog's bowels. No, not by night.'

Guillaume needed time and the darkness denied it him. 'All right. Leave at first light. Lady

Christiana will attend mass; you must reach Sir Thomas long before the men reach the rendez-vous. Ride ahead – is there one of your men who can lead the others?'

'Aye, I can choose one. Master Guillaume, what's happening? Is there trouble?'

The young squire hesitated. How much of his lord's affairs should he tell the common archer? 'Tell Sir Thomas I ride north and west with Lady Christiana and the children and a small escort. We seek to cross the Rhone and return to Normandy.'

It made no sense to Longdon. 'Normandy? Is there a reason? My Lord Blackstone'll press me for an explanation.'

'Deliver the information and tell him I'll ride as slowly as I can.'

'You want him to find you?'

'Just give him the information. What he does with it is his decision.' There was nothing more Guillaume could tell him. 'When you leave, do so quietly. Don't raise suspicion. Behave as if you're going to scout ahead. Give the authority of leading the others to one of your men. Understand?'

The archer nodded.

'I'll pick a better horse for you. Ride hard, and earn my gratitude.' Guillaume stepped away. Longdon would do as asked, if only to keep Sir Thomas's squire in his debt.

The mountain mist was slow to clear, clinging tenaciously to the valleys as Guillaume checked his bridle and rein, wishing he too could linger. By the time Christiana had attended mass Will Longdon was already away from the kinsman's sanctuary, leading the men towards Blackstone. The old man begged Guillaume to change his mind.

'All routes are dangerous; you'll ride into more routiers. They're seeping out of France like pus from a squeezed boil.'

'My lady asks for my protection; I can't deny her.'

'Wait here a few more days – let Sir Thomas make his way back and convince her otherwise.'

Guillaume shook his head. 'If I don't escort her and the children she'll ride off alone.'

'High-born or low-, women will ruin a man,' the old man said. 'I swear they're Satan's gate.' He paid no heed to the young man's look of disapproval. 'She's your master's woman, but if I were you I would tie her to a stake and keep her here until he came back for her.'

The escort of a dozen hobelars waited as Christiana climbed into the saddle, and a household servant lifted Agnes into her arms. Marazin scowled and, ignoring the young squire, strode towards Christiana.

'Madam, you place yourself and your children in harm's way. I beg you to reconsider. I have given my pledge to Father Niccolò, and am obliged to the Holy Father to secure your safety as you pass through these mountains,' he said, grabbing her horse's rein.

'I thank you, Lord Marazin, but I have a journey of my own,' she said.

'You commit a felony by not obeying your lord and husband. I have the right to detain you until word reaches him,' the old man answered.

Christiana spoke kindly to him: 'My husband's squire would then be obliged to stop you in my defence. You outnumber us so he, and these men, would die. The enmity from my husband would never be erased. You've shown us kindness and offered your protection, and I've prayed in the chapel of our Holy Mother, the Virgin Mary. I lay myself upon her grace as any mother would do. Beyond that my life rests in Master Guillaume's hands.'

'Very well, madam, but you'll take heed of the advice I give to him? He needs a better route from here than you've planned,' he said.

She nodded her assent.

Marazin returned to Guillaume. 'You've barely a chance to reach the river. Go north – then west. There's more than one mountain trail. I'll send a guide with you,' he offered.

'I'm grateful, my lord; that was my intended route. I've already sent word to Sir Thomas in the hope he'll intercept us,' Guillaume said quietly.

'Then you've more sense than I gave you credit for. We'll offer our prayers for your safe delivery into Sir Thomas's hands.'

Lord Marazin's guide led them from the fortified

manor's sanctuary. The old man watched as the stubborn mist closed about them.

Like ghosts of the unforgiven, they were gone.

De Marcy's slow-moving train of horsemen and wagons, clerks, monks and whores who straggled behind his main force, needed an uncontested route through the mountains to a place held by one of Visconti's commanders, Alfonso Girolami, who held a fort that guarded a pass into Visconti's territory. It needed few men to hold such a castle, because the narrow valley allowed enemies to be easily halted.

Less than half a day's ride from the Savage Priest's column, Lord Marazin's guide found that the intended route was blocked by a rockfall; there was no alternative but to turn back and find another way. He took Guillaume and his charges across a high ridge, a steep but shorter route to the other track, and while silhouetted against the skyline they were seen by a group of de Marcy's scouts. A half-dozen men, a woman and children were of little interest, except that the Savage Priest had alerted his outriders to watch out for Blackstone. If these stragglers proved to be Blackstone's family who had been left to catch up with his main force, de Marcy realized that the great English knight had made a grave error.

Hours later Guillaume's horses picked their way down the hillside, and then settled more sure-footedly on the track. Guillaume turned back to watch Christiana, who needed to balance herself and Agnes as her horse swayed downhill. It was then that a group of de Marcy's men simultaneously attacked both ends of the track. Panic gripped Guillaume's party, restricted as they were to fighting on the narrow road, unable to retreat back up the hillside or plunge downhill on the other side of the track.

Guillaume reached for Christiana's bridle and yanked the horse to him to keep her close. The escort was outnumbered, but the narrowness gave them an unexpected advantage, allowing them to defend against the dozen men at each end whose horses jammed and shouldered each other. Two lost their footing and slid downhill, unseating their riders.

'This way!' Guillaume cried, wheeling the horses to the weakened end of the track, taking the lead with another hobelar to drive a wedge among the enemy's panicking mounts. The ferocity of their attack, and their deliberate blinding of the horses as their first strike, caused the congested riders to flounder. Screaming horses reared and fell; men tumbled onto stony ground as Guillaume's sword blows maimed and killed. They had fought their way clear, but had lost half their men. Spurring their horses, pursued by the surviving enemy, they galloped hard. The road ahead swept downwards and the guide shouted for Guillaume to swerve into the spindly new growth of a forest. Christiana cried out as she almost lost her grip on Agnes. Guillaume reached out, snatched the child and pulled her to him. Christiana fought the horse, holding the pommel for balance, and then whipped its flank with the reins.

Riding hard, they could see that their pursuers had slowed, for losing sight of their prey meant they in turn could be ambushed; but Guillaume urged his group on to the lower reaches of the valley. If they could make the open ground and ford the small river that lay below, they would have the advantage of turning and facing vulnerable horsemen. It seemed they were going to make it, but as the horses barged around the final bend of forest track, Christiana's horse stumbled again, and she fell into the bushes and undergrowth. Guillaume reined in his horse, and turned back as Christiana painfully got to her feet, the frightened horse already cantering into the forest.

'Go! Save Agnes!' she cried.

Guillaume's hesitation, and that of the men around him as they wheeled their horses, lost them their slender lead. Three of their pursuers were upon her as the others slowed and halted. Guillaume's men had their backs to a rock face; their only escape still lay in the valley, but de Marcy's men now held the high ground.

'Surrender and live!' one of de Marcy's men called.

'Attack, Master Guillaume,' one of his men urged. 'Drop the child and go at them.'

Before Guillaume could answer one of the men held a knife at Christiana's throat. Agnes screamed, Henry urged his horse forward, but one of the men grabbed his reins. 'It's too late for that, lad. They have us.'

As Guillaume and the men threw down their weapons, the guide turned his horse and galloped for the valley. De Marcy's men let him go; he was of no interest to them. They already held the prize.

CHAPTER 35

Will Longdon's horse shivered with exhaustion, its flanks lathered white with sweat, its blood-filled nostrils flaring for air. The poor beast had been whipped by one of the archer's arrows as he urged it across the demanding terrain for hours on end in a desperate attempt to reach his friend and warlord. Within minutes of him finding Blackstone and Killbere breaking camp at the burnt-out village, it went down on its knees and shuddered in its death throes.

Longdon's gaunt face showed the strain of what must have been a terrifying ride. Blackstone listened to the message sent by Guillaume. He rested a hand on the archer's shoulder, his thoughts desperate to understand what might have prompted Christiana's decision to ride back to Normandy.

'Tell me everything that happened when you got back to the men,' he instructed Longdon. He recounted the instructions he had been ordered to relate to the young squire, but then his hesitation in the telling of it made him realize that he must have played some part in the events that followed. Blackstone saw the shadow of doubt cross the man's face.

'I may have spoken out of turn, Sir Thomas. I reminded her that we had fought together, as common men, as archers. I forgot the hatred the French held for us.'

Blackstone considered for a moment and then shook his head. 'She holds no malice for us now, Will. She's not a frightened girl any longer. Did she say anything when you told her?'

Longdon shrugged, and then remembered. 'She asked if I had really fought at your side, at the crossroads that day.'

'What?' said Blackstone. 'The crossroads? When?'

'Normandy. The ambush,' Longdon answered tentatively.

'You told her about that?'

'Yes,' said Longdon, seeing Blackstone's look of concern.

'Why?' Blackstone asked uncertainly.

Longdon couldn't explain his need for the acknowledgement of being more than Blackstone's comrade-in-arms. 'I . . . gave her the cloth, Sir Thomas. The one you carry with you. You dropped it when we fought in the forest.'

Blackstone's hand involuntarily went to his jerkin, already knowing his wife's token would not be there. 'You returned it to her?'

'Aye. I told her how you'd cut it from the dead knight's jupon. As a talisman.'

Blackstone groaned, as if the sky and earth were millstones and he the grain of wheat between them.

'Jesus, Thomas. What's wrong?' Longdon asked, forgetting rank, remembering the boy who rode at his side.

'Oh God, Will. You weren't to know. I learnt when she nursed me that her father had sent her to the Harcourt family for protection. That cloth was a gift from her. I never cut it from him – the man I killed that day was her father.'

Killbere shouted from the mounted men that they were ready to move. Will Longdon's stricken face roused Blackstone's compassion. 'I lay no blame on you, Will,' he said, placing a hand on his shoulder. 'Get some food and drink, and catch up with us.'

Blackstone turned towards the waiting men and climbed into the saddle. Blanche de Harcourt and Killbere realized that Will Longdon had brought news from the men at Marazin's.

'Will Longdon rode ahead of the others. They're hours behind him. Guillaume sent word that he and a dozen men are escorting Christiana and the children.'

'On their own?' Killbere asked. 'Is he stupid?'

'No, Gilbert, he's fulfilling a pledge to protect my family.'

'Where is she?' said Blanche de Harcourt.

Blackstone shook his head. 'In one of the passes. He's buying time for us to reach him.'

For a moment no one spoke, bewildered by the task of finding a small group in those unknown mountains.

'I'll take twenty men,' Blackstone said, 'and backtrack. We'll meet at de Montferrat's castle.'

Killbere spat into the grass. 'Sweet Mother of God, Thomas, we can't sit on our arses while you search for your missing woman! We could be there for days. How many damned needles in haystacks do you find in one life? No, we'll all go because if de Marcy is within farting distance we'll smell his stench or you'll be nailed to a tree with your balls in your mouth and I'll be without a damned contract with the Italians.'

Killbere did not wait for a response but jammed his heels into the horse's flanks. Blackstone saw Longdon find a fresh horse, ready to lead them back. 'I should apologize for him, Blanche. He smothers his emotions with blasphemy and curses but he has my interests at heart.'

'He's an Englishman, Thomas, there are not enough apologies in the world for that,' she said, wheeling her horse. 'I only make one exception for your barbaric race – and that's you.'

The valley was a place of staggering beauty. Snow had already fallen on the high ground but thousands of feet below the peaks the sun shone warmly from a clear blue sky. A meadow this high in the passes should have been bereft of any alpine flowers, but this place was known for its beauty where the sun lingered. The plateau of wildflowers, protected by the distant giants and the warmth of the forest that encircled it, laid a welcoming carpet for any traveller or pilgrim.

A jangling bridle and a choking man who kicked, face bulging, as the rope squeezed the life out of him, broke the cathedral-like silence.

Christiana wiped the tears from her eyes. 'These men guarded me under orders; hanging them serves no purpose,' she said.

De Marcy rode next to her. 'The purpose, Lady Christiana, is that it gives me pleasure,' he answered.

When his men had brought her to him he had touched her face. Her smooth skin peach-gentle beneath his calloused fingertips. She had recoiled and lashed out at him but he had snatched at her neck and gripped it, ready to crush it. And then relented. He would think on how to deal with her but whatever he had once felt was already charred ash on his tongue. She was of no use to him now other than as bait for Thomas Blackstone.

Guillaume and the remaining man, bound and tethered by rope to a routier's pommel, had been forced to keep up on foot with the horses. Five men from the escort had already been hanged every hundred paces on the approach through the forest to the fortress that guarded the pass. Now, de Marcy prepared to hang the sixth man. Guillaume sank to his knees in exhaustion. Most of the condemned men had been dragged beyond their endurance to keep up. There was no struggle left. As they pulled the man to his feet he cried out in a final attempt to save his life.

'Will you spare me? I will fight for you as I fought for him.'

'You didn't fight that well, otherwise you would already be dead. What use is such a soldier to me?' the Savage Priest answered as his men placed the noose about the man's neck and took up the slack, readying themselves to haul him up.

'I have information, my lord. About Sir Thomas's lady!' the man cried desperately.

De Marcy's gesture stalled the execution. He nodded. 'If the information has worth and serves me, then I'll let you live.'

The man nodded, ignoring the chafing hemp on his neck. 'I was an escort on the barge that took us to Avignon—'

Christiana's despair broke involuntarily: 'Say no more! I beg you. He'll kill you anyway.' Her horse was startled, but de Marcy grabbed its bridle and easily brought it under control. He smiled at her.

'You have secrets from me, my lady?'

The soldier tried to approach but de Marcy's men kicked him to his knees.

Guillaume cried out: 'Finn! Listen to what she says! He'll hang you no matter what you tell him. Go to God with a clear conscience, man.'

De Marcy looked down at the man. 'Buy your life,' he said.

'She's with child. One of the men on the barge

raped her. John Jacob, my sergeant, killed him and swore us to secrecy.'

Guillaume's shock couldn't be hidden. Christiana turned away in shame, but de Marcy gripped her chin and forced her head back. 'So, Blackstone's wife is a whore carrying a bastard child. You're worthless to me now. He'll never come back for you.'

'My Lord de Marcy, he will come! He will come for his children!' Guillaume cried out, knowing he might not save Christiana's life, but that there was still hope for Henry and Agnes. 'He gave his oath to the de Harcourt family that he would serve and protect her for as long as he lived! You know he will come!' Guillaume's desperation had created the lie. Blackstone was never likely to have made any such pledge. But he also knew his sworn lord.

De Marcy said nothing. He turned his back on the condemned man, and those at the end of the rope heaved his kicking, choking body into the branches.

The rope tightened on Guillaume's wrists as he was yanked behind the horse. They rode into the valley towards the fortress, presiding like a stern gatekeeper over a rare beauty. A thousand and more of the Savage Priest's horsemen trampled the flowers into the ground.

Alfonso Girolami held the fortress with barely a hundred soldiers. The narrow pass beneath the castle walls needed no greater defence and the garrison was as much as the remote villages could sustain. Beyond the stronghold was a dangerous route into Lombardy known as 'La Porta dei Morti'. For those who survived its rigours and reached the warm land of the Italians, it was said they would never return to the world they had known through this Gate of the Dead.

Village women cooked, and whores were kept to service Girolami's men. The ongoing track through the mountains was treacherous, and the monks who lived nearby served as guides: a service that gave them protection from Girolami who held the fortress in the name of Visconti.

Christiana had been stripped of her dress and left wearing only an undershift. She shivered, aching with the cold, held with the children in a cage in the castle's main square. Henry and Agnes slept, embracing for warmth. Thirty feet away Guillaume was slumped on his knees, hands tied behind his back secured to a stake in the square. His breeches and shirt were bloodied from being dragged across rough ground. The cold night tightened like wet rope on his muscles.

'Guillaume,' Christiana whispered, face pressed against the bars, fearing that even her plumed breath would attract a guard from the ramparts. 'Guillaume . . .'

She waited until her voice slipped into his mind, then saw him raise his head. That brave young face she'd known for so many years, that boy who had served de Harcourt and then Blackstone,

612

lifted and smiled at her. His parched lips offered no words, but he nodded silently.

They gazed across the moonlit square, both knowing they were to die.

'Forgive me, Guillaume. It was I who brought you to this,' she whispered, praying he could hear her plea for absolution. 'There has never been such allegiance as yours and you deserve an honourable death. My children and your sworn lord will speak your name whenever words of loyalty and courage are needed.'

His head slumped back onto his chest, and Christiana snuggled up to her children, the silence of the night taunting her thumping heart.

As sunlight flooded the square, de Marcy strode out flanked by men and the Italian, Girolami, a stocky man of rough features with wind-burnt face and cropped hair, his jerkin buckled tight against a swordsman's chest. Despite the castle being his domain he walked a pace behind the Savage Priest.

'Cut him down,' de Marcy ordered, and then walked to the cage as men cut Guillaume's ropes and supported him.

'How shall I kill him?' he asked Christiana, who knelt like an animal, unable to stand in the small cage as Henry shielded Agnes.

'Don't kill him. He's worth ransom to my husband. He has gold and he'll pay for his squire's life.'

'Answer the question or I'll slit his throat now,' de Marcy said without emotion.

Guillaume's eyes found hers. He nodded at her. 'Let him die with a sword in his hand,' she said.

'But he's weak, look at him, he can barely stand, and if a man is to fight he must have strength. So I'll help him. I shall be merciful and give him the vigour he needs.' He stepped back, allowing two soldiers to open the cage and drag Christiana into the square. Agnes cried out for her mother but Henry held her close to him, whispering words to soothe and reassure her. The villagers, whores and soldiers crowded around the square's edge as a soldier placed a knotted rope into the Savage Priest's outstretched palm.

'We shall see if punishing the whore that he was sworn to protect will spark a fire within him,' he said as the men threw Christiana onto the ground. 'You will crawl for forgiveness around this square twelve times beneath my punishment, which is the ritual laid down by the Church, but if you beg for mercy, then I shall kill him where he stands.'

De Marcy lashed the knotted rope down onto her back, the pain punching through her ribs. She cried out, trying to smother the scream that would terrify her daughter, and as each bruising blow fell, forced herself to remain silent, allowing little more than a gasp to escape her lips.

De Marcy worked his arm in a rhythmic thrashing until she could crawl no more. Her discoloured skin and blood-flecked welts showed through her linen shift, and blood from a misjudged blow seeped through her auburn hair. The exhausted

Guillaume begged de Marcy to stop the beating and, perhaps tired of the monotony, the Savage Priest granted the wish. Guillaume knew it would hasten his own death. De Marcy had Christiana taken to the battlements and Guillaume released into the meadow, where several hundred men camped on the castle's flanks jeered at his enfeebled state.

De Marcy followed and tossed Guillaume's sword at the squire's feet.

'My men want entertainment, Master Guillaume. They need to see how I kill. It is a requirement that they understand my cruelty. Fear of me condemns them to a life of service. Do what you can before you die,' he said.

Guillaume picked up the sword thrown at his feet. Exhaustion was banished from his mind. How often had he and Blackstone sparred until both could stand no longer, and how many times had they fought against the odds, denying fatigue until their enemy lay defeated?

He attacked.

De Marcy was taken by surprise. His own skills with a sword were better than most, but Guillaume struck with the heart of a veteran fighter. The Savage Priest was forced onto the back foot, fighting hard against the raining blows. It was Guillaume's weakened body that finally betrayed him. He parried a blow, but where once he would have shouldered his enemy off balance, his strength now deserted him. De Marcy wheeled and plunged his sword into an unprotected shoulder. Guillaume dropped his sword, and fell to his knees. De Marcy stepped back, not yet ready to kill.

'Come, boy, you're still alive. Your pain tells you so.'

'Guillaume!' Christiana cried from the battlements.

De Marcy glanced at her. 'The whore cries for her lover. Did you take your pleasures with her once she'd played her part with a common soldier on that barge?' the Savage Priest taunted him.

Guillaume grasped the sword's grip in his left hand and lunged, but de Marcy was waiting, parried the blow and then forced his blade into Guillaume's thigh muscle. He fell, squirming face down in his own blood, and de Marcy's voice came from behind him: 'Your suffering is not yet finished.'

Guillaume's young life's memories were as fleeting as a valley mist burned away by a searing sun. He tried to cling to them, but they melted and left him only with pain.

A crushed flower nestled in the grass close to his face, a teardrop of dew still on its petals.

CHAPTER 36

Blackstone's men and de Harcourt's routiers emerged from the forest a couple of hours before nightfall. As they faced a broad reach of meadow, a hundred men-at-arms emerged from the distant trees.

They advanced in line across the open space. Two banners were unfurled in the late daylight: three castles against an azure background fluttered next to a white flag struck with a horizontal red *ordinaire*.

'That's Marazin's banner,' said Killbere of the three castles.

'And the other's de Montferrat. Something has happened,' said Blackstone and spurred his horse forward.

The guide had followed de Marcy's column for several miles until his intended route became obvious. He returned to his master and gave him the news, and the Seigneur Marazin ordered a rider to summon his kinsman de Montferrat and, with fifty men apiece taken from their garrisons, set out to warn and help the English knight.

Blackstone's worst fears were realized.

Aiding Blackstone helped line their own pockets, but seeing the Countess's extra troops, de Montferrat realized he had an opportunity to seize Alfonso Girolami's fortress; control of another mountain crossing increased a prince's power.

Blackstone questioned them tirelessly about the route and the fortress's strengths and weaknesses. Of the latter there were none, according to de Montferrat, but Blackstone saw where the greatest risk lay and knew that if they took it then the fortress would be breached. He called his captains and told them they would be riding by moonlight, and how he planned to attack. The most dangerous part of the plan, with the most risk of failure, he gave to John Jacob, who would need archers.

Will Longdon – for the first time in his life – volunteered.

Countess de Harcourt's men, with Marazin's and de Montferrat's soldiers, followed Blackstone's two hundred. They filtered through the forest on a broad front, like beaters on a hunt. When they were within sight of the forest edge, they stopped and settled into gulleys. Only Blackstone's men would go beyond the trees. The long and punishing ride had not dulled his impatience to reach Christiana, but he had waited for his scouts to report back on the strength of his enemy.

The fortress stood foursquare, its walls so deep it was doubtful that any assault could break them down, built on sheets of granite, its contours following the natural line of the rock face, its flanks protected by de Marcy's routiers. The rear of the fortress, which rose sheer from the rock, with a fat belly of a lake lapping against its base, was lightly guarded. Above the battlements flew a great banner, its size declaring power and strength with its image of a coiled viper swallowing a child proclaiming it a stronghold of the Visconti of Milan. The approach to the castle lay through the avenue of trees leading to the open meadow, and it was here that Blackstone found the bodies of his men who had escorted Guillaume and Christiana.

As they rode beneath the macabre sight they finally came upon a gibbet built within sight of the battlements. Spread-eagled on roughly hewn wooden beams were the remains of Guillaume Bourdin. He was naked; two deep wounds, one in his shoulder, the other in his thigh, had blackened, but he had been blinded and tortured and his evisceration soured the men's throats. Killbere and the others held back as Blackstone rode forward to stand beneath his squire's corpse.

Not a man spoke; a few spat the taste from their mouths as Blackstone eased his horse slowly around the body. Tears stung his eyes. Through his rage and despair he quietly cursed God for His cruelty in giving a creature like de Marcy the will to commit such an atrocity.

He looked back to where the men kept a respectful distance. He and Guillaume had fought and travelled together over the years and now the boy's lifeblood soaked into Italian soil, so far from home. Many had fallen at Blackstone's side but the brutal slaying of Guillaume seemed in that moment to be the worst. It no longer made any difference for what cause a man fought, what mattered was who stood with you. And Guillaume Bourdin's courage had shone brighter than burnished steel.

Blackstone's shoulders slumped. The tears welled from deep within his chest, choking his breath. In the long nights of his recovery after Crécy, he had wept bitterly for the loss of his brother and it had been then that Christiana came by candlelight to soothe and hold him. His spirit had been broken, but had risen again to become a ferocious force. Now, as he touched the cold flesh of the tortured man, it was more than grief that raked his heart; his slumped shoulders caged the rage in his chest.

De Marcy stood with Girolami on the battlement beneath the mighty flag that cracked in the breeze. He watched as Blackstone stayed motionless in the saddle. The stench of his squire's death and the manner in which he died would blind Blackstone with despair and rage. And that weakness would deliver the Englishman into his hands. The day had finally arrived when Blackstone would die under de Marcy's hand.

Blackstone suddenly spurred his horse towards the castle walls, his eyes seeking out the man standing beneath the banner. The Savage Priest was unmistakable. De Marcy gazed down at him and pulled free his gauntlet, then held out his hand, palm outwards. The stump of a finger was plain to see.

'You are legend, Blackstone. Your squire made a feeble attempt to taunt me before he slithered into hell. He said we had met once before,' the Savage Priest called down to him. 'You're a common man who gained respect and honour through your sword. But I'm the better man because I have already beaten you. I have taken from you everything you hold dear and from today you will be less than a shadow. I tortured your squire to death. He fought well but he didn't carry your rage or my cruelty. He screamed when I took my knife to him. And as I cut his eyes and his tongue and split his body, I laid claim to being the most brutal of God's creatures. I sell my destruction to the highest bidder. Will you turn back and retreat into France and join the defeated or shall we settle this here?'

'I challenge you to single combat,' Blackstone called, his words echoing against the walls for both armies to hear.

'You'll fight on my terms, Blackstone. To reach me you must first test yourself against four of my best knights. Honour plays no part in this. I want you dead, but I want your suffering to be witnessed. Your debasement will live on by the time I've finished with you.'

'Send a hundred men with them, de Marcy,

nothing will keep me from killing you. What of my family?'

De Marcy signalled; the men at the ramparts moved aside so that Christiana and the children could be brought forward. Christiana's face was bruised, and he could see the blood had dried on her scalp. He wanted to call out and assure her, but he had no desire to expose his fear for them to de Marcy. Henry looked brave, his jaw clenched, his eyes locking onto his father. Agnes had been weeping, and she trembled.

'Allow my squire a Christian burial,' Blackstone urged de Marcy.

'No,' de Marcy said. 'He can rot. You care so much, I'll nail you next to him.'

'Then you're a fool!' Blackstone answered. 'I wish it for the sanctity of his soul, but if he stays exposed like this, then you'll inflame my men beyond hatred, and as few as we are, your own men will be attacked with a ferocity that would put any other battle to shame. And if that happens, we will not meet in single combat.'

De Marcy's men held ranks on either side of the castle, but he could see that Blackstone's men bristled to attack. Despite their two hundred being so few against his fifteen hundred, their captains held them back. Their force was too puny – and de Marcy knew it – but the English were unpredictable. If they attacked, Blackstone was right: he would die in the slaughter. The Savage Priest would be denied.

De Marcy thought on it for a moment: 'Be quick. The breeze has already turned his stench towards us. And be ready when the bell tolls,' he said. 'You will fight me when you have first fought my champions.' De Marcy's cruel face twisted into what was a smile. 'I only fight those I consider worthy opponents.'

He watched as the scar-faced knight turned away without another word or backward glance at his family.

They buried Guillaume's body wrapped in a blanket, covering the grave with stones and rocks to deter scavengers. Blackstone knelt at the graveside in clear view of the castle walls and the men who waited behind him. Blanche de Harcourt knelt at his side and Killbere stood ten paces back, stubbornly refusing to kneel within sight of de Marcy. There'd be time for prayers once the killing was done.

'I thought my revenge was over,' said Blanche. 'But I'll stay here until this Savage Priest is dead. Let us raze this place to the ground, Thomas, and trample his bones into the ashes.'

'Blanche, you must keep your men back with Montferrat's,' Blackstone told her. 'Stay hidden until the right moment. We have to buy time.'

'They'll be hidden until you or Sir Gilbert command otherwise,' she said. 'We still avenge those who were ours, Thomas. Live long enough to see it through.'

A bell rang out from the castle's tower. The heavy gates opened and four knights rode out, armed with mace, sword and axe.

'De Marcy wants you beaten and wounded and then he'll kill you himself. For God's sake, let's risk what we must and strike them now,' said Killbere.

'And lose my family?'

'Dear Christ, you think he's going to let them live, whatever happens? They're already dead. Let's finish this. Let me go out there,' Killbere urged him.

'Not yet, Gilbert. He has to see me fight and he has to know he can beat me. That's the only way we can lower his guard.' He called Elfred forward. 'Your men know their positions?'

The older man nodded. 'I'll have fifty Englishmen with a hundred arrows apiece, divided each side of the field. If they come we'll send the first lot of bastards to the devil. Then it's up to Countess Blanche and the others or we'll be dog meat.'

'Trust each other, Elfred. It's how we've always won,' he said.

'Aye, that and having bull's balls,' Elfred answered.

Blackstone settled into the saddle and said nothing more. He gathered his shield and Killbere offered his flail, the three-spiked ball held by a length of chain to its handle.

'Take my holy water sprinkler, it's always good for a first strike, then it's the axe and sword. Kill the bastards, Thomas. Maim them and then kill them, and we'll piss on their graves.'

Blackstone nodded and spurred the horse.

'There's little time for John Jacob and the men,' Blanche de Harcourt said to Killbere as she watched Blackstone gallop across the field.

'Jacob'll do what's asked of him and then we'll slaughter every one of these pig-shite-filled dogs when he does. Provided Thomas survives long enough.'

'Whether he does or not we must save Christiana and the children,' she added.

'Aye. If we must,' Killbere answered, though he saw no point if Blackstone lay dead on the field of combat.

The meadow became an arena, the late flush of the wildflowers a surge of colour before the season closed in. Snow-capped peaks, like pavilions on a battlefield, cast long shadows across the forests, as the opposing routiers held the perimeters and watched the lone knight wait for the charge against him.

Killbere and Blanche de Harcourt rode back to the treeline and Blackstone's men. Behind them in the gulleys several hundred more waited, hidden from view. Elfred looked up to the battlements where soldiers crowded to view the contest.

'That's right, you sons of whores, you keep looking this way,' he muttered to himself. 'Sweet Jesus, keep an eye on that idiot Will Longdon, he needs your blessing and strength today if Thomas's family are to live.'

★   ★   ★

At the rear of the castle John Jacob led forty men stripped down to shirt and breeches. They had waded through the slime and bulrushes that fringed the cold waters of the lake for the past hour – the time the burial had bought them. Will Longdon had ten of his archers with him, their bow cords kept dry beneath their caps. Their war bows nestled in sleeves bound with cord and smeared with pig fat, as were their arrow bags. The English archers were vital to the success of John Jacob's task. Each of the other men was armed with a sword and a fighting axe whose bevelled blade would help in scaling the cliff. Sacking bound their feet to give purchase on the rock face. By the time Blackstone rode out to face his enemy the men were already clinging to the wet granite as Jacob reached up and smashed the blade's edge into a fissure. It rendered the cutting edge useless but its haft gave him grip. The shivering men trod water as he hauled himself upwards and found a meagre foothold. If he could reach the point where the castle's walls met the rock face he could lower the coarse rope slung around his body. The soaking men waited as he crawled agonizingly slowly upwards, his fingers desperately seeking every purchase. As a distant roar went up Jacob heaved himself onto the narrowest of ledges. The master builders who had constructed the fortress a century ago had needed a foundation for the cut stone; the rib of granite that remained was enough for him to press his heels into and brace his back against the castle's wall. He lowered the rope and took the strain, and prayed his strength would hold. One of Jacob's men lost his grip. He slithered down the rock face, his body torn, his screams broken by the violent impact on his face, but the roar from the battlefield smothered his final cry. Slathered in sweat despite the cold, the men pressed themselves against the stone, desperate not to lose their own footing. Jacob's hands were already cut from his efforts and the weight he'd borne from the men on the rope laid a welt, speckled with blood, across his back.

'Nearly there, lads. Keep going. Ten feet more and we're in,' he gasped through clenched teeth.

CHAPTER 37

The huge banner filled the sky, rippling in the chill breeze off the majestic, snow-capped peaks. As the standard curled and fluttered above the fortress its image seemed all the more alive. The coiled body devoured its prey in a symbol of power and authority, warning any challenger that death awaited those who dared oppose the will of the Visconti family, Lords of Verona. Behind the fortress walls was the cruel and merciless killer who once served John, King of France, and who now led his own army of mercenaries, men dedicated to continuing war in their pursuit of slaughter and plunder under the Visconti flag. More than fifteen hundred of these vicious soldiers stood ready at the castle's flanks awaiting the command to fall upon and annihilate the two hundred men who stood a few hundred paces away behind the solitary figure of the Englishman, Thomas Blackstone.

His battered shield, like his body, showed the scars of war, but his weariness from pursuing the killer across France and into the foothills of Italy was outweighed by his desire for revenge.

The Frenchman had butchered those close to him, and now held his family captive. The two hundred stood ready to die, but if Blackstone had any hope of seeing his loved ones alive, they must stand fast. Blackstone had first to meet the challenge of single combat. He waited a hundred paces in front of his men and looked to the four knights he must defeat before finally facing the killer. If wounds or death did not claim him first.

His war horse champed its bit and eased its stance. The scent of juniper carried on the gentle breeze. Were it not for the inevitability of death it would be a near-perfect day. Blackstone turned in the saddle and looked back at his men; some of them he had known for a decade.

Had it been only ten years since he was a sixteen-year-old boy sailing to war in France? The English hamlet of his birth, with its thatched hovels and lush meadows, lay behind a veiled memory. There had been enough slaughter for ten lifetimes.

A thousand voices and more roared as four horsemen charged. Blackstone spurred his horse forward.

All those years of bloodshed had brought him to this place.

Blackstone made no attempt to avoid the first blow from the horseman who swept a battleaxe towards his unguarded face. He brought up his shield, half turned his head and, using his shoulder's strength, forced the shield forward to meet the blow. It lessened the impact; his shield took the blade's bite and as Blackstone's horse surged forward, he twisted the man from the saddle. Good fortune blessed him – instead of an axe the second man carried a flanged mace, which slammed into his unprotected side. He half turned again as the metal flukes hacked into his shoulder armour, hammering muscle and bone and snapping his head back in agony. The high-backed saddle saved him from being unhorsed. Momentum carried him forward and he swung Killbere's weapon through his pain in a roundabout sweep that caught the third man-at-arms around his throat. The chain whipped, the spikes digging into the houndskull visor. It wrenched the man's neck as Blackstone spurred on the horse, whose lunge tightened chain and spike into an unbreakable lock. The man's neck snapped. Blackstone's arm was twisted behind him, exposing his chest as he held the mace's handle. The fourth man came at the gallop tilting a shortened lance, no more than five feet long, like those the English footsoldiers used against French cavalry. Barely an instant before the lance could pierce his armour and heart, Blackstone whipped his shield across. The lance smashed into it, the impact caught him off-balance and he was pitched from the saddle. A roar of victory went up from de Marcy's men.

Blackstone lay unmoving.

De Marcy's hands gripped the battlements. His

orders were clear: the men he had sent out were only to beat Blackstone's strength down so that he would be sufficiently weakened for the Savage Priest to ride out and kill him. He was anxious that the surviving men-at-arms did not forget his command. The first man Blackstone had unhorsed was on his feet and running, sword raised ready to strike the fallen Englishman. It would be a killing blow. De Marcy ordered the crossbowmen who stood by his side to kill him. They loosed their bolts without question and the knight below fell ten paces from Blackstone.

The two knights who remained faltered; the warning was clear.

Blackstone eased himself onto his side. The fall had winded him and pain shot through his back. He breathed shallowly, letting the short gasps feed life into his body. The knights dismounted and strode towards him with shields raised, swords ready to strike.

'You'll never kill him,' Christiana said, turning to face the man who had beaten and humiliated her.

'He's flesh and blood. He'll bleed and he'll die and I will be the one to do it.'

'Even if he's wounded, you'll never defeat him. You're a brutal savage, but he fights with a different kind of strength. He'll kill you slowly and you'll beg for mercy, and he won't listen. He'll kill you today. I swear it.'

De Marcy slapped her hard, splitting her lip.

She fell against the ramparts, blood pulsing from her nose. Agnes cried out, but Henry pulled her to him. Christiana held fast, desperate not to fall to the ground, but to stay defiant – as Blackstone had always told her.

'You and your brats will die before I kill him. I'll throw them down and the rocks that tear them apart will break him.'

The men below ran the last few paces towards Blackstone, who was groggily trying to get to his feet. Their visors were up, the need for cooling air greater than any threat from the downed man. Wolf Sword lay on the ground, out of reach as Blackstone raised himself onto one knee, levering himself up, using his battered shield as a crutch, his body bent in pain. The swordsmen would hamstring a leg, bone-cut his arm, make him barely able to stand against de Marcy.

De Marcy's routiers chanted for death, their blood-lust wanting to see Blackstone finished. Killbere could barely restrain the desire to go forward. He's unarmed, for Christ's sake, he said to himself. 'Take up the sword, man! TAKE UP THE SWORD!' he yelled, but the first man had already lunged and Blackstone had still not reached for the forged steel with the mark of the running wolf etched onto its blade. An axe seemed to appear in his hand as if by sorcery, but it had been held in his crooked arm beneath the cover of his shield as he feigned injury, and as the knight struck at him, he moved deftly to one side, a movement so quick that his attacker faltered. Blackstone swung the axe down, striking between poleyn and greave. The armour that protected the man's knee and leg split, and the severed leg spewed blood across the grass. As the screaming knight went down the axe fell again across the open visor.

The second man faced Blackstone, who had still not retrieved his sword. He had no need; the axe rested in his hand, his battered shield ready for any blow. The knight knew the better man faced him and that to advance another step could signal his own death. A thousand raucous voices settled into an unearthly silence.

Blackstone gazed back at the knight.

'You think they care if you live or die?' he said, meaning the massed routiers. 'You think they understand honour?' Still the man did not move, weighing his chances. 'You can live. You've fought well. You can join us. De Marcy is going to die.'

The knight shook his head. 'I've seen him fight. He's better than you know. And you're injured,' he said.

The lance had caught the flesh on Blackstone's side; the gash was held by his mail, but the blood seeped through and the wound would hinder him. He knew that. And so did the man facing him.

'If I step away his bowman will cut me down before I make five paces,' said the knight. It was a statement that couldn't be countered. The man dropped his shield, lowered his visor and gripped his sword with both hands. 'Defend yourself,' he said, and attacked.

The men watching could count the seconds before the knight died. One: Blackstone braced. Two: he threw his shield at the surprised man who sidestepped. Three: the axe struck him between neck and collarbone. Four: the man fell under the impact. Five: Blackstone cleaved his armour and mail with three more mighty blows. The dead man's head fell.

Blackstone tossed the axe away and turned to face de Marcy.

Killbere, the belligerent knight who had fought the great battles for the greatest King, raised his sword arm and marched forward. 'Now!' he yelled and hundreds of men surged from the trees and raced to where he stood twenty paces ahead. Blackstone was a hundred paces beyond that, and the Savage Priest's men two hundred further on.

'I will kill you for your savagery, and your abominations,' Blackstone called to de Marcy.

The Savage Priest saw Killbere stride forward and the trees spawn men. No longer did he hold the power that only minutes ago was his. Blackstone's men might still be outnumbered but their blood-lust would inflict a punishing damage before they were defeated. If he did not fight Blackstone those who followed him would turn their backs, denying him the Visconti's wealth and power. Gilles de

Marcy would have nothing after all these years, except that which he could steal from the dead.

'Hold her!' the Savage Priest ordered his men. Two soldiers grabbed Christiana. She screamed, knowing what he was about to do. He snatched Agnes in one hand and grabbed Henry's collar and hauled them onto the battlements, the sixty-foot drop a toehold away.

'Blackstone!' de Marcy bellowed. 'Choose! Which one should live, which to die?'

Blackstone stared up at his children being held teetering on the edge.

'Choose! Or they both die.'

Blackstone knew everything had been to no avail. De Marcy would kill his children. Agnes's plaintive voice drifted across the battlefield.

'Papa . . . help us . . . Papa . . .?'

Blackstone's desperation shook him. He pulled his archer's knife and cut free the leather straps that held what little protection he wore on his legs and sword arm. 'De Marcy! I'll fight you without armour. You have the advantage! Leave them!'

The armour fell to the ground, exposing his wound and his vulnerability.

'Suffering cleanses the soul, Blackstone; you have not suffered enough before I send you to meet your maker. Choose! Now!'

Blackstone knew there could be only one choice. He needed his son to carry on his name. Agnes had to die.

'It's all right, Father! Henry called, his voice

wavering in fear, but finding courage enough to be heard clearly. 'Save Agnes. Save her, Father!'

'All right, boy! You stay strong. Stay with your courage!' he called back.

De Marcy pushed his arms forward, the children nearly losing their footing. The men below gasped in anticipation. 'Well? Who – shall – live? Who do you save?'

Beyond love, necessity demanded Blackstone choose Henry, but the moment he made the decision he knew that de Marcy would kill him. It was a game of bluff.

'Who do you give life to?' de Marcy bellowed impatiently.

'Agnes,' Blackstone answered, knowing de Marcy needed to inflict the most pain. Agnes was a moment away from death. Then Christiana shrieked. The child fell backwards; something had happened on the ramparts. Men screamed; the children disappeared from Blackstone's view.

John Jacob.

'Bowmen!' a voice cried out, the alarm ringing inside the castle walls.

The first six men each side of the Savage Priest died from Will Longdon's archers, the others turned to face the ragged, soaked men who had already loosed another volley. De Marcy lost twelve men before the shock of the attack turned soldiers and crossbowmen to face the invaders. John Jacob and his men ran along the ramparts;

a hundred paces behind them Longdon and his archers killed more men on the walls. A dozen more of Jacob's hobelars fought in the courtyard, slaying guards with sword and blunt-edged axes, hammering skulls, hacking bones.

Christiana let her weight fall from the man who held her, the sudden dead weight forcing him off balance. Longdon's arrow took him in the throat; he tumbled backwards onto the rocks below. Killbere's men roared.

Men still died from the English archers and hobelars. There could be no victory from within the walls. Jacob's men reached the gates. De Marcy made no move to escape. If Blackstone's men had wanted to kill him they would have done so already. A thickset, broad-shouldered, crop-headed man, older than Blackstone, his shirt matted with sweat and blood, strode towards him, a gore-slicked falchion in his hand.

'John!' Christiana cried, pulling the children to her. She and the children were still close enough to de Marcy for him to strike out. They could not reach Jacob without passing him on the narrow rampart. He lunged for them but Jacob had fore-seen the threat and stopped his advance, the falchion poised, ready for a maiming blow. De Marcy abandoned his attempt to snatch Christiana.

'Are you one of Blackstone's routiers?'

'I'm his captain and sworn man.'

De Marcy allowed a sigh, and nodded. The man could not be bought.

Jacob looked over the battlement, letting Blackstone see him.

A thousand men bellowed.

The castle gates swung open.

Blackstone pressed Arianrhod to his lips – and lifted Wolf Sword from the bloodied grass.

CHAPTER 38

John Jacob and his surviving men, with Longdon and the archers, escorted Christiana and the children, riding palfreys, from the castle gates.

Blackstone had not moved. He waited for the Savage Priest.

John Jacob stopped ten paces from him.

'All is well, my lord,' John Jacob said.

'Thank you, John. Will?' he said, seeing a bloodied Longdon being helped along by two other archers.

'Aye, Sir Thomas?'

'I'm pleased to see you.'

Will Longdon smiled, the compliment easing the pain. 'And I you.'

'You'll mend?'

'Providing you find me enough brandywine,' he answered.

Blackstone nodded. 'We will. And have these men given an extra ration. Tell one of the captains to send a hundred men into the castle and secure it.'

Longdon smiled and hobbled away.

Blackstone looked up to his son. 'You made my heart swell with pride, Henry.'

He could see the boy's tears forming, but Blackstone's stern look gave him no permission to yield to emotion. He lifted Agnes from Christiana's arms, flinching from his wound. 'Were you scared?' he asked the child who clung to him.

She nodded, nuzzling his neck.

'So was I,' he told her.

'You're never scared,' she said.

'Always, if I think of anything happening to you.'

'But I'm all right now, Papa.'

He kissed her forehead and returned her to her mother's arms. He could see bruises and welts through Christiana's grubby shift.

'We have clothes for you, and a physician,' he said, laying a hand gently on her thigh.

'You would have had our daughter killed,' she said.

Blackstone could not bring himself to answer the accusation.

'It would have been better had he killed me. He beat your whore with knotted rope and had me crawl around the yard a dozen times in penance,' she said. 'A woman raped who conceives a child is complicit in the act. De Marcy took my last shred of dignity, Thomas. And I am left with the guilt of an honourable squire's death. I mourn Guillaume more than my own shame. He was the best among us.'

The men stepped away; only Jacob stayed close, holding the lead to her horse, deferentially turning his face away.

Blackstone ignored his presence. 'You're my wife, mother of my children, lady of my house.'

She tugged the love token from her cuff and tossed down the embroidered cloth, the winged bird still entrapped – as were they by their destiny.

'My father's coat of arms. Did you know?'

Blackstone knew denial was useless. 'Some years later, yes. It was my burden.'

Neither spoke. Whatever they had was lost in a long sorrowful look. She finally nodded and kicked the horse forward, tugging the lead from Jacob's hand, forcing him to step aside. Henry's horse followed skittishly.

At the forest's edge, Blanche de Harcourt shook her hair free from her bascinet and rode forward to meet Christiana. Blackstone and Jacob watched the beaten woman press her mentor's hand to her lips.

'She'll be cared for, Sir Thomas. Her wounds will heal,' Jacob said.

'Yes,' Blackstone answered. 'You'll have more than my thanks, John.'

'I'll take friendship as payment if it's on offer, Sir Thomas.'

'Given,' said Blackstone.

Killbere cantered his horse forward. 'The castle?' he said looking at Jacob.

'Eighty or more of his men dead. Will Longdon's archers did most of the killing. I've left twenty men at the gate; they're guarding de Marcy and Girolami. Ten of ours dead. Some wounded. His plunder's in there. Wagon-loads.'

'Holy Blood of the Cross, a bargain at that! We'll

live like kings. Right, Thomas, are we to fight these dog turds? There'll be enough slaughter today to last us a while.'

'Get to your men, John. Be ready for de Marcy's routiers, they'll want their plunder one way or the other.'

'Aye, my lord,' Jacob answered and ran back towards the line of men formed up for battle.

'Gilbert, they'll strike whatever happens to me. They'll come at you straight on, at the run. You've told the men what to do?'

'A dozen times and more. You need to be at their front, man.'

'De Marcy first. Then we'll see.'

Blackstone's weariness showed. He folded Christiana's token against the wound in his side and secured it by tightening his sword belt.

'Cut the bastard's throat and be done with it. Let it go, man. What's the point?' Killbere urged him.

'I want him under my sword.'

'Thomas,' Killbere groaned. 'Thomas . . . sweet, merciful God, he's a stain from the devil's loins. Tie him to a stake and burn him if you must have revenge, but you're hurt, and those men you killed took their toll. In truth, you're in no condition to take him. And he carries as great a hatred as you.'

'Gilbert, I've known you since I was a boy, and you've always been a belligerent, conceited bastard with an unmerciful heart.'

'This is no time for compliments, Thomas.'

Blackstone lifted the sword. 'So if he kills me, show him no mercy and slaughter him however you choose.'

Killbere made no humour from it, but nodded and spurred the horse away. Thomas Blackstone would face his own destiny.

Memories of men standing before their enemy, calling out for a champion, appeared like a vision in his mind's eye. Drums and trumpets, ten thousand banners, lances held high, armour embellished by surcoats of every hue. Pomp and ceremony declaring war as, shoulder to shoulder, men jostled for position to be the first to attack, to seek the glory that would live on in their family history and be recounted by troubadours.

Not this day.

Two belligerent forces faced each other across three hundred yards of open field. Men lost to peace, devoted to war without glory, intent only on profit. No banners or royalty, no surge of pride for a king, a prince or a cause. They were there for the killing, for those who slaughtered the most would sell their skills to the highest bidder.

The Savage Priest strode out of the gates wearing mail without armour, ready to strike hard and fast with agility. He seemed bigger than Blackstone remembered – his sallow face more gaunt, his dark-ringed eyes sunk deeper into his skull. His shield bore no markings; his black surcoat covered his mail. He appeared from the shadows of the great gates, as would the Grim Reaper.

Gilles de Marcy stopped ten paces away.

'I will punish your mortal body, Thomas Blackstone, and inflict more pain than you have known, and when you beg for mercy I'll cut out your eyes and tongue, and render you blind and speechless. And then, in front of your wife and children I will cut out your heart and leave your corrupt flesh on this field for the crows and ravens. Without Christian burial your soul will be damned.'

Blackstone had no doubt that a demonic force sheltered within the Savage Priest, but he had cut him once before in the darkened streets of a captured city and he bled like any other man. De Marcy's words had no effect. He raised his shield and, as split and battered as it was, its declaration, *Defiant unto Death,* could still be seen. Blackstone gripped Wolf Sword and strode forward without challenge or battle cry, chilled by his own hatred.

The Savage Priest ran at him and the two men struck, shields clashing, followed by vicious, hammering blows. Blackstone's weight and height gave him a brief advantage, but de Marcy's knights had weakened him against the strength and skill of a fresh fighter. He feinted, half turning from his wounded side, trying to draw de Marcy in, but the killer priest stepped back, found his balance and struck hard. The blow stunned Blackstone; he went down on one knee and the roar from the routiers surged across the field, but still de Marcy did not press home his advantage. Again he stepped back, waiting for the moment Blackstone was half raised, off balance. Then he struck again, two massive blows that cut through shield and broke mail. Blackstone's shield fell. De Marcy's men edged forward, war dogs on a leash, wanting the kill. Their captains screamed to hold them back, de Marcy's rank and reputation enough to hold them in check. The Savage Priest would kill Blackstone and then, when his head was hoisted on a lance, Blackstone's disheartened men would be vulnerable.

Blackstone took a blow on Wolf Sword's crossguard, twisted, and threw himself against de Marcy, so that they stood face to face, the priest's glowering black eyes glinting in the darkness of his visor. Their chests heaved desperately for air, grunting with exertion as, sweat-soaked, they grappled, neither yielding. Blackstone rammed his shoulder against de Marcy's shield, forcing strength into his legs, making the killer take two paces back, but he quickly retaliated and barged Blackstone, striking hard and fast, grunting with effort, determined to take the man's legend as a trophy. Five, six, seven times he powered his blade onto Wolf Sword, but Blackstone twisted, half turned, used the sword's pommel to crack down against de Marcy's helmet. Stunned, the Savage Priest faltered, regained his stance, brought up his shield and struck down again and again. Blackstone took the punishment, feeling his arms weakening against the power of the blows, knowing he risked death but wanting to tire his attacker.

And then Blackstone felt the surge of fresh strength settle within him, as if those he had vowed to avenge now bore witness. He moved in quickly before de Marcy delivered the next blow. His free hand gripped de Marcy's scabbard belt and he yanked, tipping the man down. Wolf Sword smashed away the black shield; then Blackstone kicked up the man's visor. De Marcy's distorted face revealed the shock from the blow, but his unrelenting desire to kill Blackstone fed the hatred to retaliate. He rolled clear with a vicious swipe that cut through Blackstone's leg mail. It was not a crippling injury and the pain made no impression. De Marcy followed his advantage and rained down blows, grunting and cursing with the effort. Blackstone deflected every strike and then stepped to one side as de Marcy delivered what should have been a maiming strike against his sword arm. He backhanded de Marcy with Wolf Sword's pommel and felt bones crack in the man's face.

Flat-footed, de Marcy was rocked back by the impact. His sword arm barely half-raised, Blackstone swept his blade down against his opponent's gauntlet, shattering his wrist. De Marcy's body crimped with the excruciating pain. Blackstone rammed the Wolf Sword's narrow point through mail into the vulnerable shoulder and de Marcy cried out in agony. Blackstone kicked his legs away and as the priest thudded to the ground he dropped his full weight onto the man's chest. A fine spray of bloody air plumed from the stunned priest's face. De Marcy's eyes blinked in disbelief.

'You bastard knight . . . you archer scum,' he gasped. 'You'll . . . die on this . . . field with me.'

A blurred image through sweat-streaked eyes showed Blackstone a bellowing mass of attacking men. Their faces contorted, their roar muted in his mind to a dull, flat gathering of sound like a wave about to break. His knee crushed down; his crooked left arm pressed against de Marcy's throat, forcing his struggling head back into the grass.

Blackstone pulled free his archer's knife, held the Savage Priest's eyes with his own. 'Then die under an archer's knife,' he grunted; then he slammed down the visor and pushed the blade through the slit. In his steel tomb the Savage Priest screamed as his feet drummed on the bloodied ground. His body bucked, but Blackstone kept his weight on him and pressed the knife harder. De Marcy's black eyes dimmed, his last sight in this world the face of the man who killed him. Blackstone turned his gaze away before the dying killer's stare sucked his soul into hell.

The breaking tide of men was within twenty paces. Blackstone reached for his sword, but was overtaken by the whispering hail that fell and then thudded into their bodies. He saw that a hundred men must have fallen in an instant, and, as another storm of arrows reached further into the attacking routiers, Killbere and John Jacob surged past with Meulon and Gaillard beside them. Blackstone stood across the Savage Priest's body and let the men swirl around him.

The day was already won.

The battle lasted two hours, the fight so vicious that many were executed while begging for mercy. Few prisoners were taken. Once Killbere's men and John Jacob's Gascons hurled themselves in the vanguard of the battle, Blanche de Harcourt's men became the unstoppable tide of destruction. Many of de Marcy's men ran into the high forests to escape. Few stood their ground once their advantage was lost.

Afterwards, Blackstone allowed nearly two hundred of the Savage Priest's men – Englishmen, mostly veterans of Poitiers, and another sixty Gascon survivors – to swear fealty to him. The most vicious, whose crimes he learnt about from de Marcy's clerks, he hanged on a bleak, wind-swept day. Twenty-seven Englishmen and eleven Germans and Hungarians kicked their lives away on the end of a rope, the driving rain across the valley tightening the hemp, contorting faces into grotesque gargoyles. The monks and whores would join the camp followers' train, as did two French physicians who had been captured by de Marcy.

Most men who fought accepted death, but the greatest fear of even the most vicious among them was that they might die unshriven of their sins. Cistercian monks from a nearby abbey went among the dying to grant absolution. Monastic scribes recorded that a mass grave was dug before the winter snows fell on the pass. Several hundred bodies were interred from what became known as 'La Battaglia nella Valle dei Fiori'. Months later the events at the Battle at the Valley of Flowers found their way back to the English court where the story of Thomas Blackstone, outlawed knight, soon became a greater legend.

The camp followers, their base lives worthless without the soldiers, went out from the forest to help the wounded. Christiana allowed one of the whores to wash her and a physician to tend her wounds. Blackstone was still on the field of battle with Killbere and the aftermath of the fighting. She did not allow the woman to bathe Agnes, which she did herself. Her daughter was fed and clothed and then slept the undisturbed sleep of childhood. Henry had made his way from the forest to find his father.

'There's no knowing where our hearts take us, Christiana,' Blanche de Harcourt told her. 'You chose him when he was the scourge of our nation. Now, he's my family's friend, and your husband. You should stay with him; he hasn't condemned you for the violation, and he'll stand by your shame. Why desert him now?'

'I cannot explain what cripples my heart, Blanche. It is a small death that grows colder each day. My father was a gentle knight who nurtured me as a child when my mother died, and then saw me safe into your care.' She looked down at her dirt-encrusted, broken nails, still caked with blood. 'The filth clings to me as does the thought of his death at Thomas's hands. That, and all that has happened. It changes everything for me.'

'He didn't know that at the time. Godfrey de Harcourt fought his own family for the world to see, but we reconciled. It was war,' Blanche de Harcourt said, seeing the dullness in her friend's eyes. Christiana was slipping away into that dark place of loss and grieving where no love can reach. 'Once he learnt the truth did you expect him to tell you? He's just killed the man who was the very reason your father sent you to us for protection. Thomas has closed the circle that was your destiny. Keep his name alive, Christiana. Have more of his children,' she urged gently.

Christiana shook her head.

'Listen to me,' Blanche said brusquely, desperately wanting to make Christiana realize what she was going to lose. 'He can command you! He has guardianship over his children. If you challenge him he can take them. He could have beaten you and cast you out when he learnt what happened on the barge.'

'He won't do that because of his affection for me. I know him.'

'Then you don't deserve him,' Blanche told her.

'I know,' Christiana answered, tears stinging her

eyes. 'Will you offer me and the children sanctuary and your protection?'

Blackstone went among the men, sending the physicians where they were most needed, only then allowing one of the Cistercian monks to dress his own wound and remove Christiana's piece of linen. The wide-eyed soaring bird on the token of affection now looked to be panicked, drowning in his bloodstains. Henry rode alongside his father, seeing the slaughtered men being dragged into the pit, entrails and severed limbs hooked with pole-axes and spears and tossed in after them. His father watched for his reaction but the boy remained stoic.

It took three days for the weather to clear, during which time Christiana did not speak to or see Blackstone. The plunder was divided and each company given its share. Every man knew what every other had received. Blackstone offered release from his service to any man who desired it. Thirty or so men decided to return to France, most of them with the women they had seized along the way. The core of Blanche de Harcourt's retinue who had survived the battle – 173 men-at-arms – would escort her back to her fiefdom of Aumale in Normandy, her rightful place of inheritance.

Blackstone and Christiana stood in the forest; beyond them, scattered groups of men and women loaded pack horses, and armour and weapons were

651

stacked aboard wagons. In the bright, clear light of the meadow, where Montferrat's banner flew from the castle ramparts, Killbere and the company commanders organized their men into formation. The killing had reduced their ranks to several hundred, but they were expert, well-disciplined fighters, worth more than twice that number of untried men.

'The country of the Lombards is not my home, Thomas,' Christiana told him. 'You'll have an itinerant life of war now; I want my children to find a refuge and a home. If you will release us, Blanche will take us back.'

Blackstone sought the words that might embrace her, but the struggle seemed uneven. 'I'll soon have wealth, and be paid as a *condottiere* by Florence – such a contract is generous. The hard fighting is over. A home with land and servants awaits us. I stand ready to do anything that will keep you and the children with me,' he said.

'You can't stop fighting,' she answered.

'It's what I do,' he said.

'You command men; you do not have to fight.'

'That day will come soon enough – until then, I earn their respect.'

'And risk losing mine.'

'I always thought I had that in equal measure to your love,' he said quietly, reaching for her hand, feeling her small fingers beneath his own. He sensed she might be drawn back to him. 'That river we once crossed was so dangerous, but we

clung to each other and we reached the shore. This is just another river, Christiana. Hold tight and trust me again.'

'I cannot. I need time for this torment to abandon me. We will be safe and I'll pray for your well-being, Thomas. I beg you, do not force me against my will. Let us hope our time will come again.'

She raised her face to his, and kissed his cheek. 'Goodbye, Thomas.'

The horsemen gathered on the trampled, blood-stained meadow. Blackstone rode at the head of his men, as did Blanche de Harcourt at hers.

Each went forward to bid the other farewell.

'I'll keep her with me; perhaps she will find some respite,' Blanche de Harcourt told him.

'Send me word,' Blackstone answered.

He looked across to Henry who sat on a courser a pace behind the Countess, with Guillaume's dagger – which he himself had retrieved – tucked into his belt. Blackstone tied the dead squire's sword and scabbard to the saddle's pommel. 'Remember, son, never relinquish a sword taken in battle. Sir Gilbert told me that.'

'I didn't earn it, Father,' the boy answered.

'Every man here saw you earn it with your courage, as once did Guillaume Bourdin. He was the bravest man I have known and fought always at my side. It carries honour with it. That's why it is given to you.'

He reached for the boy's hand and held it fast for a moment. 'I want you at my side. You would soon be my squire.'

He saw the boy's conflict. 'Father, who will care for Agnes and Mother if I am not with them? When they release me, I will find you – I promise . . . my lord.' He turned his horse away to find his place at Christiana and Agnes's side.

'I'll place him with a good family, close to my own, and he'll be given the finest of skills, Thomas. And when he's of age, then I'll send him to you,' said Blanche.

Less than an hour earlier he had held Agnes for the last time, feeling her tender body against his own, telling her a story about a great journey that must be undertaken, of how he had to travel to find out tales of goblins, faeries and monsters, and places where angels lived in the mountains.

'And then you'll come home and tell me?' she asked.

'I promise,' he told her, feeling the sadness of all that had gone before and the desperate pain of what he was about to lose. There was little left except the brotherhood of his men and that sustained him. 'On my honour,' he whispered.

She traced his scar and kissed him.

There were no words left to say. He turned his horse towards the mountains with his men following his banner carrying the device of the gauntlet grasping the sword.

★   ★   ★

The Marquis de Montferrat claimed the fortress as his own and sent word to Pope Innocent that no routier would pass unless a tribute was paid, half of which would be given to the papal coffers. Girolami, wounded in the battle for the castle by an unknown archer, was treated by a physician and sent back to his master Galeazzo Visconti with the news that the powerful Milanese lord had lost control of the western approach into his territory – and that the man who had inflicted this defeat was the Englishman, Sir Thomas Blackstone.

It took days before news of the battle reached the Pope, and another ten before Father Niccolò Torellini heard of the event. Florence was at war with Milan and fighting men were needed if the Visconti family was ever to be beaten. Father Niccolò thanked God that it had been he who had once absolved the dying Englishman, for it seemed God had now placed him ready to serve. The messenger related how the English knight had buried his squire and cut the stone himself to mark the grave, and then chiselled a memorial into the rock.

This stone marks the resting place of Master Guillaume Bourdin, esquire to the English knight, Sir Thomas Blackstone, cruelly slain in defence of the helpless by Gilles de Marcy, the Savage Priest.

The scaffold that had held the young squire was reinforced so that in seasons to come it would still stand and bear the remains of the man strapped across it, whose shield was bound with wire and hung from his neck. As flesh rotted, the wire would bite onto bone. The etched inscription across the black shield bore witness and warning.

Here hangs the body of this cruel murderer, killed in single combat by Sir Thomas Blackstone. So will all evil perish.

Blackstone led his men away from the valley: Killbere, John Jacob, Meulon and Gaillard with their companies; Elfred and Will Longdon at the head of their mounted archers. The breeze whispered through the valley and rattled the Savage Priest's shield in gentle mockery.

Blackstone did not look back.

HISTORICAL NOTES

When Thomas Blackstone raided north of Bordeaux the attack was inspired by the Gascon Jean de Grailly, the Captal de Buch, who in January 1356 collected a mixed force of Gascons and Englishmen and seized a number of vital castles and then moved on with six hundred men to capture the city of Périgueux. Prince Edward had already begun his great raid into southern France.

I pushed Blackstone further north and created the fictional stronghold which became a spur for the French King to seek retribution and employ the services of Gilles de Marcy, the Savage Priest. During my research I came across Arnaud de Cervole, the son of a minor family who had been stripped of his benefice in the diocese of Périgueux. My character de Marcy was not based on the brigand Cervole – who became universally known as the Archpriest – but the connection was too good to miss, so in a way he kick-started the Savage Priest into life. Arnaud de Cervole fought at Poitiers and then led a mercenary force of two thousand men who threatened Avignon. Eight years later he was murdered by his unpaid Hungarian mercenaries.

It was difficult to accurately place Blackstone in Paris in 1356 as fourteenth-century landmarks have changed so much. I looked for historical records of where the guildsmen practised and read various accounts of the city with the aid of a medieval map of the city. Very few streets were named, but there was at least one broad boulevard that ran north past Les Halles, the marketplace and burial ground. The churches I named in the book exist or existed, and as Paris expanded it did so beyond the original Roman walls.

When Charles of Navarre, the French King's son-in-law, had Charles de Cerda, the Constable of France – and friend of the French King – murdered at L'Aigle in Normandy in 1354, it opened a new chapter in the French conflict. Events that unfolded over the next two years nearly destroyed the French nation. Navarre himself had a legitimate right to the French throne, but his continuing playing of one side against the other made him one of the most distrusted characters to emerge from that time. Edward III was prepared to deal with him and the Duke of Lancaster was given authority to negotiate. Not once but twice, Navarre changed loyalties, and even as Edward was discussing a possible alliance Navarre was already talking to agents of King John II. Yet Edward never quite ended his association with Charles of Navarre. In